TURBULENCE

A Novel of the Atmosphere

Giles Foden

ff

faber and faber

First published in 2009
by Faber and Faber Limited
Bloomsbury House
74–77 Great Russell Street
London WC1B 3DA
This paperback edition first published in 2010

Typeset by Faber and Faber Limited
Printed in the UK by CPI Bookmarque, Croydon

A CIP record for this book
is available from the British Library

ISBN 978-0-571-20527-1

4 6 8 10 9 7 5 3

For Julian, with thanks

It is rescue work, this snatching of vanishing phases of turbulence, disguised in fair words, out of the native obscurity into a light where the struggling forms may be seen, seized upon, endowed with the only possible form of permanence in this world of relative values – the permanence of memory.

JOSEPH CONRAD, 'Henry James, An Appreciation' (1905)

DATE: 22 January 1980
POSITION @ 0600 LOCAL (GMT):
  Latitude 54° 26' South, Longitude 3° 24' East
  Alongside Bouvet Island
DEPARTED MAWSON STATION: 11 January
NEXT DESTINATION: Cape Town
ETA: 1 February
DISTANCE TO GO: 1277 nm
CURRENT WEATHER: Overcast and cold
SEA STATE: Frozen
WIND: 15 kt Easterly
BAROMETRIC PRESSURE: 975 mb
AIR TEMPERATURE: −1.9°C
SEA TEMPERATURE: −1.5°C

Yesterday, very early in the morning, something unexpected happened. I went up on deck to find the *Habbakuk* covered with a thin mist. Darts of morning sun were lancing through. As I walked along the wooden sheathing, a gigantic phantom rose suddenly out of the sea. I started backwards from a tall figure projected against a wall of ice. The wall was an iceberg – and the phantom, I slowly realised, was my own reflection, enormously enlarged.

I was staring at myself mirrored on the ice, magnified by some trick of the light as it came through the mist. When I moved my arms or legs, the figure on the berg reproduced the same movements, changing its posture as I did. Said joined me, laughing. Soon the whole crew, Arabs and Baluchis, even Schlomborg and the Sheikh were at it. All moving their limbs. All laughing. Ghosts of gaiety. Then, with a hissing noise, the mist burned off and the visions were gone. Such is human life.

Of my own I shall tell only the substantive part. Four years ago I was approached by the associates of an Arab sheikh. He was seeking scientific advice concerning the towing of icebergs to his own country, in order to deliver fresh water to the desert. Using his considerable resources, he had tracked me down as the last surviving individual to have a copy of Pyke's plans for a berg ship.

A few simple calculations told me that it was not a feasible idea to tow a *pure* iceberg to the desert. However, if Pykrete were to be used rather than pure ice, the idea did not seem so fantastical – no more fantastical, at least, than Pyke's original scheme for the *Habbakuk*, which was formulated in the 1940s. (Pyke's secretary had misspelt the name of the Old Testament prophet used as a codename for the project in Whitehall, and I saw no reason to change it.)

Ninety-nine per cent of all the earth's ice is concentrated in Antarctica – the fringed white veil of the world, the untarnished region. It was the obvious starting point for our venture, since going north from there via the East African coast leads directly to Saudi Arabia, our intended destination. The work was done during the Antarctic summer, between mid-November and the end of January, over three consecutive years.

Among Antarctica's great shimmering floes and black-basalt rocks – they stick out like feet from under the white burnous of the glacier – I watched our bright work grow, littering the virgin scene with lengths of timber, nets of steel trellis, gargoyle-like pumps, macerators, chipping machines.

The visual information of the place was dizzying. So much light. It was as if one was gazing at the world through the eyes of another species – one of the albatrosses that circled forlornly above the site, at one with the whirling cloud and the white fog-smoke. Under this gauze, real ice-bergs floated in a concourse of currents; they looked like tombstones, monoliths, monuments of a world destroyed.

All this was in the open. What remained hidden was my great fear that this grand project, this 'Mammoth Unsinkable Vessel', as Pyke once called it, this veritable white elephant resurrected from a war grave, would melt away before it reached its destination.

But the maths said it wouldn't. However I shook them, kicked them, beat them, the equations stood up.

The ship was built in the Australian claim at Mawson

Station – that is, between the Dismal Mountains and the Amery Ice Shelf. Mawson sits on an isolated outcrop of rock. Its main climatic feature is the katabatic or gravity-fed wind, which results from drainage of cold air down the steep slopes of the ice sheet. Thousands of emperor penguins compete for space with flocks of southern giant petrels, Antarctic fulmars and skuas.

Insulated huts were erected to house the members of the expedition. As we worked, I wondered what some future archaeologist would make of all this, discovering the huts and other equipment under a flour-mound of snow many centuries hence.

The efficiency of the construction was impressive. Many of the crew had worked on desert oil rigs, or in the scrap-metal yards of Sharjah, or been shipwrights in the Gulf, so they were well acquainted with industrial processes. But the cold must have been an intense shock to them and, of course, *Habbakuk* was something unprecedented. Something out of this world – or at least beyond prior human experience.

Apart from wood pulp and ice, our materials were timber, steel girders, sea water and below-zero temperatures. I shall never forget the sight of all those dark faces in white-trimmed fur hoods, or the gloved hands spraying salt water from hoses onto the hull of the growing ice ship, constantly building up its thickness and smoothness. Some of the Pykrete was made naturally, using ice slush skimmed off the surface of the ocean and laid out in huge, forty-foot-square trays into which the pulp was poured. The mixture for smaller blocks was prepared in cement mixers.

It was very hard work for those Baluchis, tough as they were. 'Our limbs are numb,' they complained. The expedition doctor devised a procedure to see how insensitive to cold they had become. It involved successive pricking with a needle

3

from the ankle or wrist up; 'testing peripheral neuropathy', he said. Something like that. I am afraid to say the Sheikh's ganger treated them no better than the weather. Eight of them died.

We built up the first part of the ship on large timber rafts, using the larger squares of Pykrete (66 per cent ice, 34 per cent woodchip), stacking them up and fusing them together with freezing water just as Pyke had intended all those years ago. The whole was then gradually sheathed in timber and a layer of insulation (a type of mica) pumped into the narrow cavity between the ice hull and its wooden skin.

The chance of my involvement in this tale is just as narrow. The Sheikh had previously sought the advice of Godfroy Wildman-Lushington, a post-war director of British Petroleum and the very man who, as Brigadier Wildman-Lushington, had run the original Habbakuk project in the early 1940s. This time round, the Brigadier suggested Julius Brecher as a suitable chief scientist, but Brecher declined and pointed the Sheikh in my direction. More or less everyone else involved was dead.

I got down to work in my now abandoned rooms at Trinity College in Cambridge, drawing out the plans in ever greater detail. I did so in combination with various bright young sparks from the technical academies of Saudi Arabia, with whom I communicated by the miracle of fax.

One of my major concerns was that the motor nacelles would generate too much heat and begin to melt the structure, but mounting them externally appears to have solved the problem, since water passes over the shell of the nacelle and cools the engine inside. The vessel is steered by the motors on port and starboard, accelerating or decelerating as necessity dictates. There are fifteen nacelles on each side of the ship – we had them made by Westinghouse and shipped out.

I still have Pyke's plans. Enshrined memories, wriggling on

the desk in front of me as I write. Caught in gimballed lamplight, they seem as old as biblical scrolls. I roll out the yellowing volute and read, holding down the edges of the paper with a coffee cup and my tobacco tin.

Sometimes Pyke strayed into the realms of fantasy. He believed that if the Pykrete fleet carried tanks of supercooled water, this could be sprayed onto enemy shipping, whereupon it would freeze instantly and create a bridge for boarding. Or, he dreamed, the gelid water jet could be used to seal up guns. Another of his ideas was to create ice fortresses onshore, freezing explosive booby-traps in their walls which would detonate if any attempt were made to melt them.

But the basic idea behind *Habbakuk* was sound, and when we cruised out of our Antarctic harbour we were as near as possible to reproducing it, taking advantage of whatever new technologies had come along since the war.

On the day we sailed (11 January 1980), scientists from various research stations across Greater Antarctica showed up to wave us off. There were even some Chinese from Zhongshan Station – a helicopter ride across the ice shelf from Mawson – and also some Japanese and Russians. It is a mark of *Habbakuk*'s uniqueness that they all turned out, as the scientists in these different claims are by nature fiercely competitive and secretive.

I remember them standing under the orange glow of the sun amid the sparkling purity of the snow as we slid away. Human figurines with a mass of emperor penguins moving behind. The penguins reminded me of scholars at an academic conference, sipping tea in loose, casual groups during an interval as they waited for the return to seated order of the next plenary session ...

Oh, how I remember those Cambridge days. McClintock and Summerhayes, Yazikov and Lewis, vying to be editor of the *Journal of Fluid Mechanics*. The abjects who gathered themselves against me, returned in just one puff of my pipe. Better another: if only *she* could return to me like that for real.

The ship was cheered, the harbour cleared of balaclavas, bright-hued survival suits, sunglasses. Of flesh and blood only the penguins stayed. Behind them stood the sheds and hangars of Mawson, backed up by lines of sastrugi: ribbed rows of frozen, gale-borne snow, all aligned with the direction of the wind. All as straight as we are on our course to the desert, though the water twirls round us like dancers on a stage.

That twirl involves turbulence, the last great problem in classical physics. As Einstein is supposed to have put it: 'Before I die, I hope someone will clarify quantum physics for me. After I die, I hope God will explain turbulence to me.' (Another version of this story, which is also ascribed to Heisenberg and von Kármán, has the speaker adding: 'But I wouldn't want to embarrass God by asking him.')

With Schlomborg at the wheel – really a series of buttons and knobs controlling the nacelles – we have reached Bouvet Island, an uninhabited pile of rocks, gravel and glacier where we are replenishing our ice supplies. Bouvetøya, as the Norwegians call it – Norway has dominion over this desolate spot – is said to be the remotest place on earth, i.e. furthest away from any other land.

As I write, chinstrap penguins are diving for krill outside the porthole. The island is also home to thousands of vast elephant seals, which kill the penguins by shaking them inside out.

From here we will set a northward course to Cape Town, where supplies will be taken on board, as again at Dar es Salaam in Tanzania. We will then continue along the Kenyan and Somali coasts up to the Arabian Gulf.

Schlomborg wears the full brass-buttoned, navy-blue uniform of the Swedish merchant marine. He seems to be unaware that the ship he captains is made of ice, affecting a weird indifference whenever I bring up the issue of the vessel's structural integrity, the guardianship of which is my main purpose on board. But he plays the nacelle steering panel like a first-class organist.

The fellow who paid for it all, Sheikh Issa, is a dark little man with eyes full of fierce determination. He wears a billowy white robe. I presume he must have woollen long johns underneath, as it is bitterly cold in the Southern Ocean. The wind sweeps down the length of a ship like an animal trying to fasten on its prey. Now and then some small discrete item, such as someone's boot or hat, is gripped by this great wind and lashed along the deck. By the time it reaches the stern it is out of sight and the thought filling your head as you lean into the blast is that you too could be punched and slapped along the deck like that before being blown off clear.

Into an immense anonymity of foaming waves.

Rollend in schäumenden Wellen.

Rolling in foaming billows, as the aria which narrates the making of seas and rivers in Haydn's *Creation* puts it.

There are about twenty officers on board, mainly young Arab engineers and cadets from the Saudi naval school. No women. For all that, the young Arabs on the ship are obsessed with a heartbreaker called Olivia Newton John. I have seen posters of her on the doors of their cabins.

There is a fitness centre, a library and a small cinema on the ship, playing mostly old films. *The Searchers*, *The African Queen*, *Gone with the Wind*. Seeing the last again made me think of Krick.

There is also a little mosque, its minaret competing for verticality with radar apparatus and radio aerial. All is otherwise much as Pyke imagined it, except that rather than the hull being full of planes, as he'd envisioned, it contains very large tanks of supercooled water. This water, as well as the structure of the ship itself, is our cargo for the desert. The plan on arrival is that the supercooled water will be drawn off by pump. Then we will go into dry dock, suspended over mesh and more tanks. The structural ice will be allowed to melt naturally into the tanks, with the fibre in the Pykrete being sieved out by the mesh.

Grease ice, pancake ice, sea-ice sheet, ice floe – we have already fallen in with every kind of ice and through all of it the disgraced Swedish merchant captain has sailed as if born to the task. There is something a bit doltish about him, with his vast bulk and red monarchical beard, but I can't fault his navigation. He seems very tranquil up on the bridge, issuing orders to Said and his other officers. The only thing that has upset him was the appearance beside the ship one day – it was during lunch – of a sperm whale, but I think that was simply because he wanted to finish his meal. Garlanded with phosphoric radiance, the beast moved alongside us for an hour or two. Or rather, it was as if we were moving alongside an illuminated, saucepan-grey promontory – some piece of lonely land, like this Bouvet Island we're moored off, but stretching into the sea with a necklace of light.

Said is the Sheikh's son. He likes to falcon off the deck, hoping to catch other birds. Mostly young skuas which put up a good fight. Handsome and clever, with an aquiline nose, he has become a particular friend. One day, coming into my cabin and seeing before me this blotted memoir of my wartime days, this other vessel on which I've embarked to pass the time at sea, he asked, 'What are you writing?'

I told him what, and showed him some, and also pages of the dog-eared diary from which I'm working up the book. And so the custom has begun of him taking and reading the successive chapters as I finish them each day, progressing in that story as, looming out of frozen mists, the *Habbakuk* makes its way north. I drink tea or whisky, smoke my pipe, listen to cassettes of Haydn oratorios – and write. Now and then I am called upon to give judgement on a scientific issue relating to the ship but otherwise my time is my own.

Sometimes I overdo it, for an old man. One morning Said found me asleep in bed – among my papers, with manuscript sheets scattered around me. The top of my fountain pen had come off in my lap. The ink had run into the bedsheets, turning their cryptic creases as blue as the ocean through which we are sailing.

This happened, that happened . . . The question of where to begin is always hardest. A deep breath is needed before making that decision. For, as Ryman himself said – *all mistakes proceed from initial conditions.* In the end I chose not my birth or childhood but another journey, undertaken many years ago, when as a callow youth I made my own way north, to see the Prophet.

January

1

The Prophet was a scientist called Wallace Ryman. He was a conscientious objector who devised a special 'number' in which the government was interested during the Second World War. Many great scientists have had a number named after them, usually defining the state of a particular physical process. The Mach number, which expresses the speed of an object moving through air divided by the speed of sound, is the one with which most people are familiar.

The Ryman number, by contrast, is a criterion by which the turbulence of weather systems and other flows can be measured. It is dimensionless, which means it can be applied anywhere as a co-ordinate of comparison across space and time. A low Ryman number (less than one) indicates significant turbulence; a higher score (above one) indicates a more typical, 'stable' state.

These dimensionless numbers are all about information. They are used as a way of gauging information received. There has been an occasion in my life when (to cut a long and complicated story short) I think I may have had some significant historical influence in employing the Ryman number in this way. The context of this was the meteorological preparations for Operation Neptune in 1944, the first phase of Overlord – or, more popularly, D-Day.

In winter that year I was sent on a special task by Sir Peter Vaward, director of the Meteorological Office. From its reluctant originator I was to discover how to apply a range of values of the Ryman number to a fifty-mile-long invasion site on the coast of France or Belgium. The Ryman number has a direct effect on weather forecasts, because turbulence is associated with patterns of expectation and uncertainty.

Ryman lived in Scotland. Sir Peter had organised a place for me on a meteorological reconnaissance plane on its way from London to Prestwick, which then served the city of Glasgow and the large volume of air traffic arriving from America. It was late January when I set off, and snow was blowing across the airfield as I made my way to the plane (a Halifax), whose propellers were already turning.

In the absence of meteorological information in areas where the enemy operated, a large number of these reconnaissance flights flew daily on sorties all round the British Isles. The plane I was flying in was due to continue from Prestwick to Stornoway on the Isle of Lewis, from where it would fly on the BISMUTH sortie towards Iceland. The aircraft was part of Met 518 Squadron and carried their famous badge painted on its nose – a fist grasping a key with *Thaan iuchair againn-ne* written underneath, which is Gaelic for 'We hold the key'.

What did I think was going to happen, as I climbed into the cabin with my suitcase? Did I have a sense of knowledge about to dawn? What did I *feel*? It's very hard to get back to all that. It doesn't just come gushing out. I often didn't know what I felt at the time; I often don't know what I think now. So many of our deepest feelings, in any case, come to us as doubtful, tangled, compound experiences. Events themselves as they happen condition the way we see previous events, making us recalibrate the chain of causation even as we teeter along it, casting all the while a speculative eye at a web of possible futures . . . This is what living – conscious living – is.

As we took off at around ten I could still taste the baked beans I'd had for breakfast. No doubt about that, even after so many years. I remember the old advertisements, too, with their

'Always ready to serve' slogan (more patriotic in those troubled times than '57 varieties', I suppose) and picture of a soldier eating. And then: *Don't think Heinz are making less. We are making more! Fighting men must be fed first; so civilian supplies are limited. But those with a quick eye for the famous name . . .*

Something like that.

I sat up front. The cockpit was cold and draughty. Like the pilot, I had a throat mike and a flying helmet with earphones and goggles – through which, once we were underway, I watched the blizzard increase. The snow hit the glass in loosely defined units, then moved across it fast in a joining mass before being whipped off to the wingtips, where it whirled round like a thick vapour and was flung into our trail. It was in my nature to plot the journey of each snowflake in my head: p = the pressure, h = the height, x = the mass of water per unit mass, v = the velocity per unit mass, y = the entropy . . .

'You want to avoid cumulonimbus,' I said to the pilot, after a while watching the snow clouds. 'Very bad for turbulence.'

'To the deuce with that,' he said, pushing the joystick. We went into a sharp dive. The plane began to spin, a phenomenon at first oddly lacking in turbulence, since it was controlled. Nonetheless, it was terrifying.

I knew that if there was a 'wobble' severe turbulence would soon occur and we could lose control of the plane. I had done experiments on this sort of thing while at Cambridge – throwing boomerangs on the Backs and seeing when they would lose aerodynamism, or spinning beach pebbles on wooden surfaces and judging when they would fall.

We continued to drop. A penetrating noise sounded through the riveted aluminium of the cabin. 'What the hell are you doing?' I shouted.

We were still heading down, diving through one cloud layer after another, the engine roaring – 6,000 feet, 5,000, 4,000 . . .

'Are *you* telling *me* how to fly?' came the reply through the headphones. 'I've been flying cunims since you were in short trousers. This is nothing! I've flown in weather in which even the birds were walking.'

I clutched my seat, feeling the beans and bacon rise in my stomach. 'That may be so,' I said, 'but . . .' My voice dried up as wordless terror filled my bones.

He stamped on the pedals and pulled out the throttle to full. The nose was still pointing down. I looked at the altimeter in horror. The engine screamed as aero-fuel shot into it – and then in another swift movement he centralised the joystick.

Suddenly we were upright and calm. The needle began to creep round the dial – 2,000 . . . 3,000 . . . 4,000 . . . then he flattened out, allowing the instruments to acquire level values for a minute or two, before starting to climb again steadily.

'What did you do that for?' I said angrily as we regained height. 'Is that your idea of a joke?' With the increase in height came a faint feeling of my intestines being squeezed.

The pilot laughed. 'Simmer down, old chap. I was doing a thumb.'

'A thumb?' I asked, my heart still racing. Something familiar rubbed at the back of my mind. Not 'thumb' – THUM: Temperature and Humidity. The manoeuvre was a legitimate one to record those values at successive heights. But there was no need to do THUMs over the English Midlands.

I spent most of the rest of the journey in sullen silence, staring into the oncoming snow. There was not much I could do. The joker was a Lieutenant Geoffrey Reynolds, who proceeded to tell me about a noteworthy engagement in which he had become involved. Flying back from his sortie he had spotted a U-boat on the surface. The U-boat crash-dived on seeing him but Reynolds attacked with two anti-submarine bombs that exploded just ahead of the wake . . .

'The U-boat was virtually blown out of the water, rearing up stern first before sinking. I was bloody chuffed with myself, I can tell you, and headquarters were pretty pleased, too.'

I imagined the U-boat sinking in a widening slick of bubbles and oil and flotsam. 'They wouldn't have been quite so happy if the U-boat had had time to call in air support,' continued Reynolds. 'Mind you, nothing's so hairy as picking up damaged instruments from weather ships. The crews sling them out in a waterproof bag on a line attached to a buoy, and we have to fly down and pick up the line with a hook lowered from the undercarriage. Then come round again and throw the new gauges down to the crew. You don't want Jerry creeping up on you in the midst of that malarkey. It seems a lot of trouble to go to for a broken barometer. I don't really understand why they don't just throw the bust ones over the side rather than have us haul them back to be repaired.'

The reason was that these instruments were very expensive and hard to make, but one couldn't expect an airman to appreciate that. There was often a bit of friction between these pilots and us forecasters, especially on the more remote bases. The pilots depended on us for good information, and they could often be very rude when they didn't get it, or a forecast went wrong. The issue of authority was complicated by the fact that some forecasters wore RAF uniform and some didn't, depending on the type of operation in which they were involved.

I had just been promoted to technical officer, but that was a Met rank, not an RAF one. Just the previous week, prior to Sir Peter's intervention in my life, I had been a lowly meteorological assistant, a plotter of synoptic charts, a sender up of balloons on £110 a year (£6 income tax).

Mine was an odd way into meteorology, as few practical meteorologists have also been academics. I had been in the Cavendish Laboratory at Cambridge, and I got there at an early age. I was awarded my PhD in 1938, at which time I was twenty-two years old. My thesis was in fluid dynamics, focusing on turbulence and other complexities of flows or 'dynamical systems'. One encounters a lot of these in continuum physics – it's all the stuff that's shifting around, the material that's hard to quantify because it's always moving.

In the absence of any particular girlfriend, I'd fallen in love with turbulence while an undergraduate. It is really just the study of whirls and eddies, in particular those that make up, on different scales, the atmosphere in which we all live. Fluid dynamics is also keyholder of our lives in a more intimate way, in that it governs the flow of blood and chemicals through the locks and weirs of body and brain.

I listened to the hum of air passing softly over the machine, blowing past the wings in a whine that was clearly audible despite the *whoof-whoof-whoof* of the engines. Out of an intense, blue-gleaming whiteness, snowflakes whirled up from the nose. Now and then through the endlessly changing air we fell into patches of larger alteration. Troughs of turbulence, like potholes in a street in an African town – such as where, from under the dirt-stiffened pleat of his shirt, a beggar might reach out a hand for coins.

Those are all the people I have time for now, since G— is gone, those millions of Africa for whom Overlord meant nothing, to whom the generals then and nearly every politician since cast hardly a glance.

G—. I cannot even write the name. Even thinking it causes a sharp, tender shock to spike into my heart.

Flying north, I watched the white flakes spattering the screen. Their shapes, distinct only for a moment, commingled with the thread-like wisps of my thoughts as they came and went. It was as if both were being blown by a wind that would permit no stillness. Everything was swelling, dispersing, happening again and yet not again – for while each thought and each snowflake was different and had its own identity, each was being carried along in the same medium of incalculable change.

War – that altered everything too. The cosy Cambridge world of teacakes and sporting the oak began to disintegrate, chipped away in fragments. One could not just stay at one's bench in the lab. I saw an advertisement for a training post at the Meteorological Office and, wanting to serve my country in the best way I could, I applied for the job.

On being accepted I was sent to the Central Forecasting Unit at Dunstable. There I studied under Charles Douglas, the senior forecaster. He was an eccentric man but a kind one, and a brilliant meteorologist. He had a phenomenal memory – and some kind of nervous affliction. Something terrible had happened to him during the first war: he was a meteorological observer with the Royal Flying Corps and had been shot down in a dogfight. I once saw him get up in the middle of a meeting and run three times round the table.

But Douglas gave me the best on-the-job training anyone could have got. By 1943 I was research assistant to the superintendent of Kew Observatory, James Stagg, and owner of a small flat in Richmond, having scraped together enough to buy it from savings and the little money that came to me from my parents. Stagg and I worked together on various issues relating to the reflectivity of clouds. Like me, he would be plucked out of his post when the planning for D-Day began.

As we came into Prestwick, I saw that the braziers were out, lines of petrol burners on either side of the runway to aid visibility. And I must say that Reynolds, despite his chirpy offensiveness, made a good job of landing in such difficult conditions.

More snow arrived as we taxied over to the hangar – a blinding wall of wind-driven particles rising like smoke from the ground. As the wind blew, it took the loose new stuff with it, making it slide across the hard, crusted snow that had been compacted by vehicles on the surface of the airfield.

I said thank you and goodbye to Reynolds before disembarking and he grinned at me as he undid his helmet strap, so I suppose we parted on good terms in the end.

I climbed down the ladder, grateful for my Crombie and leather gloves, but very much feeling the lack of a hat as the snowflakes settled on my hair. Still, it might have been cold but I was at the start of my adventure; and besides, for me, unlike most travellers, the snow was a source of great delight. Tumbling softly or flying past fast in a jet, it made the wind visible in all its varieties – for these streams of snow passing over the trodden surface were not regular in scale: some were broad, some narrow; some ran straight, some crooked. Some stopped and flew up into the air, as if in a column. Others were clamped down, as if struck with a hammer. Sometimes these streams, which were often no more than two yards broad, acted as a kind of fence, disclosing the variable action of two other drifts of snow on either side.

Most marvellous of all were those moments when two of these corridors of snow, blown by wind coming from different directions – north and west, say – met and passed through each other, like ghosts at a crossroads.

Now I remember this image I'm struck by its significance; for it was exactly this idea of corridors and barriers, of differential borders marking out the richness and variety of weather, that I would learn from Ryman. My master, so fine and subtle, who knew things perfectly at which I could only grope, reaching for years in Cambridge the skinny hand of thought into the darkness.

Despite the dampening effect of the snow, the braziers made quite a noise, roaring yellow-blue plumes of flame into the frozen air. I noticed an American military plane on the white-shrouded tarmac, and it was an American I first spoke to on entering the airport complex. He was dressed in a USAAF leather flying jacket and cut quite a figure, being rather tall, with a scrap of thick black hair falling over his forehead.

'This will all be gone by morning,' said the man, looking out at the gale. 'It'll be like it never happened.'

As I was to discover, such optimism of prediction was entirely typical of him. Personally, I don't think he was the self-serving scoundrel some European observers have made him out to be. He just wanted the best for the world he was part of.

'I think you'll find any forecast over three days hence is purely random,' I said. 'Beyond two it's little better than gambling.'

'Oh yeah?' he said, pushing back the shock of hair. 'And who are you to say so?'

'Henry Meadows,' I said, trying not to assume an air of superiority. 'I work for the Met Office, actually.'

He laughed. 'Holy Moly, what a coincidence.' He held out his hand. 'Irv Krick. US Air Force weather service. I'm here on a familiarisation tour. What's your business?'

I gave him the alibi with which Sir Peter had supplied me. 'I'm on my way to set up a weather station in the west of Scotland.'

I'd vaguely heard of Krick – he used to work at Caltech, which in those days led the way in American meteorology – and we talked a little about developments in the field. He was on his way home to the United States, but his plane had been grounded. He went to consult his colleagues about the chances of leaving the following day and I turned to watch the storm through the plate-glass window. How was I going to get to

Kilmun in this weather? I was supposed to be taking a steamer out to the west coast in a few hours, but that would be impossible now.

I heard Krick's voice behind me. 'Me and my buddies are going to hole up in a hotel in Glasgow tonight. If you play poker, we'll give you a game.'

I considered my limited options. At the very least I needed lunch, so I joined Krick and his assistant Ben Holzman in a military car which took us through the blizzard to a hotel in the centre of the city. The journey was about thirty miles and it snowed the entire length of it.

2

By the time we reached Glasgow it was obvious that there was no chance of travelling any further that day. We sat down to spuds with mince and onions, followed by whisky and a game of poker in front of a coal fire. If I'm not careful, I thought, as the cards slapped onto the table, I could lose the whole afternoon. I resolved not to – but within minutes the whisky and the warmth had drained all the willpower out of me.

Over the card play, as coals glowed in the hearth and a waitress in an apron and bonnet supplied us with ice for the Scotch, I listened as Krick told me his remarkable life story. I had taken an unlikely route into meteorology, but his was far stranger. After taking a physics degree at the University of California he worked as a disc jockey, then as a runner for a company of stockbrokers.

'Chapman de Wolfe and Company,' he said, pronouncing it 'Volf' in the German way. 'As you can imagine, my services were dispensed with pretty rapidly after the Crash in 'twenty-nine. Though I missed the worst of it on my own account.'

'How?' I asked, leaning forward.

He grinned, slicking his hair back. 'I devised a system calibrating financial fluctuations against background randomness, according to certain physical principles. Things have changed a bit since then, but I still use the same basic idea.'

Krick's theory of stock-market cycles had begun as an innocent intellectual recreation, or so he said, but in years to come he successfully played the markets using his system. The Wall Street Crash was no accident, he maintained. It was a necessary piece of information within a larger story. Ryman, who had none of Krick's hucksterism, would have agreed. There are no accidents. Every so-called 'accident', every piece of turbulence, is part of a sequence, bigger or smaller, whose scale you cannot see. At least, you don't see it until it's too late, and then you start to panic, because you realise how foolish was your original fantasy of understanding.

During the Depression Krick sold pianos and worked as a jobbing concert pianist for the NBC Orchestra. He was also a radio disc jockey for a while. Eventually he found his way back to university, studying meteorology under Theodore von Kármán and Robert Millikan at Caltech in Los Angeles. It was uncanny to hear about these giants of meteorology in a Glasgow hotel – stranger still to do so with a glass of whisky in one hand and a busted flush in the other.

As the talk flowed, I drank more and more. I won a couple of pots. So did Krick, leaning his big face forward as he collected. The other Americans won one apiece. As the cards were dealt and shuffled and stacked, the smoke from our cigarettes and cigars swirled up the oak panelling, with its pictures of sporting scenes and moody Highland cattle. How well I would come to know their glowering stares.

Krick told more anecdotes as we played. 'Goering tried to lure back von Kármán to Europe to head up the Luftwaffe's weather forecasting,' he said. 'Von Kármán refused, simply sending Goering a drawing of his Jewish profile.' We all laughed. It was a meteorologists' joke, a 'profile' being a technical term in weather forecasting.

As Krick talked I slowly began to realise the anecdotes were diversion tactics. The tales were intended to distract his opponents from their game – and it was working. All the time he was recounting his experiences, or expounding pet theories, he was taking money off us.

The diverting stories continued. The duo had met at Caltech. Then Krick had joined an airline, as had Holzman, who became chief meteorologist for American Airlines. They began swapping tales about the aviation industry.

'I used to get in trouble in that first job,' Krick drawled, showing another hand. A pair of deuces – plus another pair of deuces. Four of a kind against my full house, and there he was scooping up our money again. 'They hadn't heard of weather fronts then, and hated me drawing them on the charts. But obviously it was more useful for the pilots. Then they could see where the action was coming from. Predictable as a corny movie.'

'Irv worked in Hollywood,' chipped in Holzman. 'He was weather prophet for *Gone with the Wind*.'

Krick grinned as he added our money to his stack. 'I picked the night they burnt Atlanta. It had to be a clear one.'

'Another time, he advised Bogart on the weather for the Ensenada yacht race,' said Holzman.

'I flubbed that. Bogie never got to Mexico. He stayed in US waters. A dead calm.'

Holzman laughed. 'Will you go back to it, Irv, when the war's over?'

'I doubt it. I was forecasting for the citrus industry before I got called up. Reckon I'll get back into it. That's where the money is.'

'Commercial forecasting,' nodded Holzman.

'Transporting airplanes is another good one,' added Krick. 'Forty planes going from A to B, you don't wanna get that wrong. One of my first duties in the air force in this war was to pick the days when our guys could fly safely across the Atlantic.'

'Days with minimum turbulence?' I asked.

'Oh no,' said Krick. 'Pick those days and our friends in the Luftwaffe would be waiting. It was more a case of just enough turbulence.' He produced a cigar from under the table and, as prelude to another tale, blew a near-perfect smoke ring over my head . . .

It has always struck me as *fate* that I met those two at the beginning of my working life. From my Cambridge ivory tower I have followed their careers with interest since the war, now and then bumping into one or other of them on trips to America. They became sort of alter egos for me, standing for all the possibilities I shut off when I chose withdrawal into academic life.

Later in the war Holzman would work on the weather forecast for the atom bomb at Los Alamos. He stayed in the US Air Force for his entire career, becoming a general and commander of the USAAF Research Laboratory. He was involved in virtually every major phase of research into missile and space systems, all through the Cold War. His security clearance was cosmic, so I didn't get to see him much.

Krick, as he indicated during that poker session, would pretty much found the new industry of selling the weather. Cotton growers wanting to know what the harvest will be like. The Edison Company having difficulties with storms knocking out power lines. The California Division of Highways worrying about snow in the mountains. The Brooklyn Dodgers wanting advice on whether they should buy rain insurance for an important game. Loggers, fruit growers, the managers of hydroelectric schemes . . .

Krick pursued all this and more. He was weather forecaster for the 1960 Winter Olympics and, the following year, for the inauguration of President Kennedy. But his biggest thing was cloud-seeding, which involved modifying weather by dispersing chemicals, usually silver iodide, or dry ice, into clouds to induce precipitation.

Krick got into this still-controversial practice in a major way, selling thousands of ground-based generators to farmers all over the US. These machines, rocketing crystals into the reluctant sky, were all controlled by radio from a complex in Palm Springs, California, where Krick himself still lives in a Moorish-style mansion in the shadow of Mount San Jacinto.

I went to visit him there once – the place had marble floors – and he was extremely hospitable, serving up frozen margaritas. But to the US Weather Bureau he became a kind of bête noire. There were accusations of quackery and exploitation. He was always very charming to me, and I never brought up something which troubled my colleagues: that he may have been the source of the rumours, still current to this day in the US, that the British teams 'failed' in their predictions for Overlord – and that D-Day was saved by Krick himself. He even maintained, somewhat astonishingly, that it would have been better to have gone a day earlier after all. I let it pass.

This was the extravagant future which lay ahead of my poker opponents. I drank far more than I should have done and lost more money than I could afford. Some time in the early hours I staggered up to bed, wallet half emptied, shoelaces trailing, mounting unsteadily a staircase, the steps of which seemed to have been frustratingly rearranged, before losing myself in a warren of interconnecting, treacherously carpeted corridors and the hiding-places of mops and buckets and boiler-room pipes. I suppose I must have booked a room in the course of that long afternoon which had stretched into evening, and eventually found my way to it, but I can't remember doing either.

3

With sheets and blankets bound ingeniously about me, competing with half-removed clothing, I woke in a vortex of nausea and remorse – the customary bedfellows of a hangover. Very quickly these old friends were trussed up themselves, tied down by an overwhelming feeling of guilt, that still older friend. How stupid to have squandered some brain cells on whisky and cards, especially when I had a further journey to make, and such important work to do. What would Sir Peter Vaward have thought of such behaviour?

I ran a bath, and as I languished in the water I recalled my first meeting with him at Adastral House on the corner of Kingsway and Aldwych in London. Having been summoned from Kew by telegram, I'd climbed the stairs to the third floor, where I was met by Miss Clements, at that time a young secretary in a cashmere jumper. Standing before the door's tall, grand panel, I waited some time in the 'vestibule', as she called it, smiling sweetly. In life's troubled mirror I try to conjure her back – before the approaching night, before the threshold, before time wrapped itself round her throat.

As it was, she left me outside Sir Peter's office. On the wall there was a large oil painting of Admiral FitzRoy, Darwin's captain on the *Beagle* and the original director of the Met Office. He suffered from depression and committed suicide with a razor in his washroom. I want to see her again, that pretty girl, but all that comes back is that damned painting.

I had no idea why I was there. The summons had come the

previous day. A Motorcycle Corps messenger had roared into the gardens at Kew, where I was preparing to send up a glob. I was handed a flimsy blue envelope marked PRIORITY. Inside was an order to be at Adastral House by 3 p.m. the next day.

Coming in to London proper, I was struck as always by the sight of the barrage balloons over the city: silver-coloured and sixty feet long, they floated about 2,000 feet above the ground, to which they were tethered by steel cables. There were also sandbags everywhere, and corrugated-iron Anderson shelters.

Sir Peter shook my hand. He had a long white face with a prominent upper lip that seemed to be missing a moustache. A watch-chain gleamed on his waistcoat, catching the light of a fire that flickered effortfully under a marble mantlepiece. The grate was piled with glowing coal, making unpredictable cracking noises as it burned.

My glance came back to Sir Peter. All in all, he was what my mother would have called 'a tidy man', but cadaverously pale – as if subject every night to some vampire-like extraction of blood.

In my lukewarm bath I watched the tap drip as his physiognomy and words reformed in my mind. 'Welcome, Meadows,' he said. 'Glad you could come at such short notice.'

Via an intercom, he instructed Miss Clements not to disturb us as I sat down, opposite him at his desk. There was a loud *bong!* The room was filled with antique clocks and as the hour turned they all started sounding, slightly out of synchronisation.

Once the noise had subsided, Vaward spoke. 'You are probably wondering why I asked you here.' A tall clock with a man-in-the-moon face gave a valedictory plink. He paused, studying me carefully. 'Before we begin, I must ask you to sign this.'

He slid a sheet of paper across the desk. It was stamped SECRET in red letters and it began 'I, ___ ___, hereby declare . . .'

This was something new. My job thus far in the war had been to send balloons carrying small radio transmitters – radiosondes, or 'globs', as we called them – into the upper air to measure pressure, temperature and humidity. They were used to forecast the weather. Weather as a set of changing conditions. Weather as a transitional state of affairs. Weather as how things were – are – will be. Weather as a source of information.

But the information is perishable, lasting no longer than the structure to which it refers, just as the bathwater I was sitting in as I recalled all this would no longer be *my* bathwater once it ran down the plughole. But perhaps that is the wrong way to think about water, anyway.

I often had to put up these balloons in thunderstorms, sweating in uncomfortable oilskins. I also worked on something called the Free Balloon Barrage, which was more exciting. It involved sending up small hydrogen-filled balloons trailing wires with small bombs on the end. The idea was that these devices, floating at about 20,000 feet, would create a sort of aerial minefield for unwary German bombers. There was no indication enemy aircraft ever did collide with any element of the barrage, although what was assumed to be evasive action by German pilots was observed on a couple of occasions, so perhaps we gave them the odd scare.

Apart from that work, I acted as a pure scientist, so whatever it was Sir Peter had in mind unnerved me.

'I assume you have no objections to signing the Official Secrets Act,' he said as I studied the document before me. 'It is merely a formality before we get down to business.'

My stomach jittered. 'Have I done something wrong at Kew, sir?' I asked.

'Not at all. In fact, that's one of the matters I wanted to raise with you. We are breaking up the Kew team. Some will go to a special forecasting unit at Bushey Park, henceforth to have overall control of developments on the continent. Others will be sent to the chemical warfare station at Porton Down on Salisbury Plain. The rest will be distributed about the services as we see fit.'

I found myself signing the paper as he spoke. I didn't want to go to Porton.

'Many civilian Met Office staffers will be mobilised into the RAF – so you will see a lot more blue uniforms about the place.'

'What about Dr Stagg?' I asked, thinking of my superintendent at Kew.

'His knowledge and experience will be used to direct a forecasting issue of acute national importance,' Sir Peter replied smoothly, leaving me none the wiser.

'And the readings?' It was also part of my job to tend to the vast bank of meters, dials and other equipment under the Kew observatory's dome.

'A skeleton staff,' said Sir Peter, gruffly. 'Enough. Be it accepted that for you I have other plans. They involve a stay at Kilmun, in Argyll.'

'Is there a weather station there?'

Sir Peter laughed. 'You could call him that. You will set up your own operation as a blind, but be attached to a Met station nearby.'

'I'm sorry, sir. I'm not sure I quite understand.'

'Listen, Meadows. Before I tell you any more I should point out that, if you accept this position, it will mean promotion to TO. It seems to me that you are not best employed at Kew. You won the Sheepshanks Prize at Cambridge, for goodness' sake.' He lit a cigarette, fixing me with his eyes over the flame. 'You're not a conchie, are you?'

'Absolutely not, sir,' I protested.

'It's all right,' he said. 'There are many ways a man can help his country. What I am about to propose is not dangerous. It does, however, require a certain cunning, and a nose for snooping around. It is most definitely scientific work, if of a surreptitious nature.'

He waited, as if expecting me to say something in response. I said nothing.

'We want you to set up an outstation from Dunoon at Kilmun, on the banks of the Holy Loch. It's not entirely a cover; the Royal Navy have made a submarine base in the loch and we run a weather station in Dunoon itself for them, attached to HMS *Osprey*.'

'I see,' I said. 'And that's my job?'

'Not exactly,' said Sir Peter, leaning back in his chair. 'Have you heard of Wallace Ryman?'

'Of course,' I said. 'The originator of numerical weather forecasting.' As well as being one of the foremost theorists of turbulence, Ryman had invented a system of weather forecasting based on mathematics.

Sir Peter looked at me, as if expecting me to continue.

'The Ryman method involves describing every weather situation in figures and making a mathematically informed estimate of how it could develop,' I said. 'He divides the atmosphere into three-dimensional "parcels" of air and assigns numerical values to each aspect of the weather within them. Then he uses maths to see where things may go.'

The Met Office director interrupted me. 'But it doesn't work. Ryman himself got it wrong. He tried out the scheme during the first war and it went awry.'

'So I understand. But the impossibility was in the computation, sir. The theory itself is sound. In principle, this kind of prediction is possible.'

'Maybe so. I hope it is, for our sake. Anything else?'

'Someone told me Ryman used to work for the Met Office,

but he protested when it was taken over by the Air Ministry. I don't know why.'

'He's a Quaker,' said Sir Peter, with barely concealed disdain. 'His conscientious objections led to him leaving the Met Office in the 1920s. He was always a difficult man . . .'

Sir Peter stopped, as if suddenly aware of having said too much. He reached out a bony hand for the paper I had signed, folded it once and placed it in a drawer of his desk, turning a key on it before speaking again.

'The truth is, Meadows, he's not an easy man but he is a brilliant one, and the British meteorological community has felt the lack of him keenly. Now we come to the nub of the thing. Are you acquainted with the so-called Ryman number?'

I was coming to the limit of my knowledge. 'Only in the most basic sense, sir,' I admitted. 'It explains the dynamic relationship between the two types of energy, kinetic and potential, that change weather.'

Sir Peter nodded. He did not seem surprised. 'No one has got much beyond the basics. That is what I am sending you to Scotland for. Though I once used some of his work, I myself know only a little about this side of things.'

'Why do you need to . . .? If I may ask . . .?'

'The Ryman number is of enormous significance because it defines the amount of turbulence in a given situation. Of the few that know about it at all, no one but him knows exactly how to implement it . . . it changes in different contexts, as you might expect. The government wants to use this number for a particular operation. Airborne and amphibious and enormous in scale. The long-expected invasion across the Channel into mainland Europe. We think Ryman himself is the only man alive who really understands how a *range* of values of his number might be practically applied – around a specific geographical area and over a particular time window

33

– but he has not responded to my letters.'

'What about the Germans?'

'They have convened a special group of forecasters whose task is to predict the date of the Allied invasion. It is led by Professor Ludwig Weickmann and includes men such as Baur and Wagemann, of whom you will have heard in the course of your academic studies. And Prandtl is somewhere there in the background, too. They have certainly heard of Ryman, we know this from citations in scientific papers.'

He paused, looking at me with pellucid eyes. 'So it's important we ourselves understand his number properly before preparing the meteorology. We cannot, in this issue, rely on providence. Dr Stagg has been selected to lead the forecast team for the invasion. If you play your cards right . . .'

He watched me, gauging my reaction. I remember I tried to keep my features impassive, waiting for him to speak again, but he did not elaborate.

'Well . . . we believe Ryman has been working on his coherent programme in secret, applying his number to other lines of research. Now it's all very well to have free thinkers in the scientific community, but in wartime nothing that might bring about victory should be kept a secret from the government.'

I remember being intensely aware of the furniture polish on all the clocks in the room. A familiar smell of beeswax, recalling in turn African servants smearing it on the parquet floor of our home at Kasungu in Nyasaland. Cloth-shrouded hands dipping into the yellow pot. Our dog Vickers sliding across the floor on spatchcocked legs. Towards French windows, well-cultivated lawns, flowerbeds, and a bounding stand of bluegum trees, together with a single baobab in which large numbers of white storks nested.

Further beyond the high windows were the flat expanses of the tobacco fields of the Kasungu plain, where, through the large, pale-green curling leaves, a moist wind called the *chiperoni* blew – and no doubt still blows.

'You will go to Kilmun and set up a weather station there. An outstation from Dunoon, as I say. The equipment has already been sent, to a building near Ryman's house, where you will live. Whybrow is the super at Dunoon. In addition to your normal duties you are to become friendly with Ryman. Find out what he is up to.'

A cooling bath in the Cross Keys Hotel in Glasgow. The commanding voice of Sir Peter Vaward in an office on London's Kingsway. Wind in the tobacco fields of Kasungu. Days gone by, existing only in the place of memory. Days that are fading like light in the bluegums at dusk. Days that will soon be gone for ever.

'Discover what the relevant range of values of his number is to an invasion front of, say, fifty miles. Learn how to apply them practically. Assume that you have about two months lead time in which to make rolling forecasts before you launch your invasion, and less than a week between making the critical final forecast and the invasion date.'

He paused, as if to make sure I was paying attention. 'And Meadows?'

'Yes, sir?'

The flames in the grate licked about, searching for their portion of air.

'If you can persuade him to abandon his pacifist principles and help us defeat the Nazis, all the better.'

'Is that likely?' I asked.

'It's more likely the king will invite Hitler to eat shepherd's pie at Buckingham Palace, but you must try nonetheless. There is too much at stake for Ryman to be allowed to keep his research to himself. By the way, you'll find a chap from Combined Operations Experimental Section at Dunoon, as well as our regular Met people. You know about the Experimental Section, I take it?'

'As much as anyone does,' I replied. It was a kind of asylum for professors run by Mountbatten's chief of staff, Wildman-Lushington. The activities which took place under its auspices – all sorts of odd scientific research for the military – were the subject of much speculation by other government technical departments.

'Well, there is a bright person from that section in Dunoon who may be able to help you. His name is Pyke. He's an expert in ice.'

I couldn't see what ice had to do with it. There was quite enough to be going on with already. In fact I wanted to be sure before I left that the job was quite so large and forbidding as it was beginning to seem.

'So just to be clear, sir. You want me to come back here with hook, line and sinker on the Ryman number. You want me to find out how wide a field of adjacent zones of turbulence – Europe, the Atlantic, the Irish Sea, wherever – we need to know about in order to make amphibious landings across the Channel. And you want me to come up with a practical method of putting the uncertainty of all those zones, with the varying time series of their weather systems, into a single coherent scheme?'

'Yes. Well put, Meadows. You should know that I have chosen you because of your academic proficiency and the excellent reports Douglas and Stagg give of you. Are you up to the challenge?'

I nodded assertively – in truth a laughable response to such a question, but there it is.

Perhaps Sir Peter sensed this. 'Don't think it will be an easy leap,' he said. 'Ryman is stubborn, somewhat peculiar. He'll be cagey. He won't be cajoled or charmed. You will have to make him respect you. That is another reason I have chosen you – because, if you don't mind me saying, you share some characteristics with him.'

I suppose, looking back, he meant that I had a tendency to become technical and a capacity for obsession.

'You may find the best way to him is through his wife,' Sir Peter continued. 'You yourself should keep secret anything you discover. Guard it close, because this is the big one. You may find this file useful. It contains meteorological various papers written by Ryman in the days when he used to publish.'

It may have been thumping as I remembered all this, lying in the bath in that Glasgow hotel, but as he spoke my head was swelling with heroic visions. I had left the director's office under no illusion that I was to be anything but the indispensable saviour, someone who had been chosen to perform a vital job of individual service for the nation.

The water cooled round my body. Already, I reflected, I seemed to have stumbled. I had tripped over the jumble of impulses which nature plants in an individual to make sure we can never conceive our own personalities as well-organised information. From within as well as without, disorder is always waiting to pounce. Failure is always at the ready. All it takes is a little push at the brick of one's self-possession and the whole enterprise is threatened. Sometimes memory is the only thing left holding the individual together: the crypt that is also the keystone.

Yet one cannot live in the past. One has to allow oneself to grow. Indeed, that is why the threat of complete disorganisation is necessary: it promotes the foliage of unformed states, of those strategic mental camouflages which work to increase our statistical protection from future risk. If the mind-system were closed, if there wasn't *always* a threat of loss, it would run down through inanition.

In this thoughtful frame of mind, I hauled myself out of the bath and stood naked in front of the mirror, kneading my hair with a towel, then getting out my shaving kit. I had quite a trim figure in those days – rationing saw to that – and, despite the continuing effects of the previous night's dissipation, I managed to face myself in the glass with something like equanimity. For a second, looking at my own dark eyes in the mirror, I saw the face of the boy who had run beneath the bluegums in Kasungu, scattering the storks from their tree of assembly, setting it awhirl.

As the black bristles came off, flecking the coils of soap foam, I began to recover some of the urgency I would need to resume the task with which Sir Peter had entrusted me.

I pulled aside the curtain and looked outside, to check the weather. The snow had almost completely gone, just as Krick had predicted. There was even a bit of sunshine. All that was left of the blizzard were puddles and dripping masonry, with occasional dubs of white sitting on sheltered lintels or between sequestered tiles.

A mongrel dog, spotted and barred, was nudging its way through wind-tipped rubbish bins along the waterlogged back alley behind the hotel. It was turning up damp pieces of this and that, testing their edibility before trotting on through the turmoil to the next unidentifiable item. Unidentifiable from where I was, anyway.

Turmoil, *tohu bohu*, turbulence ... there too the issue of perspective is crucial. You might well ask again what it is, this thing which has been my life's work. At one level it is simple. Turbulence is the jittery, swirling behaviour of a gas or liquid flowing round an obstacle (which could be another gas or liquid). More puzzlingly, it's a predictable process seen from one perspective that becomes disordered and unpredictable viewed from another, or when observed over a different time period.

I put on my shirt and suit, knotted my tie – a dark-green spotted number – did up my shoelaces and repacked my suit-case. In a way things had worked out well, what with the Yanks giving me a ride in their car like that, and bringing me straight to a hotel.

By the time I had gone downstairs, eaten breakfast and drunk two cups of strong coffee, I was ready to go. I looked around for Krick and his crew as I paid my bill, but there was no sign of the Americans. Must have already gone to the airport, I thought, before walking out myself into the sodden embroilment of the pavement.

Filled with a fray of business folk and shoppers and service-men, the street was surprisingly busy. Watching the morose crowd tramping through the melted remnants of the storm, it struck me that Scotland might as well be a foreign country to one such as myself. But then I often felt like that in England, too, as did many of us who had grown up in the colonies. It was as if we had returned to a home different from the one we had been holding in our heads all that time.

I couldn't stand all the posh officers but the oiks seemed just as coarse and stupid. Many of the intellectuals were generally dismissive of science, which enraged me. I suppose I also felt distinct because I was raised as a Catholic and was half-Irish; but if I was anchored anywhere at all it would be in central Africa.

After some political difficulties at home – his family were merchants in Tralee in Co. Kerry – my father had emigrated to Africa, where, after numerous adventures in South Africa, Kenya and elsewhere, he eventually became manager of a tobacco farm in Nyasaland. My mother was the daughter of a British copper miner from Northern Rhodesia, a widower who moved to Nyasaland to prospect for gold and more or less dumped my mother in my father's hands. It was she that was the Catholic, not him, despite his being Irish. The Meadowses were Protestants. So right from the start I came out of a mixed marriage.

Suitcase in hand, curling hair still slightly damp on my head, despite the vigorous kneading of half an hour ago, I stood for a moment watching the lugubrious Glaswegian throng – then tugged up the collar of my coat with my other hand and went on my way.

4

The place I was headed for was in the Cowal, which is a district of Argyll. A ragged peninsula on the west coast of Scotland, the Cowal lies between Kintyre on one side and Glasgow and the Firth of Clyde on the other. As one could do in those days, I caught a paddle steamer, the *Fair Maid*, from the Broomielaw quay in central Glasgow. It was an old excursion steamer, doing special service for the Navy and painted wartime grey.

There was great hubbub as passengers – many of them soldiers with kitbags and rifles – and vast amounts of cargo and coal were loaded on. Then with a blow on the harbour master's whistle the gangplank was rattled back on board. A warp of rope was thrown off the bollard by a fellow on the quayside. Vibrations thudded through the vessel as the engine engaged. Then the great paddle wheels themselves began to turn, making criss-cross patterns in their boxes, water gushing down.

The ship gave two toots of its horn, steam jetting from its funnel, and so we were away, moving quickly through the bustle of Glasgow towards Clydebank.

At first I just set my suitcase down beside me and leaned over the taffrail, watching the sights. Pennants fluttering, we sailed out past miles of mills and warehouses, coal yards and cranes. We came through the roar of the Clydeside shipyards, which were full of red steel and tiny figures – ant-like creatures on the hulls of half-made dreadnoughts and cargo ships. From there we passed towards Greenock and Gourock and the tranquil lower Clyde, where the Firth opened up into a filigree of blue lochs and green hills.

Hence over the water was the Cowal shore. It was there, in a village called Kilmun, that I was to solicit – from a pacifist, on behalf of the military – the secret of weather forecasting.

The present weather had improved enormously since yesterday. Even though it was still cold, blue sky was showing through shifting, toothy clouds which moved over the crinkly sea as if to comb it. I sat down on a slatted wooden bench and watched the milky froth of the double wake of the ship trailing out behind. On either side of the water, thickly wooded hills enfolded churches and cottages and farmhouses.

After a while I pulled out the file Sir Peter had given me and, keeping a close hold on the flapping pages, boned up a bit more on Ryman and his work. I remember trying to place him in the context of what I myself had been doing at Kew, and to understand how his theories might really make a difference to an invasion. Most of the file contained scientific papers Ryman had written, but the first page was some kind of personal biography, which I suppose must have been supplied to Sir Peter by the intelligence services:

RYMAN, WALLACE. Mathematician, physicist, meteorologist, sociologist. Conscientious objector. Has travelled in Norway (1922) and Germany (1939). Has developed mathematical techniques of weather forecasting, expert in fluid dynamics, meteorological technology. Hobbies: none known.

Born 1892. Only child of Catherine Garnett and David Ryman. A prosperous Quaker family. David Ryman running a successful tanning and leather manufacturing business. At age 12 sent to a Quaker boarding school, Bootham in York, where

received an education which apparently stimulated
an active interest in science. In 1909 went to
Durham College of Science, where took courses in
mathematical physics, chemistry, botany, and
zoology. Two years later, gained scholarship to
King's College, Cambridge. Graduated with double
first-class honours in the natural sciences
tripos in 1914. Joined as a Quaker the Friends
Ambulance Unit same year. In 1932 married Gill
Blackford (b.1906), daughter of William
Blackford, chief engineer at the Saunders-Roe
seaplane factory in Cowes. No children.

Career:
Friends Ambulance Unit in France (1914-1918)
Researcher, National Physical Laboratory (1918-
1919)
Lecturer, Paisley Technical College (1919-1920)
Researcher, Scottish Peat Company (1920-1921)
Researcher, National Physical Laboratory (1921-
1926)
Senior Lecturer, Manchester College (1926-1927)
Met Office. Eskdalemuir Observatory (1927-1930)
Met Office. Benson, Oxfordshire (1930-1931)
Head of Research, Saunders-Roe, Cowes (1931-1933)
Professor, Paisley Technical College (1933-1939)
Resigned from Met Office when it was absorbed
into Air Ministry, stating conscientious
objections as reason. Currently living off modest
private income following inheritance from
parents, incl. shares in Ryman's Tanning &
Leather Ltd, York. Pursues personal scientific
and some sociological research, i.e. causes of

war and how to prevent them. In 1937, elected to the Fellowship of the Royal Society.

What struck me most about this was how restless Ryman was, changing jobs every couple of years. Also how determined he was to keep himself not just out of the Oxford and Cambridge scene (which, with a double first and a King's scholarship, he could have easily entered) but also away from London. It was as if he wanted to keep himself pure. If he had not had those spells at the Met Office, would anyone have heard of him at all? As it was, he was a square peg in a round hole so far as the rest of the meteorological community went, although I had often seen respectful mentions of his name in the literature.

At that time, weather forecasting in Britain was practised by following the evolution of physical quantities based on measurements taken at various stations around the country, then applying them mechanistically to the next two or three days – as if one were taking the recipe and ingredients of a cake and predicting what it would look like and taste like, which might be done with a fair degree of accuracy. Beyond three days it became a question of the relative probabilities of various weather narratives: the cake might turn out this way or that way or another way, depending on how it was cooked.

Ryman was the first person to have mathematically connected eddy motion across different scales, from the smallest gyre lifting a leaf in a corner of the garden to those of great storms, hundreds of miles across their turning diameter.

But his equations were so complex we had not yet been able to use them at the Met Office. The arithmetic required to solve them took too long. Even sitting there on the boat then, I remember having to stare at a single line of calculation in one paper for a full ten minutes before I understood it. I can often remember having to kick myself for being too stupid like that.

As I was number-crunching, my attention kept being distracted by the marine paraphernalia further down the deck. Winching equipment waiting for its moment. Coils of rope lying on wooden palettes like sleeping cobras. The ensign flapping at the prow. The face the life-ring's open mouth made where it hung on the bulkhead. The derricks poking their noses over the side. Most of all the two paddles, milling over and over, just like my thoughts themselves.

I don't want to give the impression meteorology was in the dark ages during the war. Our radiosonde balloons, such as I sent up at Kew, did allow us to make synoptic charts – 'maps' of weather, which is more or less what you see on the television news nowadays. Synoptic means 'seen at the same time' and refers to measurements taken simultaneously in different locations. From extrapolation of these simultaneous measurements, the map of likely future weather emerges, moving across land and time.

But apart from synoptics, which came in not long before I joined the Met, our methods hadn't changed radically since they were first devised by our suicidal founder, that same Admiral FitzRoy whose picture graced the wall outside Sir Peter's office. The lack of change was despite the partial adoption of various new methods which distinguished between different types of air 'mass', originating in the poles or the tropics. Using the term for a battle line, the Norwegians had invented the idea of 'fronts' to mark the edges of these bundles of weather.

Fronts are a graphic representation of the moving limits of weather systems; they try to put a discrete edge on shades within the continuity of the total. They are a kind of spectral lockdown, as if one is imprisoning the ghost of change in a line; but for all that they are very useful, giving a sense of emerging pattern.

Once again my attention was distracted, this time by the foghorn of another vessel. The most conspicuous aspect of that journey, I remember, was other ships. The water was thick with them. Puffers and dinghies and tugs, motor launches, supply barges, frigates, troopships ...

The troopships were the most impressive of all, being as stately as their names: *Queen of Bermuda*, *Aquitania*, *Empress of Britain* ... Filling the air with grey smoke, they were carrying armies from the Empire and the United States, either to ready themselves in training camps in the Cowal and points north, or on their way out to fighting in various theatres of war.

Ryman had set out to develop a numerical system that would complement the FitzRoy and Norwegian methods and possibly supersede them, by manipulating the quantities and limits of weather systems mathematically. His number, more properly a ratio, as I think I have said, was at the heart of this. It showed the *rate* of turbulence in an evolving weather system, dramatising the relationship between wind and heat as a number on a positive or negative scale.

Surrounded by all that rope and ships, I suddenly saw an easy way to explain it all to myself, as a kind of springboard for the more difficult task that lay ahead. When the Ryman number is positive, turbulence is decreasing, because the flow is dynamically stable. Cold air is reducing the roughening effect produced when wind goes over surfaces or when one wind hits another coming from a different direction. It's like a tug of war – a rope being pulled between these wind irregularities and the calming effects of cold – and the cold is winning.

When the number is negative, turbulence is increasing. The flow is dynamically unstable. Buoyancy effects associated with higher temperatures combine with wind irregularities to produce larger, faster-spinning eddies. Then it is like a race between two ships. The ship of wind-generated turbulence versus the ship of temperature-generated turbulence.

But just as there must be a finishing line to a race, so turbulence always becomes exhausted, locally speaking. It cascades down from big eddies to small ones before the process begins again somewhere in the wider system. Effectively, as I had said to Sir Peter in my interview, the kinetic energy of eddies in one place is converted into potential energy that will make turbulence in another place. It is like expelling a troublemaker from one school only for him to join another and make trouble there – not that turbulence should always be considered as trouble. Far from it.

Hearing shouts, I looked out across the water. Thronging the decks with their green helmets and uniforms, soldiers were waving to us from one of the vast troopships. Some of the other passengers waved back, and then the shock of the leviathan's bow wave reached us and began rocking the *Fair Maid*. Soon I would see the anchorages of some of these monstrous ships in Holy Loch (my own destination) and Loch Long.

As we moved from side to side, it struck me that the difference between the two vessels was nothing compared with the difference between what I understood then, concerning Ryman and his number, and what I would need to understand and be capable of if I was really to supply what Sir Peter wanted: Ryman numbers for a geographical space that might be subject to any number of contrasting, altering weather systems over a five-day window.

The maths alone was mind-boggling. The time period over which the evolution of any eddy can be predicted is generally comparable with its own life-span, which is why averages are used in weather forecasting. But what Sir Peter wanted was very specific, and you just can't use averages to predict the *specifics* of the next generation of eddies, any more than you could use an average to predict the life-story of an individual human being. All you can do is show the likely dominance of one pattern over others . . .

As this thought went through my head I became aware that we were approaching the settlement of Dunoon, sometimes referred to as the 'capital' of Cowal. But before we could pull in we had, like all the other ships, to pass through the naval boom. This was a barrier of mines and deep baffles which stretched across from Castle Rock at Dunoon to Cloch Point on the Renfrewshire coast. Its purpose was to prevent enemy U-boats attacking the naval bases, anchorages and training facilities in the lochs above. An armed tug – the boom boat, as I'd later learn to call it – had the job of opening a gate in the cordon to let us in.

Once this had been done, we swung in to Dunoon pier. A majestic Victorian construction made of thick wooden planking, it supported a pier house painted brown and white, with a clock tower on top, together with a balustraded promenade running from one side to the other. Underneath the promenade were tobacco and sweet kiosks, together with toilets, a ticket booth and the harbour master's office. There were gulls everywhere, stalking the wooden decking or skulking among the barnacle-encrusted uprights which supported it. Beyond the pier was a large green mound with a small castle on top, its flagpole flying the saltire. This mound dominated the whole town which spread out below it.

Dunoon had long been a holiday resort for Glaswegians, chief jewel in the necklace of villages and towns strung along the Firth of Clyde below the Cowal hills. Most of the passengers disembarked here – along with sacks of coal, bundles of ironware, mail bags and crates of beer. I had hoped then to continue my journey to Kilmun, which was just across the opening to Holy Loch, but was informed by the steward that Kilmun pier was closed for repair. I would have to get off at Blairmore, just a little 'furth' doun the watter', as he put it.

It was no great delay. In a few minutes, passing under some of the finest mountain scenery I'd seen outside Africa, the *Fair Maid* was cranking towards a craggy foreshore where, with foam washing under its stanchions, Blairmore's own pier jutted out into the foot of Loch Long.

I decided I would go straight to Ryman's house, reasoning that, if the building in which I was to live was nearby, I could make myself known to him in the course of establishing myself in my new home.

5

I stood motionless on the planks of the pier, squinting at the plume of smoke rising from the stack of the departing *Fair Maid*. Its decks were still full of folk bound for Arrochar at the head of the loch and other destinations in between. A fine sight, that pillar of blackish-greyish-whitish smoke and steam – leaning at first then streaming backwards, so that it lay horizontally against the clouds.

The plume began to move eastward, back towards the Firth and Glasgow. It would, I knew, break up during the twenty-five miles between here and the city, separating as atmospheric diffusion took effect. I watched only the first stage as the plume bent at the near end, becoming like a question-mark in the sky.

A large, dark seabird – a great skua? – flew among the swirling shapes, to the disintegration of which its own powerful wingbeats were contributing further dispersive energy. Soon the objects of this dark interpreter's attention – I could hear it calling now, a harsh *hah-hah-hah* – would become something else, chemically and physically altered by the more powerful forces of the surrounding air.

As I walked up the pier, from behind the little stone hut at the end a strange sight appeared. An anachronism . . . a horse and trap . . . The animal was stamping and steaming, blowing a little bubble of froth from its mouth. I stared at the little spoked wheels of the trap. It took me a few seconds to rationalise it. Blairmore time, it seemed, was a long way behind London time – by a half a century at least!

Stepping out from behind the horse, a rough, gypsy-looking man in his forties completed the Victorian picture. Lifting his whip in salute, he gestured to the back of the trap. He wore a tweed cap and chewed on a pipe – it stuck out of his unshaven, windswept face like a branch from a pollarded tree. He struck me as a not very prosperous farmer, with a dash of drover or poacher.

'The Ryman house, Kilmun, please,' I said, as he stowed my heavy leather suitcase in a net in the back of the gig, which already contained several parcels and a crate. I climbed aboard, he sat beside me, and with a touch of the whip the wheels were turning and we were on our way.

His name was Mackellar – he gave no first name – and he was, as I had guessed, a farmer. 'I meet the boat whenever she comes in,' he said. 'Pick up the messages, passengers. The messages I pick up for nothing, passengers are fourpence.'

He gave me a hard, sidelong look. 'Ye have it?'

I nodded, gripping the black-lacquered wood of the seat as we clipped along by the lapping water.

'You'll be the weather man, is that no' right?' he asked.

'How did you know?'

'They've put in a' this equipment for you. On my land. My building as well. Compulsory order. No rent, mind, but that's the government for you, war or no war.' He gave the horse a tap with the crop and our pace increased with a jolt.

I shifted in my seat. 'Sorry about that. But it is important work, you know.' I tried to think of a simple way to describe it. 'If there is to be rain, we forecast it to warn the soldiers.'

He gave me another sidelong look, and tapped the horse's flank again. 'Dae the soldiers no have mackintoshes, then?'

I smiled and turned my attention to the passing country. Once we had left the little hamlet of Blairmore, my spirits were lifted to see the loch beach on one side and the high hills thick with trees on the other. Scattered scraps of cirrus, the thread-cloud, garlanded sunlit, spruce-covered hilltops. Some showed signs of forestry work, with gaps where trees had been cut down.

'First time up in these pairts, then?' asked Mackellar.

'Yes,' I said. 'I was brought up in Africa.'

'Africa, eh? That's a fair distance, eh? Well, you'll find difference, tha's for sure. Sun and cloud always smirring each other here.'

Coming round Strone Point – which separated the foot of Loch Long from the opening into the Holy Loch – we passed into a long strip of road half covered with vegetation.

'The folk here call this Midge Lane,' said Mackellar, who seemed to switch randomly between Scots and English. 'Fine now, but gin the wind dinna blaw nae mair, the midgies come. They ging oot for biting the incomers.'

There was a pause as I tried to translate this to myself. During the hiatus the clipping noise of the horse's hooves filled the hedge-lined lane. A dog barked as we passed a gate and the horse shied, pulling at the leather traces.

'Don't be frichtened,' Mackellar said, softly. 'He disnae like the dugs. Nor the midgies either. Great smokin' crowds of them, we get here.'

'I saw something like that in Africa,' I said eventually, remembering my boyhood in Nyasaland. 'On a large lake there, they have big clouds of midges.'

Mackellar gave a low chuckle.

'Ah dinna ken aboot Africa, but ah'll tell ye whit's whit aboot the midgies here. Ye'll see if ah'm wrang. I swear if ye leave the midgies alane, they willnay bother ye. They come tae where there's chappin' in the air, so though they micht dance aboot ye, keep still yersel. Every dunt ye gie them, they'll gie ye back wi interest. Whit's mair, they love the mochy weather, so gin the sun comes oot, ye gae oot too. And they dinnae fly ower salt watter.'

He gave the horse a proper crack with the whip and round the bluff, as if by inches, Holy Loch angled into view. I saw the heads of two seals stick up out of the water. They looked like soldiers' helmets.

'Why's it called Holy Loch?' I asked.

Mackellar shrugged. 'Thair's mony a tale.' He did not elaborate.

The Loch was dominated by the sight of three grey navy ships, each with a covey of submarines moored alongside. The village of Kilmun was strung out in front of them.

We weren't supposed to talk about ship names then – there were warning posters about this everywhere – but I would soon learn that the mother ships were HMS *Forth*, *Titania* and *Alrhoda*. From here the submarine clutch would disperse on their deadly and dangerous missions into the Atlantic Ocean, many never to return.

'Ye have business wi' the Prophet?' asked Mackellar.

'You mean Professor Ryman?'

'We ken him as the Prophet.'

'Oh.'

'He gies us advice,' said my nut-brown chauffeur. 'When tae plant oor crops. When the moon'll mak a cow drap her calf. When the salmon run'll start. How tae mak your ain weedkiller and whit'll keep the midges aff ye. That sort a thing.'

'But surely country people know all that anyway?'

'Auld wives' tales,' he said dismissively, upturning the prejudice I had formed of him. 'Folklore and the like. God knows, my wife has faith in it. She thinks milk boiling o'er means somebody is going to fall ill, that snails an' smoking are unlucky, an' maist of a' that if the burds skirl before a flaw, a stronger blaw's on its way, sic as could tip ye heelstergowdie.'

After asking him what 'heelstergowdie' meant, I deciphered all this as meaning something like 'if the birds whirl around before a squall, a stronger wind is on its way, such as might tip you head over heels'. He invariably spoke the Scots more quickly than the English.

'But I prefer the Prophet's predictions,' he continued. 'He goes about with a gun. Ye'll see for yourself soon enough.'

The earlier sun had gone. The Holy Loch looked cold and grey now, its surface flecked by a raking pattern of white cat's paws, every rippling line and distortion derived from physics and chemistry, even the clouds reflected in its waters.

'That's where the Prophet lives,' said Mackellar, pointing with his whip as we approached a solid, square, magnolia-painted house set among gardens and situated a little way back from the road behind a stone wall. 'My ain farm's just beyond.'

On a hillside above Ryman's home (which was Georgian, I suppose, with two bay windows), I saw another wall and beyond that a farmhouse and outbuildings. There were also stables and a cowshed and a barn stacked with hay, together with some glasshouses. In the field between the farm and Ryman's house stood a much older stone building, beside a trough at which two Highland cattle were drinking. Higher up ran a stripe of beech trees. Mackellar told me there was a stream in the middle of the beech wood, with a small bridge across it.

Further still up the hill was the forestry: line after line of forbidding spruce, broken only where logging had taken place – and also by a long steel chute. It looked like a child's slide. 'The foresters use tha' for getting the wood out,' explained Mackellar, seeing me looking.

We had stopped at the wrought-iron gate of the Ryman house, which was decorated with a solar design surrounded by signs of the zodiac. I wondered for a second if I had strayed into a location with laws other than those of Newton, a place of signs and wonders, a glen of omens. But then I saw a sundial in the garden and also a large telescope on a pedestal, and somehow with those instruments rationality reasserted itself.

'That building next to the tree, the auld cot-house, that's where they put your kit,' said Mackellar, pointing up the hillside. 'There's a bed, but I cannae say it looks very comfortable. I'll take you there.'

'No, no thank you,' I said. 'I may as well pay the professor a visit now I'm here. But if you could take up my suitcase, I'd be most grateful.'

'That I'll dae,' said Mackellar gruffly.

I climbed down from the trap.

'Now the Prophet,' he said, raising his whip for emphasis, 'he disnae like folk to bang at the door.' He paused. 'So you must go in sleekit-like. He'll like you mair, if you make it so,' he added.

The farmer followed this statement with a thrusting movement of the other hand that needed no interpretation. I searched in my pocket for the fare and gave it him. As the trap made its way up to my new home I walked up to the front door of Ryman's house.

I was about to knock when I remembered Mackellar's warning. I pushed against the heavy black door. It was locked.

Behind me, from somewhere across the loch or deep up the Firth, I heard a ship's foghorn sound. It was like the groan of a dying mammoth or mastodon, as if some early drama of evolution was being played out across the archipelagic waters of the Cowal. I stood and waited, feeling uneasy again. This really did, after all, seem an odd, obscure place for the logical transparencies of science to have triumphed, as far from the mechanistic projections of the Ryman number as could be imagined.

6

Hearing a sound, I turned to see a tall woman emerge from an outhouse behind me. Her blonde hair was scraped under a scarf and she wore a woollen jumper, corduroy trousers and wellington boots. She was carrying an empty hand seed sower, an instrument that allowed one to control the flow of seeds through different outlets. There was something about her that was immediately reassuring.

She gave a start when she saw me, then smiled. 'I'm supposed to be propagating cabbages,' she said, lifting up the sower's funnel-shaped spout and peering at me mischievously through it. She held out a hand. 'But I've lost the packet that the seeds are in. Gill Ryman. And you must be . . .?'

'Henry Meadows. I'm from the Met Office. I'm staffing the radio equipment in Mr Mackellar's field.'

Gill Ryman. Eyes the colour of the sea and just as changeable, but brighter. Lines of care on her brow and, yes, she looked tired, but she was intriguing as well as reassuring – most of all those eyes, which were filled with the fierce energy of true believers. I didn't know, then, quite how unquenchable was the faith of this bright-eyed huntress of seed, whom I would so terribly harm. It was her faith that saved me, not my own. And it was her intelligence which cracked the number. But on first meeting her, I got no sense of either of these things; she was, instead, the object of misdirected melancholic longings, feelings that I only half understood myself.

Her hand was cold and slightly calloused as I shook it. I noticed there was scrollwork on the front of her jersey. She was attractive, quite a big woman overall, but also, in an odd way, angular. The mixture gave a sense of strength and frailty in balance, as if she were both fern and flower; it made you wonder what lay beneath.

'Oh, that's you, is it?' She took off the scarf, shook out her locks, then looked me up and down, like a farmer inspecting a bullock at market. 'We noticed the men from the ministry had been busy. My husband once worked for the Met Office.'

'Well, that's why I'm here,' I said. 'I mean, at your door. I'm a follower of his weather work.'

'Really? But he gave all that up ages ago. He concentrates on his peace studies now.'

Peace studies. How strange that sounded in wartime. A blasphemy. For a moment I was lost for anything to say. I didn't want to arouse suspicion.

'All the same,' I said eventually, 'I am very interested in his mathematics.'

'I can't promise he will see you, but do come in.'

I stepped towards the front door again.

'Oh, we don't use that one,' she said. 'This way.'

I followed her round to the back. I found myself gazing at her well-covered form. She had a roundness across the hips; otherwise she was bony, all knees and elbows and shoulders. Behind the house, stretching up a hillside towards the low stone building and Mackellar's, were vegetable gardens in which I noticed a tall labourer digging.

'That's the cot-house up there,' she said, gesturing at the old stone building as she opened the back door. Cot-house. Mackellar had used the same odd term, which I later learned was just an old word for a dwelling on agricultural land. The little black Highland cattle I'd seen earlier had moved closer to the stone structure. Now they were gathering round it, angling down their malevolent-looking horns as if they might lift it from its ancient foundations.

'Those are our gardens in between.' My gaze drew back down nearer, to the old man, digging.

'Parsnips,' added Mrs Ryman by way of explanation as I followed her into the hall. Directly, something hit me on the head.

'Sorry. Should have warned you. That's my husband's special heating system. It hangs from cables. Don't ask me how it works.'

A series of pipes, supported by wires, ran down the centre of the hallway. The whole place smelt strongly of steam and chemicals. I followed her through into a large country kitchen.

'Cup of tea?'

'Yes, please.' The kitchen was rather spartan. 'Excuse me, but – is your husband here?'

'He's always here,' she said. 'That was him, digging in the garden.'

'That was Professor Ryman?' I was amazed.

'Yes. He does most of the heavy digging. Though we get Mackellar to scythe the grass. I hope he was pleasant to you on the way up from Blairmore. It's a pain, our own pier being out of action; usually you would have been able to walk.'

'Mackellar? Pleasant enough.'

'He can be a little surly. And as for his wife . . .' I was surprised she was so candid.

The kettle whistled loudly. She turned her attention to making the tea – not a pot, just a mug with a steel diffuser in it – then vanished into an adjoining room.

She returned with a bowl of broad beans. 'Hungry? Go on, try them. They're delicious.'

I took a couple of beans. They had been boiled and sprinkled with salt and were surprisingly good.

'We don't keep sugar in the house, I'm afraid. Or biscuits. Wallace says there is as much glucose in a broad bean as in a spoonful of sugar.'

I wondered if that was true. It sounded as if it might be, though with so little sugar available at this stage of the war it would have been hard to verify the issue.

'There now,' she added, handing me the mug of tea. 'You drink that up and I'll ask if he will see you.' She went out into the garden.

I sipped my tea, which was a bit too strong, then peeped into the drawing room. The walls were whitewashed, and it was plainly furnished with antique black-oak furniture. Sideboards and dressers and the like: the sort of thing people inherit – though I had received nothing like that. It all stayed in Africa.

There were also two threadbare armchairs in the Rymans' drawing room, and a chaise-longue upholstered in pink satin – a rare hint of luxury. The overwhelming impression was one of self-denial, although in one corner of the room there stood a large rocking horse. There were indentations in the wall opposite its head and ears, clearly made by too-enthusiastic usage.

Apart from the chaise-longue and the rocking horse, the only other softening touch was a piece of embroidery in a wooden frame behind glass. It was the kind of fancy lacework you might see displayed in Madeira or Nantes, or even in Nottingham long ago. I realised it was a child's christening gown.

'I'm afraid my husband cannot see you now,' said Mrs Ryman from behind me. She had returned from the garden without my noticing. There was a little chill in her voice. We both looked at the gown for a moment and she gave a blink. 'He has some calculations to do once he has finished digging. He doesn't like unexpected visitors.' She expelled air from between her lips. 'Unexpected anything, really.'

In light of this rebuttal I recalculated my own options, trying at the same time to cover my annoyance. 'Oh. What a shame. Another time, perhaps?'

'Sunday lunch,' she said. 'Do come. The minister will be there.'

I shook her hand, and then she said, with a curious smile, 'I look forward to it.'

7

The Met Office had been busy in Mackellar's cot-house. As I approached the building I noticed a green motorcycle leaning against the wall by the door, its handle pressing against lichen on the stone. Inside I found my suitcase, a desk, and about five torpedo-like hydrogen cylinders. There were also a large number of labelled wooden crates, some drums of caustic soda and several new cable points. Electricity had been run up from the road on wooden poles. A stove and sink stood in one corner; in another a door opened to a small bathroom with a red-tiled floor.

On the desk was a letter from Gordon Whybrow, my immediate notional superior at the main station in Dunoon. Typewritten in a distinctive font, it listed the materials that had been delivered. The note also detailed the charting and plotting that would be required of me. It added that the motorcycle outside was for my own use as I had a balloon schedule involving releases in some quite remote locations.

Having read it, I felt a bit glum. It was all very well Sir Peter giving me a cover under which to spy on Ryman, but the cover itself would mean quite hard work. How was I going to manage it all? Still, there were compensations. I had never been on a motorcycle before.

So the first thing I did was I tuck my trousers into my socks and go back outside to try it. I fell off a few times, skidding about the field and frightening the cattle, but it was tremendous fun. I'd more or less got the hang of it after an hour.

Spattered with mud, I went back in to inspect the crates.

I read some of the labels: EDDYSTONE RADIOSONDE, ROTATABLE ADCOCK AERIAL SYSTEM, RADIO TRANSCEIVER ... There was also a teleprinter for contacting the main station at Dunoon, plus an AO, an oscillator device for comparing the radiosonde transmissions against a known frequency.

I picked up a hydrogen cylinder and shook it. It was empty, which explained the drums of caustic soda. From these and other ingredients, I was to make my own hydrogen. I had never made it before, but I knew this was common practice on sub-stations, unlike at Kew. It would have been impracticable to deliver pressurised ready-filled cylinders to observers in rural locations.

Realising the unpacking was going to be a big job, I walked down to the village shop to buy some bread, cheese and pickle and other provisions, then set to work on my return. It would take me the rest of the day to sort it all. I began splitting open the crates with a crowbar – labelled CROWBAR, in inimitable Met Office style – and I finished around midnight. The floor was covered with splinters of wood; they looked like arrows and spears left over from some terrible colonial massacre.

That night, as I lay in the darkness, with the cattle coughing around me in the field and bits of slate dust falling on my face from the roof when the wind blew, I actually found myself looking forward to plotting some charts. Brain work rather than brawn work. But, having unpacked the equipment, I still had to prepare it.

The next morning, after doing my ablutions, I went up to Mackellar's farm to scrounge some milk. The gruff old farmer – pipe sticking out of his mouth even at that early hour – gave of it freely, taking me to the dairy and dipping a steel jug into a bucket.

'You keep that jug and come here in the mornings, do the same thing yersel'. Never you mind if my wife comes bawling. Tell her you have the permission.'

'Righto,' I said cheerfully, and made my way back down the grassy hill, carefully holding the milk-slopping jug in front of me with both hands.

I had some breakfast, then began testing the audio oscillator. The regular sounds it produced were compared with the altering transmissions from the radiosondes that hung beneath each balloon, which I could pick up on the high-frequency radio set. The signals varied in pitch according to the height of the balloon, thus enabling me to get a fix on its position as it recorded meteorological phenomena.

The oscillator was quite loud – it made a series of pips – and could be heard outside, even though it was standing on the desk in the cot-house. It soon attracted the attention of the cows in the field. They gathered round the building in a circle, which made me vaguely uneasy. The sight of them provoked a memory.

As a young man I once helped round up cattle on a farm somewhere on the earth road between Blantyre and Zomba, where one of my father's friends had tried his hand at dairy. Those animals, feeding on yellow grass amid clusters of native huts, were a cross between Friesians and African zebu and they were pretty lively. These Scottish beasts, spikily horned, impishly black, seemed far less tractable. They regarded me moodily, with a certainty of interspecies difference that reminded me of the way baboons would face up to lions. Where was Vickers when I needed him, to give them a nip?

By the end of my first full day in the cot-house I had got the HF set playing big-band music from the Home Service and the teleprinter, switched into receive mode, churning out observations and forecasts. Combined with other readings from the local area, my own information would be telexed from Dunoon to Met Office operational headquarters and fed into the general weather picture. This, in turn, would be the basis of briefings to the Allied forces all over the world.

The teleprinter made a *chuh-chuh* noise as its keys hit the paper, which jerked out off the roll and snaked to the floor. It was heartening to think of all those Met observers and Waafs and Wrens punching in their messages. The meteorological realm presided over by Sir Peter Vaward was very well organised. It had to be. Consider just for a moment how the constant changeability of the weather had to be gauged, now and in the future, against a background of the chaos and upheaval of war.

But having global weather information is one thing; using it is quite another. If your measurement is even slightly wrong – as we now know it always will be – there's a danger of the data degrading very rapidly. There's also a more basic problem of measurements (which are mental artefacts) being taken on certain sizes of eddies (which are physical artefacts) and not others. There are always scales and dimensions that are being ignored. And this is dangerous because the whole point is that all these sizes of turbulence are interconnected; they are both separate and continuous, feeding energy from large to small then back again.

Each scale must be viewed as information that contributes to understanding the likely pattern of the whole; and they don't last long anyway, these eddies, even when you do spot them. New information, yes, but now it's changing, now it's gone – and what have you understood?

Ryman's method did not solve the missing dimensions problem but it went closer to doing so than anything done before. But the Ryman number was clearly not something one could tick off on one's fingers. So although it was frustrating to have to wait a week before I could see him, I was grateful for an interval in which to marshal my thoughts and try out his techniques as best I could, using Channel weather as a proving ground.

I spent the second night in the cot-house, as I would many over the forthcoming four months, doing calculations – sometimes in my head, sometimes with a wooden slide-rule, notched and ink-stained, which I still possess. Squeezing precision out of continuous domains in a mustering tumult of differential calculus – such was my life in that strange time.

Lying on the bed doing calculus. Sitting on the crapper doing calculus. Shaving doing calculus. Doing calculus while listening to the radio, hearing what was going on in the war or, for preference, some classical music. Doing calculus while eating. Doing calculus while squeezing the toothpaste tube.

Squeeze, squeeze, squeeze. I am sure I even did it while I was sleeping. Sometimes that can happen. You can go to bed with a problem in your head and wake up with it solved.

But not this problem: how to supply, on the strategic scale and with enough lead time, a safe weather forecast that would allow thousands of men to land by sea and air on a stretch of the French coast on a single day at the optimum time.

8

Early on my third day I set off on the motorcycle to Dunoon, in order to report to Whybrow. I had left it rather late, telling myself the important thing was to ready myself for the encounter with Ryman. Presumably Sir Peter had given Whybrow some indication that I was also doing work other than local observations.

Feeling the wind-chill on my face and hands, I rode along-side the water, past the row of large loch-front houses which constituted Kilmun itself, passing an old church with a tower in its graveyard. I then turned left under bumpy green hills, travelling for several miles (and at one point falling off) until I reached Dunoon.

It was a busy place. As well as local residents there were an awful lot of people in one sort or uniform or another. Colonial troops and Americans as well as British servicemen. On asking where I might find HMS *Osprey*, where Sir Peter had said Whybrow was based, I found it to be one of the shore-based establishments – in this case a former convalescent home – which the navy insists on calling a ship. The floor is referred to as the deck, right starboard and left port. Even to leave by the front door is to take a liberty boat.

As I arrived, a flag-raising ceremony was taking place out-side the building, complete with buglers and ratings in blue and white uniforms. The event was unpopular with the towns-folk as it brought the main road to a standstill.

We stood waiting and watching, our way barred by sentries

with rifles. At the crucial moment, much to the amusement of civilian onlookers, an old fellow in a blue jersey, who was selling fish and oysters from a wheelbarrow, shouted out 'Loch Eck herrings, fresh Loch Eck herrings!'

Once the performance was over, it turned out my wait had been for nothing, as on gaining entrance I learned that the Met station at Dunoon was actually inland rather than on *Osprey* itself. Yet even this second site was still conceived as part of the 'ship'.

I remounted my motorbike and eventually found, on the outskirts of the town, a group of Nissen huts dotted around an old white-painted farmhouse. There was a cookhouse and a washhouse and a hydrogen shed (formerly a grain barn), some dormitories and not much else. The conditions were quite primitive. There was mud everywhere. The sight of it made me shudder.

Gordon Whybrow was bald and short-sighted, with a pair of thick-lensed spectacles balanced on the end of his long, thin nose. I first found him in the Ops Room, as the farmhouse drawing room had been rechristened. He was wearing RAF uniform, like all Met staff who have been conscripted, even if they're actually working in another branch of the services, as he was on *Osprey*. I was still a civilian employee at this stage.

Bent over a desk bearing the large typewriter on which, I presumed, his letter to me had been written, he was studying another machine, or part of it. I recognised it as the switching mechanism on a new type of radiosonde.

Three inflated red balloons bumped on the ceiling of the room, their strings draping over Whybrow as he peered at the device. Behind him, on a large board on the wall, a Waaf was plotting combined readings. A slight brunette, she was reaching up for strings – held in place by brass 'mice' – which showed the directional lines of balloons released from different stations.

Little red flags marked the positions of weather ships in the Atlantic, the Channel and the North Sea, while lines of green flags marked the tracks of the met recs, the meteorological reconnaissance flights which took off from airfields all over Britain each morning.

Another Waaf, plumpish with short fair hair, was kneeling on the floor, reading data to her colleague as the teleprinter roll spilled down. Her chubby face was dotted with freckles. She was the only person in the room to notice my entrance, smiling pleasantly and brushing a hand against her skirt as if doing so would compensate for the awkwardness of kneeling.

'You have to set the switch sequence before you put on the windmill,' I said to Whybrow's bald head. He looked up with a face full of surprise, swiftly followed by irritation, whether at my remark, which I suppose was a bit know-it-all, or simply my arrival I could not tell.

'Henry Meadows. The director probably mentioned . . .'

'Ah,' said Whybrow, straightening. 'There you are at last. Our man of mystery. I noticed you had hooked up the teleprinter yesterday. Why has it taken you so long to report in?' He seemed to speak through his long nose.

'I wanted to get myself established first,' I replied. 'Seeing as the equipment was all there . . . And as I'm sure you know, Sir Peter has given me some other duties, too.'

He blinked through the spectacles. 'Other duties, eh? How about that? Yes, the director did say you had a special project you were working on for him.' He turned to the two Waafs. 'A special project. How about *that*, girls?'

'Allow me to introduce Gwen Liss and Joan Lamb,' said Whybrow, pointing at each in turn. 'I say, he should have come here first of all, shouldn't he, girls?'

I ignored him. One of the women giggled. It was Gwen, the thin brown-haired one, whose cheeks were rather drawn in.

68

This gave her a look of passionate austerity. Joan, meanwhile, was fair and broad, Germanic or Scandinavian in appearance if one had to put a label on it, but with dark eyes. With her blonde hair and freckles, the combination was also rather striking.

Whybrow waved a dismissive hand at the Waafs. 'Give us a minute, will you.' He gestured peremptorily at the red balloons on the ceiling. 'Send up one of those and get me a cloud height estimation.'

Without saying a word, Joan tugged on one of the strings, Gwen seizing the balloon as it came down. It more or less filled the doorway as she took it out, holding it before her as if she were a waitress with a tray. Joan followed.

Once they had left, Whybrow turned to me, folding his hands on his RAF tunic with the air of someone about to make a speech. 'I don't quite understand why a Type 3 outstation need be set up in Wallace Ryman's garden, but who am I to reason why? Apparently you are a "bright young thing" who needs careful handling. A real scientist, Sir Peter said, as if the rest of us aren't. Well, young man, I'll be expecting the very best from you, as from any other observer.'

'Of course, sir,' I said, putting a deliberate meekness into my voice. Whybrow was more or less irrelevant so far as my true task was concerned, but there was no point in antagonising him for the sake of it. And there could, after all, I thought then, be some way in which I might need his help.

'Right, then. Let's get down to brass tacks. Have you sent up any sondes yet?'

'I haven't any hydrogen.'

'We sent over all the requisites.'

'I have never made it before. The tanks came ready supplied at Kew.'

He laughed abruptly, as if pleased to discover I wasn't such a know-it-all after all. 'Then you had better come with me.'

Leaving the farmhouse, we walked through the mud that divided the Nissen huts, all of which were of uniform height. The hydrogen shed was much bigger. From a kind of gable at one end of it, the tower of the cloud searchlight rose, giving the whole complex the air of a makeshift airfield.

'Gwen! Joan!' shouted Whybrow.

He called again. A red balloon appeared from behind one of the huts. Eventually the balloon entered the cloud.

'Three hundred and ten feet, sir,' said Joan emerging from the hut, followed shortly afterwards by Gwen.

They both, I would later learn, came from landed families in Norfolk. The sort of stylish women to whom everything came easily, they seemed odd candidates to be stuck up in this backwater. But then, war did that to all of us, moving us around its chessboard in ways we never expected.

'Jolly good,' said Whybrow nasally. 'Now, I'd like you, one or other of you, or both, to show our new arrival how to make hydrogen. Then send him to Mr Pyke up at Loch Eck.'

He turned to me. 'Sir Peter said I was to introduce you to someone from Combined Ops' Experimental Section who is up here. Strange fellow, Pyke. Very hot to use science for war, and clever with it. Anyway, good luck!'

On this oddly cheery note, Whybrow made his way back to the Ops Room, his square back framed in the rectangle of light between two Nissen huts. Without saying anything to me, the two women began walking in the direction of the tall hydrogen shed.

Falling into pace behind them, I couldn't help noticing their fine shoes were covered in mud. They were court shoes, but fine ones, not the standard, pump-like things that most of the Waafs wore, which looked like comical black frogs.

'Shame to cover such nice shoes in mud,' I said to their

backs. 'They look rather expensive. You ought to be in wellies, with this lot.'

'Not likely,' said Joan over her shoulder. 'We wouldn't be seen dead in wellies.' It struck me as odd that she should speak for them both.

'Hydrogen shed,' Gwen announced bluntly. They both spoke in this clipped, staccato manner. She pushed against the door and I followed them inside.

The lights flickered on to reveal a large warehouse-like space. At one end were some stairs leading up to the gable, out of which a mezzanine floor projected. There was a balcony there with something vertical behind, just showing in the darkness above the lights: a suspended row of aluminium-shaded lamps, looking like soldiers' helmets hanging from wires. The floor space below, empty in the centre, was lined with steel drums of caustic soda and piles of cylinders for storing hydrogen.

'This is the generator,' said Joan. She indicated another drum, smaller and thicker than those in which the caustic soda was stored. It was sealed with a screw-down lid, out of which projected a black rubber tube.

I stubbed my toe on something and swore. The women laughed maliciously. I peered down to see what had injured me: a lozenge of lead. 'That's the safety weight,' explained Gwen, her tone kinder than before. 'We're always doing that. We have a whale of a time doing that.'

She pulled on some rubber gloves and fetched a lump of caustic soda, holding it up to the light as she walked back towards me. It looked like a cake of salt. 'You don't want to get this horrid stuff on your skin.' She put it in the generator, along with some water. 'Fill to two-thirds.'

'Add a cupful of iron filings,' said Joan, leaning over.

'Ferrosilicon, really,' said Gwen, watching Joan pour the

71

catalyst into the cylinder. Then, as Gwen moved quickly to screw down the lid, Joan picked up the lead weight next to my foot. She placed it on the rubber tube where it emerged from the lid. Steadying herself by putting out a hand to Gwen's shoulder, Joan stood on the weight, first with one foot then the other.

'You have to do this or the weight can come off,' she said, as the reaction began. Balancing, arms outstretched, she looked like an outsize Christmas fairy. Next to her, inside the cylinder, the recipe for hydrogen fizzed and gurgled.

The reaction came to a peak. Gwen produced an empty balloon from her tunic, knelt down beside the canister and began rolling the nozzle over the stubby tube. 'You have to thread it on quite carefully,' she said.

'Or it can all go wrong,' added Joan from her pedestal.

I watched the balloon begin to inflate.

'Hydrogen,' said Gwen, holding the sides of the balloon with her palms as it filled up. 'Lightest element in the universe, ta-ra ta-ra.'

'And the most abundant,' said Joan, stepping down from the lozenge as the reaction came to equilibrium. 'Fifteen pounds of it in every human body.' They sounded like music-hall comedians, limbering up for a punchline.

Gwen unrolled the nozzle of the balloon from its umbilical tube, knotted it and let go. It danced up past the row of lights, rising to the apex of the ceiling.

'How will you get it down?' I wondered aloud, watching.

'We'll show you,' said Joan. 'Come on.'

I stood in the centre of the shed. 'Isn't it highly explosive? It could burn on those lights.'

'Only if there's a spark,' said Gwen. 'Come along.'

I followed them across the cavernous shed and up some narrow stairs that led to the gable end and the balcony.

Climbing up through an open trapdoor, I saw there were several steel sheets bolted to the wooden floor as foundations for some kind of structure. It was quite dark up there, but I made out the base of the cloud searchlight tower. Beneath it were two thin mattresses side by side, with pillows and blankets. I was surprised, my mind raced . . . they surely hadn't brought me into a bedroom?

'We sometimes take turns to have a nap up here while on duty,' Gwen said, by way of explanation. She turned on a little lamp: just a bare bulb fixed to one of the wooden rafters.

In the new light I saw two little bowls of make-up on the floor and a full-length mirror draped with clothing. Under the mirror was a small pile of shoes. There was also an easel and a stack of canvases, together with a palette covered with hardened oil paint of various hues, jam jars full of paintbrushes, and a wooden tray of half-squeezed tubes of paint.

'We paint up here too,' said Gwen. 'We're artists, you see.'

Even more surprised, I looked at the picture on the easel. It showed a long yellow beach with rolling breakers curved along a bay. Among puddles of seawater in the sand, a couple of black dogs jumped about, chasing salt-wet tails. The dogs' tails and the curling breakers mirrored each other, as if the intention was to convey a relationship between them. Behind the dogs, blues and yellows and greens of varying relationships blended into the glow of the horizon.

'That's pretty good,' I said, aware of them looking at me in expectation of an opinion.

'Not good enough,' said thin Gwen, and I wondered for a second if she was referring to my response rather than the painting itself.

'Never is,' said Joan. 'Would you like some tea?'

'Oh, yes please,' I replied. 'Which of you did it?'

'We do them together,' Gwen said proudly.

'That's unusual.'

'Maybe. It's our thing. We hope to apply to the Slade, if this horrid war ever ends.'

'What do you think we should call it?' Joan asked me.

I looked again at the painting. 'Dogs in Foam?' I ventured, and they both laughed, hooting loudly.

On a low table next to the mirror was everything needed for brewing tea. Joan put a small kettle on. The three of us stood slightly awkwardly, waiting for it to boil.

'What does Whybrow think?' I asked.

'What about?' said Gwen.

'You two having this little den.'

'Oh, he doesn't mind,' said Joan, pouring hot water into a teapot.

'He daren't,' Gwen said. 'We think he's scared of us.'

'Really?'

'He says we make him anxious,' said Joan, pouring, then handing me a mug.

'Why?'

Neither replied. As we drank our tea, I studied the metal-grid pylon-like tower which rose out of the floor towards the roof, where – bolted on either side of the pitch – there were two more trapdoors. The glass of the searchlight and some meteorological gauges were suspended on a trackway in the middle of the grid, which was raised by a geared winding system.

'Can I see it work?' I asked.

'It's not worth turning on in the day,' said Gwen. 'And at night it attracts bombers, but basically we undo these . . .' She climbed onto the grid of the tower and unbolted one of the trapdoors, which fell down with a bang. Cold air rushed down. I could see the sky – and Gwen's calves.

All in a pickle, I quickly looked down again, trying not to catch the eye of Joan, who was standing next to me. I didn't quite succeed. I was sure she was smirking. The suspicion began to grow in me that the whole thing had been done for my benefit. Or theirs. Had I been had? I was beginning to see how Whybrow might find them perturbing. They seemed to be the kind of women who could turn men round their little fingers, and enjoy the sport of doing it.

There was another bang as Gwen let down the second trapdoor. Joan grasped a metal handle and began winding the worm gear which raised the tower. It ascended like a theatrical device. I watched as Gwen rose further with the tower until her head poked out of the roof. Her silk-stockinged ankles were now level with my face. I felt overcome by simple lust.

'Jeepers it's nippy up here,' she called.

I stared. There was something hypnotic about the way – like a graph curve, like a continuous function – the material followed the flow of skin and bone.

Things were made worse by Joan's hand brushing my back as she reached for the handle of the worm gear. 'You could help,' she said, starting to wind. 'This thing hurts my wrist.'

So I wound the tower – and Gwen – down again. Joan was right. It was quite hard, in spite of the gear.

'In summer,' said Joan, 'we can smell jasmine up there on the wind.'

'Very romantic,' I said.

'Whereas in winter we get chilblains,' said Gwen crisply, climbing down beside us. 'Joany, we'd better get that balloon.'

I looked over the balcony to the balloon on the ceiling. The suspended lights shone a peculiar red through the rubber, like torchlight through fingers. Gwen appeared, holding a pole with a hook on the end – like a boat gaffe – and Joan leaned out over the balcony to deftly hook the balloon.

'Yes,' said Gwen, as she and I descended to the ground floor. 'No, hand it down. I'll do it.'

She took the other end of the pole from Joan, who then climbed down herself.

Gwen opened the door of the shed to let the gas out of the balloon, sounding a long, slow exhalation. I imagined the molecules of hydrogen spreading out into the atmosphere and combining with other elements.

'Whybrow mentioned seeing Pyke from Combined Ops at Loch ... Loch ...' I said, frowning and moving my weight from one foot to another as I tried to remember the name.

'Eck. I'll show you where to drive,' said Joan. 'It's not far. Pyke is usually on the loch at this time. If he's not there he'll be at the Argyll Hotel in town.'

I was pleased it was her. For I have to admit, it was Joan who (in the midst of my ignorance) was stirring my pot then, more than Gwen, despite the business with the stockings. How they will laugh if they ever read this!

We walked through the mud and the old farmyard towards the gate.

'How will I recognise Pyke?' I asked.

I swung my leg over the motorcycle.

'There's no mistaking him,' she said. 'He has a messy little beard, wears specs. Looks a bit peculiar. Holes in his suit jacket.' She giggled. 'You better watch out or that's what you will become.'

'Why?' I asked, affronted.

'All you scientists end up that way.'

'What do you mean?'

'You have no style. All you think about are your equations.'

'Ah,' I said, rising to the challenge. 'But that is just it, don't you see? The style is in the equations. Some people write ugly proofs, others do it with panache. I like to think mine are as beautiful as, as – well, anything!'

I watched her face become aghast. 'Anything? Anything is

76

not beautiful. Only special things are beautiful.'

I felt embarrassed at my inability to express myself. 'All right, Miss, if you say so. But one day I'll show you some of those equations and you will see what I mean.'

'I look forward to it.'

After giving directions to the quay at Loch Eck, she said goodbye to me, then turned and headed back to the station.

I managed to stall the motorbike after just a few yards. As I was sitting in the middle of the road, kicking the starter, I became aware of a detachment of troops marching towards me. American infantry. It was too late for me to move. They separated on either side of me before rejoining; exercise-hardened faces giving no acknowledgement of my presence.

I sat frozen to the seat. I have never seen a statue of a man on a motorbike but that's what I was, a monument around which they flowed with the molecules of the air. After the rupture, when the men reformed, it was as if there had been no disturbance. Turning on the saddle to watch the soldiers grow smaller down the road, I thought again about the invasion of which they might become a part, for which I was supposed to help predict the weather by unwrapping the mysteries of the Ryman number.

I kicked the pedal. Under gunfire on a beach . . . I did not envy them that. I kicked the pedal again.

Starting the engine, finally, I was shaken by a grave doubt as to whether anything I could do as a meteorologist could match what would be asked of those soldiers.

9

Loch Eck was a sombre place. Shadows cast by cloud sat on dark green hills rising steeply from black water edged with reeds and rushes. One cloud in particular caught my eye, perched above its hill. It was a member of a class of clouds termed lenticular, so called because they often look like a thick lens with a hole in the middle. They're unusual in that, although the locality and shape of the cloud remain the same (they frequently cap mountains), the air comprising it is always changing.

I continued on my journey up the loch, at one point having to show my paperwork to a sentry. After riding by the shore for a mile or two, during which time I also passed some navy cadets in a heavy wooden rowing boat, I came to an old stone quay, just as Joan had described. Gathering my thoughts, I propped up the motorcycle on its stand and began walking down the ancient blocks of stone.

My eye followed the grey edge of the quay to where it was interrupted by a broad stairway down to the water. At the top of the stairs stood two men, one of whom was holding a pair of leather reins. Something was waving in the wind above them, echoing the shaking rushes by the edge of the loch.

'Hullo, lend a hand, will you?' he shouted, seeing me watching.

The speaker was a long-haired, bearded, sallow-faced man in his fifties, possibly older. His greying beard was like a scrappy piece of bush; it was as if it was fighting with his skin rather than growing out of it. The leather reins he was holding stretched out into the loch. Out there, a creature was moving through the water, pulling the leather taut. I walked down towards them.

It was an aerial that I had seen waving. The other man – younger, in his early thirties, and almost shaven-headed – held a handset attached to a radio set in his backpack. The handset had red and yellow buttons. Both men wore tweed suits, which in the younger man's case looked rather odd; it's not something you expect, to see the skull beneath the skin of someone in a tweed suit. Next to the two men was a crate containing two dozen or so herring – and next to that stood a tea flask resting on some greaseproof paper, which was half wrapped round an unfinished sandwich.

Without explaining further, the older man handed me one of the reins. The moment I took it there was a sharp jerk that almost sprained my wrist.

'He tends to get a bit excited in tight places,' said the man.

'What is it?' I asked, bemused, resisting the tug of the rein.

'It . . . is Lev,' said the man. 'Short for Leviathan. We're testing the effectiveness of sea lions in guarding harbours against attack. Give him a zap, Julius, will you?'

The other man pressed a button on his radio transmitter. The rein in my hand slackened. Very soon after, nearer to us than I expected, a whiskered face broke the water.

'If there's a mine down there, he'll find it,' explained the fellow with the reins. 'I'm Geoffrey Pyke, by the way. Combined Ops Experimental Section. This is my chum Julius. He's the youngest don in Cambridge. Studies blood. And this is Lev. Come on!'

I thought it strange, considering the secrecy of his department, that Pyke should openly identify himself to me like this, but that was the sort of unconventional, wilfully unorthodox man he was.

He called again at the sea lion and made a signal with his hand. Lev began to frolic in the water beneath us. Pyke made the signal again.

'And you are . . .?' he said, without looking at me.

'Henry Meadows. Met Office.'

'Met, eh? Yes, someone said you might be dropping by.'

The sea lion flopped onto the wide steps that rose along the side of the pier and started to climb them, levering itself up with its tail, step by step.

'Gradus ad Parnassum,' said Pyke, holding up a herring.

The animal wore a harness, behind which it dragged a wretched tangle of reins. Gulls began to circle above the herring and the sandwich.

'We must do something about those reins,' said the man called Julius.

'Soon there won't be any,' said Pyke. He turned to me. 'Sea creatures, Mr Meadows, are far more intelligent than we realise. Especially the whiskered mammals. And the dolphins, of course.'

Lev reached the top of the stone stairway. Pyke gave him a fish. He lay at our feet, raising his black, sleepy-looking eyes to us as he chewed, slapping his tail on the slabs in what seemed like satisfaction. His thick hairy coat was covered with glistening droplets. He had extraordinarily long ear-lobes, which made him look as though he were wearing a Tibetan hat.

'How can we help?' continued Pyke. 'I say "we" – in fact I'm the only person from Combined Ops up here at present. Julius is just helping out for a few days. But if you have a specific problem . . .' He began unclipping the reins from the harness. 'Discoveries, isn't it, Lev, my lad? That's what we're after. At least, that's the plan.'

'Discoveries cannot be planned,' said the shaven-headed don, in a tone of only half-jovial reprimand. 'They tend to show in the most unexpected places.' He had an accent. I later learned his surname was Brecher. He was one of those German scientists, many of them Jews, who had fled Nazi persecution.

'That may be, Julius. But perhaps we should turn our attention to more pertinent matters, like how can we be of assistance to our man from the Met. What are you working on?'

I told them a little about my work in fluid dynamics and at the Met Office, mentioning in passing Ryman's method of applying differential calculus to the physical quantities of weather. Pyke had already heard of it. Then Brecher said much could be learned about biological systems from studying them mathematically in a similar way. 'In all these disciplines there is a flux of identification and differentiation, as the system seeks rules by which to govern itself. The system's own context is part of that. Think of the relationship between blood flowing in a capillary and the other tissue around it.'

When I knew Brecher in later years – we would often play billiards in the Baron of Beef in Cambridge – I would come to recognise such statements as typical. Of all the brilliant men I met during that peculiar wartime winter, he was the most able to express his ideas with philosophical cogency. But in the end it was always blood with Brecher. I don't know how many times I saw his serious, energetic demeanour bent down over the cue, or listened over the click of the balls to him giving voice to some theory of the blood.

I tried to ignore him because it was all so seductive. I mean biology: you have to keep some areas of intellectual enquiry off-limits, pretending they are an uninteresting lumber room off to the left.

Otherwise you end up wandering down a maze of interconnecting caves until you enter the cavern of the central mystery. A place filled with sublime terror, where there is regularity but no fixed criteria for judging it; a place where you know the terms in which the mystery might be stated but not what it actually is. I suppose knowing the horror of this is the price of the relativity Ryman and other more famous thinkers have bought for humankind.

At the time I had no such fears. 'I'm actually hoping to work with Ryman,' I said. 'He lives up here. I wondered if you had come into contact with him. Sir Peter Vaward, our director, said you may be able to help me in this regard.'

Pyke's eyes widened. 'Ryman . . . yes, I knew he was in these parts. The king of turbulence! I once went to a fascinating seminar he gave – we were at Cambridge together – but I've never met him socially. Not sure I can be of any use to you.' He knelt down and rubbed the sea lion behind the ears. 'I thought Ryman was a conscientious objector, anyway. Wouldn't have anything to do with the war. How come he's letting you work with him?'

'It's a bit complicated,' I said, thinking on my feet.

'Mind you, I might need your help myself,' said Pyke. 'With a fluid dynamics problem . . .'

'Involving sea lions?' I asked, bemused.

Pyke laughed. 'No. Another project. Lev works in all weathers.'

The animal opened its mouth to display a ferocious looking set of teeth. 'He can see in low light, which allows him to dive very deeply.' I looked doubtfully into the sea-lion's cloudy eyes.

'There's another team training dolphins, down in Devon,' his trainer continued. 'At Ilfracombe. Teaching them to carry tools to divers. They're also using them for hydrodynamic studies, to improve the performance of torpedoes. Lev here, his job will be to find mines on ships and be a prophylactic against attacks by frogmen.' Pyke talked very freely, I thought again.

The sea lion roared, as if in appreciation of his master's voice. It was a spine-tingling noise at such close quarters and the beast's breath did not exactly make you want to kiss it. But when he flapped his Tibetan ears, all the fearsomeness went out of him.

'Toss him another herring, Julius,' said Pyke.

The other man did so. 'Human and animal in perfect harmony,' he said as he threw it.

'Julius is an idealist,' said Pyke. 'But now and then he stoops to earth. He's using crystallography to uncover the structure of haemoglobin. The secret of life is hidden there, isn't it so, Julius?'

Brecher pulled a face, then shrugged.

'In blood?' I prompted.

'In blood,' said Brecher. 'And other proteins. Cells in general. After the war it will be the job of scientists to unlock that secret more fully. We will be like explorers looking for a new continent.'

'Inspiring, isn't he?' said Pyke, slapping Brecher on the back. 'I keep asking him to join Combined Ops, but he won't. Why don't you come to Canada with me, Julius, to work on Habbakuk?'

'Habbakuk?' I asked.

'Ah, sorry, old chap, that's the other project. Can't say too much about it right now. But as I say, we might need a fluid dynamics man. I'll bear you in mind as there don't seem to be that many people about with a grasp of these issues.'

Suddenly Lev roared again. He leaped into the water, springing off with all four flippers, causing an enormous splash. With a valedictory turn of the head and a last look at us from his deep black eyes, he disappeared. I wondered why he should not do so for ever, but I suppose sea lions, just like humans, become inured to patterns of behaviour.

'Yes,' Pyke replied, when I asked if he came back because they fed him. 'But I like to think there is affection there, too.'

'Cupboard love,' said Brecher.

'Your English is improving,' said Pyke.

Brecher laughed. 'Let us go for a drink, my friend.' He turned to me, the aerial wafting above his head like a giant wizard's wand. 'You will come? There is a good pub just up the hill.'

Pyke picked up the half-finished sandwich and tossed it into the air, where a gull swooped on it. At once I was back on Lake Nyasa, where, out in our boat, my father used to wave *chambo* that were too small to eat up at the fish eagle, who would lift from his hieroglyphic lakeside tree and break magnificently out of the sublimely blue sky to receive the gift full toss. *Chambo* is like a perch or bream, but there are plenty of others to choose from: there are more species of fish in Nyasa than any other lake on earth.

But it was by Loch Eck that Brecher knelt down to gather the sea lion's reins, and the rare fish in that place was powan or freshwater herring, the descendant of saltwater cousins trapped in the loch when glacial moraines blocked the route to the sea. Looking back, I don't know which type were the fish we fed the sea lion. I hope it was not that survivor from the age of neanderthal caverns.

'You can bring that,' Pyke said, pointing at the crate containing what Lev had not consumed. 'I'll have some for supper. Actually, they serve pickled ones in the pub, if you're hungry. Roll-mops.'

So I picked up the crate and we walked away from the quay up a steepish hill. On the way, Brecher told me more about his work with crystals, but what I found myself thinking about again was Gwen and Joan's painting. I think it was that the notion of herring roll-mops reminded me of the picture's curling dog-tails and breaker tops . . .

How foolish I was about those two, how foolish I was altogether. In days since I have often read about Liss and Lamb in the papers. I saw them in London a couple of times, at their house in Limerstone Street in Chelsea, and once in the 1960s they dropped in on me in Cambridge and we had tea in my rooms. They were exuberantly dressed in kaftans and beads and taffeta skirts. I remember one of the porters staring at me in surprise from under the rim of his bowler hat as we walked across Trinity Great Court.

We must have made another strange trio, coming up from Loch Eck to the pub: Pyke carrying the tangle of leather; Brecher with the radio on his back; me with a herring crate. Perhaps Joan was right about scientists. We can seem odd to others – but the truth is that like any part of society we are a mixed bunch.

The pub was called the Whistlefield Inn. A sign outside showed an old-time drover with his sheep. Pushing open the door, we were immediately surrounded by company: ancient locals in shabby brown jackets, white shirts and wellington boots, and a number of young men with short hair, dressed in US Navy uniforms.

As well as the ornamental bronzes to be found in most pubs there were buoys, lobster pots, fishing nets, coils of rope and other, stranger objects hung from the ceiling and walls, such as a blunderbuss, a trombone, a sailor's cutlass and a brass deep-sea diver's helmet. There was even a small pram. There were framed brocades and unframed oil paintings, all sorts of ivories and other colonial monstrosities, carved from stone and wood, and shelf after shelf of old books covered with dust.

'I love the chaos of this place,' said Pyke. 'There is always something else for the eye to settle upon. You two get us a pew.'

We shouldered our way through. The locals of the Cowal were talking loudly in soft Scottish accents, emitting vast clouds of smoke from distended cheeks as they spoke. The sailors, murmuring in low tones, were bent over their pints of heavy, staring at the contents – which resembled molasses or motor oil – with consternation.

Pyke, Brecher and I sat down to drink more of the same. I noticed a wooden tailor's dummy standing in a corner of the room, unclothed except for a Kitchener-era helmet and – a recent addition in honour of the town's guests – a Stars and Stripes flag over its shoulders. There was also an unusual ebony cabinet with two serpents painted on its doors, their heads facing each other and their bodies joining and separating at intervals in the design.

'The caduceus,' said Pyke, seeing me study the conjoined serpents through the smoke. 'A symbol of the opposing forces of the universe. The endless dance of life. It's why the best solution to any problem is always to be found in the most extreme form of the contradiction that constitutes the problem.'

He drew a figure 8 with his finger in some foam which had spilled on the table. The number disappeared before it had been written.

'Eight. Or infinity. The snake that chases its tail. Probably the most important number in the universe, eight. Don't you think so, Julius?'

'I think the universe is pretty oblivious to what we think important or not,' came the reply.

The discussion continued, as pub discussions do, in desultory fashion. Describing his research, Brecher mentioned the passage of rhesus antibodies from mother to baby in the blood. Individuals either have or do not have the rhesus protein on the surface of their red blood cells.

'There may be danger to the fetus when the mother is rhesus negative and the father is rhesus positive,' he said. 'The first pregnancy might run smoothly, but it becomes problematic with each subsequent one, as maternal antibodies attack the rhesus-positive child. Sadly, these mothers may never carry a child to term. They tend to miscarry earlier and earlier.'

'Rhesus was king of Thrace,' Pyke said gravely, with beer on his moustache. 'Came to a bad end by not staying on the *qui vive*.'

At some point or other in the winding course of the conversation I quizzed Pyke about a subject – for I was innocent of it then – which had been puzzling me since we were down on the quay. I felt it was only fair, since I had filled them in on Ryman.

'Tell me about Habbakuk,' I said. 'You mentioned it before.'

'Habakkuk,' said Pyke, '– with a b and three ks – is the name of a prophet in the Old Testament.'

'A magus,' said Brecher.

'A wonder worker,' said Pyke, slurring. '"For I will work a work in your days, which ye will not believe, though it be told you."' They both laughed, as if in recognition of some private joke.

'On the other hand,' said Brecher, 'Habbakuk – with two bs and two ks – isn't.'

They both laughed again, pleased with their pedantry.

Cross at being shut out like this, feeling as if I was being pulled down by some Lev-like creature into a swirling sea of alcohol, I abruptly made my excuses and left. The wind had got up and the sign outside the pub was creaking as it swung to and fro. I stumbled down to the quay and rode steadily back to Kilmun on the motorbike, grateful for the freshening air on my face.

On the way I passed a lorry carrying timber down from the hills. There were steel chutes like the one by Mackellar's field all round these parts. A trio of foresters sat on the long logs on top of the lorry, the wind fluttering their hair and the green fabric of their overalls. When I got home, night had fallen. All along the Holy Loch, searchlights were probing long fingers of light across the water.

10

'Home', of course, was the cot-house in the field. Throat wooden, head buzzing from the beer, I threw myself onto the bed. As the clouds passed over the moon up beyond my uncurtained window, I thought of Lev the sea lion, Habakkuk the prophet – and again of Ryman, that other prophet whom I had not yet met.

Through the window's film of moisture I watched the blue-grey clouds perform their intermittent veiling of the moon – restlessly gleaming and quivering, sometimes seeming to streak the darkness, sometimes to be streaked with it.

Lying there, staring at that deceptive dance of light and shade, my thoughts passed to my own old home . . . How once my mother had opened the door to our holiday cottage on Zomba mountain and a snake had shot out from under the draught/dust-excluder – some piece of vulcanised rubber, scuffed leather, something, nailed to the bottom of the rickety old door. Our dog Vickers chased off in pursuit.

There is a snake in every childhood. But mostly we had happy times. At harvest time I liked nothing more as a young boy than going to the tobacco auctions in Blantyre with my father, watching the great yellow bales he had grown and gathered being unloaded and sold. The auctioneers were mostly South Africans or Rhodesians. As they talked the prices up and down in the argot of the auction room, it was like listening to a strange music.

Once the sales were over we would go to the club in Limbe

and I would drink a glass of squash while father had whisky and soda with his chums, their talk largely of the turn of the tobacco, which was not its curling leaf but the difference between the buying and selling price, and who would win next month's cup at the races over in Salisbury. In those days people travelled about Rhodesia, Northern and Southern, and Nyasaland itself as if they were a single country.

There were wooden ceiling fans spinning as these discussions took place, moving the air around us. I remember these made a big impression on me. I wonder sometimes if they were the source of my interest in turbulence, but that probably had much more to do with the African weather – something emerging darkly from the apron of stirring cloud which tumbled off the edge of Zomba mountain plateau. Zomba and Mulanje are Nyasaland's two great mountains. We visited both, to get away from the flat expanses of tobacco fields near Kasungu, and to escape the heat.

In later years, as the tobacco price rose, my father could afford to buy a cottage on Zomba. It was a green-painted building hidden halfway up the mountain in a grove of tall trees. What I remember most fondly is the preparation to go there, back in Kasungu, the antecedent excitement of my mother packing cardboard boxes with provisions, my father putting bullets into the magazine of a hunting rifle, or preparing his fishing flies for the trout streams. There was water everywhere on Zomba. It was like a giant scoop or sponge sucking down the storms that pressed up from Lake Nyasa, with thousands of trickles and streams running through the forest, keeping everything in a luxuriant, dark-green harmony.

Other times we would go to Nkhotakhota, or Monkey Bay, and other places along the long strip of Lake Nyasa itself. It was called the calendar lake because it was 356 miles long and 52 miles wide. Sometimes we used to travel on a dented white steamer called the *Ilala*, which carried passengers and cargo up and down the kingfisher-blue expanse.

On one voyage to Monkey Bay, Vickers went crazy, leaping off the ship into the water in pursuit of some goats and chickens that were being unloaded into canoes. Rhodesian ridgebacks are good swimmers, and ours swam all the way to the shore and disappeared. With the help of some good-natured fishermen who were sitting cross-legged mending their nets, we eventually found him at sunset, running about on the sand with piebald dogs from the villages. They were all barking and jumping over each other, as if they had gathered for a celebration. The image has always stuck in my memory.

There were often waterspouts on Lake Nyasa – vast moving pillars of air and water whirling about a low-pressure core. They seem like divine manifestations but share, scientifically speaking, the characteristics of both the tornado that wreaks such violence in the United States and the street eddy that in cities across the world turns up leaves and dust and paper into a recognisable column. I could watch such visitations all day – they are hypnotic – but the event which was to determine my future interest in weather took place, as I say, in Zomba, in 1931.

I was fifteen years old, and the first I knew of it was Vickers barking outside, followed by a sound in the distance, like a waterfall. Then one of my mother's pickle jars trembled on a shelf in the cottage, before falling to the stone floor and smashing. I realised there was something wrong with the light coming in through the window.

Both my parents were outside in the garden. My mother was tending her flowerbeds: she loved a flower called the ixia, which had white petals with a prominent dark-purple streak in the middle. It was sweetly scented, particularly in the evenings. Nearby where she knelt, trowel in hand, my father – hair slicked back with Brylcreem, pipe in his mouth – was doing his accounts on a rickety old table.

I suppose, until he lifted his head, Vickers was curled up next to the table. He usually was, now and then rising to stretch in the sun, allowing my father to reach down and ruffle the peculiar line of fur that ran up his spine – against the grain of the rest of his coat – and gave his breed its name.

'Jolly good fellow,' my father used to say, whenever he patted him on the furline like that.

I stared at the smashed jar, then ran outside, ducking back into the stone recess of the porch as soon as I saw the vast wall of mud bearing down the mountainside. Darkening the fall of light, it was simply roaring towards us and nothing – nothing! – was going to stop that. I watched as, twenty feet away, my parents, the one still kneeling in front of her ixias, the other throwing back his chair as he suddenly stood up, were trapped by the waves of mud. There was no chance of them getting to me, though they tried; it all came down too quickly. A chunk of masonry from the cottage fell off near me and I pretty much resigned myself to dying in the mudslide.

But I didn't. Instead I watched my parents drown in it: half a million tonnes of clay mixed with water which slid down Zomba that day, slumping from an area of felled plantation forest after a flash flood from a river. Liquefied mud, thick, rocky mud, mud spilling down a hillside and over your loved ones as if it were chocolate. Coating their skin, covering their hair, filling their lungs.

Nobody wants to remember that – your parents rearing like tethered horses as they try to reach you – and I have tried to paper over the event in my memory. So completely that some-times I am persuaded that I did not actually witness it, that I passed out and have imagined the whole thing retrospectively. I have no idea what happened to Vickers: I know I heard the bark beforehand, and I know he was, or would have been, sitting at my father's feet; but after that not a glimpse, not a sound. Nothing but mud.

So far as verifiable facts go, I do not even know how I was rescued, only that I was removed by the colonial authorities to an orphanage at Cape Town in South Africa. From there a cousin of my mother's took me on, paying for my continuing education at Douai in Berkshire and later funding me at Cambridge.

Laminar flow and whirling flow, I had seen in a single terrible instance the regular predictable straightness of the one and the viscous, unpredictable evolution of the other. I had also experienced difficulties relating to the vantage-point of an observer: that positionality in time and space which, along with the two types of flow, is central to fluid dynamics.

What I hadn't understood, except in the most immediate and tearful sense of personal bereavement, was the full human dimension: how the event would distort my perceptions of – and relations with – others. How it turned me into this inward, unreflexive creature, this truculent, obtuse, curly-haired character I now look askance at in the mirror in my cabin on the *Habbakuk*, lifting my head from the page.

Of course, the hair is white now, whereas once it was dark. The blank paper too, it strikes me now, is also like a mirror. But a cloudy one, as if the flux of human thought condenses when one tries to put it into words.

I wasn't the only one to suffer. Hundreds died in the Zomba mudslide of 1931, but I count it as the moment when psychic night – and the physics of the atmosphere – entered my head. It has been a kind of dizziness in my life and oddly enough I was not the only one to feel it. For months after the mudslide there was an epidemic of dizziness – involving twitching tremors and falling down – among the local Chichewa. Some

92

kind of psychosomatic response to the mudslide among those who survived, it spread like a contagion through the populace. It was often followed by nosebleeds. I had something like it, too, doctors said, and perhaps that is why the whole period is so hazy in my memory.

For all that, I miss Nyasaland greatly. It is part of what has formed me, and I would like to return there one day. I loved the rows of tobacco where they hung, lion-tawny, in the curing sheds. I loved the palm-fringed lake shore and those wicker baskets the weaver birds made their homes in, up the flashing ribbon of the Shire river – where, under towering gulfs of green, the boatmen pole their canoes to the rhythm of a soul-shuddering song.

What happened to the past? Why was it taken away from me? Who siphoned it off, like the mosquitoes settling on the boatmen's backs to suck their blood?

11

At the end of the week, as instructed, I presented myself at the Ryman house for Sunday lunch. The Prophet greeted me himself. My first impression was of a man in his early fifties with an intelligent if somewhat anxious face supporting a mass of unruly, starting-up grey hair. Under a prominent forehead and over a small, flattened nose he wore black spectacles covered at the bridge with sticking plaster, a black tie under a starched, round-cornered collar, and an old-fashioned grey suit. The creases of his trousers were extremely well defined. The toe-caps of his shoes shone like billiard balls. This was unusual. In my experience, scientists tend not to look after their shoes.

My eyes travelled back up his body. He was tall, I realised, his forehead high and smooth, his mouth downturned. He did not seem like the jolliest soul. In fact, apart from the wild hair, Professor Ryman looked like an undertaker.

'I'm sorry I could not see you when you last called, Mr Meadows; I was gardening,' he said. 'A beautiful theory, without any mercy, has had me in its thrall and I find the garden the best way to escape. It is now finished. At least, I have written it down. Come through.' His voice was an odd mixture of smooth and rough, beginning mellifluously and ending in a kind of cough, as if he were a singer who had found a crumb in his throat.

I followed him down the hall, under the strange array of strings and pipes on which I had previously banged my head and past a large pier mirror, improbably grand for that spartan household.

'May I ask what it was about, your theory?' I said, man-oeuvring myself around a large stove which stood, oddly and inconveniently, at the foot of the stairs.

I received no reply.

We entered the drawing room, which was dominated by a grandfather clock and a piano. Mrs Ryman and a cleric in a dog-collar were conversing by the window. 'That is the gnostic position,' I heard the minister say. 'An unfolding. The disclosure of what appears to be secret.'

Ryman paused for a moment. His shoulders hunched appreciably but he did not look round at me. 'The latent roots of a matrix,' he said abruptly, in answer to my question, which I had almost forgotten asking.

The minister, a florid gentleman, was continuing his own discourse. 'So that what's inside is equivalent to what is outside. But the equivalence itself is the secret. In the Orphic rite, you know, the mystic was he who kept his mouth shut. The mute. *Muein* in the original Greek, giving rise to *mustes*, mystic. Do you see?'

Mrs Ryman nodded. I stared at her, startled by the feelings which were rising in me. The skin on her face was so luxuriantly healthy I had a curious desire to lick it. I tried to put this bizarre idea out of my head, but my attention then became fixed on her generous body as she listened to the clergyman. She wore a green cardigan and tweed skirt and a white blouse with something gold pinned over the left breast. It was too homely a look to be alluring, I told myself, but this was more than compensated for by her youth. She was, it struck me, about twenty years younger than her husband. Such disparities of age were more common then than now, but I still wondered, at the time, how they could have come together.

'I am afraid I cannot offer you sherry,' said Ryman. 'We're abstainers here. Some apple juice, perhaps?'

I accepted and smiled at Mrs Ryman as she brought over her guest to meet me. The minister was dressed in black, apart from his dog-collar.

'Minister Grant,' she said. 'This is Henry Meadows. Our young man in the field. He is working for the Meteorological Office.'

'Literally in the field,' I said, shaking his hand. 'We've established a small weather observation centre in the field next door.'

'How lucky you are,' said Grant. 'To be under the very gaze of a titan of your science.' He had a red face and rheumy eyes. I suspect he missed the sherry even more than I did.

To break the ice, I thought it might be amusing to tell them all about Pyke, Brecher and the sea lion.

'Ingenious,' said Grant, when I had finished. 'Train up a seal.'

'Sea lion,' said Ryman frostily. I was getting the distinct impression he did not like Grant. 'Surely they do not plan to use these animals on attack missions?' he asked me. 'Men may be stupid enough and callous enough to kill one another, but there is no need to involve innocent animals as well.'

'I don't believe attack is part of the plan,' I said. 'The idea is for them to detect mines. Mr Pyke said they can see in very low light, diving down as far as six hundred and fifty feet. The potential is incredible.'

'The word "potential" should be used only in its strictest scientific sense,' said Ryman. He paused, looking rather pleased with himself. 'In all other cases it is misleading.'

Perhaps he was right. In any case, I did not want to cause any more friction. 'I believe you would quite like Mr Pyke, Professor,' I said. 'He's rather clever. He said he was at Cambridge with you.'

Ryman looked sceptical, but I persevered. 'And Julius Brecher, who has made some fascinating discoveries about the structure of the blood. He has unpicked haemoglobin. It is very important medically, I understand.'

I was mainly parroting what Brecher had told me on the way to the pub. I was talking out of my depth – quite a bit out of my depth, actually – but Sir Peter had said a certain degree of cunning was necessary in this work. If deception must be employed, the higher morality of war work should cancel out the fault.

The stratagem worked. 'Tell me more,' said Ryman, suddenly filled with interest.

'Each red blood cell contains approximately six hundred and forty million haemoglobin molecules. Haem is iron in the ferrous state, as I am sure you know. Brecher found that a tetramer of globin chains join together with its own haem group in a pocket.'

'Fascinating,' said Ryman, his usually lugubrious face animated and full of light. 'Do continue.'

'The job of a haemoglobin molecule is to load and unload oxygen as it travels through the body. Its total journey, during a lifetime of one hundred and twenty days, is said to be three hundred miles.'

'Did he say anything about the rhesus factor?' asked Mrs Ryman, to my surprise. For some reason I did not expect her to be so scientific as her husband. My mind flicked back to something Brecher had said about incompatibility of blood types between mother and baby.

'Gill,' Ryman said in a soft but admonitory tone. She looked meekly into her glass of apple juice.

'Yes,' I said, warily. 'He did mention something of that.'

There was a brief silence. Then, firm again, Mrs Ryman said, 'Where is Brecher based?'

'He's at Loch Eck at the moment,' I replied, 'with Pyke; they stay at the Argyll – but his main work is at Cambridge.'

I waited for either of them to elaborate, but once again there was silence. Grant, who had become distracted during the discussion, was inspecting the brass workings of the grandfather clock; I hung expectantly on an explanation of the reprimand.

Hung on so long, in fact, that even Ryman, who was clearly largely impervious to social convention, was driven to reply. 'We recently gave blood to the transfusion service,' he eventually said in an airy tone. 'Shall we go through to eat?'

Mrs Ryman sat opposite me, with Grant and her husband at either end of the table, which was almost as highly polished as Ryman's shoes.

At once, Grant started banging on about mysticism and religion again. The substance of his views, though spoken at a volume suitable for general address, continued to be directed at Mrs Ryman. She was more concerned with ladling soup into our bowls out of a deep white porcelain tureen, but Grant didn't seem to notice his listener's lack of attention.

I took my opportunity. 'What strikes me most, Professor, about your work – is the distance-to-neighbour aspect of things. It seems to me that measuring the relative distance between particles rather than measuring them from a fixed point will be an increasingly important tool.'

Ryman beamed, apparently now glad to oblige me. 'Yes, and not just with particles. The relationships between social groups, sets of ideas, even words themselves might be measured this way.'

'Ideas?'

'Yes. I have often thought ideas pass through society in something of the manner of an ocean eddy. And like most things they are best considered differentially rather than as absolutes.'

'By ideas you mean . . .?'

'Equality, liberty, justice. That sort of thing.'

'That sort of thing,' said the minister, looking up from his discussion with Mrs Ryman, 'is dispensed in heaven.'

Ryman ignored him. 'We think we know what these ideas mean but actually they are like clouds in our heads. The best way to understand them is to classify them by charting the distance between them.'

'Scripture says love passeth all understanding,' came the view from the other end of the table.

As the two men bickered, I became aware of Mrs Ryman's brown, enquiring eyes studying me across the table. Her face was glowing. It was a frank look she gave me but there was no tenderness in it, or anything remotely erotic. It was the look of someone inspecting produce at a market stall.

'Delicious soup,' I said, leaning forward in my seat.

'From the garden.' She lifted up the ladle. 'Have some more.'

'I'll save myself, thank you.'

She gave a sly, sidelong glance at Grant. It was as if I was meant to see this.

'Handy during wartime,' I said, 'to grow your own veg.'

'We were growing our own vegetables long before the war.'

Grant snorted at a remark of Ryman's. 'Have you not read your Isaiah? "My ways are above your ways, my thoughts above your thoughts." Our Lord is beyond even the very idea of the absolute. We judge by human standards, but it is only within the perfection of his law that we can understand the reason for evil. Till kingdom come and we join in that perfection, there's a limit we cannot cross. Thus, we cannot understand an abnormal phenomenon like Hitler.'

'The present war is not about evil,' said Ryman, in the tone of someone talking to a child. 'It is about armaments.'

'On the contrary, Professor. Hitler *is* evil. Invading countries. Suborning the rule of law. Interrogating with torture.

99

Killing thousands of civilians. I would call that evil. I would say he presents a danger that only faith can answer.'

'Rubbish! Faith itself is the dangerous thing,' said Ryman. He relaxed slightly in his chair, like a chess player sensing victory. 'Especially Christian faith. Christians are worst of all for fighting. The figures speak for themselves. I have them all down in my *Statistics of Deadly Quarrels*. Through history, there have been fewer wars started by adherents of Islam than by adherents of Christianity.'

Grant fell silent, as if stumped by this information.

'Tell me, Professor,' I said, 'why did you make the switch from meteorology to the study of war?'

He put his hands down on the table to deliver what seemed a well-rehearsed reply. 'In the midst of my Cambridge course on natural science I was hesitating whether to specialise on the physics or biology, when someone told me that Helmholtz' – Helmholtz was a German scientist – 'had been a medical doctor before becoming a physicist. It occurred to me then that Helmholtz had eaten the meal of life in the wrong order. I decided I would like to spend the first half of my life under the strict discipline of physics and afterwards apply that training to researches in biological and social sciences.'

'What sort of researches?' I interjected, perhaps too rapidly. I suppose I was hoping that he might let slip the secrets of applying the Ryman number by explaining why he'd left the work behind.

It was too negative a way to seek revelation. Ryman just smiled as he recalled his non-meteorological triumphs. 'A range of issues. The submissiveness of nations. War and eugenics. The measurability of sensations of hue. Many other topics of that type. Also psychology . . . quantitative estimates of sensory events and abstract relations. The application of measurement to continuums. Getting pain and pleasure, touch and smell, aggressiveness and tranquillity down to equations. Say you were to begin by tapping someone softly with a horsewhip on the thigh – how many times and how hard would you have to hit before it became painful?'

As I considered this odd idea, his wife brought through the main course, which was roast chicken. Grant began chattering to her again. I stared for a second at the yellow bird, which sat on a platter in a pool of gravy, before turning back to Ryman. 'Do you regret not taking your meteorological studies further?'

'I continue to dabble. I recently worked out how to detect the distance of thunderstorms from the number of clicks their electromagnetism makes on a telephone line. Do you mind carving? It upsets me.'

Taking the carving knife and fork from him, I also decided to take the bull by the horns, or grasp the nettle, or whatever figure of speech is appropriate for a stubborn meteorologist. I stood up, ostensibly to perform my job of dissection, but also to ask him the question outright.

'The thing I have been wondering about is – how can you apply the Ryman number to adjacent zones with different background means . . . how do you connect it all up?' I wonder now if this question was what gave the game away.

To my surprise, he stood up from the table himself and walked to the window. From the way his shoulders hunched he seemed to be suppressing a burp. Or even laughter. Then he said, with his back to me, 'The personal attribution is embarrassing. Others named it.'

I did not feel this was a proper answer to my question, so said nothing, hoping he would continue. But Ryman did not speak, instead staring out into the garden, up into Mackellar's field beyond. As I continued to carve, laying successive slices of the feathery white meat on the side of the platter, Gill Ryman carried in steaming dishes of vegetables. She set them either side of Grant, who, on seeing the curls of steam that came out of holes in the lids, exclaimed – in the tone of one declaiming a biblical quotation – 'The tails of two smoking firebrands!'

Coming back to the table as I passed out the chicken-loaded plates, Ryman produced a fountain pen and notepad from his jacket pocket. He began sketching and jotting down figures. Standing up as I was, I could clearly see that the designs and numbers were of a meteorological nature. I was confused. I felt as if he were toying with me.

I sat down, feeling deflated. I decided to press on by indirect routes again. 'Do you not feel,' I asked him as he wrote, 'that there is some mismatch between the precision of mathematics and the inexactness of psychology and social science?'

Ryman looked up from his notes with an irritated expression, as if I had no right, at his own dinner table, to disturb him from his calculations. 'I am aware of the difficulties you describe,' he replied, directing his remarks to me with his pen as his wife served out vegetables.

'But I believe they can be overcome. Mathematical expressions may be applied usefully to all sorts of activities and study. Translating one's verbal statements into formulae compels one to scrutinise the ideas expressed therein. And the possession of those formulae makes it easier to deduce the consequences of one's original statement.'

I must confess I had to stifle a laugh at the highly formal manner in which Ryman expressed himself. 'When did you first begin to apply mathematics to this kind of material?' I asked the Prophet, trying in my tone not to reveal anything of my true intentions.

He smiled – still holding the pen poised, like someone taking the temperature of the air but with a medical thermometer. 'A long time ago. As a young man I had to find out for the

102

Scottish Peat Company how channels in peat bogs should be cut, in order to remove the right amount of water. I realised that a broad-brush approach must be found, one that converted the exactness of differential equations into something more approximate.'

I knew about this part of Ryman's work. 'You relate changes in the y axis to the small distances over which they occurred along x.' After pouring on some gravy, I began cutting up my own chicken and eating.

Far from becoming suspicious, he seemed grateful that I was familiar with at least one area of his studies. 'That's right. And that became a way for me, in many spheres, for solving practical problems that do not lend themselves to smooth curves and continuous functions. But this kind of thinking has been at the heart of my weather work, too. For example, I ask you the question: does the wind have a velocity?'

It was a subtle question. It depended which part of the wind you were talking about; yet the wind was one thing, absolutely. Heaven's breath, but discontinuous as we humans experience it. 'Not an easy question to answer,' was all I said at first, while continuing to ponder the rich array of possibilities.

As I thought, I looked out of the window at the ridge above the cot-house, where the beech trees stood, dwarfed by the massed dark green ranks of the firs of the forestry timber plantation higher up. There was something about the sky above the trees that threatened new weather.

'A line squall coming,' said Ryman, as if reading my thoughts. 'One hour.' He put back the notebook and pen in his pocket. Mrs Ryman and Grant were continuing to talk about religion.

'The wind's velocity . . .' I mused, crunching on a roast potato as I returned to his question. 'I suppose it all depends on what you measure – where and when you start, where and when you finish. The process of measurement must have a beginning and end. The establishment of those points has an effect on the outcome.'

He seemed satisfied by my answer. 'That's one way of putting it. The wind's velocity is not continuous, even if it might seem so as you stand at the end of a street and a gale howls past you. In fact the various parcels of air are being blown hither and thither. The function is jagged. So at the molecular level, we cannot say the wind has a velocity, even though we regularly measure wind speed with our instruments.'

As he spoke, he was cutting up his own chicken into equal-sized pieces. He then bisected each roast potato and severed his floret of cauliflower down the middle. It had a look of someone's brain.

'I wonder,' I asked, 'what on earth made you leave Cambridge? I mean, the space in which to think, the facilities . . .'

'Too many people – I like to work alone, following little-used tracks, testing out my own theories with small-scale practical experiments. Take the peat. I could only satisfactorily determine its porosity as it lay in the bog, using peat's own original structure.' He lifted up his water glass. 'So I made an apparatus. A cup of peat . . . I carefully cut it out of the sod with a narrow-bladed knife, then I put water inside and noted the rate at which it ran through.'

Grant's voice rose at the other end of the table. He was still explaining something about evil and the war to Mrs Ryman, poor woman. 'God, in himself, does not cause wars. He takes no pleasure in the extinction of the living. It is the devil's envy which brings death into the world, as those who follow him will discover.'

Silence fell on the table. Out of the window through which Ryman had been staring, the trees looked black. They moved with the clouds that hurried by beyond them. Inside the room, the minister's rheumy gaze settled on Ryman, and the two men looked at each other for a moment.

It seemed the duel of views was set to continue, and this time the professor took up the challenge in good heart. 'I think I have shown, Minister, that religion itself is the worst cause of war. Followed by the armaments industry.'

'I thought you were a Quaker!' said Grant in a tone of hurt exasperation.

Ryman smiled in response. 'I am, but a biological one. I think God is the accusative of the verb to worship – the addressee of a biologically necessary process.' A gleam came into his eyes. 'So don't say, "Lift up your hearts!" Say, "Reorganise your hypothalami!" Now, if you'll excuse me I must go to the loo.'

We sat in silence for a few seconds before Grant spoke. 'Given he has such opinions, it is strange the professor comes to church at all, Mrs Ryman.'

The colour rose in her cheeks. 'My husband is rather outspoken. I apologise. It's hard to explain. I am a Quaker, he is a scientist. He shares with me and all true Christians a yearning towards something larger and better than ourselves.'

I was amused at this outbreak of piety but, watching her speak, something else fizzed and sparkled through my brain – or through that still deeper place where emotions, thoughts and feelings join in a single experience. It was a perception that there was something beautiful about Gill Ryman. It had to do with the line of her jaw as she was speaking, the incline of her head, the way her lips parted over white teeth as the words came out.

As I was entertaining these speculations, Ryman returned, which provided the opportunity for Grant to resume battle. 'So how would you define faith?' he asked bluntly, as the professor sat down.

'Believing in a vacuum,' Ryman replied, just as bluntly. 'Ignoring the evidence. Waiting till enough people develop the same conviction.'

'There is no need for an argument,' I interjected. 'I am sure, Professor, that the minister does not want to be like those Victorian bishops who condemned Darwinism any more than you would want to exclude all spirituality from human affairs. I'd like to ask some questions about your work.'

Ryman took off his spectacles. 'I am sure you would,' he said. 'But now is not the time.'

I looked at Gill Ryman and she looked down, plucking three times at her napkin. 'I should fetch the pudding,' she said, standing up to go to the kitchen.

I also rose. 'Excuse me.'

'Don't flush,' called Ryman to my back. 'We don't flush unless it's visually necessary!'

Passing a lamp and table in the hall, I climbed the stairs to the toilet. Below, I could hear Gill moving pots in the kitchen and Ryman and Grant resuming their argument. It didn't, in my opinion, seem to bring either of them closer to what they desired, which I suppose was scientific truth on the one hand and divine revelation on the other. I found the ding-dong faintly exhausting – but where would mankind be without disagreement? Without that grand family row between organisms and then species and then inherited human traits (harmful or helpful as we see them in retrospect), without that complex of conflicts known as natural selection, we'd have remained a lump of mucus in a prehistoric fjord – invertebrate, hardly possessing cells, oozing silent juices instead of language.

I pushed open the door to the lavatory.

12

Ryman's urine was still in the bowl. It was the colour of pale wheat. The whole room was filled with the savoury scent of it. The toilet was of the German or Danish type used for stool-gazing. I mixed my water with his and flushed the chain, watching the eddies evolve.

Hearing a shout from downstairs, I cursed softly as I stepped out onto the landing. I'd forgotten not to flush. There was something automatic about the way one's hand went to the handle.

The door to Ryman's study was ajar, and I could not resist the temptation to step inside. The walls of the room, which was fairly large, were lined with labelled box files. I baulked at the idea of rifling through his papers. For one thing, there were far too many of them. Those on the desk, I could see at once, were weather charts and tables of algorithms.

So he hadn't really stopped meteorology completely; Sir Peter was right to think he was continuing his programme.

I was acutely conscious of my hosts downstairs, just floor-boards and a ceiling away. But I could not resist the safe, its door inexplicably open. Inside were two book-sized type-scripts. I flicked through them, hoping to find any mention of the Ryman number. But they were both to do with his peace studies. One was entitled *Arms and Insecurity: A Mathematical Study of the Causes of War*; the other was the *Statistics of Deadly Quarrels* which he had mentioned.

I looked at the books on his shelves: Batchelor, Prandtl, Napier

Shaw, everything you'd expect in a meteorologist's library. There was also a small open cupboard with pieces of string hung across, on which were suspended a number of pairs of spectacles. They were all identical to the ones he was wearing. On the cupboard frame were some faded labels – 20, 30, 50, 100 cm – showing the working distance for which each pair of spectacles had been designed. I chuckled at all this. Was there no area of his life to which Ryman did not apply his zeal for classification?

On a small oak table to the side of the writing desk stood some scientific instruments, including a brass microscope and a system of rotating pivoted rods. I spun the weighted rods. Their purpose seemed to be the demonstration of the conservation of angular momentum. Very important thing, which one sees in skaters and dancers. But its most important proof is astronomical. The way the planets wheel round, waiting to come into alignment.

Fretting that I would be missed downstairs, I quickly scanned the white labels of the box files for anything relating to the Ryman number.

Solving Boundary Problems by Surface Integration.

Atmospheric Stirring.

Wind above the Night-Calm at Benson.

Quantitative Estimates of Sensory Events.

All these labels were written out in Ryman's neat hand.

Then I saw it. Between *The Deferred Approach to the Limit* and *Chaos, International and Inter-molecular* was a box marked simply *Number*.

Was this what Sir Peter was looking for?

I opened the box to discover not the sheaf of papers I was hoping for, but eight brass shell cases. They were arranged in a sequence of ascending size, in a cardboard mould stuck with green baize. Just as with the spectacles, they were numbered, 1 to 8. Their length and girth was also recorded.

'Would you kindly like to tell me what you are doing?' said a voice behind me. I turned to see Mrs Ryman, oddly round in profile as she regarded me over one shoulder. She had clearly been walking past and stopped in surprise, having seen me.

'Oh God,' I said, trying to put back the box and catching it on the bottom of the shelf. It fell open, scattering its contents, each shell case rolling in a different direction. I turned again to where Mrs Ryman stood watching me, then went down on my knees to pick them up. They seemed to rattle a bit.

She had entered the room, calmly watching my frantic search. Eventually I stood up, with three of the larger cases tucked under my left arm, a medium-sized one in my right hand.

I tried to speak, but could think of nothing appropriate to say in the circumstances.

'What on earth are you doing with those?' she asked, staring at the objects. It was as if she had never seen them before.

'I'm so sorry,' I finally gasped. 'I just stepped in here . . . I'm fascinated by your husband's work. The number—'

'Number?'

'I mean the equations,' I struggled. 'I wanted to see some. The box said number.'

'The box said number?' Slowly, incredulously, as if there were gaps between them, she repeated my words.

I took a step back. Flailing a hand behind me, searching for the box file, I knocked over the display of pivoted rods. They fell to the floor with a clatter, rolling about among the remainder of the shell cases.

'Oh God,' I said again.

'Are you unwell?' asked Mrs Ryman. She knelt down and picked up the fallen box file. 'Give me those, you clot,' she said. One by one, I handed her the shell cases. 'Now please go downstairs,' she said, starting to put them back into the box.

It was excruciating. Again I tried to find words to explain, but in the end I left her crouched over the box, arranging the shell cases by their size.

13

Ryman seemed oblivious to my absence. 'That accommodation between religion and science you spoke about earlier,' he said as I sat down, red-faced and sweating. 'We might have seen a way forward to it. You could say faith is action on a hypothesis, with a view to its verification.'

I wondered how I would ever face his wife again. Should I simply make my excuses and leave right now? I felt an overwhelming need for a cigarette, but we still had to finish the meal.

The main-course plates had been cleared away. 'It's just a variant on Pascal's wager,' Grant said dismissively. 'Distinctly unchristian, if you ask me. It makes one doubt the keystone of one's belief. It's not a definition of faith that I can accept.'

The two adversaries seemed to have made an accommodation of their own. 'Interesting man, Pascal,' said Ryman. 'Went looking for God and found statistics. And the variation of pressure with height.'

At that point Gill returned, carrying some bowls and the pudding, which was suet with custard. I fancied she gave me a slight nod, but could not be certain: my eyes were fixed very firmly on the shiny brown table, which showed the face of an idiot. Simply to give my hands something to do, I picked up my spoon and began eating the sticky mass of suet.

'Maybe he did,' Grant was saying of Pascal. 'But it's still not a true definition of faith.'

'I don't mind what definition *you* use,' said Ryman. 'So long as we understand each other. That means my not committing theological solecisms and you having a proper respect for the fundamental concepts of science – a respect which, if I may say so, you did not exercise in church this morning.'

Maybe I was wrong about a mellowing between them because, on hearing this, Grant threw down his napkin and abruptly left the room. I thought he had gone for good, but there was a rattle of the cistern upstairs.

'Don't flush!' roared Ryman, cupping his hands towards the stairs.

'When he comes back, apologise!' his wife hissed to him.

Ryman shrugged. I sat between them in embarrassed silence – doubly embarrassed silence – wanting that cigarette even more.

Grant returned, stern-browed, but before he could get a word in, Ryman started berating him. 'The fact is, I didn't think much of your sermon this morning. If you want to repeat it next year, I can lend you some good books for beginners in science.'

The minister looked at Ryman in astonishment.

'By the way, I believe you have just had cause to use our lavatory,' continued the professor. 'You flushed it. That is permissible, as I have already explained numerous times, only if the deposit is a solid one. Otherwise, in this household we flush once daily.'

'Wallace!' cried Gill.

It was too late. Pushing back his chair, Grant left the table again. This time he headed for the hall door, which he closed behind him quietly as if to emphasise his host's lack of grace.

As Gill gave chase, Ryman let out an explosion of breath. 'The man's a fool,' he explained, turning to me as if seeking an ally. 'In church this morning he spoke of "the centrifugal force which drives everything inward to our hearts". Absolute poppycock. At least *you* understand.'

It wasn't long before Gill returned, slightly out of breath. 'He's gone,' she said. 'He's sure not to come back now.' She stamped her heel in frustration. 'Why do you always do this?' She gave me a sad smile, as if imploring me to speak and somehow rescue the situation. But I didn't know what to say. All I could think about was our secret – if it was to be a secret.

Ryman was determined to justify himself. 'My dear, in one hundred years' time the world will be facing a catastrophic water shortage. If all the civilised world was over the coming century not to flush its lavatories, not to water its lawns, it would go a little way to alleviating the problem. Of course, there are many more effective scientific processes . . .'

'Wallace, I do not want to hear about a scientific process . . . You made a guest leave our house.'

'He's an ignorant buffoon – isn't he, Meadows?'

I squirmed in my chair as their eyes fell upon me, each expecting a different reply. 'I must say,' I said, 'that his views on centrifugal forces are a little unorthodox. Still, it's a common mistake among laymen. And the clergy, it seems.'

Neither of them seemed very impressed by my answer. 'I've never been so embarrassed,' said Gill, which was ironic considering how I was presently feeling. Soon enough Ryman himself would know of my poking about in his study, for it would be only natural for a wife to tell her husband of such an event.

In the window, the light darkened suddenly. There was a rumble of thunder, swiftly followed by a bolt of lightning, cutting across the sky like a scar.

Ryman looked at his watch. 'One hour, near enough.' He stood up, then cocked an eyebrow to the window. 'That squall I referred to.'

His wife looked at me across the table. 'Will you excuse me? I ought to do the washing-up.'

I nodded, looking back into her eyes. Now something told me she wouldn't sneak, but you never know what goes on between a couple.

As his wife left, I joined Ryman at the window. The south-western part of the sky was filled with dense low cloud. It was the colour of vintage champagne, yellowing the triangular green tops of the forestry plantation. Amid the cloud I could make out dark, rolling oscillations or whirls, rapidly increasing towards the north-west, and growing visibly as they moved. It was an amazing sight, since it had progression in it, framed by the window. The window's curtailment of view gave a starting point and stopping point for what we were seeing. And what was on display there – it was nothing less than that sequence of states along the temporal and spatial axis which is at the heart of all weather. It is seldom seen so plainly.

As soon as the cloud hit the line of beech trees, streaks of rain suddenly began to fall, then stopped just as abruptly. The tops of the trees, slowing the horizontal movement of the cloud, had momentarily produced turbulence and stronger upward currents.

Ryman put it more elegantly than I ever could have done. 'One might compare the cold air to a chisel laid flat on the table, then pushed forward to shave up the warm air in front of it, with its cutting edge. The amount of rain is of the right order for such an explanation. In any case, I've seen this phenomenon before.'

We returned to the table. I could hear Gill washing up. 'Over this ridge, many times,' her husband continued. 'And in France once, too. In 1917, between Nancy and Belfort.'

He gave a little shudder, then handed me the sketch he had made earlier. It was a rough reproduction of the scene we had just witnessed. 'That squall – it could be up over the top of the country along the east coast and down into the Channel by Tuesday. A real storm.'

'But the weather in the Channel is good at the moment.' As it happened, I had seen some charts that very week.

'That makes no difference. Conditions can change very quickly, and this is something even meteorologists often forget. I forgot it myself in France while I was writing *Weather Prediction by Numerical Process*, which is why there's a big mistake in that book.'

He paused for a moment and looked at me with searching grey eyes. 'Now tell me, Meadows, why has the Met Office set up an observatory on my doorstep?'

I felt a surge of panic. 'Do you know, the truth is, sir, I am not quite sure,' I said with as much smoothness as I could muster. 'One just goes where one is sent.'

It was a thoroughly unsatisfactory answer. Anyone with the least meteorological knowledge could see that Mackellar's field was an inappropriate place for an observatory, however small. I wondered if he already suspected me. He must have done.

Ryman drained a glass of water which was on the table, then set it down heavily. 'Come on, it's stopped raining.' He stared out of the window for a second. 'Let's go for a walk.'

14

There was a tennis court behind the house, as well as the large vegetable garden I'd seen earlier. Ryman obviously enjoyed growing vegetables, for he insisted on showing me not just each plot but several plants individually. He then invited me to admire a still he had made that used solar energy to evaporate seawater.

We walked on, up through the wet field towards the cot-house. He asked me if I had any crackers or lizards, two older types of observation balloon used by meteorologists. I said I had, in case the more modern balloons got caught up or something went wrong with the transmission. Ryman asked me to fetch one cracker and one lizard, in order to see what the wind was doing at successive levels: when one is studying air moving across the horizontal it is convenient to define a mean wind whose velocity varies only with height.

'For old times' sake.' His voice was full of wistfulness, as if, despite protestations to the contrary, he actually regretted the days when his passion was hard meteorology rather than the more nebulous if nonetheless noble science of peace.

He followed me into the cot-house and looked over the meteorological equipment, while I began inflating the balloons with some hydrogen I had made according to Gwen and Joan's recipe. I was embarrassed by the general squalor of the place, the piled ashtrays and empty beer bottles, but Ryman was only interested in the equipment.

'You don't mind me looking?' he said. I shook my head. As

he poked about, I continued filling the balloons. I didn't want to get it wrong. There had been enough embarrassment for one day.

We carried the balloons outside. They only just fitted through the door. Waving them behind us like a couple of kids, we continued walking up the slope of the field, towards the beech trees. Beyond them, at the top of the ridge, the fir plantation loured over us, its black trunks like soldiers preparing to march down and attack the intervening line of beeches.

'I often do this walk,' he said. 'Gill calls it my beech tree walk.'

There was a good wind blowing in our faces by the time we reached the line of beeches – which as I say effectively divided the field from the plantation.

'There's a little stream and bridge in the middle,' Ryman said. He took me into a glade in the stand of trees, and sure enough a stream ran through them, bisected by an old wooden bridge. 'Mackellar's father built it,' said Ryman, as we stood on the giving planks. 'I find it a good place to observe eddies.'

We looked down into the running water, watching its elusive folds and detours round stones and mossy branches. A stickleback darted across. 'Straight from God's hand,' said the Prophet. 'Come on.'

Going back into the field – with some regret, for the glade in which the bridge stood seemed like a special place – I took in the view. The steel chute used to get the timber out went down the side of the field to the shore road; a hedgerow and the outflow of the stream bordered the other. Across the middle of the field was the dry-stone wall separating Mackellar's property from Ryman's. In one corner the black cattle had gathered: a convocation of horns. Beyond it all could be seen the bumpy green hills of the Cowal, interspersed with fragmentary glimpses of loch. It was like being on an archipelago.

With his cracker streaming out behind him, Ryman said, in a modest mumble, 'I invented these, you know.'

He began to explain to me how he had developed the cracker, in which a small explosive charge, triggered by an altimeter, goes off to alert the observer that the balloon has reached a certain height.

It turned out he had also invented the lizard, a more basic version of the same instrument, in which the balloon's tail is encased in a chiffon tube. This girdle forces the balloon to expand vertically – until it presses against a physical trigger and the tail is released, again as a signal.

'Hence the name lizard, from the habit of some of these animals to drop their tails when attacked,' said Ryman.

'Geckoes,' I said. I remembered them vividly from Nyasaland, sprinting up the wall after insects.

'Yes,' he replied. 'I suppose we should have called them that.'

We worked on in silence for a minute or two. The sun had come out, making the foresters' steel chute glint. I became aware of the sound of the wind sliding between the leaves of the beeches and – a different sound – over the grass of Mackellar's pasture. This also shone slightly, as if every blade of grass had been polished up by a diligent attendant.

'I miss all this,' Ryman said, as we continued preparing the balloons. 'But my life now is concerned with the relative frequency of wars and how to prevent them.' He laughed. 'That is my war effort. To encourage submissiveness. Like Mr Gandhi.'

Gandhi was admirable, no doubt, but as a policy Ryman's so-called war effort sounded too weedy for any self-respecting male to sign up to. And rather self-satisfied. But obviously I couldn't say that to him. 'You mean you want us to submit to Hitler?' I asked, instead.

'It's nothing personal. Hitler, Churchill, Roosevelt, Stalin.

Actually all one system. We are all part of a single self-aggravating system.'

'I'm afraid I must disagree.'

He sighed. 'So do most people.'

'If it were not for our airmen, our bombers and fighters, the war effort generally, we should now be part of Hitler's Reich.'

'The bombers and fighters are part of the problem. If Germany had not built up its Luftwaffe in the 1930s, which it did to counterbalance our own naval power, there would not have been a war. The weapons should not have been accumulated in the first place. For a similar reason, I have a safe in my study, in which I keep my most current manuscripts to protect them from fire, but I leave the door unlocked, so if any burglars came they would not use explosives.'

'They might still steal them,' I said, my stomach churning as I remembered the dropped shell cases. 'Anyway, suppose that by 1935 Britain had developed armaments on a massive scale, as we have now. If we had built up our arms then, we would have been able to hold the Germans down and get our own way all over the world.'

'A childish ambition. Because, don't you see, then the whole world would have allied itself against our superiority? This war just would not have happened if arms had not been assembled. It does not make any difference by whom the process is started.'

Ryman was a great mathematician, but as we stood there under those yawing, whispering beeches, with weather balloons pulling in our hands, his pacifism struck me as hopelessly naïve, if not downright irresponsible.

I tried not to lose patience. 'If there had been no armaments, we would have gone to war with our bare fists.'

He just laughed. 'Listen to yourself. You sound like someone in a Kipling book.'

Finding ourselves at an impasse of argument, we stood unspeaking, face to face, both listening to the wind as it passed through the trees, making them stretch out their melancholy limbs.

There was another sound – air moving over the rubber of the balloons. A whining rasp, and I could tell from his face that it had provoked thought in him as well as me.

It was Ryman who spoke first. 'That, and it is to the point, my young friend, is the sound of friction. You know, general friction will do more against Hitler even than General Patton.' He gave another little laugh at the joke. 'Because along with turbulence, friction is one of the most important things in the universe. Perhaps they can be described as cousins, even brothers. Or actually the same person, appearing in different profile.'

A lone magpie, flying away from the sun, landed on the grass in front of us. I remembered suddenly how my mother on seeing one – well, she did it with the piebald crows in Africa – would immediately cross her thumbs and call out:

> I cross the magpie,
> The magpie crosses me,
> Bad luck to the magpie,
> Good luck to me.

'Friction!' exclaimed Ryman as the bird flew off. 'You see, Meadows, nothing can start without something to push off from. But good comes even when there's no positive action. Blocking, delaying, braking . . . these things create value just as the mixing of turbulence does, enabling the birth of new systems and the death of old ones, the transfer of energy from one place and time to another.'

'But friction is mostly a negative force, socially speaking. It reduces efficiency.'

'Yes, but that negativity prevents bad plans as much as good ones. That is why Hitler will eventually fail. Look, shall we fly these things or not? You're not tight there.'

He took a piece of paper from his pocket and folded it inside the chiffon sleeve on my lizard, which had worked its way loose.

'They never came loose on the original balloons,' said Ryman. 'Gill made the sleeves. We tested them in a wind tunnel on the Isle of Wight. Mr Blackford, her father, is chief engineer at the Saunders-Roe seaplane factory in Cowes. I worked there for a while with him, doing research on aeroplane wings. That was how I met Gill.'

So that was it. We released the balloons. Up they went then, cracker and lizard, red against the tall dark shapes of the beeches. Despite the wind there were no fierce vortices, and the balloons rose steadily at about 500 feet a minute, following the angles of the wind as it came in different layers over the green rooftops of the fir plantation. I remember a feeling of exhilaration watching them ascend.

I could see that Ryman was similarly enraptured. Like master and pupil, we watched until at 800 feet there was a sharp explosion – a flash in the sky. At the same time, the tail of my lizard came loose, plummeting down. The igniter from the cracker left a puff of smoke in the air. This dispersed as it fell, floating over the trees like a gauze.

Ryman and I then had a technical conversation about the implications of averaging out the different horizontal winds to produce a mean and what was really entailed, philosophically, by classing turbulence as a deviation from this already artificial measure. He said the nature of an eddy was difficult to define precisely because its identity was involved with its context; and that despite the mean's artificiality, eddies could not be specified independently of it.

It soon became too dark to continue, so we agreed to go

home. Ryman seemed pleased with the balloons and we parted on good terms. He invited me to visit again soon.

'Maybe we might do some work together?' I ventured, aware that I had not got very much out of him about the Ryman number.

He gave me something half between a nod and a negative shake of the head, as if he wanted to say no but was trying to be polite.

I thought I should try to insist. 'It would be an honour for me if it were possible. Is there a chance?'

He looked at me mistrustfully. 'Perhaps. But as I say, I have found I do my best work alone.'

As he spoke, the heavens opened again. (What a curious saying that is! As if there were a vault above. Levers and a hinge, operated by a divine magnet . . .) I desperately wanted to get an undertaking from Ryman. But it was soon raining heavily. Without further ado we ran across the field for shelter in our respective houses.

As the rain battered the slate roof of the cot-house, I dried my hair and boiled the kettle for a cup of tea. Having drunk it, I lay on the bed, smoking, worrying about what I was going to do. I wondered whether I should write a letter to Sir Peter. He had already written to me asking how I was getting on. I needed to reply. The invasion was ahead. But what would I tell him? The truth was that I'd got nowhere.

My mind turned to the flimsy blue missives from my parents that used to arrive at my boarding school. The mathematical gift had showed itself relatively early, and I won a scholarship place at Douai, a Benedictine public school in Berkshire. It was a wrench leaving Nyasaland and I looked forward to my holidays like nothing else.

My early schooldays were plagued by bedwetting and sleepwalking. My fellow pupils use to tease me, imitating my sleepwalking during the day. I apparently walked completely erect, but head down, with my chin on my chest. Once, on the eve of a test of French verbs, I climbed out of bed and wandered downstairs in a trance and started banging about in the kitchen, opening cupboards and throwing aside the battered tin pans in which we were served rice pudding. On being discovered by a member of staff and asked what I was doing, I told them I was 'looking for *je suis*'.

I wasn't much good at French, but in sciences I was a bit of a phenomenon at school. I had less difficulty with German and Latin, and this was a good thing because in those days you had to pass a Latin examination to get into Cambridge, and many of the most important scientific papers of the time were in German.

Once the holidays finally came, along with other colonial children I would join a ship of the Union Castle line to Cape Town. I would then take the mail steamer up the coast to Dar es Salaam in Tanganyika, where my father would pick me up. It will be strange to see that place again.

The drive across to Nyasaland across a highland escarpment which marked the edge of the Rift Valley was always very exciting; though being somewhat long and arduous the journey was of great concern to my mother as she waited at home on the farm. With the image in my head of her greeting us, one time or another – wearing a dress printed with flowers as the mud-spattered Alvis pulled up outside the verandah, Vickers jumping manically up beside – I fell asleep, secure once again in those happy times, before the event. Before the *kizunguzungu*, which was the Swahili word for the spinning dizziness to come.

I don't know what the Chichewa word was. We spoke kitchen Swahili to the servants because that's what my father had picked up in Kenya. I ought to apologise for it now, and I will happily do so, but at the time such an apology would have been inconceivable.

That was just how it was in those days. Whites didn't give politics a second thought. I myself certainly had no conception, as a boy, that it might be better not to talk to Cecilia and Gideon and the others in a *lingua franca* of command which was as foreign to them as to us. Everyone in the house spoke English well enough but, ridiculously, it was used only when pidgin Swahili failed either them or us. Now, looking back, remembering Cecilia's mothering of me and Gideon's fond scolding of Vickers, I wish I had learned Chichewa. Some boys did, but they lived on farms even further off the map than ours.

We were all in the Great Rift, that long strip of African country which, mostly let down through faults and slips and sudden fallings away, stretches from the lower Zambezi in the south to Ethiopia in the north. Related rifts continue across the Red Sea into the Jordan Valley. But beginning with Lake Nyasa and bifurcating at its top end into Lakes Tanganyika, Kivu, Edward and Albert on the western side, and a vast series of mountainous gulfs and plunges up through towards Lake Rudolf and beyond in the east – my rift, the Great Rift, was formed when rigid basement rocks buckled during the last continental shift, lowering and raising great blocks of land as if they were nursery bricks. In between these two arms sat Uganda and the vast basin of Lake Victoria, and volcanic extrusions such as the Ruwenzori.

Ugandans, Kenyans, Tanganyikans, Nyasalanders, the white settler on his farm, the Indian merchant selling soap and sugar at his *duka* – we were all turning in the lava that runs in the splits between cultures, all spinning and tumbling as we fell like scraps of paper into those running streams. Some individuals were burned in an instant. Many whole tribes were choked and scorched and incinerated. Some were bloodied by floating boulders. Others there were who were overwhelmed simply by the smoke of distant battle.

But of the white tribe we can say one thing with certainty. We were the most stupid. Some of us had no idea whatsoever it would ever end, no conception at all that at imperial sunset another formation might appear, rising like a sea monster out of the molten depths.

Out of the fault.

The Rift.

The Great Rift.

There is every cause to believe that there is more extraordinary geological activity to come in the Great Lakes region. A man named Bullard who had been a research student in Rutherford's laboratory, and was still at Cambridge when I turned up there, did some fascinating work on this subject. He showed that gravity is lower than it ought to be in some of these Rift lakes. This negative gravity means there is material down there that's lighter than its surroundings, material that's longing to rise – and would do so in an instant were it not for side-pressing rocks holding it down like a pair of pliers. Bullard's anomalies mean some of the Rift is not just foundered valleys, the consequence of a fall.

Some of it must have been pushed down. If there is a shift of plate tectonics, that material will come flying up.

15

A week after my lunch with the Rymans I was working over some charts in the cot-house when there was a knock on the door. It was Gill. She was carrying a round wooden tray on which stood tall tumblers full of ice and a jug of straw-coloured liquid. She was dressed in a skirt and blouse: some kind of heavy, yellowish, iridescent silk for the skirt and another material, the colour of limestone, for the blouse. Her figure seemed fuller, somehow, as if it were a fold one might enter. I felt a shiver of desire.

It made me nervous to see her. Although taking any opportunity to see Ryman himself, I'd been keeping a low profile so far as his wife was concerned, for obvious reasons.

'I thought you might like some lemonade,' she said.

'Lemons? At this time of year? In Scotland?'

Her high heels ticked across the tiled floor. I had never seen her in anything but flat shoes before.

'We use lemon essence, actually. And citric acid. Wallace makes it.' She came over and put the tray down on the desk where I was working, peering over my chart as she poured a glass. 'What are you working on?'

'Some rather intricate upper-air conditions.'

'Oh,' she said. 'That.' She went to the bed and sat down, smoothing her skirt. 'You know, Wallace once had a plan to chequer the globe with reporters who'd send in upper-air data to computers in his forecast factory, all calculating away.'

In those days the word computer was used to refer to

human beings with slide-rules. Effectively, back then, it meant mathematicians. It was another term she used which seemed strange to me at the time. 'Forecast factory?' I queried.

'Yes, a large hall like a theatre in which all the computers, men as well as women, would sit doing their calculations, keeping pace with the weather as it was reported – by telegrams.'

'That would mean a lot of telegrams.'

'Or by radio. Or telephone, though that would be expensive. Every three hours each of the sixty-four thousand computers would receive a message from his or her area of the world.'

'Sixty-four thousand people? In one room?'

'Yes, working in parallel as the weather moved across the globe.'

I humoured her. 'It would have to be an awfully big theatre. More like a football stadium.'

'He has in mind something like the Albert Hall, overseen by a conductor.'

She stood up and swept her hands across the room. 'A map of the world is painted on the walls of the chamber: the Arctic on the ceiling, England in the gallery. In the upper circle, the tropics. Dress circle? Australia. Antarctic in the pit. Desk by desk, each computer attends to the mathematical quantities, broken down by type – pressure, temperature, humidity – for his or her region. Then works them through the appropriate equations. Do you see?'

'Sort of.' I took a hesitant sip of the lemonade. I was right to be doubtful. It was frightfully bitter and chemical. 'Each computer passes the solution to his equation to his neighbour, and so on.'

'Oh no, it's much better than that. On each desk is a visual display showing the values for that equation once it is worked out. These are read by one's neighbours and by a higher official who co-ordinates the work of each region and maintains communication throughout the system, reporting to the central conductor.' She paused. 'All the basic-level computers wear a uniform to encourage discipline – though I don't suppose Wallace would want it to be anything like a military one. Perhaps something like the police, with the higher officials displaying special chevrons to distinguish them from the ordinaries. No one speaks, it's all done by writing on slips.'

It took me more than a few seconds to absorb all this. As I was doing so, with ever more animated gestures, Gill explained how the 'conductor' would co-ordinate information about the future weather as it flowed north and south, east and west, each flow mirrored by what was happening on the floor of the forecast factory.

It was a pretty bizarre scenario, effectively treating men as machines working in parallel, but it was the issue of representation that puzzled me most.

I put it to her. 'How does he think they mirror the variability of the real world? The fuzziness of a cloud, the rate of evaporation from foliage, the vorticity of one eddy as compared with that of its neighbour? Not to mention all the other myriad things which affect weather.'

'Wallace has quantities, symbols in the equations, for all those things. Each one. Even one for fuzziness. I think he calls it "turbulivity". Or "scatterivity". Anyway, that's by the by. All those numbers, resolved down to quantities more familiar to the public – wind, rain, temperature – will eventually be broadcast to the nation, but the whole thing has to be properly organised before that is possible.'

She moved to the centre of the cabin. Again I was struck by the fullness of her figure. 'From the pit, the Antarctic region, a pillar rises. In a pulpit at the top stands the conductor. His instruments are the human computers in their adjacent geographical zones. Time is of the essence. Or rather, it's the medium that they're working in. Chasing real weather almost in real time as it races round the globe.'

Her heels might have been on the wooden boards of the cothouse, but her head was in conceptual clouds. Pointing here and there with one arm, then the other, she was lost like a child in the game of the thing. 'The conductor shines a beam of rosy light on those who are running ahead of the rest, a beam of blue light on those who are behind.'

As she moved through the room, I found myself watching the contours of her legs and back and shoulders, most of all (and strangely) her abdomen, until she inclined her head towards me with a smile – 'Well, what do you think?'

What I thought, uncomfortable suddenly, was that a husband's scientific scheme was being offered me by his wife as a kind of seduction. But there was something even stranger than that. In the distance, from high on the hill, I heard the sound of one of the foresters' chain saws. Looking at her body I was struck by her beauty again, but also something else, it suddenly occurred to me that she might be pregnant. What a fence post I was, I think now. But then most men are in these matters.

'Well, it's certainly a system,' I said, puzzled. 'It would work for world domination if it doesn't work for weather prediction. How are people told about this factory's forecasts?'

'The conductor has a senior clerk, lieutenant . . . come, you be him.' She held out her hand, and I rose to take it, as if for a dance. 'The clerk dispatches the future weather by pneumatic carrier to a room where it is transmitted to the public. Obviously there is a lot of information. Wallace is quite anxious about the amount of data. Messengers carry piles of used computing forms from the lieutenant down to a cellar, a storehouse for data . . .'

Mimicking the action of the lieutenant handing the messenger a pile of forms, she suddenly fell hard against my chest. I fell back onto the tray and the jug of juice crashed on the floor. The next moment Gill and I were hunched down among the broken glass and fake lemonade.

There was a strange theatricality about it all, as if she had always *meant* to push me. Then she leaned over as I was about to pick up a shard and pressed her hand hard down on top of mine. Again it seemed entirely deliberate, though surely it must have been an accident, I thought.

'Oh God, I am sorry.'

She had almost made this apology before the event happened. Certainly before I let out a howl, lifting up my hand to look at the shard embedded in it.

'I'm sorry, I'm sorry,' she said, whipping out a white handkerchief – it was a man's handkerchief, one of Ryman's, I suppose – to mop up the blood running down my wrist. She grabbed my wounded hand to remove the shard, which she dropped into her own empty glass. She continued to mop at the wound till the handkerchief was fairly soaked. Then, without a word, she rushed for the door, leaving me bleeding, blood dripping on my charts.

Flabbergasted, I found an old towel to staunch the remaining flow. As I was doing so, I heard a vehicle start up. I went to the door just in time to see Ryman's car disappear down the hill.

With the towel still wrapped round my wrist, I wandered down the field, at a loss to understand what had happened. There was a smell of burning. As I got closer, Ryman emerged from the smoke of a bonfire he was tending. He was a little way from me, across some roughish ground that divided the bottom of Mackellar's field from the Rymans' garden. He was carrying a fork and wearing an old straw hat.

'Your wife!' I shouted, walking towards him.

Dressed in wellingtons and an old trilby hat, he stared at me through his glasses. 'Yes?'

'She's gone. She brought me a drink. Citric acid. It dropped and I cut myself. Then she fled.'

'I think she has gone in the car. What had you been discussing?'

'What?'

'What were you talking about?'

The smoke of the bonfire began to envelop us. Plumes of it were curling over the brim of Ryman's hat, giving him an obscure, spectral aspect.

'Your scheme,' I said. 'The Albert Hall. Your complicated scheme.'

He gave an odd, bitter smile. 'The scheme is complicated because the atmosphere is complicated.' And then, like an enchanter or stage illusionist, he folded himself back into the smoke.

16

For some time after this strange incident, I kept my distance from the Rymans. I didn't know what to do. In any case, I was busy. The flow of work from Whybrow had increased enormously. A barrage of messages emanated from Dunoon, and Whybrow took quite an obnoxious tone if you didn't jump to it. As well as my usual observations, barometer readings and so on, I had to provide Met plans for flights from a local airfield. I was also occasionally asked to do prospective calculations relating to smoke screens for defence artillery units.

I found it frustrating to spend so long doing all this extra work, but I couldn't exactly refuse to do it outright. There was an element of Whybrow trying to impress the authority of his little fiefdom on me, but that was only part of it. The nature of war – and weather – meant that the work's very existence was an indication of its importance, even if it was not as important as my authentic reason for being in Kilmun. Still, I did cut some corners here and there and this caused Whybrow to flap a touch.

So I did not have much time to visit Ryman, even though Sir Peter's instructions remained uppermost in my mind. At least I think they did ... Another part of me was in a kind of reverie, unable to think on any scale except the one I was within, there in the backwater of Kilmun. Despite all the soldiers and ships, it seemed a very long way from any invasion of mainland Europe.

It crossed my mind that I should simply again ask Ryman –

outright – to explain exactly how to use his wretched ratio. My psychology wasn't suited to all this subterfuge. I was almost grateful for the heavy workload I was under, since it at least gave me reason not to consider my failure to get what Sir Peter was after. By now I had sent the director a bromidey sort of letter, saying I was beginning to make progress.

The whole situation was peculiar. I had come to the conclusion that Gill's attempt to maim me was definitely deliberate – but I could not for the life of me understand the reason. Or why, if she really was pregnant, she had come on like the temptress older woman? And what, in the house of a pacifist, were those shell cases for? In the face of all these mysteries I was grateful for the bluff simplicity of Mackellar.

It became my habit, once the day's work was over, to meet him for a smoke and sometimes a nip of whisky on the dry-stone wall that ran along the edge of the field in which the cot-house stood. I smoked cigarettes. Mackellar had his pipe, an authentic cherry-wood briar, such as I myself have now taken up, eschewing cigarettes in my old age.

Sometimes one or two of the foresters joined us on their way down from the hill. Bearded, bony-faced taciturn men in green overalls flecked with woodchips, they spoke, if they spoke at all, in a Scottish accent different from Mackellar's. He said most of them came from the Highland estates, from families that had done this sort of work for generations.

Long-limbed and slightly forbidding – as if they might cut a man's throat without a thought – the foresters made up for what they lacked in conversation by bringing along square tin flasks of some sort of hooch they distilled themselves up in the camps. There was a comforting lack of excitability to these gatherings and nothing was said in them worth recording. We all just sat there making staccato observations, often un-acknowledged – about weather and wood, animals and landscape and tools – until the tobacco and the alcohol did their job of unfolding the knots of physical (or, in my case, largely mental) activity that had made up the day.

One night, I remember – hard to get a precise sense of time after all these years, there are difficulties for the mind there – it was too cold to sit on the wall so Mackellar invited me inside the kitchen of his farmhouse. It had a splendid wooden fireplace. I noticed that carved into the black wood of the frame was an X with three horizontal bars below it.

'It's an auld thing,' said Mackellar, when I pointed it out. 'Supposed to stop witches coming doon the chimney. I canna say it's worked.' He let out a harsh laugh.

Mackellar had got the fire going and we were drinking when his wife walked in. I'd seen her from a distance but not yet properly made her acquaintance. She was some years older than her husband and wore a stained and ragged coat. It was bright red.

'Filling the hoose wi' fumes, again, Mackellar,' she said, 'you and your freen.'

Meg Mackellar wore a tight blue woollen cap on her head, from the sides of which shot forth curly strands of white hair down to her shoulders. But the most remarkable thing about her was that red coat, which was of the most lurid colour imaginable.

'Ye'll be hawkin the morn's morn,' the garment's wearer continued. 'And the efternoon an aw, and aw nicht long, and so on till ye are deid wi' it!'

I stood up to introduce myself.

'I ken who ye'are,' she said dismissively. She still had her herd stick in her hand: a stubby little piece of hazel for marshalling calves.

A little drunk, I declared, 'Scientific opinion is fairly divided on the effect of smoke on human health, Mrs Mackellar.

Besides, tobacco excites the intellect. It also does wonders for constipation.'

Mackellar roared with laughter, snorting until his face was as red as his wife's coat, but his wife waved her stick at me. 'A man who smokes is a man who will perish.'

Grumbling to herself, she began to make tea at the range. As she did so I noticed a strong smell of manure, mixing in with our tobacco. I glanced down at her heavy boots, from where the invisible current came.

Some currents were more visible. All the while I was reading the signs of turbulence, as I am accustomed to – the spirals, involutions and curlicues of Mackellar's pipe smoke, mixing with the tendrils, cochleae, and volutes of my cigarette smoke – until the straight jet of the kettle steam, beginning to turn vermicular itself, joined the whole circumbendibus. Here, if it were to be sought, was Ryman's working model of the universe.

Mrs Mackellar put two cups on the table in front of me and her husband. The chipped cups sat on the linoleum tablecloth for a minute or two, cooling, and not a word was spoken among the three of us. Cup steam joined the circus of kettle steam, cow shit and smoke.

Finally we drank the tea, sip by sip. The heat of it was a sensation different from the fire of the whisky. Another flame on the tongue. Once the tea was drunk, in softer tones than I thought her capable of, Mrs Mackellar offered to read my leaves. It seemed rude to refuse.

She stared for a long time at the bottom of my cup, then wrinkled her brow and shook her head. 'Keep those around you close,' she said. 'They are in danger.'

'What did you see?' I asked nonchalantly. Part of me wanted to laugh, another part felt chilled.

'I saw what I said,' she replied, in a tone of quiet finality.

February

1

It began with a dull roaring sound. At first I thought it was something to do with the mechanical felling of timber above. Then, growing much louder, it brought me running out of the cot-house – and what I saw was a thin stripe of duck-egg blue cut across the sky. The aeroplane was moving fast. I watched it swoop and curve at the end of its run. Only then did I understand it was the enemy.

Passing and turning, the plane came over several times . . . Good use of the throttle in a short space, I thought, watching, before becoming concerned – dully, numbly – about being shot. I scuttled back inside the cot-house.

The plane returned two weeks later. This time I really did expect its guns to open fire, so I kept under the eaves of the cot-house as I watched. Looking, though, I realised it was a meteorological reconnaissance plane, a specially converted Junkers – a Ju 290, by then the main long-range reconnaissance vehicle of the Luftwaffe. It was making the kind of low-level photographic sortie known in the RAF as a 'dicey do', meaning an uncertain dice with death, as delivered by anti-aircraft guns.

On the plane itself, I knew, there would be telephoto lenses in the wing-tips for photographing cloud above bomb targets. I wondered why he was so low: I could actually see the psychrometer strapped to the aircraft's nose. It was an instrument used to measure humidity – along with a barometer and an air-speed indicator it was part of the fundamental equipment used by meteorological reconnaissance flights on both sides. Geoffrey Reynolds had had one on the plane that flew me up to Scotland.

The morning after the Junkers appeared for the second time, I got up, shaved, made some porridge and tea for breakfast and went as usual to check my instrument screen. I'd had to get Mackellar to build a wooden fence around the louvred box to protect it from the cattle.

I first checked my grass minimum – that is, the temperature recorded when the thermometer is exposed to the open air on forked twigs stuck in turf, so called because the thermometer bulb is just in contact with the tips of the grass blades. Its purpose is to show the reduction of the temperature (by radiation to the night sky) of the layer of air closest to the ground. The next thing was to check the rain gauge.

I had a psychrometer of my own, or hygrometer as they are also called. It was a fiddly business, but not so much as for meteorologists of the past, who had to mess about with a human hair that expanded and contracted according to relative changes in humidity. Now we just use two thermometers, one which is kept wet, the other dry, and note the difference.

As I took the reading, I heard the clank of cow-bells in the distance, so afterwards I went up to the farm to find Mackellar, to ask him if he had seen the Junkers.

The atmosphere in the dairy was thick with the sweet, relaxing smell of milk. Mackellar's lurcher – which didn't seem to have a name – was curled up in a corner, while its flat-capped owner sat on a stool.

'I seen it before,' he said of the plane. 'Pass us that bucket.'

The cows shifted in their stalls. I asked if I might have a go at milking one. He sat me down by an old cow, which was likely to be more patient with a beginner. I did rather well, though I spilled some of the precious liquid on my trousers.

Later that morning I joined Mackellar as he took the milk down to the local creamery. Sitting in his trap, with the milk slopping in churns behind us and him giving the horse a little tap with the whip now and then, we wound our way through the hills that loured over the Dunoon road. Once again they were encircled with cirrus, looking this time like the eyebrow tufts of an old man.

I felt happy, with only one slight reservation. The second sighting of the plane troubled me, but I didn't know why. How could I? How was I to know it would be quite so damaging to me personally? Or that it was part of a whole dimension of weather intelligence that has largely remained secret even to this day?

There was just a niggle at the time, a suggestion from the corner of the picture, prevising me of danger through the whole. Even though it was full of preparations for war, Kilmun did not seem like the kind of place that might actually be violated by actual conflict. Yet here the war had been, flying above us, as if on an inspection. It meant something, surely; that plane was here for a reason.

The wheels of the trap crunched over the road beneath us, their rhythmic noises blending with the patterns of my thought. Beside me Mackellar's face was like a broken-up layer of rock, furrowed and dark brown, except for his lips, which were paler.

The creamery manager, an aged gentleman in blue overalls going by the name of David Rennie, said he too had seen the plane. Apparently the Home Guard had been put on alert. Rennie himself was a member. He said he was surprised the plane had not been shot down on its way westwards.

Mackellar was unruffled by all this. It was as if nothing could disturb the land for him. For this was his atmosphere, and he knew it. He knew the fields divided by thorn hedges garlanded with wild flowers. He knew the treeline where the forestry ended. He knew the shoreline where his boat was pulled up, its interior like a scoop for air, its rowlocks winding spools for his mackerel lines.

In the wind, the feathery lures, brightly coloured, fluttered at the end of the lines: flags on a medieval battlefield. That is what I think of right now, looking out of the porthole at the star-spangled banner flying from the bridge of a United States ship that has come alongside us. It's a NOAA research ship, a National Oceanic and Atmospheric Administration vessel on its way from Cape Town to the Antarctic to study the forces that affect global climate variability. The opposite direction to us, in other words.

What else did Mackellar know? Let me see. Without much conviction of success, I try to conjure back that vanished atmosphere of history, which even as I sit here threatens to slip back into obscurity – or, at least, that wood-panelled corridor of time whose very varnish promises distortion of memory. But what was there . . .

The long windbreak of beeches that the Rymans called the beech tree walk, though Mackellar's father had planted it. Also the sound the beechmast shells made, crunching beneath our feet. He knew, too, that the cot-house compulsorily occupied by the Met Office was the oldest building in the area. And he knew that Ryman's house was built on the site of an old rabbit warren, and that now the rabbits had moved further up the hill, nearer to the beech trees.

Mackellar said he could call them closer to him in order to shoot them, by imitating their young. I did not believe him when he first told me this, but many times later I saw him on moonlit nights, hunting rabbits by the beech tree walk. Sometimes he used snares and nets, sometimes a .22 rifle and lamp. I heard shots in the night and the strange, high-pitched noises he also made up there on the hill, the sound of them mixing in with the whistling of the wind as it passed through trees and thistles.

A week or so after our trip to the creamery I saw him strangle a rabbit he had caught in a snare. I watched, with horrified fascination, as he took out a knife to remove its intestines. He fed them to his dog, then quickly, expertly, peeled back the rabbit's skin. What was left after the unfolding was something terrible, fetal. I watched as he removed the backbone, cutting away lumps of meat.

I was glad not to be able to accept his invitation to supper that night. I had a good excuse, anyway: the Waafs from Dunoon, Joan and Gwen, had invited me to a dance.

I gunned down to Dunoon on the motorcycle, full of erotic expectation, with the tails of my greatcoat streaming out behind. The dance was being held in an ornate oriental building called the Pavilion, which was decorated with fading posters of the entertainer Sir Harry Lauder, who was a local resident, and a group of high-kicking showgirls called the Glenmorag Follies.

The girls were there to greet me, both fabulously dressed in very bright frocks and made up to the nines. We gave in our coats and I acted the cock of the walk as I strolled into the dance hall, a girl on each arm. Heads turned to look at us, I believe – there were lots of servicemen in the hall. But for all their uniforms, I felt most resplendent in my simple black suit and tie. I remember how the girls' dresses switched enticingly over their calves.

After downing a few drinks I asked Joan to dance. Pushing aside a blonde lock from her forehead, she smiled sweetly, nodding in assent, and I really thought my luck was in – for I had heroic visions of myself in the romantic department as well as the meteorological.

But as soon as we took to the dance floor, it was clear these hopes were to be dashed. The dance orchestra was called 'The Flying Yanks' – they were a US air-force band – and of course they played American music: jive, swing, jitterbugs and that sort of thing. I did my best, but it was hopeless. I felt stiff-armed, moving like a marionette, whereas Joan seemed to have the hang of it right away, turning with an easy grace, confident in her crossings and recrossings, as if she were as naturally cut out for the pursuit as her brightly sashaying dress.

Things went no better with Gwen, on whose toes I twice trod, and soon, clearly bored with trying to teach me the steps, she called it a day. The pair peeled off, danced with some officers, then mostly with each other. I hung round the bar consoling myself with beer, then bought a bottle of whisky to take home. I felt angry, feeling as if the girls had led me on, but the truth was I had no right to demand special treatment. The young can be so unreasonable in what they expect from the opposite sex.

2

Leaving the dance hall, I wandered about with the bottle of shame hidden under my coat. The whisky, I remember, was Whyte & Mackay. Eventually I elected to sit under the statue of Highland Mary, from where I watched the ship lights on either side of the boom that was stretched across the Clyde. I sucked at the neck of the bottle – sucked at it like a baby at the pap while watching the moonlit white clock face on the pier house, or casting jealous glances down at the couples emerging arm in arm from the Pavilion.

I'd had a few girlfriends in my early years at the Met Office, but none of them had turned out right. We'd had the usual hand-holding in the cinema and kisses and increasingly bold delvings, but it always seemed to peter out. Partly it was that I always went for upper-class or bohemian women, I suppose because they were furthest from my own experience and therefore most desirable. Most eventually said they found me too obsessive, which was strange because I took the view that a girl might find it attractive for someone to ramble on in a likeably boffinish way. It was still an effort for me to 'perform' this rambling: I'd effectively been emotionally withdrawn since my parents' death.

In any case, it seemed I was inept with girls. It wasn't that I didn't have any sex. I took what was on offer (I'm ashamed to say I lost my virginity while conducting an affair with the land-lady of the boarding-house I lodged in at Dunstable during my training), but at this stage the grand passion eluded me.

Though the landlady shrieked with pleasure, the moment of losing the blessed thing was unsatisfactory to me. What I remember most was the cherry-coloured curtains in the room. Afterwards she said: 'There, you've done it now.' Or it might have been: 'There there, you've done it now.' One would think these moments stick more firmly in the memory, but as time goes by it seems to get harder and harder to fish things out of the river.

Maybe – I remember thinking this – the problem was that I was actually in love with the weather. Most people might just exchange greetings and chat about that subject, but I have to get technical. Surely there had to be other people like me. Maybe, I thought, taking another slug, I just needed to find a woman who was like that.

Fragments of broken music rose like wisps of smoke from the Pavilion, creeping into my ears, or waiting a while before doing so to mix with the sound of the waves washing against the pier stanchions, from where a strong smell of fuel oil emanated. I felt unmoored, adrift, dogged by failure.

Wrapped in my Crombie, I sank back on the grass and stared at the woman above me. Erected in 1896, the statue remembered Mary Campbell, a locally born individual famous for becoming the tragic lost love of the poet Robert Burns. Though Burns was already married and his wife expecting twins, he and Mary exchanged vows on the banks of the River Ayr, swapping Bibles over running water. This is said to be a Scottish tradition (so long as the stream still runs and Bible stays true, the love too will hold), but it all came to naught as she died of a fever. Well, it was appropriately under this embodiment of doomed love, ten and a half feet high, surrounded by railings a year after it was built to keep off vandals, that within a few turns of the hands of the clock, I emptied that whisky bottle and drank myself into a stupor.

3

Freezing cold, head thumping, I woke up at dawn to see the boom boat moving aside the gate in the line of mines across the water, all under a deck of stratus, the sheet- or layer-cloud. The boom boat was admitting a grey frigate. I was watching the warship's wake, that perfect expression of turbulence in action, and wondering through the agony of my hangover what I would think in future of last night's fiasco and this whole strange situation I found myself in, when I suddenly realised there was something wrong with the way the wake was bubbling up. There was a line of extra foam down the middle of the frigate's serrated trail. What *I* saw was the retrograde fur on the back of a Rhodesian ridgeback.

For a moment I thought it was the remnant of my drunken odyssey, making me hallucinate, but then I was certain. There was something else down below: it could only be a U-boat, using the frigate as a shield to get through the boom into the network of lochs in the Cowal. Getting to my feet unsteadily, I ran as quickly as I could up Argyll Street to HMS *Osprey* and informed the sleepy rating at the reception.

'You're drunk, man, I can smell the whisky off you,' he replied, looking at me cold-eyed. 'Had too much of a good time at the dance, did you? You better bugger off quick or I'll have you arrested.'

'I am *not* drunk,' I shouted across the desk, though I expect he could indeed smell alcohol as he said. 'Come on, go tell them now. I'm in the Met, I know what I saw.'

Grumpily he went into the depths of the 'ship' before returning a few minutes later. 'Well, I told them, chummie. I don't see as they're going to take any notice of you, seeing as I also said you smells like a still, but I 'ave told them.'

He had hardly finished speaking when a loud explosion sounded on the water. We both ran outside to hear another explosion and see a large column of foam erupt from the river. Then another came, and another, and finally a much louder noise, shattering the windows of houses along the quay. A siren sounded and air-raid wardens with gas masks and helmets began to run about.

The rating grabbed me by the shoulders and shook me, making my head – already reverberating from the boom of the depth charges – ache all the more. 'You were right! You were right! There was an enemy craft below. We've got 'im.'

So it proved. The all clear was given. With a gathering crowd of townsfolk and naval staff emerging from *Osprey*, we watched as a large pool of oil and pieces of debris began to float up in the vicinity of the explosions. The frigate, standing by to pick up survivors from the stricken submarine, gave several blasts on its foghorn and a large cheer went up throughout the town. My hangover rapidly dispersing on account of adrenaline, I felt as if the cheer were for me in person. Visions of a medal flashed before my eyes, of congratulations from Sir Peter, of adulation from Gwen and Joan, from the whole female population of the Cowal, in fact. There was no need to return to London with the Ryman number pinned on my chest. I could just live here all my life, being bought drinks in pubs, fêted for ever as the man who saved Dunoon.

And it was beginning right now. Not so reluctant now, the rating pulled me over to meet the officer he had informed – tall, strikingly handsome Captain Scott-Clark, who shook my hand enthusiastically. 'Very clever of you to spot that. We've had a lot of difficulty with subs hiding from radar in the wake of ships. Now, I don't want to take anything away from what you did, but we did know the U-boat was following. It was a trap – we just had to get her far enough away from the mines of the boom before setting our charges.'

As quickly deflated as I had become elated, I slunk off and found the motorcycle where I had parked it by the Pavilion the previous night. Riding up Argyll Street, past FH Carey the tobacconist, Abel the chemist, Muirhead the grocer, and then the NAAFI run by the local scout troop, I wondered if I was ever going to distinguish myself. Mathematics? The Sheepshanks Prize felt a long way away. I certainly wasn't excelling as an amateur spy, and now my efforts as a spotter of submarines had been dashed.

Maybe, I reflected as I chugged under the hills between Dunoon and Kilmun, I would have to become a tobacconist, chemist or grocer. Or even a Scoutmaster.

I passed Kilmun church. What about a priest? I could give up all idea of sexual conquest and become a priest. A monk like my teachers at Douai. But I could hardly remember my Hail Mary in those days.

In the course of the ride home, as my hangover returned with a vengeance, the Virgin merged – across an imperceptible mental boundary – with that other Mary, she under whose statue I'd had my appointment with Messrs Whyte & Mackay.

That was a long time ago. But I can still remember that hangover coming back, borne like Satan on the clouds of my pipe smoke. It was painful. It was superfluous. It piled Pelion on Ossa. It was nasty – like a sneak thief returning to steal something that had belonged to him in the first place, left by accident at a premises he has already burgled. Yes, it was a supreme hangover, as only a spirits hangover can be.

The remainder of the month passed in a similar alcoholic fug. Alcohol and nicotine, too. My household gods. I remember looking at a piled-up ashtray of cigarette ends and bottle tops and thinking what a salad of despair it was.

March

1

According to my diary, I worked begrudgingly on local upper-air forecasts for Whybrow, my calculations punctuated by meals and the thump of logs coming down the chute. I wrote that this noise reminded me of the sound the African villagers' pestles made in the mortars in which they ground their maize, which first had to be laid out and dried on straw mats in the sun, each kernel having been picked off the cob by hand.

The foresters worked hard, too. Sometimes I'd see them passing to and fro, carrying tools or provisions for their camp. I myself ate well in Kilmun (much better than I had in London). With scones or porridge for breakfast next to my tea, corned beef sandwiches for lunch and mutton or herring or haggis for supper, it was as if the whole providence of Scotland was in my mouth. Now and then I grilled a lamb chop, and there was always fresh mackerel from the loch to be had. Ryman sometimes left vegetables from his garden on my doorstep.

But despite all these kindnesses I felt beached, becalmed. The only respite came from my beginning to study, in what would soon seem in retrospect a very amateur way, the weather patterns that would relate to an invasion across the Channel. It made me realise again how tough the challenge was going to be, with or without the help of the Ryman number.

One Saturday, in search of entertainment, I went with Mackellar to Dunoon, where there was a race meeting and fair. He had his dog in tow, I my equations – and my frailties, for

I'm embarrassed to say I got blotto again in the course of this expedition. But some things still stand like cromlechs in the memory through the haze of whisky and beer. Mackellar writing out his bets with a licky old stub of pencil. The trainers with their trilbies and medal-like passes. The jockeys' coloured silks fluttering in the wind. Little men carrying big saddles out of the weighing room, leading their mounts into the parade ring, their hard human faces contrasting with the beauty of the horses'.

Round the edges of the racecourse, excited children capered through the inexhaustible fair, sucking on ice-cream cones, chewing on liquorice, jumping on the merry-go-round – I remember it was painted in uncontrollable swirls of gold and yellow – and pelting small wooden balls at a coconut shy. Soldiers with roll-up cigarettes in their mouths were walking their tottering sweethearts into tunnels of love or showing off on test-your-strength machines, lifting up the heavy rubber mallet to send a projectile up a column – at the top of which a bell sounded, if reached.

Ignoring the bustle around them, a pair of pipers played, the distinctive mournfulness of their appalling noise – it was like a cat being hit with a poker – quite at odds with the chaotic jollity going on around them.

Though no boundary could be distinguished between them, the two crowds – the crowd of racegoers and the crowd of fairgoers – moved round each other independently as if in a kind of dance. I have often thought since that the movement of crowds might be analysed in the same way as particles in a weather system. That day, more foolishly, I thought the same kind of approach might be taken with a horse race.

Mackellar and I took up a position on the rail, near to the starting line. Finally the hullabaloo of those around us was silenced by the sound of the starter's call. It was David Rennie up there on the rostrum, not in milk-spattered overalls nor his Home Guard uniform, but sporting now a splendid set of tweeds. The sight of him, hand aloft, made me think of Ryman's weather conductor, the wizard of storms, the king of turbulence, controlling all from his pulpit in the Albert Hall. And then of Pyke – that was the tweeds, I suppose. It struck me then that Pyke was the opposite of Ryman. Two geniuses landed on the Cowal shore, one hot for peace, the other for war.

It is said a horse's face will tell you about the outcome of the race in which it is about to participate. This was one of Mackellar's methods. He looked for 'generous eyes', he said, and I guffawed, not realising he was offering this homespun wisdom only in response to the abstract idiocies with which I'd regaled him on the way here, and the sums I'd been feverishly scrawling on the back of the racecard since we arrived.

He had breathed scepticism as he sat in front of me in the trap, and he exuded it now as he stood next to me on the rail, watching me do more calculations on the back of the card. Of course I lost, as many times as he won.

When we got back from the course, having celebrated Mackellar's successes in the pub, his wife was waiting for us, leaning over the gate with her long white hair hanging down like bunches of bleached-out seaweed. The sun shone through it, the last of the light, for dusk was advancing.

Mackellar held up a fistful of notes. 'And you say he brings bad luck!' he said to her.

She gave me a look, half-mad, half-sneering. 'I didnae say he brought bad luck. I said he should keep them round him close. I said that they could be in danger.'

Uttering an indecipherable curse, Mackellar punched her on the shoulder. 'Am I in danger, wummin? Stoap yer nonsense.' Mrs Mackellar slipped, staggered, and then fell down, dirtying her red coat in the mud.

It must have been quite a forceful blow as she was a heavy lady. She pulled herself up on the gate, staring at me with fire in her eyes, then turned and walked back to the farmhouse. Mackellar followed her, looking as if he meant to beat her further.

It was a wretched scene, turning my gut. I realised I had as little notion of their marriage as I did of the Rymans'.

I didn't have much idea about making hydrogen either. I was cooking some up in the cot-house, a couple of weeks after the trip to the races. Distracted by all that had happened, and depressed by my continuing failure to elicit anything useful from Ryman, I overdid the catalyst.

The noise in the drum was terrific. The reaction was too violent. I had put my foot on the safety weight but it blew off all the same, throwing me to the floor. One of my feet was soaked in caustic soda up to the ankle and I had to be rushed to hospital in Dunoon. An ambulance came to pick me up.

The whole episode was both embarrassing and extremely painful. The doctor said I would have a scar on my ankle: one prediction, at least, that has been proven true. The only bright spot in the whole story was that I received a lot of visits and fond attention from Joan and Gwen. One or other, and sometimes both, came and sat by my bed each morning.

I was there for about a week. Whybrow visited and gave me a ticking off, saying he hoped I would learn from the experience. What a snake that man was. Constantly removing and replacing his spectacles as he spoke to me, saying he had had 'so many complaints' about my dealings with other Met staff, and that on visiting 'the scene of the accident' he was 'dismayed' to find so many empty bottles of alcohol lying about. I felt like telling him next time I'd leave some full ones there for him.

Ryman was equally critical when he arrived to take me back

to Kilmun. 'Very silly thing to have happened. I've cleaned up the place for you. Neutralised the caustic soda.' I was so miserable I didn't even reply when he said this next to me in the car, still less start harping on about his bloody number again.

It was strange, returning to the cot-house. Once Ryman had gone I lay on the bed, feeling sorry for myself. Looking back, it seems rather melodramatic. I suppose at base I felt my career was not progressing and that I was spending the war stuck in a bog. I was beginning to wish I had never come to Scotland at all, and instead stayed with Stagg in Kew. But, of course, he wasn't there any more either. He'd moved to an American air base near Twickenham, from where he was preparing for the invasion forecast.

I had recently had a note from him, but not about D-Day. It was something related to our previous work together which had been passed back to him: a problem which defence radar was beginning to get on cloud reflections – at that time they were described by the radar people as 'angels' – and the scattering of radio signals in the lower atmosphere. I was able to give a satisfactory answer, which I suppose stood me in good stead with Stagg later on.

My mind went back to our farewell, which took place between my meeting with Sir Peter and my flight north in Reynolds's plane. I'd been a bit nervous about telling Stagg I'd taken another job. He was quite a puritanical character, deadly serious, and a dedicated worker.

So it was with some trepidation that I'd approached him across the lawns at Kew with the news that I was leaving his team. He was up in a tower checking instruments at the time, and as his gaunt, tall frame descended the iron rungs of the ladder – he looked like a machine unfolding – I expected to be spoken to in harsh tones. Super-conscientious, Stagg did not like to be interrupted.

'What is it, Meadows?' He began brushing fragments of rust off the sleeves of his suit jacket.

I swallowed, looking into that ascetic face. 'Yesterday I was summoned to Adastral House by an urgent telegram. To see Sir Peter Vaward.'

Stagg gave a curious smile. 'Oh yes? I did see that you hadn't lodged a docket from that glob.'

I swallowed again. 'The thing is, sir . . .'

'It's all right, Meadows,' Stagg said pleasantly, and began to walk back to the main observatory building. 'I know all about your new appointment. Good to be out of the city, I should think.'

As I followed him, I wondered how much he knew of Vaward's instructions to me. I thought it best not to mention it. Then Stagg, walking quickly, dropped his own bombshell.

'Try to do it right, whatever Sir Peter has set you to. I have requested that you join me later as my clerk – I need someone who is proficient at maths – but he told me he has given you another assignment and you can come to me only if you fulfil it.'

Lying there in the cot-house, listening to the ships moving in the loch – sometimes a signal gun would sound – there seemed little chance of living up to Stagg's and Sir Peter's expectations. As darkness fell, half drifting off despite my throbbing ankle and cawing of crows outside, I experienced a tremor of panic, as if I were falling – backwards, endlessly down a mountain slope engulfed in mud.

I was not dreaming. Somehow I was cognisant, perceptual, as well as being half asleep . . . and what I perceived in this twilight world, in the course of my own tumbling fright, were the crawling, stumbling figures of my parents. Pallid forms floundering, resurrected skeletons reaching out from the deep, noisome mud.

Behind them stretched a road crowded with African bodies, all struggling in ghastly pandemonium, inhaling mud as the boundary stones of the road flew up on either side on them.

April

1

Spring came, but it didn't seem like a blessing to me. I listened to the wind singing in the beech trees, mournful even though winter had passed. The midges arrived very early that year, swirling round me like a personal cloud as I walked, then landing and biting ferociously, raising large weals on the skin. Their movements in the air seemed random but, just as Mackellar had said, they responded to perturbation, accumulating where a body caused agitation in the air.

In the middle of the loch, over salt water, the sailors on *Forth*, *Titania* and *Alrhoda* were free of these pests, but on shore no one was safe. Ryman gave me some of his home-made midge repellent – a mixture of rosewater and petroleum jelly – but I still had to make sure I kept as little skin exposed as possible. I was constantly squirming, wriggling, swishing my body like a horse's tail. On some evenings, when they descended in swarms, the only way to escape was to jump in the bath and lie there until the weals mollified.

I did this a lot, wondering as I lay there how I could get the information I needed out of Ryman. I felt trapped, immobile, passive. It is astonishing how little that experience is recorded in the annals of human time – I suppose because it is so common and what we want from our observers of history is the drive towards the active and the extraordinary, as opposed to the usual swimming against the flow of the river, getting nowhere except older.

The truth was, I didn't really want to stay in Kilmun any

longer, but I didn't want to admit failure either. Not, now (I had grown up that much, at least), because I craved success, but because of sheer stubbornness. Because of a kind of friction against the world. Because of not giving up as a virtue in itself.

But a recipe for midge repellent was hardly likely to satisfy Sir Peter. Thus it seemed – then as always in my mind – that he was likely to remain unsatisfied, waiting for me to explain.

Sometimes, after the midges had subsided, I emerged from the safety of my bath and walked bare-chested outside, as if feeling the night-time breezes on my body might free me from the trap I was in. There is a Nyasaland tribe whose witch-doctors think the future can be predicted by the sensation of wind on their skin. There is a certain folkloric common sense to this, but it would not do for the generals, even though I suspected that they understood no better the science they demanded in its stead.

Applying the Ryman number properly was the key. Like the chorus in Haydn's oratorio, it told the heavens. It was the code that showed how weather fitted together, the variance and the invariance – and really I was no nearer to breaking it than I had been when I first arrived. Even though it was a beautiful place, Kilmun had come to seem like a bleak hermitage to me.

But I wasn't going to give up. I was resolved to see the thing through. I pursued Ryman like a demon, contriving reasons to visit him, ask him things, chancing to bump into him at every opportunity. Slowly, like a piece of ice beginning to melt in a glass of gin, he began to relent, to admit me into his life.

Nothing more was said of the shell-case fiasco, nor of the strange incident concerning Mrs Ryman and the citric acid. She blushed slightly when – in the course of my importunings of her husband – I next saw her, but otherwise it was as if nothing had happened.

The situation was all made more odd by the growth of a

firm conviction in me that Gill was a very good person, a real Christian. She was concerned by such problems as famine relief and was keen that we should not be too beastly to the Germans if we won the war.

It wasn't just talk, her goodness. She often used to have the poorer children of the village into the house for buns and tea (it was they who used the rocking horse), and gave some of them piano lessons. One day I passed the window of the house and saw her standing listening to one of the children play a tune I recognised as Debussy's 'Clair de Lune'. She had her hand on her stomach and this confirmed to me my suspicion she was pregnant. I put my belief that she had been trying to seduce me down to male arrogance; it's a fact that unless we receive very clear information to the contrary, men believe all women want to sleep with them.

Sometimes Ryman joined in the sessions with the children, especially if they had questions about science. I remember once watching him, having been asked about the points of the compass, magnetise a needle in his laboratory and float it in a bowl of water to show how it spun round.

Another day in April, so my diary says, Ryman showed me on my own the collection of glowing valves and electric wires by which he had once hoped to calculate the vast field of future meteorological phenomena. The circuitry was mounted on a piece of ply drilled with holes. (Ryman called it a 'breadboard'.) He showed me how variable resistances and the switching on and off of the valves could represent different inputs like wind strength, temperature, pressure and so on. Even different height levels in the atmosphere, something we were only just getting to grips with on paper in the Met Office.

'Sometimes,' he said as we bent over the breadboard, 'I think machines on these lines are the only way my forecast factory will be realised.'

'Your Albert Hall scheme?'

'Yes.' He twisted a piece of wire round a capacitor. 'But I doubt it will happen in my lifetime.'

I helped him to resolder some circuits which had come loose, dripping the bright molten metal onto the brush-like ends of the wires. Later I wondered whether I should tell Sir Peter about this rudimentary calculating machine. But it was theories the director wanted, not electric toys. I had by this stage sent him a report containing summations of what I gathered about Ryman's work, hoping he would agree I was making progress.

Working inside on the breadboard was unusual. Most of the time I spent in Ryman's company we were outside, messing about with smoke plumes and seeds and the parachutes of dandelions and such things, seeing how the wind affected them and what we could infer from that. On one occasion he told me to go into town and buy sixty ping-pong balls, but I couldn't find even one in Dunoon. 'All right,' he said when I came back. 'We'll use parsnips instead.'

We dug them from the garden then took them down to the pier at Blairmore, where my steamer had come in when I first arrived. We chucked them into the water, two by two, measuring the distance between them, the relative motion . . .

It was a calm day, specially chosen. What we were testing was eddy diffusion in water, so we didn't want the wind to disturb the process. We confirmed another law Ryman had discovered. The general law, stating that diffusion of objects in a turbulent stream rises in proportion to the original separation – i.e. how far apart you throw them in. But it wasn't the Ryman number, it wasn't the real secret revealed in all its nakedness.

Ryman adjusted the depth at which different-sized parsnips floated by pushing nails into them, like weights on a fishing float. He knelt on the wooden planks of the pier with a bucket of seawater beside him as he tested each of our thirty pairs for relative weight. He noted everything in a little black book, even the percentage of rotten parsnips.

The man was a one-off. I had never met anyone who tried to apply so rigorously, so widely, the strictures of quantification and measurement. Not just in the obvious areas, but in everything. He even wrote a paper on fashion, explaining how to predict the likelihood of one colour succeeding another as the shade of the moment.

He was always seeing things in relative terms, seeing in base 17 or 60 what we'd see in base 10, seeing in hogs what we'd see in corn, seeing shillings in dollars, methuselahs in measuring spoons – seeing, indeed, 'we' where 'we' would see 'them'. That was the source of his peace work. The idea of any interval or gap in humanity was anathema to him.

I felt he would have extended the same courtesy to all living species so far as he could; even to matter, both organic and inorganic; even to the atmosphere itself.

'For what is the air,' he used to say, 'but something we make part of ourselves every day? The atmosphere is where all of us live – it lives inside us with every breath.'

2

I am perhaps giving the impression that I was always by Ryman's side. That would be mistaken. Whenever I got on with my own weather-observing duties he would for the most part keep away, mindful, no doubt, of my military connections. Mostly I worked alone, sending up balloons for Whybrow. Fairly frequently this involved stepping into cowpats as I ran clutching the launching string of the balloon, with the copper wire of the aerial trailing behind.

But Ryman did seem to have mellowed, and when he was undertaking his own experiments would often call me to join him. In one, we tested the wind's velocity – that complex issue he had referred to during lunch that first Sunday – by shooting into the air with a special meteorological gun metal spheres of different sizes: three spheres the size of an apple, five the size of a plum, fifteen the size of a cherry.

It was my job to pace out the distance to the landing site of each shot, if it could be found. I remember standing under a tree – wet knees, wet shoes – thinking, 'What the bloody hell am I doing here? Why don't I just give up?' Then Ryman bellowed through a megaphone from the other end of the field, telling me to hurry up. I ran back to him across the grass, nearly falling over in my haste.

'Good analogue of the effect of friction on human affairs,' he said.

'What?'

'Running through tussocky grass.'

It was then that the Junkers converted for meteorological and photographic operations appeared in the sky again, coming down low over the field. I could have sworn the pilot was looking at us as he swooped by, but Ryman dismissed the idea. Perhaps it brought the war too close for comfort.

He was equally dismissive as, ducking down, I told him I had seen the same plane twice before. The only action he took was to throw down his meteorological gun on the grass, I presume so it would not be thought an offensive weapon.

'Do not mistake randomness for intention,' he shouted over the engine noise as the plane made another pass. 'Conventional sapience has it that because we have an enemy, he has turned up in this particular spot of air to fight us; it is just as likely he happened to be flying overhead.'

I was astonished he could talk such nonsense, at such a time. 'Don't you think we had better find cover?' I shouted back, cowering under the sonorous clatter of the plane.

But Ryman stood stock still, his silhouette a perfect target. Not wishing to appear cowardly, though that is what I felt, I straightened up and followed suit. We waited for the plane to bank again at the end of its box of sky. But it didn't, instead continuing into the middle distance.

'No need,' said Ryman, watching the cross of the wings and tail. 'It's going now.'

He was right. Its growl diminishing, the aircraft progressed in the same direction until it merged into the horizon.

Only when the noise of the engine had gone did I speak again. 'Common things are common. Rare things are rare. As I've said, I've seen this plane twice before. It's rare to see a German plane over Kilmun. That suggests it is here for a reason, not by chance.'

Ryman shook his head and bent down to pick up the gun. He began reloading it with metal spheres. 'You are exhibiting a very human tendency – to underestimate randomness.'

'But it's not random!' I said in frustration. 'This is the third time he has been here. The Home Guard has already been alerted. We should get someone to come and shoot him down.'

'Not under my auspices.'

I could not believe that someone could continue to hold such ideas when Allied troops were dying. 'Don't you feel it's your duty to fight for your country?'

'On the contrary. It's my duty to stop the fighting. Or at least, to minimise the harm done by fighting. But that doesn't mean I'm a coward. I joined the Quaker ambulance corps in the first lot, you know. Nobody in the Friends Ambulance Unit was a coward.'

'I didn't say you were a coward,' I mumbled, suddenly unsure of my ground.

He ceased counting ball bearings for a moment. 'But I can tell you I was frightened. It was the most terrifying experience of my life.'

'What did it involve, being in that unit?'

'Our job was to bring the seriously wounded from the *poste de secours*, in the forward trenches, back to the nearest hospitals. I will never forget the stench of charred flesh and the poor men in the back crying out every time you went over a pothole. The traffic was pretty chaotic in the roads behind the trenches. Staff cars, lorries, ambulances like ours, tanks, horses and carts, too, and the wounded tramping through the mud. Once, during a bombardment, I ran over a man with an amputated leg. He had a crutch and this . . . stump. The bandage unwound from it, trailing into the puddles . . .'

Clearly distraught, he took off his glasses and rubbed his eyes. 'I rather hoped to get a leg knocked off myself. Then I could go home with a clear conscience. I was so sick of seeing things smashed and burned. That cursed war! After a while nothing happened in it but casualties. It seemed to go on largely because of inertia; the original causes, though not forgotten, faded into the background. There could have been peace much earlier if the leaders had agreed to have it, rather than carrying on so that they could say they won . . .'

He paused and looked at the ground as if to recover a distant scene, not from memory but from hell.

'Sometimes, going down Dead Man's Alley, as we called it, I had to drive round the bodies of sentries and horses that I'd seen alive on the way up. I was a bad driver, anyway, because I saw my dream instead of the traffic.'

'Your dream?'

'The system. My theory of numerical weather prediction. I wrote the first draft during the battle of Champagne. Lost it for a while after that, then found it in my living quarters under a heap of coal.'

'I'd love to read through some of your equations,' I said, sensing an opportunity. 'Is that when you came upon the Ryman number?'

He took off his glasses again and looked at me searchingly. 'I told you – I don't call it that . . .'

'I have to confess that I don't exactly understand how to connect up a range of its values,' I said, pressing on.

I could see him studying me, looking me in the face. Did he suspect something? 'It's just a measure,' he said evenly. 'A measure of changing conditions. Surely you know that?'

I wondered if I'd said too much, for he looked me in the face again and fell silent then, which I took to mean we should resume our experiment. After about another half an hour we packed up and I followed him back towards his house, neither of us speaking. Mrs Ryman was watching us from the drawing-room window. With a ray of sunlight falling on her, her pregnant profile was clear now. The light, which gave her hair an auburn, reddish tone, seemed to form an envelope around her.

Glancing at me, Ryman said goodbye and, carrying the meteorological rifle over his shoulder like a soldier, hurried inside.

As I walked back up the hill I turned and saw, framed in that same window, bathed both in that self-same light, him and Gill embracing.

3

I didn't see much of Ryman during the next week. Whenever I tried to manoeuvre myself into a position in which I could ask him more about the number, he began making excuses again. I was sure he was now deliberately avoiding me.

After a few uncomfortable days of this, I simply accepted the stalemate. Maybe if I sat tight, things would change. But they didn't.

I continued with my cover job as a meteorological observer, now and then dropping down to Dunoon to buy food, pick up my wages or collect more supplies for making hydrogen. I was more careful about that now. On these occasions I always sought out Joan and Gwen, and they invariably welcomed me with a cup of tea and a chat and showed me their latest painting. I suppose I was still hoping I would end up in bed with one or other of them.

It still seemed there might be a chance of that, despite the fiasco of the dance. One Sunday they came for a walk with me in the plantation above the cot-house. I had not yet been into the forest, despite being constantly reminded of its presence by the logs sliding down. The idea was that we would find the foresters' camp on their day of rest. I'd imagined they would greet us in their silent way, and perhaps brew up some coffee.

Well, it was supposed to happen that way but I hadn't quite realised how thickly the trees were planted. The forest was impossible to walk through, because the old stumps of cut trees still stood between the rows, and it was gloomy anyway.

The girls had soon had enough. So we came back and stuck to the beech tree walk, going along by the stream and over the bridge, chatting as we strolled. Entering the glade that was there, I again felt it was somewhere special. A place of mysterious peace. I think they felt it too.

Gwen was particularly friendly to me and it was she who suggested we try sliding down the chute for a lark. I got in first but there was too much friction and I couldn't get down. Then Gwen got in front of me, between my legs, me holding her shoulders. Still we didn't move. Even though I knew that the foresters didn't work on Sundays I began to worry that a log might come down and hit us. Only when Joan joined us did we start to move, slowly at first and then quicker and quicker – 'Hold on tight!' Gwen cried – until we came out of the forest and into the sunlit field, speeding past Mackellar's farm and the cot-house and finally Ryman's. Laughing wildly, we tumbled out by the wood stack next to the road.

The jolly mood continued later that evening when I returned to Dunoon with them, and after getting something to eat in a dining room in the town we all went up to their little den in the hydrogen shed. They made Martinis and talked to me about art, now and then getting out crayons and paper and sketching something – a horseman, a fragment of statuary, the torso of a woman with flowing hair – as an explanation of what they were trying to tell me. Or they would refer to the beach picture of the dogs in the breakers, which was still up on the easel.

That picture exerted a powerful influence on me and at the time I could not tell why. Now I realise it was because of Vickers.

Most of their arty talk went over my head. But we continued chatting away until suddenly there was a loud boom in the distance. At first I thought it was another U-boat in the Clyde but it was too far away. We opened up the trapdoors and raised the tower to have a look.

Across the water the searchlights above Glasgow were criss-crossing to and fro, like the limbs of a preyed-upon creature frantically trying to stave off the all-devouring dark. Nearer was a large mass of light, something burning with a terrible blue colour. Hearing the sound of planes above, and then Dunoon's siren wailing, we climbed down.

'You better stay here,' Gwen said. 'It will be too dangerous to ride back and you've probably had too much to drink anyway. You do rather overdo it.'

I saw them exchange a glance. I thought for a moment that my dreams had come true, but what they meant was that I should sleep in the hydrogen shed and they would go back to their quarters, which is what happened, me bedding down on their biscuit mattresses, driven wild with frustration by Gwen's and Joan's residual perfume in the rug and cushion they gave me to sleep on.

When I emerged the next morning there was another smell on the wind. Something like scorched malt. Whybrow spotted me as I crossed the courtyard. He asked what I had been doing in the hydrogen shed. I explained about the raid.

He nodded grimly. 'Yes, they bombed the sugar factory in Greenock. People have been rowing across the river all night to escape the flames. Most of the town has been down at the pier helping them. And you have been doing what?'

Without waiting for an answer, he turned on his heel, leaving me wondering exactly what he was accusing me of.

The answer came about a week later, when I returned to Dunoon, ostensibly to collect supplies for making hydrogen but also hoping to see Gwen and Joan again. Not finding them in the main office I entered the hydrogen shed and called up to the little boudoir. There was no reply. I began collecting my hydrogen supplies.

As I was doing so, I heard a voice behind me. 'Actually,

they've gone out. Your girlfriends have gone away for the day.'

I turned to see Whybrow's face, regarding me with malicious glee.

'Hoping to see them, were you?' he jeered. 'Up there.' He gestured up at the mezzanine as if he were trying to swat a fly. 'Well, you can't. They've gone to Glasgow – to meet some other man, no doubt. I've half a mind to have them transferred. Or better still, kicked out.' His eyes popping, and both hands gesticulating now, he looked as though he were about to have some kind of seizure. 'They are disgusting, in my view. And you . . .' He interrupted his ejaculation to poke a finger towards me. 'You are no better. Chasing after them. Going about like a slavering puppy. You're days behind with your charts. Let me tell you, young man, that you are running out of time. If you don't buck your ideas up I shall put you on a charge to Sir Peter. He might think you're a genius, fit to mix with the likes of Ryman, but I think you're just workshy. And lecherous.'

He began to splutter, raising both hands now, as if he were a ghoulish puppet-master directing invisible marionettes. The poor man worked himself into such a frenzy that he had to pause for breath. Not knowing how to respond, I took the opportunity to gather up my supplies and leave the shed.

'You're running out of time, Meadows,' he shouted again as the metal door banged behind me. 'Out of time, let me tell you!'

4

Driving back to Kilmun on the motorcycle, I considered the quantity on which Whybrow had so eloquently discoursed. Time was not something so easily reducible to definition as the old fool seemed to think. It has been described as a river which carries us along. Or – and this was my present state on the pillion, amused but also unnerved by my superior's outburst – a road on which one travels. Neither of these explanations is adequate, especially for those highly absorbent events which return unbidden to mind years later, like my parents' death. And, I remember thinking, it's not just the most important events that return like that . . .

My philosophical divagation was interrupted by the sight of Pyke, kneeling by the roadside, changing a tyre on his Humber motor car.

'Can I give you a hand?' I said.

He was glad of the help, but said very little as we replaced the tyre.

'Anything the matter?' I asked eventually.

He straightened up. 'Leviathan, my sea lion, is dead. Blown up by a mine. My mine. Bits all over the bay.'

'I'm so sorry.'

'As I am. It was my own fault. A failure of science.'

'What will you do now?'

'I'm driving down to London. Mountbatten has got the go-ahead from Churchill and Roosevelt for my project.'

'That thing you called Habbakuk?'

He nodded. 'Can't say anything else just yet, but I may be in touch.'

'And your friend?'

'Julius is back in Cambridge. That reminds me. We had a strange visit from the wife of your man Ryman. She brought us a blood sample. Some of it in a test-tube in a solution of citric acid. More on a handkerchief. She wanted Julius to test them.'

'For what?' I asked, alarmed.

'Rhesus compatibility. Blood groups. Julius recently made some new discoveries about blood structure, though I don't know she knew that. Rather odd. He took it all in his stride, of course.'

'She does know,' I said, my mind whirring. 'I told her myself.'

'I'm going to be late,' said Pyke, looking at his watch. 'Must get on. I'm down to see Lord Louis, as I say. The only person in authority who has ever listened to my ideas. God knows, sometimes you'd think the government wants actively to prevent the use of science in this war.'

He threw the jack into the boot of the car, slammed it, and came round to the front to take his seat. 'Goodbye, then, Henry.'

I put my hand on the window-sill. 'Wait. Julius . . . did he test the blood?'

'I don't know. He took it to Cambridge with him in a thermos flask. I don't know what he told Ryman's wife.'

He started the engine and drove off. I remounted my motorcycle and continued my journey.

A little further on, puzzling over what Pyke had said as I rode along, I was signalled off the road by two army motor-cyclists coming towards me. They demanded I show them my papers. Important dignitaries were coming by shortly.

'Brass hat parade,' one of the soldiers explained. 'You'll have to come off the road.'

178

We stayed on the verge to watch the convoy past. It was quite a spectacle. Two more motorcyclists. An open army truck full of soldiers with Sten guns. A Rolls-Royce, a Buick, then four more motorcycles behind.

'Here,' said the man, as they passed, handing me a pair of binoculars. 'Have a butcher's at the VIPs.'

I caught a glimpse of two hunched, coated figures in the Rolls and a mass of uniforms in the American staff car.

'Churchill,' said the soldier, unable to contain his excitement. 'And Eisenhower. He's a big cheese on the Yank side. They're visiting the commando base at Ardentinny. Right, better go.'

He kicked his starter and drove off, bumping over the short cropped grass between clumps of furze before speeding up to tail the convoy. I stayed for a little while, leaning on my own motorcycle, smoking, watching the sky above the hills, wondering again about what Pyke had told me about Gill Ryman and the blood sample.

My eye was caught by a cold-looking tarn in a bowl of fritted rock. They say water is the eye of a landscape, but I was none the wiser. I was confused, in fact.

Very quickly, as if in confirmation of my train of thought, a mist descended, rolling like gauze across the gorse and boulders and turning the sun into a fuzzy spot. It was a real Hound of the Baskervilles number, though meteorologically one would have to term it a thick sea mist. Or was it a valley fog? When the valley is next to the sea, such nomenclature could tax the ingenuity of our Lord himself. I decided to hurry back.

But I had one more unscheduled meeting yet to make, a few miles further down that misty road. It was Mackellar, in his trap. He had a passenger, and although the mist was very thick now I could just make out the figure of Gill Ryman, wrapped in a shawl. She had a blanket on her knees.

I slowed down and looked up at her. 'Going somewhere?' Not, I must admit, the brightest question, but it had been an odd sort of day, and was about to become more so.

'The Isle of Wight,' she said.

'In Mackellar's trap?'

The look she gave me matched the stupidity of the question. 'Wallace is remaining at home. He can explain.' She paused for a moment, as if deliberating and then relenting her reticence. 'I am having a baby. He cannot bear it again. Nor can I, for that matter.' A snap came into her voice. 'Now I'm afraid we must hurry for the boat.'

Mackellar – my erstwhile friend, wife-beater, Mozart of the pipe – gave me an inscrutable look. Then he cracked his whip and drove off, into the grey.

5

It had certainly been an extraordinary day – an extraordinary few days, I reflected, arriving back at the cot-house on the motor-cycle. And what had happened to spring? I lit a fire to drive off the effects of the sea mist/valley fog and made myself a corned beef sandwich. Later that night there was a knock on the cot-house door. It was Ryman, and he began by begging for a drop of drink like a Glasgow tramp, though not exactly in the manner of one.

'Would you by any chance have any alcohol in the house? Something has happened again which must make me break my ordinance of self-denial.'

I settled him down with a whisky in the most comfortable chair I could find. He stared at the floor for a long time.

'Gill has gone,' he muttered finally.

'I know. I passed her in Mackellar's trap. I'm surprised you didn't take her in the car, given her condition.'

'You know that too, then. Petrol ration. We've run out.'

'I could have got some from Dunoon for you.'

A look of misery passed over his face. 'This is her seventh pregnancy, Henry. All the others have resulted in miscarriages.'

Something landed on the slates above us – a rook? a wind-blown branch? – but it was as if the very sky had cracked. He began speaking quickly. All that was interior came into the open air. 'We always wanted a child. She's thirty-five now; she'll try again next year, too, if this one does not survive. She says it's her duty and she will not shirk from it. That is why she has gone south.'

'To the Isle of Wight.' I said.

'Yes. As you know, the Blackfords, her family, live there. They usually nurse her afterwards. The miscarriages are happening earlier and earlier, so she has gone down in good time, in expectation of the worst.'

'Perhaps it will be different this time.'

'I doubt it. It is a matter of faith alone for us now. There is clearly some scientific reason for what has been happening. It is do with blood and how it is structured into different groups. The rhesus factor, which you know about. A very new area of study. So . . . we have sent samples of our blood to that man Julius Brecher, whom you mentioned.'

'And mine, too, I hear,' I said.

Ryman looked sheepish. 'Ah, yes. Sorry about that. It was Gill's idea to do it like that. She reads a lot of novels. I myself would have asked you directly. The point is, we thought . . .'

His voice trailed off. I put another log on the fire and waited for him to continue, which in due course he did. 'The point is that we hoped, if it happened again, if the baby died, you might, er, stand in. We wanted to get your blood tested for the purpose.'

'Stand in for a baby?' For one bizarre moment I thought they meant to adopt me.

'What? No. We mean, we wondered . . . if you would . . . with Gill. We wondered whether would you . . . with my wife, in order that she might conceive a child? If it all goes wrong this time, I don't think either of us could go through it again. So . . . well, we have at least established your blood is not contradictory. Mine is, you see.'

Shocked, I took a large gulp of whisky and stood up to pat my pockets nervously, searching for cigarettes.

'That's very bad for your health,' observed Ryman from his seat, watching me light up once I had found them.

I gave a burst of laughter at this. He gave me a hurt and angry look and rose to his feet himself.

'I'm glad you find this all so amusing,' he said, facing me.

'Wait.' I put a hand on his shoulder. 'I just thought it was funny that you should be thinking about my health at a time like this. I meant nothing by it.'

He sat down again, sniffing. 'I see. Well, it's natural that the mind should seek refuge at times of distress in its most familiar habits, and one of mine is to tell people when they are doing things that are bad for them.'

Then it was his turn to laugh, bitterly. 'There I go again. Gill says I am always doing this. Analysing future outcomes. She thinks it is because my mind's always working so hard that we are not able to have children. As if my whole body were taken up with thinking.'

Tears ran down his cheeks as he spoke.

'That's nonsense, sir,' I said, as kindly as I could manage.

He took out a handkerchief and blew his nose, smiled weakly at me, then abruptly stood up again and left.

6

I spent the night in turmoil. In the morning, further to discomfit me, as it seemed, the Junkers rumbled over again. So much had taken place that I had almost forgotten about it. I jumped out of bed just in time to watch it whoosh over my head, the cameras on its wingtips clearly visible this time. The rest of the day was spent drawing charts – not because I was mindful of Whybrow's incontinent warning but because I had to take my mind off everything that had happened – in particular the thought of poor Gill and the baby, and Ryman's peculiar request. The two seemed in no way commensurate.

There was no sign of the Prophet and, not wishing to confront in my mind his outlandish suggestion, I didn't seek him out. The whole affair was quite beyond me. There was, in particular, something ghoulish about the idea of arranging, even if provisionally, to put another child in a woman's belly when the one that was already there was not yet dead. It would take great mental and emotional detachment to do that, I thought. Detachment or desperation.

Without stopping for lunch I got my head down again until I was up to date with my work. Whybrow could stuff it all down his gullet for all I cared, but I didn't want him denigrating me to Sir Peter.

I made supper. Potatoes and carrots on the stove, a mackerel Providence had reserved for me at the end of Mackellar's lines. Plus a bottle of beer, and a cigarette for pudding. It was only then, in a tobacco trance, that I conceived of a simple plan to strike back at the German plane using a series of cracker balloons.

I seized upon the notion with dangerous fervour. Now that I look back at this stupid idea, I realise its emotional impetus may have come from Whybrow's implication that I had been neglectful in not helping those people who had rowed across the Clyde following the bombing of the factory in Greenock; and, of course, from wishing to displace from my mind the business with Gill and the baby. The role of displacement is, it seems to me, just as important in consciousness as it is in the environment, though whether something similar to the distributive working of turbulence takes place in the brain I could not say.

Whatever its mental roots, the practical conception for the plan was derived from the not dissimilar Free Balloon Barrage that I had worked on in my early career at the Met Office. Because the government had ordained it, I didn't think the idea stupid at the time. Now, of course, older and marginally wiser, I would take the fact that the government had ordained it as a fair indication of its likely stupidity.

As to the plan itself – each balloon could be primed to go off at a different height. If I set them up right, perhaps in a line behind the beech tree walk, and detonated them at the correct periods, I might be able to create a barrier into which the Junkers would fly and damage itself. For added nuisance value, the length of the copper-wire aerials beneath the balloons could be increased, in the hope that one of them might get caught up in the plane's propellers. It would all require precise timing – and a lot of balloons.

I broke open all of my crates and worked late into the night, filling balloon after balloon. I used up my whole supply of hydrogen materials, then settled down to sleep with all the balloons nestled around the bed. No smoking now: I'd weighted them all with small sealed cartons of motorcycle oil, mixed with a little petrol. For extra explosiveness, I attached a collar of magnesium to the cartons, which were themselves connected by fuse to the main cracker charge.

I had no idea if my plan would work, but it was surely worth a shot. Calculating the likelihood of one of the balloons actually being hit by the plane was impossible. There were too many variables.

But there could be no harm in trying. That is what I thought, at any rate. Underneath the thought, however, was the vision of a brilliant spectacle, something that would rescue my part in the war and be talked about for generations to come.

7

In the light of day, I felt a twinge of unease about what I was planning. I worried about the waste of materials and the trouble I would get into if it didn't work. Or, indeed, if it did work. But by then, with no clear idea of the significance it would have, I was already committed to the idea. I went to the beech tree walk to set a series of tether switches to which each of the balloons could be attached, enabling them to be released in sequence. I then came back carrying one balloon at a time, each weighted with extra incendiary materials and trailing an extra-long copper-wire tail.

It was quite hard to put all this in place, as a high wind was blowing and each balloon had to be tethered with its burden and tail neatly laid out, to avoid tangles. The tether switches were strings attached to a fuse and a ground-pin, like a tent-pole – I had rigged it up so that each fuse would ignite its neighbour.

I did not finish until eleven, when who should appear but Ryman, walking along the opposite bank of a stream that ran under the beeches. He was wearing corduroy trousers and a thick woollen sweater and carrying a bottle of milk. I quickly crossed over.

'What are you doing?' he asked, eyeing the bundle of leftover tether packets under my arm.

'Oh, this and that,' I said casually, which was not perhaps the best way of deflecting attention from my activities. 'I have been thinking about what you said the other evening,' I said tactically, in order to distract him.

His response was to look as if he were having a thought: one thought after another, in fact. Then he repeated, 'What exactly are you doing?'

'I'm laying a sequence of cracker balloons.' At any moment he might have walked through the long line of red balloons on the other side of the beeches, so I thought it best to tell him a little of the truth.

'What are *you* doing with that milk?' I said as another diversionary measure.

'Come,' he said. 'I'll show you.'

We walked alongside the stream, towards the wooden footbridge. The whole place was filled with green mossy light and the smell of vegetation. Inside the glade, where the wind had less effect, the midges were greatly in evidence, and I was soon slapping and itching. The sense of peace and composure I'd felt in that place was no longer in evidence. Quite the reverse.

As we leaned over the bridge, which sagged slightly under our weight, Ryman began pouring milk from the bottle into the running, turning water, making a cloudy vortex on one side of a rock and a white-lined plume on the other.

He chanted a ditty as he poured. 'Big whirls have little whirls that feed on their velocity. Little whirls have lesser whirls and so on to viscosity – in the molecular sense.' He paused, before continuing in his ordinary voice, 'And this is the gospel of the Lord.'

I watched him pour more milk into the stream, where it turned in the opalescent eddy of itself, before being swept away by the surrounding water.

'Or it might not be the gospel. Unfortunately, we cannot see the whole picture, and must carry on our business on premises that are still in the hands of the builders. That business is the search.'

His mixing of both milk and metaphor apparently over for the time being, he paused again before looking at me very directly. 'I think you, too, Henry, have been searching for some kind of answer.' Below us, the water riddled through the stones. 'How to use my so-called number in war is what you're after, I suppose?'

I gave a disconsolate nod of confirmation.

'Who sent you?'

It was pointless to try to cover up any more. 'Sir Peter Vaward.'

'You've really been spying on me, all this time?'

'Not very successfully.'

He put his fingers to his brow. 'I had an idea from the first it might be something like that. You do make things complicated for yourself. Why didn't you just ask me?'

'It's war work,' I said vacuously. 'I was afraid you might have conscientious objections. And anyway, I did ask you, several times.'

The Prophet shrugged. '*Sir* Peter Vaward, eh? One of the gas men at Porton Down, he used to be, before he got so grand . . . He used some of my equations to find out how quickly poison gas would disperse.'

'He's just trying to do his job. The Met Office needs to comprehend turbulence in a single coherent scheme. The truth is, they need it especially for the landings on mainland Europe.'

'I know what those will mean,' Ryman said sternly. 'I know what killing is.'

I saw the Prophet in the cruel delirium of the trenches, half mad with horror, the crazy Albert Hall vision rising as if on scaffolding out of that mess of dead men and horses, only to be lost under a pile of coal.

'But you'll tell me?' I pleaded. 'Even if it goes against your principles?'

'The practical application of science is an individual's moral choice. The theory itself is neither moral nor immoral. See here, for goodness' sake!'

As if he were watering a flowerbed, he poured the last of the milk into the stream, where – though not exactly – it swirled round as before, until its behaviour became unsteady, particles of milk and water enmeshing in little puffs of diluting white as they flowed over rocks and through weed.

Ryman spoke with an air of authority – although it was the authority of a man unburdening himself. 'Weather energy goes round in circles, runs down corridors, cascades down stairways. It diffuses, regathers, reforms, diffuses again. It moves in jets and trickles, is divided by layers thick and thin – layers that themselves can be throughways as well as shields. It's always moving through one system to another, taking different shapes over time. That's why there'll always be the unexpected. The number will not help you solve that problem directly.'

He paused to grip the rail of the bridge before resuming speaking more quickly, with a brighter timbre to his voice. 'But if you want help with your war, I will give you some peaceful advice. The extent of unexpectedness can be modified, increasing the probability of prediction. You must focus on the layers and boundaries between weather systems to draw out that predictability. Each layer has a different predictability. You must concentrate on the barriers between these differently characterised flows. The width of the flows is key, but also their depth, and how long they last. So the spacing – in time and geographically – of where you make your observations therefore becomes crucial. Don't think of the date for your invasion, or you will make a prison for yourself. Think of your data instead. How does it fit into the surrounding context?'

I slapped my neck. Was he really just saying we had to measure better? If he was, it was a preposterous thing to offer up as the secret of weather forecasting. I felt like pushing him off the side of the bridge, into the water.

I lit a cigarette to counter the midges – and to give me the courage to speak my mind. 'What Hitler is doing is wrong. Morally wrong. Surely you must see that. If you really cared about avoiding murder and death you would help me.'

'Very well.' He pointed at the stream with the empty milk bottle. 'Look. There is no milk there now. The important thing to remember is that, in itself, turbulence decays, until it is regenerated by new energy sets. This is where questions of range and context come in. Barrier questions, boundary matters, timing issues. Beginnings, middles and ends. These are the important things. These are the limits which affect the predictability of different atmospheric layers. You need to find the so-called Ryman number for each part of the story. The problem is, it has already changed by the time you come to the next part. The time meter is always ticking as you move about spatially. More or less everything comes down to that basic relation.'

I guess this was the moment of revelation, though it didn't seem like a revelatory experience. I felt unsatisfied. The knowledge I was after was, if anything, more elusive than ever. Perhaps I was foolish to have expected that the answers could just come like logs down a chute. Yet I clearly owed him for something.

I took his hand and shook it. 'Thank you. I think I understand better now. But I do have some other questions.'

He looked at me coolly, as if I was pushing my luck. 'Go on.'

Everything I'd been thinking about came out in a rush. 'To invade a piece of France or Belgium, how much of the adjoining coast would we have to do the forecast for? How long before the invasion day should the critical forecast take place? How far beyond the immediate vicinity, one or other part of the Channel, should weather systems evolving from elsewhere be considered?'

'Oh for goodness' sake,' he said, raising his eyebrows. 'The edge is always dangerous. You must try to track *all* the limits, *all* the barriers. That is what I've been trying to drive home to you. Remember this, too: that a barrier between two weather patterns might also be a narrow corridor for a third. Watch out for what's flying down that narrow corridor, Henry. That can change everything for miles around.'

'But I don't know how to make these distinctions! I have a fifty-mile stretch of beach and I am not sure where your beginnings, middles and ends of the various weather systems fall on it.'

He sighed. 'You just must use your common sense, taking care how you relate the different zones. Where you cannot measure, you must sensibly approximate. Use randomisation judiciously.'

I seemed to hear something by the back of my head. Something very distant and apparently insignificant but in fact prodigiously imperilling. But I did not understand what it was, at least I didn't right then. I thought it was a midge, maybe, or some whining mechanical process taking place in the hills or on water. The Cowal in wartime was full of such noises.

His voice warmed a little. 'Don't pretend to the military that it can all be computed, Henry. It can't. Not yet. We don't have the brain power. Not even if every member of every Allied met office sat side by side doing one tiny part of the calculation each, as in my Albert Hall fantasy. We need machines to do it.'

With that he turned away, as if to head for home, before turning back and looking at me directly, face to face where we stood on the bridge. 'I notice you haven't asked me about Gill. You will think about the matter we spoke of?'

I nodded, uncertain as he departed as to what kind of contract, if any, I had just made – but that, as things turned out, was the least of my troubles.

8

As I watched Ryman's tall figure stride across the field, I realised what it was, that half-familiar noise I'd been hearing. It was the German plane, coming in low. That is what I had heard. We both turned to look. Without stopping to think, I ran as fast as I could to the start of the beech tree walk, where I had set the first of my release switches.

The Junkers came over, already in the curve, readying itself to turn. They could have shot Ryman by now, had they wanted. Perhaps they really were just taking pictures . . .

I pressed the plunger. Up they went then, from behind the line of trees, dipping and drifting, one after another . . . a host of cracker balloons, each packing a charge, each with a sting in its tail.

I came out from among the trees to see Ryman running back towards the rising tail of the last balloon, his face full of fury. What was he doing? It was as if he wanted to pluck the offending weapon from the sky. Some of the balloons had already begun to detonate. The plane, coming in on its second pass, was now faced with a line of balloons rising through the air at irregular intervals, with the wind making it impossible to predict where they would rise.

Crack! Crack!

At every level they were going off. Large patches of red fire in the sky. *Crack!* Then white flashes as the magnesium caught and flared.

They made a tremendous noise. The sky quickly filled with

smoke and the air was acrid with the smell of burning petrol. I heard an exultant laugh come out of my throat.

Black smoke was falling. Through the pall I saw Ryman, closer now. Above him, the plane's engine droned. To my dawning horror, I glimpsed Ryman standing in the path of one the balloon wires, the last in the sequence, which had drifted down. It missed him. As it passed by him the tail made a loud pop and burst into flames. I saw Ryman flinch and duck, and then, to my relief, straighten up amid the new puff of black smoke, apparently unharmed.

At that moment, however, the wind changed. The balloon doubled back in his direction, its wire swinging from side to side, the blackened carton spinning round. Twisting as it followed the eddy-driven movement of the balloon from which it was suspended, with the remains of the carton acting as a sort of anchor on which the wind could catch, the copper-wire aerial caught him round the neck, looping rapidly round. All this happened in an instant. I watched, stupefied, as the balloon began dragging him along the field. There was a ghastly comedy in the mechanical movement of his legs.

I ran towards him. What on earth did he think he was doing?

Above us other balloons continued to blow. Flaring pieces of magnesium were tumbling onto the grass beside me. When I reached Ryman his face was bright red. His weight had anchored the balloon a little, but he was still sliding across the field. I grabbed hold of his kicking legs and pulled him down to me, clawing frantically at the wire around his throat.

I was making things worse. The wire grew tight. A noose. A killing snare like one of Mackellar's for the rabbits. My knees began to shake. I felt the *kizunguzungu* feeling returning.

Ryman was frothing at the mouth. I tried again to pull the balloon down, but now it made no difference to the tension on the wire, which had knotted itself and drawn close. Panicking, I twisted the wire tightly with my fingers, still trying to loosen it, but all that happened was that it bit deeper into his Adam's apple, crushing his windpipe. His eyes bulged and his face began turning from red to blue. Ryman's head slumped forward, a trickle of blood at his nostril.

It was no use. I needed something to sever the wire. Leaving him suspended, I ran to the cot-house to search for a suitable tool. I remember frantically sweeping everything off my desk and overturning half a dozen crates before I eventually found a pair of tinsnips. I rushed back outside in a daze to find Ryman's body still hanging from the balloon, wreathed in smoke. Stumbling and falling on the grass, the plane still swooping overhead, I ran back to release him. I snipped the wire above him and he fell to the ground, enabling me to get at the strangling copper. But I was too late. His face remained as swollen as the balloon whose aerial had just garrotted him. I think he must have been dead even before I'd run to the house. Moaning, I fell to my knees by the body. The earth seemed to quake, as if rocks deep below were being rent asunder.

The plane passed overhead again. At that moment there was another explosion in the air. I looked up. One of its engines was smoking – I assumed from drawing into its propeller housing another wire and carton, followed in short order by a hydrogen balloon, just as intended.

But there was no grand finale, at least not then. The Junkers just seemed to wobble for a moment, then sailed on imperturbably into the blue light of the horizon, leaving me and my disaster to run their course. What I did not see, what happened later, in another part of the picture, were parachutes opening, men falling to earth.

9

The rest of the day passed in a blur of ambulance men and vehicles and police. I half-dragged, half-carried Ryman's body to the cot-house, laying it on the grass outside, then went inside to make the necessary telephone calls. Afterwards, appalled at myself, I sat beside the body on the porch, unable to look at the face. Something inside me had broken.

Confirmed in a sense of personal futility, I sat on the step as the officials went to and fro. Later the Mackellars appeared – they had been at the agricultural market in the town and had just come back in the trap.

Mackellar strode across the grass towards me, the whip from the trap in his hand. Someone had obviously told him that I was responsible for what had happened. At first, craggy-faced and trembling with anger under his flat cap, he just stood there in front of me where I sat on the step. I was about to say something when he lifted the whip and began swiping me with it, uttering curses as he did so. I cowered on the step, curling fetally under the rain of stinging blows.

Eventually – and it seemed like an awfully long time – a pair of policemen pulled him off me.

I wiped blood off my face and sat back on the step, caught in a terrible immobility of misery and pain. I was almost grateful for the pain, not feeling sufficiently self-lacerated for what had happened. Just a terrible numbness and dizziness: oh yes, a vicious return of that.

The ambulance took Ryman's body. His glasses fell off as

they loaded him onto it. With tears running down my bleeding face, unable to watch any more, I stood up and went into the cot-house. I washed my face and staunched some of the bleeding with a towel. I looked awful.

Questions surged into my mind . . . What had all this been *for*? I must, I thought, send a telegram to Gill at once. But what could I possibly say to her? The prospect of facing Sir Peter also terrified me. Had I got what he wanted? If so it was at a great cost. As I was standing in front of the mirror, a policeman appeared, telling me I had to go with him to Dunoon.

From that moment a stream of further misery flowed. First of all I had to face Mrs Mackellar, who was waiting outside the door. Her wild white hair more awry than ever, and her ragged red coat flaring out behind her like the tail of a banshee, she came up to me as I was being put into the police car. She was carrying her hazel herd-stick and I thought for a second she was about to continue the work her husband had started, but all she did was lean her Gorgon-like face into the car window.

Nodding to herself more than me, she said, 'I was right about you. Dangerous.' They were sentiments that I could only agree with.

I was then driven to Dunoon for questioning. I told the inspector who interrogated me that I was doing my duty in trying to down a German plane. It was four hours before I was released. Four hours being quizzed and signing statements. In the end my explanation that the whole thing had been an awful accident was accepted. On being released I was given instructions to report to Whybrow, of all people.

I did not care very much what that idiot thought, though I was worried about the extent to which he could colour Sir Peter's opinion. But Whybrow was not full of the malevolent satisfaction I was expecting. It was as if he was as shocked as I by what had happened.

He said in mild tones that I should go back to London immediately and see Sir Peter. 'It seems to me,' he continued, 'that you've behaved extremely irresponsibly. In this as in other matters. I shall be making a full report to the director.'

I went in search of Joan and Gwen, but on climbing to the makeshift studio in the observation tower I found it quite bare. The mattresses, the mirrors, the easel and other painting equipment – everything was gone. I climbed back down and went to the Waafs' quarters to ask.

A sullen looking girl with pins in her hair came to the door. She told me that Gwen and Joan had been transferred to another unit. Whybrow had kept his promise. That was why he had been so anodyne. He must have known I would come in search of them.

I returned in a box-like green bus to Kilmun to pack, in preparation for my journey south. As I walked up through the village for the last time, someone opened a window and shouted something down at me.

'Murderer!' That was the word.

10

Dawn and the beginning of my long journey south for a reckoning with Sir Peter brought only more shame. As I was waiting for the boat to Gourock, who should appear but Minister Grant, the cleric who had left Ryman's table in such a rage.

The bombast seemed to have gone out of him. 'I did not rub along well with him myself, as you will be aware. But he was a popular figure here. Do you know, they used to call him the Prophet? So I am afraid there is a deal of animosity towards you. Really, it is a good thing you are leaving.'

I nodded distractedly, looking at the MacBrayne *Comet* as it drew close to the quay, propeller and exhausts churning up the water as the captain manoeuvred the vessel into position.

Grant told me that Ryman's body had been removed to a funeral parlour. 'He left instructions in his will that he was to be cremated. A rationalist to the end.'

'Mrs Ryman has been informed, then?'

'So I understand.'

'Will she be coming back?'

'I don't know.' And then he gave me an imperious look, full of all the authority of the Kirk. 'What I do know is that her husband is dead because of a schoolboy prank. Was that what you came here for?'

'Of course not. I came to learn – to predict the weather.'

Now the old Grant came back, the Grant of the dinner table and the Old Testament. 'You should read your Job, young man. "Great things doeth he, which we cannot comprehend. For he saith to the snow, fall on the earth; likewise to the shower of rain ... Dost thou know the balancings of the clouds, the wondrous works of him which is perfect in knowledge?"'

No.

I do not know them.

I cannot compute them.

Though I did not say that, simply nodding and turning away, towards the arriving MacBrayne, which was already rattling down its gangplank.

Once across the water I caught the boat from Gourock into the city. Light came down awkwardly through the hedges at the edge of the line.

At Fort Matilda children's heads popped up, calling out obscenities at the train as it passed.

At Greenock there were walls covered with red lichen.

At Port Glasgow there was a mill chimney.

Then came warehouses with broken windows and the cruel, careless Clyde, a depressing expanse of rippled mud now the tide was out, a lagoon of slime and seaweed which it now seemed that all the choir of heaven could not sing back to beauty. In fact, all it would take was water – rivulets of running water, pushing over the isobar-like lines of mud, cleansing, purging water, water running in from the sea.

Later – on the train south from Glasgow to London, my thoughts ebbing to and fro with the rocking of the carriage as the hours passed – the enormity of what I had done finally hit home. Someone had died. An *individual* had died. Wallace Ryman had died. The police might have let me off but there were still moral charges to answer, focused, even if only internally, on the degree of consequence and my intentions.

On consequence – well, it's impossible, isn't it? To chart it all, backwards and forwards through time and space, as one might a rainstorm. Yet I *was* foolish, I *should* have been more careful, I *ought* to have given thought to what might transpire.

I pondered the different ways in which I might be able to explain it all to Sir Peter. Really, I should have been thinking about how I could explain it all to Gill. But it's a fact that the human mind tends to run away from its true responsibilities – always seeking an exit, always seeking a place to hide.

Examining my intentions, I found that I couldn't gauge them with any accuracy. I? My? Who was I kidding? My state of mind was so agitated I no longer knew what 'I' was, what 'I' meant.

I didn't know. I just didn't know. Even now I don't know who I am.

Feeling uncertain of myself like this, I heard the Prophet's voice in my head, extemporising on the nature of the eddy. *Difficult to define precisely: for a limited time it retains its identity, while moving with the surrounding fluid – until it becomes something else.* That is how I myself felt on that train – as if my very soul were being diluted by the surrounding fluid of life, that whirl of *kizunguzungu* which is ever with us.

Outside, in one of the speeding cities of the north of England, flames burned from two towers, the light of each cross-cutting the fading daylight between them. Munitions factories, in all likelihood. Very soon, on account of the blackout, the flames would be extinguished, for dusk was snatching away the last of day, taking a little piece of not just mine, but each man and woman's life as an extra tithe.

After an hour or two more we came to a creaking, juddering halt while another train passed. Now it was fully dark. The train vibrated, hummed. The other train's passengers sped by in their lighted boxes. The carriage gave a sideways shudder, as if someone had clouted it with a piece of track they had picked up from a siding. The engine changed its tune, and with a hiss of hydraulics and a screeching jolt the train resumed its motion.

As the journey continued, I came up with resolutions that now seem inadequate. All sorts of causes might drive one (this was the manner in which I considered the issue) to the corner of one's poor little acre, such a place as I'd found at Kilmun, launching into the path of that aircraft those balloons with their fatal tails. But the causes are more or less irrelevant. The real moral issue is how much one turns in the yoke. To what extent – irrespective of the historical goad – a particular course of action might authentically be claimed as one's own.

Yes (I told myself), surely the key now was being honest about why the action was made. Facing up to the fact that I had simply craved excitement, accepting that was why I'd set a trap for the plane like that. But I could hardly admit that to Sir Peter.

Stiff and bleary-eyed, I alighted at St Pancras no more assured of my personal coherence than of the shreds and patches of steam, the bits and pieces of smoke that surrounded me. I stood on the platform for a moment listening to echoing voices of the porters and guards. A brown paper bag was drifting around under the great glass arches. Watching it fall, I noticed a half-eaten, half-rotten apple lying on the ground nearby and was struck by the aspect of a mouth it presented. Staring at it, I realised my face was hurting from the gashes on it where Mackellar had whipped me; people had looked at my injuries curiously while I was on the train. Hoping they would heal at least partially by the time I had to see Sir Peter, I picked up my suitcase and walked.

11

As I waited outside Sir Peter's office, once again Admiral FitzRoy stared down at me from his painting, this time in reproach, or so it seemed to me. There was no sign of Sir Peter's secretary. Miss Clements, as I then knew her. Still wondering how I was to gloss my tale of catastrophe, I could find – apart from the fact that Ryman may have given us what we wanted – only one hopeful note.

Perhaps here in the high castle of Adastral House, from where the grandee of British meteorology tried to direct a flock of weather forecasters across Britain and the Empire into providing coherent, standardised, reliable information not just for specific military missions, but for the prosecution of the larger policy of the conflict, perhaps here the death of a single man might not be considered of great moment.

But I dismissed the notion immediately. I might as well sign up for the Nazi Party if I started thinking like that. Even though a single death might not count in the large scheme of the war, it nonetheless had to be accounted for in the still larger moral scheme of life. With every sparrow that falls ... that sort of thing.

Eventually I was called through into the room of clocks, with its familiar smell of beeswax. The office was darker than I remembered, the overcast weather outside penetrating as if it had been piling up on the other side of the glass and only now, with my entrance, found one of its own. Little grey pearls of light – fragments of the insinuated material, fluxes of local dissipation – danced on the faces of the timepieces.

Sir Peter himself was standing by the window as I came in, looking down at the traffic in Kingsway.

'Sit down, Meadows,' said the weather magus of the war, still with his back to me. A buff-coloured folder was in his hand.

I sat in one of the big green armchairs. The fire which had warmed the room on my previous visit was unlit this time, and the sight of the empty grate heightened my anxiety. It was like a mouth with teeth, but no lips or tongue.

At last, Sir Peter turned. As if on cue, one of his clocks sounded. Then others, one after the other: a cascade of sound. Followed once more by the man-in-the-moon clock chiming on completion of its own dilatory circle.

Silhouetted in the window as he was, it was impossible to make out the exact tenor of Sir Peter's expression, but I could see well enough that he had changed. His hair was quite white now, rather than grey, and his pale face was much more deeply lined, with eczematic patches here and there, standing out like the little red flags used to mark the positions of weather ships on charts.

The number of staff at the Met Office had doubled to nearly 7,000 since I had last been in the room. This had put a colossal strain on the director, so it was later said. With Allied successes growing at last, each new military operation to dislodge Hitler's troops or their proxies demanded the appropriate meteorological forecast. The range of operational activities planned and executed was now enormous. Experienced forecasters were being shifted from one operation to another as missions evolved.

But of all these plans and plots the proposed landings on mainland Europe were the most important – and here was I with only shame and disgrace to contribute to them, awaiting a reprimand when I had expected triumph and honours, rightful laurels. Underneath it all was guilt, the pure, searing guilt of one who has taken a life. The kind of guilt which purples a soul for ever.

What was I going to say? I swallowed hard as Sir Peter crossed the room, carrying the manilla folder.

'It hasn't really worked out, has it?' he said, sitting down in the other armchair. I was surprised, both at the understatement and at the almost offhand manner in which he spoke.

'It was an accident, sir.'

Now the voice acquired the hardness I had expected. 'So you say. It seems to me a piece of tomfoolery on your part that went badly wrong. Others, such as Gordon Whybrow in Dunoon, are putting a much darker interpretation on your behaviour.'

He opened the folder. On a paper inside I caught a glimpse of Whybrow's typewriting – recognisable from the dozens of instructions I'd received from him in Kilmun – but could not read the words. 'I must say, he has developed a very low opinion of you. He seems to think you were more interested in chasing after women than doing any work. And he says that you are prone to drink.'

'That's not true, sir. Well, the point is – I worked hard for you. If it were not for the business with the plane . . .'

My voice trailed off. I leaned forward, putting my head in my hands – and then there was silence for a while.

'Don't be too hard on yourself,' said Sir Peter eventually. 'It could be argued you were only doing your duty in trying to down that plane. You know you did damage it fatally?'

I shook my head.

'The crew realised they would not make it home, so fearing coming down in the sea they bailed out. They parachuted down in Ayrshire and were soon picked up.'

'I'd no idea.'

'There's more, and it's very interesting. It might make you feel a little less guilty for what has happened.'

I could not see any way in which that could be possible, I thought to myself as Sir Peter continued. 'Among the crew was a man called Heinz Wirbel. A weatherman, an observer in the Zentral Wetterdienstgruppe. About your age and similarly overqualified, with an academic background. Anyway, Wirbel was willing to sing, and I'm more inclined to listen to what he had to say than to Whybrow or the Dunoon police. The Germans weren't just flying meteorological reconnaissance, they were trying to establish Ryman's whereabouts. Moreover, Wirbel was attached to Professor Weickmann's invasion watch group, which shows they have been following the same train of thought as us.'

I sat up. 'Really? I did think it was all rather odd.'

Sir Peter continued. 'Well it was. The death of Ryman might have been an accident, but the appearance of the plane wasn't. They couldn't kidnap him, at least not easily. They might have wanted to kill him, though Wirbel says he had no orders to do that. They certainly were looking for him, I suppose to see if he really was retired or whether his revolutionary approach to forecasting was now being used by us officially. It's all bluff and counter-bluff, nowadays, between me and my opposite number in Berlin. They try to think what we could consider a tolerable meteorological interval for a military operation, given our approach to interpreting weather, and I try conversely to do the same with them. Both always speculating on what relative analytical techniques might mean for operations. So any intelligence regarding the underlying theories being employed is useful.'

I felt a great, if bogus wave of relief on hearing all this, as if the Germans might now share my responsibility for Ryman's death. 'But how did they know about Ryman? I don't just mean citations in papers – how did they know where he lived, what he was up to and so on?'

Sir Peter lit a cigarette, the flame of the lighter illuminating his long white face. 'He was a complex man. In August 1939 – you may not know this – he went to Danzig. Just before the German invasion of Poland. I believe he wanted to witness the prelude to war for himself. As part of his so-called peace studies.'

I suddenly remembered the box file, *Visit to Danzig and Berlin*, which I had seen in the study and never looked at.

'On the way back, he visited Berlin,' continued Vaward. 'There he met the well-known Quaker Corder Catchpole. Now Catchpole is a conchie, like most of them: he served with Ryman in the Friends Ambulance Unit in the Great War. By 1939 Catchpole was Quaker ambassador in Berlin. He was trying to prevent the onset of war by keeping open some unofficial channel of communication. He was someone our agents followed as a matter of course. When he met up with Ryman, we became aware that Nazi intelligence were also on to him. They already wanted Ryman, you see, they knew about the importance of his work. Most of the great German scientists with an interest in weather, like Theodore von Kármán, had fled for America in the thirties, so they were backward in this area. I suspect there was an idea that Ryman could be turned because of his pacifist convictions. And when one of our people heard him bid farewell to his hotelier in Berlin with the words, "Heil Hitler and King George" – frankly, we began to worry about his allegiances, too. But the fact is, he wouldn't have anything to do with anything military on either side.'

I told Vaward about the box file. 'Yes, we have seen that,' he said. 'Intelligence went through the house. It's just a few newspaper articles about Danzig, including one by Ryman himself, describing the visit. We have also spoken to Mrs Ryman about her husband's sympathies.'

I felt protective towards her. 'I hope you were considerate.'

As I spoke, I felt again, in the very crypt of my soul, that immense longing which found its object in Gill.

He nodded, a forbearing smile passing over his moon-like face.

'Do you know what has happened – with the pregnancy?' I asked. 'Is she back in Scotland?' I had a vision of her back up in that bleak house alone.

'I don't know about the baby. Only that she has decided to stay in the Isle of Wight permanently.'

'Do you by any chance have the address, sir? I'm conscious I ought to communicate with her.'

'I am sure you are. But I am afraid I don't.'

He lit another cigarette, the tip of his tongue showing as he put it to his lips.

'Er,' I said, feeling emotionally exhausted, 'may I have one of those, sir?'

'Why yes, of course. Expect you need it.' He leaned across and lit it for me. The manilla folder slid off his lap and fell to the floor, revealing more pages from Whybrow's typewriter. There seemed to be acres of the stuff, fanning out across the carpet.

'Damn,' said Sir Peter. 'Pick up those, will you?'

He looked down at the papers as if they were things of no importance, and gathering them up I affected a similar disdain, making a show with my eyes of not being interested in their contents.

'Now, tell me, Meadows,' he said, once I'd handed the folder back to him. 'Did you or didn't you manage to find out anything more about applying the Ryman number to an invasion site?' He was looking at me not like the man holding out the lifeline, but the one who was in need of it.

I knew that now was my opportunity. 'I did find out something, sir. Ryman spoke to me at length just before he died.'

A flush of excitement passed over Sir Peter's pallid face. 'About how his number might help us find the right date for the landings?'

'Yes, though I think date is the wrong way of thinking about it, at least insofar as planning an invasion goes.'

'Well, what is the right way, then?'

'When I spoke to him about the landings specifically, he said the most important thing was not the date but the data.'

A tone of crossness entered Sir Peter's voice. 'What does that mean?'

'I'm coming to it, sir. He meant that it was our observations that were most likely to wrong-foot us, that we would do better by adopting a retrospective view than a prospective one.'

'The Americans are already doing that with their analogue models. Using historical data statistically to extrapolate how current weather will develop.'

'With the greatest respect to our allies, I don't think that is what he was talking about. He would say that you could have hundreds of years of data and still get it wrong. You might pick up some quasi-periodic phenomena but the singularities, the weather frequencies on given calendar days, could be completely against the grain.'

'Meadows, I am so much more aware of that than you can imagine. What exactly are you bringing me here? How does it relate to the range of applicability of the Ryman number for amphibious landings?'

'The connection is not yet fully formed in my mind, but . . . Well, because turbulence, as measured by the Ryman number, moves between one geographical area and the next, vertically as well as horizontally, the issue of adjacency is key. Ryman kept mentioning transport barriers, the layers which separate turbulent fluxes. He said that, as well as separating areas of turbulence, these barriers could also be corridors conveying it.

These throughways and fences between different weather types are very important, he said. Some might be as narrow as a hundred feet.'

Sir Peter was becoming increasingly testy. 'Barriers? Corridors?'

'They're related, sir. It's a matter of perception. Interpretation of the future depends on the medium through which one refracts the past.'

'I have no doubt it does, Meadows. Instinct tells me that probably all the things you are saying are perfectly right. But you try convincing military men of theoretical constructs like those – especially if they look at your personal record and see what a dunce you have been, practically speaking. Stagg has requested you join him on the invasion weather group and I have to say I'm really not sure about that any more. But . . . tell me again, about the corridor-barriers. What do they mean for a soldier, Meadows, or an airman?'

I took a deep breath. 'The fact that they can be corridors as well as barriers explains some of the super-fast weather changes that have puzzled forecasters in the past. We have to alter our data gathering and our models accordingly – make sure we realise what we are looking at. Look harder, and be prepared to approximate where we cannot measure.'

His moon-white face suffused with red. 'Look harder! Approximate! That is all you have learned? I send you all the way up to western Scotland and all you come back with is that things can change quickly and we need to improve our instruments and models? And, if that doesn't work, make a guess?'

I was shocked at the sudden disappearance of Sir Peter's customary leisurely tolerance, but I was determined to stand my ground. I knew in my bones that what Ryman had told me was important – even if all it amounted to was, 'Be very careful what you do with your data'.

I knew I had to stand up for myself. 'Sir, this is important. I think it is what you wanted. These barriers can be paths along which pass significant fluxes of their own – sometimes with mass and momentum as large or larger than the adjacent flows which they separate.'

'So you say, but what useful truth am I meant to take away from it for forecasting for the invasion?' His voice, challenging when he had previously spoken, then continued in a different tone, half plaintive, half bitter. 'Current discussions between the forecasters on Stagg's team are extremely dynamical, if you'll excuse the pun. The end result is the meteorological equivalent of the Tower of Babel.'

One of the clocks made a whirring noise, as if resetting a spring inside itself. As the sound ended, I suddenly became aware of an altering of positions. I realised Sir Peter was tacitly pleading with me to take away from him the avalanche of anxiety about the landings which was being piled up on him by overbearing military superiors and by weather forecasters mired in deep disagreement.

Certain of the abiding rightness of Ryman's conception, I felt able to speak with authority, as if I were not Sir Peter's junior but his equal. 'It's more of an approach than discrete knowledge. In music, it would be something like a fugue.'

The director gave a very deep sigh. 'Meadows, have you any idea what Admiral Vian, or General Montgomery, or Air Marshal Tedder, still less Eisenhower himself, would say to me if I presented a fugue as our modus operandi? All they want is reasonable practical assurance of fine weather for a period of three to five days. What I have discovered, and the reason I sent you up to Ryman, is that we don't actually have any methodology for prediction beyond a day or two – apart from the American system of historical statistics, which our people don't think a safe basis. But at least it's a system. You've made some clever theoretical points in the mid-ground between science and philosophy, but I can't see how any of it can be stiffened into practicality.'

'There is one way, sir.'

'What?'

'This. We massively increase our instrumentation within a thousand-mile radius of the invasion site, taking special care to look out for the dialogic characteristics of these barrier-corridors. An increase in the volume and flow of positional information is the only way of taking account of the increase in complexity implied by what Ryman says.'

Giving a cry of disillusion, Sir Peter flung himself backward into the depths of the armchair. 'Hah! I have got weather ships dotted between Reykjavik and New York in predetermined positions in the Atlantic. I have got daily meteorological reconnaissance flights going out under that vulgar appellation met rec from airstrips all over Britain and the Empire. You can see them for yourself on that map up there.'

He pointed at a weather map on the wall, hardly visible behind the array of clocks. 'Not to mention every RAF station across Britain, from Langham in Norfolk to St David's in Wales, from Wick in Scotland to Chivenor in Devon, doing their THUMs. I've got data coming in from submarines in the Mozambique Channel and the Red Sea. I've got daily indications of weather from the resistance fighters in France, steamship captains in the Persian Gulf and Chindits in Assam. I've access to the full weather forecasts of the Red Army and bits and pieces from both Chiang Kai-shek and the communists in China. I have all this and yet you say I am data sparse?'

If my security clearance had been higher he might have added what has since become public knowledge – that he also had Enigma's decrypts of German meteorological reports from U-boats and British weather spies in the depths of

Poland and Belgium, sending up from clandestine aerials quick-burst radio transmissions which were picked up by our bombers as they passed overhead.

Nonetheless, I was still surprised by the freedom with which he bandied about what must have been classified information. All over the country posters were asking 'Do You Know One of These?' and showing below cartoon characters such as Mr Know-All, Miss Leaky Mouth, Mr Glumpot, Mr Secrecy Hush Hush and Mr Pride in Prophecy – 'He knows what the Germans are going to do and when they are going to do it. He knows where our ships are and what Bomber Command is going to do' – yet here was a senior official talking without a care, albeit to one who had signed the Official Secrets Act.

Vaward followed up his long, baying speech by saying loudly, almost shouting, 'And do you know what? Scientifically speaking, you are right! Because, scientifically speaking, one can *never* have enough data. But these military men have a different culture – bend everything to the task, that's their view. Every piece of data gathered must work actively towards victory. That is the end of their hypothesising, not scientific truth in the abstract.'

I spoke softly, feeling like a doctor at the bedside of a patient. 'I don't want to be a pessimist, sir. I simply report to you what Ryman told me. I'm sorry. I wish it were more momentous, but there it is. His main interest was the causes of war. Meteorology, once a passion, seemed to have become a distraction.'

A clock sounded, and Sir Peter seemed to take it as a sign to calm down. 'I still think there is much more to be found out about that number,' he said, lighting another cigarette. 'I was rather hoping you'd be the one to spill the beans.' He gave a sigh, blowing out smoke. 'Perhaps it will have to wait till after the war.'

Feeling a wave of self-disgust pass through me, I watched

the smoke curls unwind themselves as they rose to the ceiling.

'Here,' said Sir Peter gruffly, seeing me look and proffering his cigarette case, which I availed myself of. 'A more immediate question,' he continued, 'is what are we going to do with you now? I have two choices for you. The first is that you join Mr Stagg again. He has taken charge of the meteorological planning for the invasion of Europe and is in dire need of a personal assistant. He has asked for you, as I say, and it's not a bad idea, given that you know him already and are familiar with complex forecasting techniques. But I have also had a query from Combined Operations. Apparently Geoffrey Pyke, whom I understand you met in Dunoon, has asked that you be the meteorologist on something they are up to in Canada. They won't tell me what, exactly, but it concerns ice.'

My mind went back to the pub. So Habbakuk was something to do with ice, then.

Sir Peter continued. 'So those are the two options. Despite your idiocy with that plane, I would be sad to lose you. My personal preference is that you help with the weather planning for the invasion. The greater urgency is there, no doubt about it. But I've always made it my policy to allow every man to choose his own destiny. That way he can find out what line of work he is really cut out for.'

I watched him write an address on a scrap of paper. 'Pyke says you are to go to this address in Smithfield.'

His tired white face regarded me in the gloom. 'Once you have done so, and talked to him, make your choice, Meadows. Let my secretary know, and she will make the necessary arrangements.'

'Thank you, sir. I will try to make the right decision.'

'Miss Clements will see you down,' he said, ushering me to the door. I felt he wanted to be rid of me now, but he had one last thing to say. 'For God's sake, try not to kill anyone else.

I've had the devil of a time extracting you from this mess.'

But there was no sign of Miss Clements when I emerged. I stood under the portrait of FitzRoy, reconsidering my options for a moment. Right then, having had more than enough of weather, it was to ice that I was tending, somewhere clean and simple without the problematical involutions of the atmosphere and the dangerous gloss of an invasion. But I owed Sir Peter a great deal for his having taken my side in all that had happened.

I pressed the button for the lift to the ground floor. The door opened and there, like a genie from a bottle, Miss Clements appeared, carrying the score for Gilbert and Sullivan's *Pirates of Penzance*. Suddenly fluent, romantically speaking, I forgot for a second the horror of Ryman's death, and the urgency of D-Day, and the ingenious plans of Pyke.

Miss Clements, it emerged in conversation, belonged to an amateur dramatics group. She had a rehearsal that evening. I knew the piece well, we used to do it at the Arts Theatre in Cambridge. Mentioning the weather duet in Act I as my cue –

> *How beautifully blue the sky,*
> *The glass is rising very high,*
> *Continue fine I hope it may,*
> *And yet it rained but yesterday.*
> *Continue fine I hope it may,*
> *And yet it rained but yesterday*

– I stood for a while chatting with her, the lift door bouncing against my open palm.

Oh to be there again, to see her *face*. Clear, fine-textured, with a hint of sensuality, such as invited one's gaze to linger longer than was strictly polite. I would give up all my lamplit answers, any number of proofs and academic honours, to heave anchor for the past and see that face again. It makes me wish I had brought a cassette of G&S, not Haydn, with me on this voyage. But it is no matter. The words come back unassisted across the fields of the ocean and the music does too: the mind's strong poetry, hoving across the deep-stretched years into this cocktail of wood and ice, this drinker of dolour and dollars, this knocker-back of riyals and heavy fuel oil, this vessel which we have christened *Habbakuk*:

> *Did ever pirate loathed*
> *Forsake his hideous mission*
> *To find himself betrothed*
> *To a lady of position?*
> *Ah yes! Ah yes! Ah yes!*

Choir-voices of the sea . . .

I take out my pipe now and remember the time we said goodbye – for the last time. Through a tobacco fog I see her again, her face as massive in my mind's eye as the back of the mysterious cetacean monster which has returned to our side, that gigantic bull of a sperm whale which appeared at the start of the journey and seemed like a moving land.

Now it seems like a continent.

12

A light, fresh breeze was funnelling down Kingsway as, jolly from flirting and still humming to myself, I emerged from Adastral House. Looking back, I am shocked I could have forgotten Ryman's death so blithely, even if for a moment. But there were distractions . . . The breeze was carrying a scent of green apples from a grocer's trolley stall and cinnamon from a baker selling hot cross buns. The buns were laid out on grease-proof paper on lattice trays. I bought one and it was delicious. I could mention the sticky glaze on top, the way the light crust broke in, but the real thing I remember was the burst of sweetness when I hit a currant.

But maybe I am being too hard on myself – eating, drinking, most of all sex, those activities ease the turbulence of the flesh, allowing us, briefly, apparent escape from the burden of soul.

As I ate and walked, I recalled something Ryman had said about consciousness being like the berries in jam – that some-times we are in the berry, sometimes in the jam, with the dif-ference being that the 'berries' are the exterior surfaces of con-sciously directed thoughts (such as one might explore while pursuing a line of research) whereas the jam is what we're mostly paddling around in. But now and then we hit upon a berry we were not expecting and that sends us down a train of associative thought, enabling us to leap from berry to berry like someone crossing a stream by stepping stones.

Eating my bun as I was, I suddenly remembered something else: a story that Ryman – who had spent some time teaching at Paisley Technical College when he was younger – had told me about boys throwing teacakes at him while he was at the blackboard. We were moving along the beech tree walk, measuring out future memory pace by pace . . . I remember his tall bush of wiry grey hair moving in the breeze as he spoke . . .

'I took the affair as a joke, but at the next lecture the bad effects of this were seen. They all brought in buns and pelted me with them. Throughout the term I got used to stale buns hitting me on the back of the head intermittently. It kept recurring. I asked each student in turn whether he was responsible and of course they all said no, so I told them that one of their number could add to his ungentlemanly qualities that of being a liar. They just laughed. Then, from the corner of my eye, I saw one in the act of throwing. His name was Patrick Latchford. In a moment of madness I seized him and made to drag him towards the door. He grabbed onto his desk and it came off its pedestal, hitting the floor with a loud bang. The lid flew open, scattering buns over the floor. There must have been at least twenty of them. It turned out his father was a baker. Anyway, that was the end of the lecture bun saga.'

Ryman had laughed then. It was good to recall him happy for once, and I found myself laughing, too, as I remembered it, though it was the kind of laughter that threatened to turn to tears in an instant. But Kingsway was busy with men and women, many in uniform, and the sun was shining through gaps of loose cloud. Maybe it was a signal one thing at least was going to go right, though in retrospect it's clear I had already received that, back at Adastral House.

I walked on a little, past an umbrella shop, a chop house, then hit Pen Corner – the Waterman's Pen shop on the corner of Kemble Street and Kingsway. In the window were fountain pens, silver and gold. They lay like bullet shells in their velvet beds and they made me think of the shell cases in Ryman's study. I really should write to Gill; but what could I say? Sorry didn't seem anything like enough. On the contrary, it seemed like an insult.

The streets were filthy, and here and there were holes where there should have been buildings. A man in a brown coat, grey flannel trousers and a shirt with an open collar passed me. His right hand was dangling down with the thumb in the fold of a book with green boards, which I recognised as *Enquire Within Upon Everything*, then a popular title. He had the look of a derelict or someone gone AWOL. Watching him pass, I suddenly became aware again of my own appearance, in particular the cuts on my face. I had not thought about them in the crucial meeting, though she would often joke about them in later years. Strange how different times can come back like this, as if the separate incidents are being reissued fresh.

Waiting for a bus, I took the piece of paper from my pocket and read what Sir Peter had written: *Morgan's, Smithfield, no uniform*. I began plotting the journey in my head, stepping closer to the kerb and being jostled by the crowd of waiting passengers. I didn't see the bus, which came close enough to me to whip the paper from my hand – and didn't stop anyway. A murmuring grumble, like the beginnings of thunder far off in the sky, went through the knot of people. They were collected round a lamp post in a way that reminded me of the cattle in Kilmun, gathering round a salty post, or the cot-house when the oscillator was pipping.

Catching my breath, I fell to my knees to retrieve the paper from where it lay in the road, flapping like the wing of an injured bird. As I picked it up I became certain that I must throw in my hand with Pyke. Despite the assertions of special knowledge I had made to Sir Peter, the truth was that I felt that grasping the uncertainty of weather in a way coherent enough

219

for the generals was too much of a challenge. No amount of forecasting skill would ever give reasonable enough assurance to send so many men before gunfire. At least with ice there was some certainty: you knew it was going to melt.

For a second I stood paralysed by the hazy glamour of the ice field which was waiting for me in the future: the wraiths of snowdrift racing from under the paws of torchlit huskies, the sledges moving across the great white desert, the boiling green sea biting at its edges, the heroism of an Amundsen, a Shackleton, a Scott . . .

Still clutching the note, I made my way towards Holborn, passing on the way a pub called The Dagger. The sign above the door showed a knife held by a disembodied, gauntleted hand – some kind of heraldic emblem – with a sort of cloud painted round the pricking-point of the blade.

A point in space – but for once I successfully resisted the temptation to go in. Outside, a Guinness delivery lorry was waiting with its engine running, tainting the freshness of the breeze with its exhaust. I watched the greasy black cloud of its emissions drift down a side street into a stand of trees, where it was enmeshed by the moving leaves and branches. The dray-man, wearing old green overalls that recalled to me those worn by the foresters in Kilmun, was evidently waiting for someone to emerge, for he began sounding his horn repeatedly, blast upon blast. It was extremely loud.

As I walked away the sound carried after me on the wind, fading until I could no longer be sure if it was a present perception or a memory. It was as if I was in a labyrinth, lost halfway between the mental and physical worlds.

13

Pyke's operation was in Smithfield Market, that ancient quarter of London wedged between Clerkenwell, Blackfriars and the City. Walking under its large, ornate hangars, in front of long ranks of butchers in white coats and bloody aprons, past glistening chops and chump, haunches and great mounds of diced beef, was like entering a cathedral dedicated to the god of meat.

At the poultry specialist, glazed duck lay in rows beneath bald chickens suspended from hooks, their plucked puckered skin hanging loose; elsewhere the splayed carcasses of cows and pigs presented their innards to passers-by. There was even a pile of pigs' trotters. I stared at it all in wonder.

Most hypnotic of all were the large mounds of stewing meat, chopped up into cubes, which the butchers were slowly moving from one place to another with what looked like garden shovels, all the while making jokes at each other's expense. It did not seem conceivable, in a time of rationing, that so much meat could exist. Did that, I wondered, explain their good humour?

I suddenly felt jealous of these men whose role in life was so clear and unambiguous. But it was not in any way shallow. The casual attitudes of these Cockney butchers, the way they strolled about with saws and cleavers, caps at jaunty angles on their heads, or stood around drinking cups of tea – tea was the potent cement between them – the barely comprehensible shouts and calls they gave, all this was simply camouflage for a high seriousness of purpose. They were working men who obviously believed in what they did.

Apart from the repartee of the butchers, the other main sound of the market was a tremendous lowing, emanating from yards behind the main halls in which the doomed cows were penned. As I walked past them, some sad-faced, some big and boisterous, I was glad I did not have to kill them myself.

Morgan's was a rather dilapidated steel vault that appeared, from the outside, to be almost completely sealed. But there was a door. The name was stencilled in a patchy red arc of paint across the metal. To one side was a black rubber button. I pressed it and thought I heard a bell sound inside, but through the market's cacophony I couldn't be sure. It was a while before the door opened, releasing a cloud of frozen air, in the midst of which was a face wearing a flying helmet and goggles.

'Name?' said the apparition, whose body, I now saw, was encased in an RAF-issue electrically heated flying suit.

'Henry Meadows,' I replied.

'Come this way, sir.' Before us stretched a dimly lit corridor with steel walls. He led me down it to an anteroom, where more fleece-lined flying suits hung on pegs, together with helmets and goggles. 'You'll need to put one of these on before I take you down.' He almost seemed to stand at attention while I changed into the heavy garment. We returned to the corridor, following it until we came to a passenger lift. The descent was a long one. Eventually, the lift stopped with a jolt and its doors opened to reveal a small square room, like an airlock. Facing us was a door, sealed like the main entrance.

'Just a minute, sir,' said my guardian, pressing another rubber button. A voice rang out from a loudspeaker grille. 'Yes?'

'Verse Six and visitor. Mr Meadows.'

'I'll just check with the gaffer,' said the voice. We waited in silence in that stifling little space until the voice came again. 'Ask him the name of the sea lion.'

My minder invited me to speak into the grille. 'It was Lev,' I said, leaning forward in the bulky suit. 'Leviathan.'

The door opened with a hiss to reveal a vast cold-store – much lower in temperature than the corridor – in the midst of which were set up differently sized blocks of ice and other materials, including wood, masonry and concrete. There were various pieces of equipment – long steel basins, electric refrigeration machines, some kind of industrial vice – but I could not work out the purpose of this strange laboratory. Suspended from the ceiling, rows of metal-shaded lamps sent pyramids of light down through the curling air.

Out of the vapours three men approached, each dressed in a flying suit. One of them had a pistol in his belt; another carried a sub-machine gun. I hesitated, but then the unarmed member of the trio pushed up his goggles.

'Meadows!' cried Pyke, clasping me by the shoulders. 'Welcome to Habbakuk!'

'So this is Habbakuk,' I said, looking around. 'I'm none the wiser.'

'Good. Let me explain. We're making super-strengthened ice for use in constructing ships. It's all happening under the auspices of Lord Mountbatten, as I think I already explained. My laboratory assistants are commandos from his Combined Operations staff. I call them Verses One, Two, Three and so on – after Habakkuk in the Bible. Or almost. On official documents it's spelt with two bs and two ks, because of a typing error.'

'What's all this got to do with making ships from ice? Is that even possible?'

'"Look among the nations, watch, and wonder marvellously; for I am working a work in your days, which you will not believe though it is told you,"' Pyke intoned, half repeating what he had said in the pub in Dunoon. 'Chapter one, verse five. Oh, never mind. Come and see Julius.'

'Brecher? Is he here?'

'Yes. I snaffled him from the Cavendish Lab in Cambridge for a few days. He's mixing up some Pykrete. That's the stuff we're making the ships out of. It was Mountbatten's idea to name it after me, not mine. Julius,' he called, 'look who I've got here.'

Brecher was rotating a large spatula in a basin of loose ice slush mixed with something else. The mixture resembled some kind of bran and the spatula, I realised, was a canoe paddle. The light of the lamps was reflecting off his shaven head.

Brecher looked up. 'Meadows! I was thinking of you the other day. That friend of yours in Scotland. I wrote to her with the result of my blood tests but she never replied.'

I was perversely glad that Gill was as remiss in letter-writing as I; although, of course, the scale of the two omissions was hardly comparable. 'What did you say?'

'Well, it's all rather personal.'

'It's all right,' I said. 'She's a friend.' The overstatement, or lie as it might be called, came out with the squirming fluency of a trout held between a fisherman's hands.

Brecher looked at me. 'Very well,' he said. 'She wanted to know whether two samples of blood she sent me had any rhesus incompatibility. I told her they probably did not, though one of the samples was very patchy and old, so it was quite hard to do the test. She sent it me on a handkerchief of all things.'

I realised he was talking about my own blood. He continued stirring the ice as he spoke.

'You see, almost all blood cells carry antibodies of one type or another and under certain conditions – for example, fetal cells crossing over into the maternal circulation during pregnancy – this can cause problems. But we don't fully understand this aspect of things.' He pronounced it *aspekt*, in the German way, with the stress on the second syllable.

'What sort of problems?'

'Ultimately, intrauterine fatality. Death in the womb.'

I suddenly saw – as if down a long passageway – the series of miscarriages, each little homunculus scampering towards Gill and Ryman, half-formed, screaming. In this field, at least, the role of science as an aid to humanity, a helpmeet for civilisation, was clear.

'This is wood pulp,' said Pyke, who had shown scant interest in my conversation with Brecher. 'What we've done is mix ice with wood pulp to increase its mechanical strength. There's a pay-off between ductility and strength, depending on the amount of pulp or sawdust you put in.'

'That should do it,' said Brecher. He removed the paddle and scraped it against the side of the tub, then left it balanced across the top so the residue of the mixture could drip back in. 'I'm off back to Cambridge now, Geoffrey. Nice to see you again, Meadows.' He gave a conspiratorial smile.

'Come and look here.' Pyke led me to another part of the room where one of the commandos was turning a block of ice on a lathe. 'A four per cent suspension of the material we are working on. Quite strong. Show him the hammer, Five.'

The commando put the football-sized block of ice on the floor and picked up a sledge-hammer. He gave it a mighty swing – but on contact the hammer just bounced off the ice as if it were steel. The commando put down the hammer and rubbed his wrist.

'Rather unforgiving,' said Pyke, grinning, his tobacco-stained teeth glowing like citrine against the surrounding whiteness. 'There's something else I want to show you.'

He led me over to a large panel of ice – six or seven feet high, three feet thick – next to which armed commandos were standing. 'Show him, Three.' The commando with the pistol lifted it and fired at the panel. Rather than penetrating it completely, the bullet entered only a few inches.

I was amazed by the mysterious properties of Pykrete. 'How did you manage that?'

'Ordinary ice,' explained Pyke, 'has a crush resistance of about five hundred pounds per square inch – whereas in the case of Pykrete the figure is more like three thousand pounds.'

The experiment was repeated with a Tommy gun, which Pyke fired himself, then with a .303 rifle. The noise of the reports was deafening in that confined space, but both times the bullets remained trapped in the Pykrete.

'Depending on the power of the gun, the bullet will only go in between three and six inches,' Pyke said. He dug out a bullet with a penknife. 'See? Do the same thing with pure ice and it would penetrate fourteen inches. And what are the other figures, Five?'

'Twenty-five inches into softwood, six inches into brickwork, two inches into concrete, sir!'

'Very good, Five. Now, come and see my only vice, ha ha.'

He took me over to the industrial vice I had noticed before. It was pressing on a block of ice no more than a foot square. I could hardly see it between the iron jaws, but the piece seemed to be resisting well: the pressure gauge above read 2,000 lb.

'A little block like that could support the weight of a motor car,' said Pyke. 'Simply because of the micro-reinforcement of wood particles. Fire at it, torpedo it, saw it, and Pykrete will resist you. We showed it to Churchill and he jarred his hand trying to split a block of it with a chopper, and then he showed it to Roosevelt. It was rather amusing. The PM had a waiter bring in a pitcher of boiling water and two punch bowls. Churchill put a piece of ice in one of the bowls and a piece of Pykrete in the other. Of course, the pure ice melted at once, but the Pykrete just bobbed about in the boiling water as if it were cork.'

'What are you going to do with all this?'

'I was coming to that. Ice warfare has not yet been developed to the levels it could reach. Remember, a bullet fired in Lapland costs fifty times a bullet fired in central Europe.'

'I don't understand.'

'Because of the transport costs. The idea is that we could build aircraft carriers and other ships from Pykrete for next to nothing. Berg ships, made in the remote recesses of the Arctic night. Refuelling depots for aircraft. Or a mid-Atlantic base from which to attack U-boats. Or ice-breakers to cut a new north-west passage and send supplies from America to Russia. Or sprayed frozen water could be used to incapacitate shore defences during an invasion of mainland Europe.'

I must have looked a bit sceptical. How much of this was true? There seemed to be no end to his technical abilities and the fecundity of his imagination, but his excitable attitude to it all was like that of a child at Christmas. It struck me again that his enthusiasm was rather similar to Ryman's – even though he was utterly committed, fervent even, about using science in war.

Looking into the clouds of ice vapour I suddenly seemed to see Ryman's face, his bushy hair and downturned mouth becoming different – exaggerated, as if redrawn by the surrounding swirls . . . becoming contorted as it had been when he was hanging from the wire. I shuddered with nausea, closing my eyes to put away the vision.

'Mr Churchill himself has said the advantages of Habbakuk are dazzling,' said Pyke, cheerily. 'We've been given the go-ahead. Workmen on Lake Patricia, Ontario, have already built a prototype berg ship of a thousand tons. She is flat-bottomed, lozenge-shaped, sixty feet long, thirty feet wide. Her Pykrete hull is sheathed in timber and pitch, and a petrol-driven refrigeration plant sends cold air through iron pipes set in the ice.'

'You *are* joking?'

'Of course not. She's stayed afloat! Brecher and I went out to see her. The plan now is to move to Corner Brook, Newfoundland, to build a full-scale ship. Will you be our meteorologist and study the effects of turbulence on Pykrete? Have a look at these numbers and think it over. For God's sake, don't let them go astray. Right, must crack on!'

He shoved some papers into my hand and began to hustle me towards the door, which in those bulky suits was not an operation that could be effected at speed. I went up in the lift, changed in the anteroom and, putting on my overcoat, stepped back out into ringing Cockney voices of the meat market.

14

I spent the next three days in a state of high excitement. Pyke's plans were as full of difficulties as fascinations, but they drove the awful incident at Kilmun from my mind. I wrote a note to Sir Peter explaining which way I had jumped. I did not go into too much detail about how I had come to my decision, but did not neglect to thank him for all the support he had given me in my career so far. At last, I thought on posting the note, I now had a clear course of action. I felt I'd reached what meteorologists call a point of occlusion: a moment – a place – where warm and cold fronts meet.

I had made my choice. I was convinced – what a young fool I was – that the self-disgust I felt at having caused Ryman's death would now subside.

In choosing Pyke's ice over Sir Peter's fire it might have seemed as though I was travelling in the riskier direction, but it did not feel like that to me then. For while, on the face of it, Pyke's scheme to build ships out of ice appeared highly fraught, despite its backing from Mountbatten, it felt like a safer proposition than becoming part of the invasion forecast. All that I had learned from proximity to Ryman only seemed to confirm the wild mutability of the weather. I didn't want to send men to their deaths.

My pied-à-terre in Richmond being unavailable – I had rented it out while in Scotland – I took a room in a boarding-house on Claremont Square, within walking distance of Smithfield. It was a nice Bloomsbury house transplanted to ugly Pentonville, where I wrote furiously into the night, smoking heavily, covering – just as I have been lately, on an ice ship heading for the desert – sheet after sheet with spidery blue writing, trying to solve the many problems of fluid dynamics associated with Habbakuk.

The problems Pyke set me concerned the ship's draught, which I would only solve when I came at it this time round. Back then, I was staggered by the ambition of the project. A ship 2,000 feet long and thirty yards wide with a thirty-foot-thick hull. The one we made in Antarctica was much smaller, but otherwise many of the details were the same. Motor nacelles mounted along the flanks – 1,000-horsepower electric motors with a propeller; generator turbines inside the hull, protected by box girders; an elaborate system of refrigeration through pipes in the ice; tanks for the oil which drove the turbines, generators for the nacelles and other auxiliary machinery . . .

I put all my questions down in a memo and the following morning set off for Pyke's workshop, with the memo folded in my jacket pocket.

It was a joy, after all that seclusion, to burst out into the leafy freshness of Amwell Street. I bought a pint of milk from the dairy there and drank it straight from the bottle, enjoying the sensation of coldness in my throat.

Then I thought of Ryman's bottle of milk and all that happened afterwards, and my gorge rose. I saw his thin hand pouring it into the stream again.

Crossing Rosebery Avenue into Exmouth Market, the atmosphere of the city changed. The sweet light of Amwell Street became smokier and more acrid, as if all the poisonous inks of the printing presses in Fleet Street and Bouverie Street, blowing northward, had begun to infect the air.

I continued on my way to the freezer unit in the bowels of

Smithfield. I walked down some steps off Bowling Green Lane, then up past a pub called the Three Kings and down into Clerkenwell Green. Crossing under the St John's Gatehouse – a stone-blocked medieval building associated with the Templars or Hospitallers or something of that order – I had the sensation of being in many different times at once. How odd that the fighting knights of Christendom once sojourned here, flaming swords at the ready! Now here I was, in 1944, on my way to a meeting about a scheme that could change the course of the war using ships of ice.

Having passed through the butchers' hall as before, I rang the bell at Morgan's. Hardly had I done so when a rather cross-looking soldier appeared from within the vault. He wore an ordinary army uniform, chestnut-coloured boots and Sam Browne belt. He didn't let me in at first, just stood with the door half-open, eyeing me suspiciously.

'Well?' he said. He had a sandy moustache and his hair was cropped very short.

I introduced myself and explained that Pyke had engaged me on a project I could not discuss.

'Which one?' he asked, warily. 'You better come in.'

'This one,' I replied, having stepped inside. I suddenly realised that the freezer vault was no longer freezing.

'Damn fool,' said the officer. 'He shouldn't have done that. Pyke has been stood down from this project. It's over. He's too much of a liability, anyway. We're closing this place and no one is coming in without my say-so.'

Behind him I could see the protective clothing in the ante-room being piled up into boxes by one of the commandos.

'But he said I might be joining his team,' I said, plaintively.

'Well I'm telling you you're not.'

'On whose authority?'

'On Lord Mountbatten's. Not that it's any of your concern,

Meadows, but my name is Brigadier Wildman-Lushington and I monitor Pyke's insanities on behalf of Lord Louis. Pyke has quite enough projects on the go at the moment. Habbakuk has been cancelled and he has been told to focus on another.'

He gave me a suspicious look. 'What service are you in?'

'I work for the Met Office,' I explained. 'I'm a weather observer, with some knowledge of turbulence. That was why Pyke wanted me.'

He looked at me as if these were inconceivably poor accomplishments for a full-blooded male in wartime.

'I see,' he said finally. 'Well, you'd better go and observe some weather, hadn't you? Don't come back here.'

He more or less pushed me out the door. I stood there for a moment, then made my miserable way back through the chumps and chops, across Clerkenwell Green, and headed in the direction of the boarding house, stopping on the way for a drink in the Three Kings. Feeling revulsion towards the world – not just to the mutability of weather but also of events, of life itself – I once again contemplated my fate through the bottom of a pint glass.

Quite a few pints, in fact, before staggering home to bed in the early afternoon. As I climbed the stairs, something which took a deal of concentration, the crone who ran the boarding house gave me a hard look. How strange it is to be recalling such circumstances while listening to the wine-harvest fugue in *The Seasons*. I had not harvested anything.

Pyke went out of my life that day, and so did Habbakuk, at least until the Sheikh's people got in touch. Pyke himself committed suicide with sleeping pills in 1948, overtaken with gloom that his post-war ideas had not been taken up. He really was a most extraordinary man, about whom there were lots of things I did not know when I encountered him during the war. I had no idea, for instance, that he had escaped from a prisoner-of-war camp in the First World War, having used statistics to analyse the reasons for the failed escape attempts of others. Or that he made (and lost) a fortune in the metal markets, at one point owning futures on a third of the world's tin. Or set up a school based on the revolutionary educational principles of the philosopher John Dewey. Or that, having been classified as a security risk by the Americans, he spent time in a mental institution in the United States.

So many unknowns in a life. It's customary to characterise a biography as having a beginning, middle and end, but what about the spaces in between? What about all the unrecorded moments that are ciphered away, never making it into history? Pile up all those, disappear all those in every human life across time – not to mention other types of life – and you build a massive head of pressure against the future, millions of Pascal units just waiting to come down on us in the form of the unexpected, just waiting to displace us, subject us, unseat us.

DATE: 1 February 1980
POSITION @ 0600 LOCAL (GMT +2):
   Latitude 33° 54' South, Longitude 18° 25' East
   Cape Town, Duncan Dock, E-Berth
DEPARTED BOUVET ISLAND: 23 January
NEXT DESTINATION: Dar es Salaam, Tanzania
ETA: 15 February
DISTANCE TO GO: 2248 nm
CURRENT WEATHER: Sunny and warm
SEA STATE: Calm
WIND: 5 kt South-easterly
BAROMETRIC PRESSURE: 1012.7 mb
AIR TEMPERATURE: 23°C
SEA TEMPERATURE: 19°C

May

I feel I could still help. If, despite everything that has happened, you can still see your way, Sir Peter, to attaching me to Stagg's team after all, I should be extremely grateful.

The failure of Habbakuk hit me like a hammer blow. It seemed to confirm that I was in a narrative of decline, rather than being subjected to a disconnected series of mishaps. I had begun to wonder if success and happiness were now impregnably concealed from me for ever.

Now I had to go back to Sir Peter on my knees, writing him another letter. I was embarrassed, frankly. It was not the most fluent piece of self-advocacy, but it was the best I could do in the circumstances.

As I walked back down Amwell Street to post it, I thought again about James Stagg – my former mentor at Kew and the man who had been chosen to lead the weather forecast for the invasion. It would be an honour to join him, but I didn't think much of my chances now.

In some ways he was quite a surprising choice for Sir Peter to have made to lead the D-Day team. Dr Stagg had been science master at George Heriot's School in Edinburgh before entering the Met Office in 1924. Like Ryman, he had worked at Eskdalemuir Observatory in Dumfriesshire for a while, but there his field had been terrestrial magnetism, auroral activity, not meteorology. He was earth sciences really, not actually a forecaster at all, though I believe he had done a little of that in Iraq at some time. He had also served on a polar expedition to Arctic Canada before becoming superintendent at Kew.

Was it there that the cold entered his heart, I wonder, or did that chill, remote air he sometimes had, that seemed to whirl about him, emanate from Covenanter traditions? For he was certainly an awkward character – rather like Ryman, in fact, but without the playfulness.

After posting the letter to Sir Peter I went into the Three Kings again. Into my own shame, feeling as if I were a hamster circling a wheel, but grateful for the all-conquering, uncertainty-dispelling booze all the same. What the alcohol did for me, I now see, was appear to suspend time; the awful sense of endlessly waiting or, equally, of being endlessly too late, became something of myself, absorbed into the ebb and flow of my own body, rather than something imposed from outside. I remember in later years – over one of the cups of strong, aromatic coffee that he favoured at a certain Cambridge café – Brecher telling me that the human idea of time was bound up with the fervid rhythms of the blood.

Some hours later – it was dusk by now – I woke up in my rooms feeling hot and thirsty and headachy, on account of the drink, no doubt. I went downstairs to make a cup of tea. I would have preferred it with plenty of sugar, which usually does the trick with hangovers, but we were having to do without that then.

Claremont Square was on a hill. If I stood on a bench I could see down into King's Cross, where a cupola of pink light – the accumulated pollution of trains and factories – was adding further colour to an already colourful horizon. How strange it is that some of the sky's most beautiful spectacles are produced by pollutant particles of smoke and chemicals. The moon was pale yellow, with a halo of fattening blue, which gradually attenuated through puffy clouds into yellow again.

Pink, yellow, blue: it was like a picture show, so pretty I could almost have forgotten that we were at war. One was always on the lookout for planes, of course, or the flash of anti-aircraft fire, but the impression I had that night was of calm, of a deadly normality. It was as if my fate were being painted up there on the canvas of the sky – and I had an uneasy feeling the painter was disguising the true perspective.

Light, colour: illuminating and entertaining as they are, these quantities can distract from the facts of a matter as they funnel into the eye – glistening, swirling, a steady stream of stimulation – filling the observer with misguided perceptions, dubious assumptions, delirious upliftments. Chief among these is the belief that everything is going to be all right in the morning.

2

But it was! It was all right. Not the following morning, which was gruesome and hangover-blighted, but one a day or two later.

I was sitting in the kitchen reaching for the ersatz marmalade – it was made with cabbage and honey – across the breakfast table when there was a knock at the door. The landlady went to see who was there. She returned with a familiar envelope marked PRIORITY in blue letters.

Through the glass of an upper window – the kitchen was in the basement – I saw a telegram boy mount his bicycle. Serried ranks of iron railing staggered his steady start.

What he had brought was, I knew as soon as it came into my hand, a missive from Sir Peter containing my fate. It looked just the same as the one which had first summoned me to Adastral House all those months ago. Leaving the margarine soaking into my toast, and undergoing a keen perception of bad news, I opened the envelope with a trembling hand.

PROCEED WITH URGENCY TO SUPREME HEAD-QUARTERS ALLIED EXPEDITIONARY FORCE (SHAEF), BUSHEY PARK, TEDDINGTON, TO TAKE UP ROLE OF PERSONAL METEOROLOGICAL ASSISTANT TO GROUP CAPTAIN STAGG.

I leaped up from the table and cheered, knocking over the counterfeit marmalade in my joy. 'I've got a job,' I cried to the landlady. 'I'll be leaving today.'

'Good. Make sure you pay your rent,' was all she said, with a sour mouth.

Once I had recovered my composure, and the marmalade jar had been rescued, I ate the rest of my breakfast in a jolly mood, certain that at last the right path had opened up for me in the tangled wood of life. I settled my account with the land-lady and went upstairs to pack.

Taking the train from Waterloo to Teddington, and then a bus to Bushey – on 7 May 1944, my diary says – was rather like going home for me. I'd lived in Richmond before the war, as it was convenient for the observatory at Kew. But now it was a home I barely recognised. Southern England was loaded with troops and materiel. There was khaki everywhere. The trains were full of soldiers and the roads packed with convoys of tanks and landing craft and endless lines of lorries with canvas covers heading for the coast.

We waited in the bus for almost an hour for a lorry carry-ing an enormous length of concrete – I later realised it was a section of one of the 'Mulberry' artificial harbours – to manoeuvre itself round a corner. There was a lot of shouting and sounding of horns by the drivers of the backed-up vehi-cles.

Then it all cleared and we were on our way, passing into a green archway of trees over the road. To me it felt a tunnel joining two segments of my life. For it was here that I resolved to stop the drinking, which had been rather building up, and knuckle down at last.

Finally, I reached Bushey. Part of the park was surrounded by high walls; the rest was cordoned off with tall fences. American Military Police with white helmets and unsmiling faces guarded the gate. As they checked my papers, I wondered again about Stagg. He had always been very good to me when I worked under him at Kew, though others found him a difficult, prickly man. Later this reputation came to dominate, but people had no idea of the strain he was under. By the time I arrived at Bushey Park he had been working on the invasion forecast for several months.

It was late Sunday afternoon when I arrived, but no one would have known it from the hustle and bustle of the place. I had quite a time getting through the various security cordons, but after numerous calls by the 'Snowballs' (a common nickname for the men in white helmets), I was escorted to the SHAEF meteorological office.

It was quite a long way, and as I followed one of these Snowballs through the temporary buildings – Nissen huts, cement storehouses, messes and troop quarters in tents and tin-roofed sheds – I was borne along in a flood of frenetic activity. Officers and men, British and American, from all the services, were rushing about with papers and files under their arms. The atmosphere was rather like that of a school on the day before a very important examination.

The Met section was situated in the main headquarters, a long, low-slung building – rather like a much larger version of my cot-house in Scotland, but built of concrete blocks, not stone – covered with a camouflage net. Stagg's office was next to the map room, the operational headquarters for the invasion. I thought I caught a glimpse of General Eisenhower, but I couldn't be sure.

The Snowball knocked on the door.

3

Stooping, Stagg appeared in the frame. Wearing a slate blue RAF group captain's uniform, he greeted me with a weary smile. 'Hello, Meadows. How are you?'

'I've been better,' I replied, as the MP marched off.

'Yes. I am not surprised. Sir Peter told me all about that dreadful business in Scotland. Ryman was a great man, but it is understandable that these things happen.'

'Is it?' I said doubtfully, suddenly realising that my role in Ryman's death was by now common knowledge in the meteorological community.

'Yes, in wartime it is understandable. Look, whatever happened, I'm glad you're here, Meadows. I desperately need some help. They gave me a list and I picked you.'

Like Sir Peter, Stagg had aged markedly, the strain of his task accentuating the structure of his thin, severe face, the most noticeable feature of which was a light moustache. The total effect was a curious mixture of strength and weakness, strong will tempered with a sense of anguish.

'Well, sir, that is why I am here,' I said, looking at his uniform. 'And I will do what I can. I see you have become a military man.'

'Ah yes. I want to talk to you about that. You'd better come in.'

He led me into the office and shut the door. It was a large, sparsely furnished room with a dark brown carpet. There were weather charts on the walls and a big table in the centre, with three telephones standing on it: one red, one black, one white.

Stagg sat at a small desk, motioning me to one of the chairs at the table. 'I'm afraid you'll have to join up, too,' he said. 'I was having a lot of problems with chaps not taking me seriously as a civilian, so the Air Ministry finally mobilised me. Our allies don't like to deal with civilians when such highly secret matters as these are being discussed. For a time I was demoted and my deputy, Colonel Yates of the US Air Force, became chief Met adviser. The American generals were not happy that a civilian should come between them and Yates. They like to have a clear chain of military command. You'll meet Yates soon. Nice fellow. Now, sit back and I'll tell you how it is.'

Looking at me over a pile of dossiers on his desk, Stagg explained that, since the middle of April, he and a team of forecasters had been producing a five-day forecast every Sunday evening for distribution to General Eisenhower and the rest of SHAEF. It related to the crossing of the English Channel in order that the Allies gain a foothold on mainland Europe – which first step to recovery of the continent was code-named Operation Neptune. The invasion as a whole was code-named Overlord.

'The forecast is for the whole week,' Stagg said. 'Every Thursday is regarded as a dummy D-Day, which is the name we are giving to the invasion date. H-Hour, similarly, is the landing time for the first airborne troops. As you've probably gathered from the number of troops moving about the country, it is likely to happen quite soon.'

He spoke in a low tone. 'I can't tell you how difficult this is, Meadows. I need you to help me with the technical work, including taking the minutes and preparing documents for each conference. Representatives of the three armed services have been trying to foresee each critical weather element for D-Day by convening a conference. I need you to examine the forecasting process.'

'What are the critical elements?' I asked, trying to focus my mind.

'Broadly, the limiting conditions are as follows.' He counted them off on the fingers of his left hand.

'(A) D-Day should be within one day before to four days after a full moon. (B) There must be quiet weather on the day and for three days afterwards. Wind to be of no more than force three onshore and force four offshore. (C) Cloud to be less than three-tenths cover below eight thousand feet; visibility three miles plus. Or as an alternative to condition (C): (D) in which case the cloud base itself has got to be above three thousand feet generally, morning mist not excluded. There are other constraints affecting parachute drops, which we have not yet tried on this scale.'

I was shocked that such a grand, important plan as Overlord depended on conditions so difficult to fulfil. No wonder Sir Peter was anxious. 'It doesn't sound very likely in any of those permutations,' I ventured.

'No,' Stagg replied lugubriously. 'That is why it's such a devil. But it must be possible. It has to be, for all our sakes. The immediate military objective is to land a force on a fifty-mile strip of enemy-held coastline. A force strong enough, and with supply lines secure enough, to resist quick dislodgement. We need moonlight and we need low tide, but the critical probabilities will be the state of the sea, which of course is mainly dependent on the wind strength on the beaches, and the amount of cloud.'

He scrabbled around for a piece of paper. 'Look at this bloody thing.'

Typed out, bearing the stamp BIGOT, the paper listed the probabilities of various combinations of the conditions Stagg had outlined, expressing them as racing odds:

LIMITS	CHANCES TO ONE AGAINST		
	MAY	JUNE	JULY
I: WANING MOON			
B AND D WITHOUT A	4	2	5
B AND C WITHOUT A	9	4.5	19
II: WITH NEW OR FULL MOON			
B AND D WITH A	11	6	16
B AND C WITH A	24	13	50
III: FULL MOON ONLY			
B AND D WITH A	24	13	33
B AND C WITH A	49	24	100

The word BIGOT, I would discover, was stamped on all Overlord documents. The rationale was that no one would go about boasting that they were reading papers with the classification BIGOT, any more than they would say they only had one testicle.

'Crikey,' I said, doing some quick calculations in my head.

'Exactly,' said Stagg. 'Not the best conditions in which to undertake the greatest amphibious operation in history.'

He took off his glasses and rubbed his eyes. 'It's all much riskier once you put in the demand for moonlight. Odds in category II are roughly three times those in I.'

I was puzzled. Surely it would be best to invade under cover of darkness. 'Why do you need the moon?'

He looked as me as if I were stupid. 'The need to have a full moon or be near one,' he explained patiently, 'is to ensure a time of low tide at sunrise on the invasion beaches, so that mines and tank traps and so on can be cleared. The RAF and US Air Force would prefer an outright full moon, so that gliders and other planes can land before sunrise – which doubles the odds again.'

'Not exactly making it easy, are they?'

Stagg shook his head. 'I don't think it's any less daunting for the brass hats than it is for me. I have to present to them regularly now: Eisenhower, Air Chief Marshal Tedder, General Bull, Admiral Creasy, Air Vice-Marshal Wigglesworth . . . and all the other chiefs and deputies of SHAEF divisions. The first time was terrifying. Eisenhower looked at me and said: "Whenever you see a good spell that would be suitable coming along during the next month or so I want you to tell us. Give us as much notice as you can."'

'And have you?'

'What?'

'Suggested a date.'

'Not yet. None of the forecasters can agree. And there isn't enough data. We don't have enough weather ships in the Atlantic. Sir Peter has promised more.'

He stood up and went to a map on the wall, showing me where ships, marked out with flags, were dispersed across the ocean. 'This whole area has no weather ships. The only good news is that the Germans are in a worse position. More or less the whole remaining Atlantic U-boat fleet is now concerned with sending weather information. They know just as we do that the Atlantic weather is what will determine the weather in the Channel.'

He sat down, taking off his glasses and rubbing his eyes with the backs of his fingers. 'Where was I? We have three teams of forecasters. At Widewing – that's the main US air base near here – there is a man called Krick and another, Holzman. Both colonels.'

I smiled ruefully, remembering the Glasgow hotel. I hadn't realised they held such high rank.

'Krick has compiled a statistical index of weather patterns in northern Europe going back forty years or so. He uses the analogue method.'

The analogue method involved selecting weather types from past periods that most closely matched the current weather and seeing what happened before. It was a bit like case law. The future is extrapolated from the past, with the forecast extending to as long as six days ahead.

'I've met them,' I explained, remembering with a nauseous twinge the poker game and the terrible hangover which followed it. 'Krick and Holzman. By chance, at Prestwick airport. Krick seems a jolly fellow, but as for the analogue method, if that is what he practises, I'm not persuaded. Nature does not repeat itself like a workshop press; identical patterns do not develop identically; and it's not really possible to forecast more than two days ahead. Three days, max.'

'Exactly,' said Stagg. 'That is just what Charles Douglas says. Well, he's opposed to anything over two, in fact. He's pretty much made that the rule at Dunstable, as you will know from your time under him there. Fancy some tea?'

He stood up again, unbundling his long limbs like a praying mantis on a leaf.

'Yes please.'

He flipped a switch on an electric kettle. 'A gift from the Americans,' he explained.

I remembered Douglas running round the table, his tie and the tails of his suit jacket flying behind him. I suppose it must have been what's now called stress which made him do this, as well as the aeroplane crash in which he had been involved during his combat training as a fighter pilot. He was wounded five times in incidents after the crash, and that can't have helped either.

Like Stagg, Douglas had a thin face and a moustache. Well, lots of people had moustaches in those days. I considered him a man of tremendous skill and judgement, and to some people's mind he is still the greatest British practical weather forecaster of the century, with Ryman taking the palm for theory.

Very sound, very careful. He tended to start with the present weather data then would apply weather memory and weather theory by common sense, rather than according to a particular philosophy.

'Douglas doesn't apply past situations religiously, like Krick, or rely totally on theory, like Petterssen,' Stagg continued, shaking loose tea into a pot. 'He allows a kind of jiggle, a wrinkle, into his system, a space for his own intuition, and he admits of theory whatever he is personally convinced by.'

All this tallied with what I knew of Douglas from my own experience. 'That's why, even though he stammers and stutters and sometimes can hardly speak his mind,' Stagg continued, 'I listen to him most – he is very aware of the complexity of any given situation, having more experience of the vicissitudes of British summer weather than the others. He is less likely to stick his neck out, which is Krick's preferred method. If you can call it that. And the Norwegian, well, he just seems to believe he's infallible.'

'That would be Petterssen?' I ventured.

'Sverre Petterssen, yes. You'll speak to him soon. The third member of the team. Rather academic, an expert on the upper atmosphere. A member of the Bergen school who has spent time in America. Passage of fronts, deductions from the upper air ...'

Stagg's voice trailed off wearily. With sad-looking eyes he stared at the tendrils of steam coming from the kettle.

'I know more about the upper air affecting the surface than I used to,' I said, trying to be helpful. 'Ryman did a lot of work on that at one stage.'

'Did he now?' said Stagg, musing. 'Well, I wish he was here now, because I often don't have a clue what Petterssen is talking about. It would be good to have someone to vet his assertions, which are made as if backed up by tons of data. Whereas actually his findings are based on quite new stuff. And as for

251

his habit of revisiting his successes, well, that just gets everyone's back up. Most of all Krick. He just loves it when Petterssen's forecasts are wrong.'

He took off his glasses for a third time, this time rubbing his cheeks with his palms, like someone using a flannel to clean their face.

'It sounds as if you have a lot on your plate.'

'Yes. Krick and Petterssen are both tricky customers, They both have irreconcilable, fixed ideas, seemingly logically developed. I can hardly make them agree on the time of day, never mind next week's weather. Oh, there's another lot, too. Naval forecasters, Wolfe and Hogben, at the Admiralty centre in London. Very skilled on wave conditions, as you'd expect, and lower air. They don't have such dogmatic views as Krick and Petterssen, and tend to agree with one another, which is a godsend in one way, but . . .'

His voice trailed off again. I realised I was looking at an almost broken man. 'So, you all meet once a week?'

Stagg straightened up immediately. 'Good God, no. These people don't meet in person, except Douglas and Petterssen, who work together in Dunstable. No, we do it all by telephone – twice a day.'

I was puzzled. 'Why by telephone . . . and so often?'

Stagg chuckled. 'You know how Sir Peter is short of forecasters? Well, these people – among the best forecasters in the world – are doing lots of other work for their respective services, in different locations, as well as preparing the forecast for the invasion. And we have to talk twice a day to keep up with Eisenhower's plans. What we say to him affects a vast network of troops and vehicles, all of them waiting to go, not to mention a host of ships hiding round Britain, from the coves of north Devon to the sea lochs of Argyll . . . That's where you were, isn't it?'

I thought of the ships and subs moored outside Ryman's house. Once again, I felt deep astonishment at my role in the death of probably the one man on earth who might have been able to reconcile the competing views of Stagg's warring forecasters. It suddenly occurred to me that Sir Peter had ordered me here in spite of, not because of, my frank letter to him. He still hoped I had learned something from Ryman. Even if I had more or less given up, he was still looking for a single all-explaining answer. It was the wrong approach; but how could the multidimensional picture which Ryman conveyed to me be conveyed in turn to military men who needed relatively simple instructions?

The generals were the least of it. The thought of casualties filled me with dread again. After my Scottish calamity, was I now going to be responsible for sending thousands of men to their deaths on the beaches of Normandy because of an incorrect forecast?

'I'll take you through the charts before the phones go,' said Stagg. 'We've got about two hours.'

'Right.'

He finally produced the promised cup of tea, and we sat down in front of the charts. They showed a map of Europe and the Atlantic, covered with isobars and fronts, together with specific pressure and temperature readings from weather ships and other sources.

Once we had finished going over the charts, which were more complicated than any others I had previously seen, Stagg brought up again the subject of my joining up.

'Now, I thought flight lieutenant would be the rank appropriate to your Met Office grade. I hope that's all right. You should have time to pick up a uniform from the commissary before the conference. Follow signs for Web 51. They should be able to fix somewhere for you to sleep, too. Don't be too long.'

4

After collecting my new blue serge uniform, which was rather itchy, and sorting out the logistics of a billet, I retraced my steps to Stagg's office. I joined him at the big oak table with the three telephones. Their chrome dials looked like flowers waiting to open. I was hungry. The timing of events was such that I had missed lunch and no one had yet mentioned dinner. I looked at the table. Next to each phone was a little black box housing a scrambler. Our conversation would be encrypted.

Stagg and I were joined by his American deputy, Don Yates. He was a spare, dark-haired little man, who would often amuse us by telling fantastic tales of his hiking, hunting and fishing exploits back home in the States. He came from a wooded, mountain area of Maine, near the Penobscot river. If he was to be believed, the area was still as full of deer and fish as it had been in the days of Buffalo Bill. It sounded like paradise: sheltered coves and mossy forests where Yates had learned how to catch his supper with his bare hands. I remember him once saying how he had reached down into a stream and felt the quivering mass of a salmon there, 'like a piece of pure muscle'.

He was a patient fellow, Yates, and a good handler of men. Like Holzman, he had been a student of Krick's at Caltech, before rising quickly to become head of the US Army's weather operations in Europe. He often had to face down Krick as perhaps only a fellow American would be able to do. He had a lot of presence and, I suspect, carried great influence in the presentations to Eisenhower. He knew when to speak and when to keep quiet. When I saw Yates and Stagg arguing, as they often did, there were times when I would quite cheerfully have belted Stagg over the head with a ruler, but Yates always kept his cool.

My very first conference call followed a pattern that would become familiar. First we set up the phones, routing the calls through a knot of exchanges run by intelligence staff. Nowadays it would be a matter of pressing a couple of buttons, but at that time to arrange a conference call on secret lines was quite a feat.

Once we had gone though this frustrating and at times amusing process, which involved a lot of 'yes, yes, yes . . .' and took about twenty minutes, Stagg picked up his handset and dialled. Immediately the two other phones rang and we picked up.

I heard a series of disembodied voices check in: 'Dunstable' (the Met Office), 'Widewing' (the USAAF and RAF base near-by), 'Citadel' (the Royal Navy at the Admiralty Forecasting Unit in Whitehall).

This telephone circuit became a major part of my life during May and June 1944. Krick and/or Holzman speaking for Widewing; Petterssen and/or Douglas speaking for Dunstable; and one or other of Lieutenant Hogben or Commanders Wolfe and Thorpe speaking for the Royal Navy from the Citadel.

Other parts of the military establishment listened in – to ensure that our top-level D-Day forecasts did not conflict with those regularly given to lower-level naval, air and army forma-tions.

On that first day, Stagg introduced me, saying, 'You'll all be pleased to hear I have a new assistant, Henry Meadows, a bright Cambridge natural sciences graduate who I hope will pitch in from time to time. He has worked with me at Kew and trained as a Met observer under Mr Douglas.'

I said hello to Douglas, who I think was pleased to hear from me, and reacquainted myself with Krick, hoping he wouldn't mention that we had played poker and got drunk together, which I doubted Stagg would approve of.

But he didn't, just drawling, 'Well I'll be damned, Henry. Welcome aboard.'

The first job of the conference was to agree on a map of current conditions, and I would soon discover that not everyone always turned up with the same map, let alone the same forecast. It often took about half an hour to sort all this out.

Once actual forecasting got underway, Petterssen at Dunstable was first to speak, his strong Norwegian accent interrupted by the occasional clicks and static of the telephone wires. It took me a while to become familiar with all the codes they were using to describe areas of high and low pressure . . . H1, H2, H3 . . . L1, L2, L3 . . .

It was standard that H stood for a high pressure area, L for a low, but the numbers to which they were attached were altered from time to time as a further security precaution, should the enemy be listening. Given the transitory nature of weather, our counterparts at the Zentral Wetterdienstgruppe were going to be hard pressed to interpret any intelligence they might receive. I wondered whether Sir Peter had been able to get anything more out of Heinz Wirbel, the scientist who had bailed out of the Junkers.

'As I forecast last time,' began Petterssen, 'L2 has moved east-north-eastwards, bringing further deterioration from the west in its wake as the week progresses. There will be increase in cloud and freshening west-north-westerly wind through the week, switching to west-south-west up to force four or five on Wednesday, as an interval, deterioration continuing into Saturday, when there is risk of rain . . .'

'Patches of low, low, low . . .,' interrupted an English voice.

'Lowish cloud along s-south-west coasts on Tuesday morning, some of these, er, at a base of one thousand feet, mixing with, with fog patches in the western Channel.' It was Douglas. 'Mainly fair to Wednesday, then G-G-God knows.'

Someone else on the line grunted. I heard Stagg sigh beside me. The echo repeated in the handset against my ear.

'I can't go along with this,' said an American, unmistakably Krick. 'You're far too gloomy, Petterssen. I see quiet, fair weather in all areas, especially from Wednesday. Considerable fine intervals, especially in eastern areas. Good visibility except for those local morning fog patches Douglas mentioned. They'll burn off quick.'

'What about that low?' countered Petterssen. 'Surely you can see that low coming? High pressure in the north-east Atlantic is bound to force it through.'

'That cyclonic cell, not very considerable in my view, will anyway collapse within two days, allowing the warm period I mentioned,' said Krick. 'There are many analogues for a settled period like this, in May 1929, for instance, and the following year. This is how it will play.'

He spoke with great confidence, with bravado, in fact. That was the thing about Krick. He did not have the intellectual power or ethical rigour of the others who sat, at least figuratively speaking, round that table, but he had something none of the rest of us had. Conversational force, and the ability to make a narrative of a scientific forecast. The latter, especially, is a really important quality in a forecaster.

But if the story's wrong then the whole team is in the soup. And there were other voices round that table that were often convinced Krick's predictions were way off beam. In their own minds, these speakers were actually just as confident as Krick, even if they didn't sound so.

'Um, not n-n-n-necessarily,' said Douglas. 'We had a

development like this in May 1931. Pressure over Europe was a little lower than now, and not so high in the north-east Atlantic. But the upshot was a period of north to-north-east winds which continued for ten to twelve days; they r-r-r-reached gale force at times in the eastern Channel.'

There was a pause in which the telephone wires clicked and whirred as if, somewhere in the depths of the exchange, a mechanism was running down.

'God almighty,' said Stagg. 'We'll come back to this. Navy?'

'We lean towards Petterssen-Dunstable on the general forecast,' said a good-natured voice with a New Zealand accent. This was Lieutenant Hogben. 'Fine weather but risk of rain on Saturday. On the maritime side of things, and I remind you this is an amphibious operation, we expect no appreciable swell. Waves less than two feet at first, probably increasing to four feet in the eastern Channel and six feet in the western Channel.'

'Right,' said Stagg. 'Well now, either Dunstable or Widewing will have to relax its view. It seems to me – and you must remember that my job is to present a single, confident reliable forecast to General Eisenhower – that the divergence rests on what happens at the end of the week. We all know how, by its very nature, the structure and processes of weather can produce interminable discussion and still spring–'

There was an unearthly moan throughout the whole complex as the generators went down and the lights were extinguished.

'Potash!' shouted Stagg.

'What's that?' said Yates's American voice in the darkness.

'I say potash so as not to swear,' said Stagg. 'It's a bombing raid,' he explained to me. 'We always just shut off the electricity because if they hit SHAEF – well, it's all over then.'

The phones themselves were clearly on a different circuit from the mains, and this enabled us to keep talking. I heard some distant explosions, but could not estimate how near the bombs were falling or of what magnitude they were.

'Some way off,' said Yates, as if reading my thoughts.

The lights came back on, but the discussion had stalled. The experts still could not agree. Stagg became quite angry, as he had to deliver a five-day forecast to Eisenhower the following morning.

Douglas disparaged the whole idea of five-day forecasts. 'You can have as m-m-many conferences as you like,' he said. 'They will make no difference: it is just not p-possible to make regular forecasts five or six days ahead that can have any real v-v-value for military operations or any other p-p-purpose.'

'Scientifically speaking, there are no reasons why long-range forecasting should not be possible,' said Petterssen calmly.

'Of course it's possible!' blustered Krick. 'Precise long-range weather forecasting requires day-by-day prediction for years ahead, and that is what my analogue sequence method provides. Look at the chart and the comparison of previous weather sequences from 1930 I sent through.'

'Pure guesswork from t-t-two days out,' mumbled Douglas.

'How dare you!' exploded Krick through the earpiece. 'I've been through half a century of northern hemisphere weather maps. Because of that, I am able to give a mathematically reliable five-day forecast.'

'There is only one man in Britain I know able to do weather prediction by d-d-direct attack with mathematics,' said Douglas, 'and even he would admit it is a p-p-process very liable to error. His name is Wallace Ryman.'

A chill went through me. I was wrong that everyone in the meteorological community knew what had happened. 'He's dead,' I said immediately, hearing my own voice in my ear a second later. 'Ryman is dead. He died in an accident in Scotland. I was working with him there.'

'Oh dear,' said Douglas. 'What a p-p-pity. I remember going to Norway with him to see your p-p-people in Bergen, Sverre.'

'Yes. I heard about him from Bjerknes, my tutor,' Petterssen said. 'I'm afraid to say he was regarded as a strange sort of character. He brought a gun with him, to measure wind shear. Many considered the gun a toy and the man himself an over-grown Boy Scout. It is a shame, though, that he abandoned meteorology before his numerical weather process could be put into practice.'

I thought of Ryman with his gun in the field. Was he not the great man I'd thought? 'Well,' I bristled, feeling the need to stick up for him, 'until his death he devoted himself to the application of mathematics to peace studies. I think many of his meteorological ideas are still valid, nonetheless.'

'Devoted himself to *what*?' said Krick, incredulous.

'Peace studies. He applied mathematics to the relationships between opposing forces to see how war might have been avoided.'

'Gentlemen, can we please make a forecast?' said Stagg. 'On exactly what issues are we divergent?'

There was a babble of voices from all sides.

'My past analogues are right,' said Krick. 'The whole US weather service is run on this basis.'

'It must be informed by theory,' said Petterssen. 'Otherwise it is worthless.'

'You must look at the prevailing pattern before you consider other factors,' said Douglas.

I felt the need to speak again, but it was as if the voice coming through me was not my own. 'Future weather is a judgement of probabilities based on physical principles which are reducible to mathematical formulae. There is one I know which relates temperature and wind speed to produce an index of turbulence. The Ryman number. You may have heard of it. Well, I could try and find its values for the Channel weather in the relevant period.'

Silence ensued. Of course, I now feel it was a mistake to have brought up the number at the first conference, but I suppose I was trying to prove myself.

'Very good, Meadows,' said Stagg eventually, like a schoolmaster congratulating a pupil. I perceived a slightly embarrassed tone in his voice. 'Do so, though in my experience weather is less reducible to numerical process than Ryman and, clearly now you, believe.'

'I don't think so,' said Petterssen. 'We are scientists and science is indeed about reducing things to their underlying values. However, since you are talking about the Ryman number, I fear, Mr Meadows, that your mental equipment is not up to the job of applying it across this situation. Please don't be offended. I could not do it either. To put in all those variables over a large area, as Ryman himself found, is currently beyond the wit of man.'

'Christ, Sverre,' drawled Krick. 'Let the boy try.' I guess this remark was why I continued to visit him after the war.

'I am not letting him not try!' said Petterssen.

'Gentlemen, *please*, can we now proceed on that basis to a working forecast, something which, if I may remind you, General Eisenhower expects first thing tomorrow morning?'

Eventually Stagg smoothed out everyone's differences and we botched together something which contained bits of all the forecasts, reducing our confidence in the last three days of the forecast to placate Douglas.

Once the phones were down Stagg gave me a weary look that required no explanation.

'Is it always like this?' I asked.

'The atmosphere of the conference is always a little . . . aggravated,' he said.

'Look, with your permission, I really would like to have a go at applying Ryman's method.'

'All right, take a stab at it,' said Stagg, though without much enthusiasm. 'But mainly I want you to take over the work of preparation for each conference and deal with any enquiries that come into the office. I also want you to go through what we've done so far, comparing our forecasts with reality. See how accurate we've been.'

We were still heading for a five-day forecast, despite Douglas's doubts. I tested the rolling forecasts as we were making them against the minimum conditions that Stagg had showed me on the BIGOT sheet. On day one, did we forecast whether the minimum conditions would be met or not? On day two, was the forecast right or was it wrong? Day three, etc.

I soon discovered that the forecasts were accurate for the first day, but became increasingly less reliable after that. For the second day they were merely useful. By the third, fourth and fifth days, D-Day itself in our model, they had entered the realms of speculative fiction.

5

The telephone conferences continued, with a view towards 5 June as the most likely invasion date. This was the putative 'D-Day' towards which all our plans were being directed. I struggled at first to keep up with the discussion and actually had very little time in which to try to apply the Ryman number on my own initiative; but during the fourth week of May I began to find my feet.

I noticed more and more that Petterssen and Krick were prepared to forecast the weather with confidence, using long chains of intricate causation, theoretical or statistical, to back up their assertions. Douglas and the navy people, Hogben and Wolfe, were more usually correct in their forecasts, but again only for one day, two at the most. It was not enough for Eisenhower. He needed five days lead time to mount an invasion.

Stagg became very irritable. I, too, began to feel the strain. I redeveloped an inconvenient condition which caused me to have embarrassing nosebleeds while under pressure. Many a weather chart bore the signs of this indisposition, and during conferences I often had to pinch my nose with one hand as I listened to the voices squabbling on the other end of the phone. Surely, I worried, I was not also to have a return to those bouts of dizziness I suffered as a young man, in the wake of the mudslide?

It wasn't just me and the other forecasters. Everyone at SHAEF was strung tight as a tripwire, from the lowliest mess waiter (there was one who invariably served us with a dewdrop on the end of his nose) to Eisenhower himself. I often saw the supreme commander smoking furiously under the fir trees near his caravan.

Beyond the confines of military bases, the roads were filling up with more convoys of men and machines on the move towards the south coast. In a few days' time Eisenhower and some of SHAEF itself would do the same.

The weather was actually favourable in the early weeks of May. There were about eighteen possible days that month. The tide was low enough to remove defensive obstacles from the beaches, the wind and moonlight perfect for airborne operations – we really could have gone. But the millions of tons of aircraft and shipping, and more than two million men who would be involved in the operation, were not yet ready. And the Germans were on high alert exactly because of the good weather. It was not until the fourth week of May that the logistical aspects coincided to produce a target date of the fifth, sixth or seventh of June.

Whether the weather would hold for any of those dates was another matter. On 28 May (a Sunday), Stagg went down from Bushey to recce Eisenhower's advance command post at Southwick House, near Portsmouth, where we would be berthed during the week of the invasion. It was assumed that the supreme commander and his chief meteorologist should be near the main bulk of troops. Before that day's first conference (led by Stagg from Portsmouth, with me listening in at Bushey Park), Stagg told me how the whole surface of the navy's main harbour, every inch of it, was now covered with a fleet of ships. 'I had never seen so many,' he told me. 'It's a majestic sight. Like a city on the water.'

As for the conference itself, generally the participants agreed that the probable lines of weather evolution were still anticyclonic, that is, veering towards settled weather, as one would expect in summer. But looking out of the window I thought even as we spoke that I could see the sky darkening – not in a unidimensional order, but in variegated fashion, shreds and patches of cloud taking on a blacker tinge as they moved across the sky. A camouflaging of light.

Sitting alone in Stagg's office, between two conferences, I looked at applying the range of Ryman numbers for the forecast conditions. It was no easy task, complicated by the fact that the moment I started the weather did change, just I had felt it would. The long spell of settled, mainly anticyclonic conditions we had been enjoying – during which the Germans had strengthened their defences along the Channel – was about to break. I went to the teleprinter to check new observations as they came in, and was horrified by what I read as the paper jerked through my hands. The new situation developing could only be described as *very* turbulent, even by winter standards, never mind those of high summer.

It did not help that we seemed to be getting erroneous pressure and wind-speed readings from a single but crucial weather ship to the south of Iceland, codenamed WANTAC. The data it sent was slightly different from that provided by other ships nearby. Was it too large a difference to attribute to a wrinkle in the instrument calibration? All wind measurements from ships must account for the airflow distortion caused by the ship itself, otherwise large errors can occur. When radioing in the readings the crew swore blind the readings were correct and that the anemometers were in a position in which they were not being unduly disturbed by the ship's presence.

Nonetheless I felt strongly there was something that needed looking at with regards to WANTAC's aneroid barometers and air-speed indicators. I sat wondering, immobile, about the ship, imagining its masts rising from the foam-barred waves of the Atlantic as if they were the immortal pinnacles of an ancient palace, archetype of that which governs mighty empires.

Stirring from my reverie, I made a mental note to speak to Stagg about WANTAC, but I was nervous as he had become ferociously bad tempered. On one occasion about this time I spilled some coffee on a weather chart he was examining. 'For the love of Mike!' he howled at me. 'Will you *please* try to be more careful, Meadows? It's bad enough having you bleed all over these things without you throwing coffee at them as well.'

In conferences, I could see him biting his lip beside me and covering up the mouthpiece to let out explosive sighs. During a second conference that Sunday night of 28 May, after Stagg had returned from Portsmouth, we tried to formulate a forecast up to Friday, 2 June and beyond to a possible D-Day. Most of us accepted that bad weather was on the way. Petterssen said he expected thunderstorms, as did I, and Hogben at the Admiralty predicted strong winds and deep depressions. But Krick was typically optimistic, still saying it was all just going to stay fine.

'You haven't taken into account the upper air,' snapped Petterssen. 'I have reviewed your forecast and found it to be correct. Except in this crucial aspect of upper-air effects on the surface, which will definitely result in thunderstorms.'

There was a short silence. The phone line wailed and clicked.

'I agree on the upper-air issue,' said Stagg, 'and my own view is that the balance of probability is against Widewing in this case.'

'Oh it is, is it?' said Krick. 'This is crazy. You are just ganging up on me because I'm American.'

Petterssen said something in Norwegian, clearly a swear-word.

So it continued for another two hours, with no agreement about what lay ahead. Amid the to and fro of argument, I forgot to ask Stagg about the erroneous readings from WANTAC.

After another nosebleed I went to bed feeling as if my head were a kaleidoscope of numbers. I was terrified the *kizunguzungu* feeling might return, but I was determined not to start drinking again. The word, which had the same root as that for white men (*mzungu*), stuck in my head as I dozed off, involving itself in its own etymology like a dust-devil chasing its tail across the veldt.

It is said they – we – were called *mzungu* because white men ran around so much and to so little purpose they made Africans dizzy. Or it was because white men came from more than one direction and with more than one motive. A third explanation was that *mzungu* and *kizunguzungu* both had their origins in descriptions of the ocean, from where foreign ships came. Some days, having whirled itself into a frenzy, the ocean is like a big, dizzy bowl of foam, impossible to decipher. That white foam is *mzungu*.

But what I saw that night as I fell asleep was the froth of a pint glass of beer, leading – like some oversized sergeant major at the head of a column of troops – a long line of whisky chasers.

6

We started again early the next morning. Monday, 29 May, according to my diary. There were fewer arguments this time, but only because we were all exhausted. Stagg finally managed to get the participants to agree he could tell Eisenhower and the other brass hats that the weather would be settled during the coming week, followed by some disturbed weather at the weekend.

Around lunchtime, having driven down to Portsmouth again, Stagg saw Eisenhower and the other generals, admirals and air vice-marshals, who were now fully installed at Southwick House.

The meeting took place in the library, 'surrounded by empty bookshelves on three sides of the room', as Stagg reported to me later. 'They implied to me strongly again that they want to go a week today.'

That would be 5 June. 'How long will the bad weather at the weekend last?' the generals asked him.

'At this time of year continuous spells of more than a few days of really stormy weather are infrequent,' he replied. 'If the disturbed weather starts on Friday it is unlikely to last through both Monday and Tuesday . . . but if it starts on Saturday or Sunday, Monday or Tuesday could well be stormy.'

The bigwigs just about seemed to accept it, he said, without saying whether his information would affect the decision to go on the following Monday.

Stagg motored back to Bushey for the evening conference.

To everyone's surprise, as soon as it began Petterssen predicted that there would *not* be a deterioration of the weather at the weekend after all. Krick, too, reversed his position, saying that Petterssen had been right in his previous incarnation and there *would* be storms.

I couldn't believe this double volte-face, and neither could Stagg. Once the phones were down, the strain showed on his face. He was shaking with anger and anxiety. Watching him, I realised Sir Peter was living in a land of fantasy. Perhaps there was nothing that I could bring to this situation that would help it. Would Ryman's own presence have helped, I wondered. I doubted it now. The last thing we needed was another view. But still I wished I could have had him sitting next to me in his crisp grey suit, advising and guiding as we fought our way through the thicket of indecision.

It was not the best time to ask Stagg about WANTAC, but the issue could be ignored no longer. Checking the ship's pressure readings at its station off Iceland during the day, I had seen that they were still anomalous: they were higher than they should be, different from what might be expected, given the readings from other ships nearby. The wind speeds, meanwhile, were marginally lower, which probably suggested the area was a conduit for calmer weather. What if these readings were the explanation for the disparity between Widewing and Dunstable? What if they signified one of those narrow tubes that Ryman had talked of? The ones that seem like barriers between two opposing weather systems but are actually corridors for a third? Either that, or the instruments were wrong. What if ice, that powerful force I now know all too well, had upset the gauges on the ship?

'I could fly up there, you know,' I said to Stagg, after explaining my concerns to him. 'I could check the tolerances of the instruments myself, and then we would be sure.'

His response was to start shouting at me. 'Are you mad? The invasion will most likely be over by the time you are back. You know how busy we are. I can't spare you. You don't seem to have got anywhere with your Ryman number and I don't see that this is going to be any different.'

'I do think those readings are important, sir. We can't just ignore them.'

As I was speaking I suddenly remembered what Reynolds, the pilot who had flown me from London to Prestwick, had said about picking up broken equipment from these ships from a floating line and dropping down new ones.

It had to be worth a try. 'You know, we replace these instruments using aircraft from the reconnaissance flights and collect the old ones for repair. What if I was to put in a request that they do so with WANTAC's? It could be done on the BISMUTH track, which goes out towards Iceland. Then the old ones could be brought straight down here and I could test them.'

Calming down, Stagg thought for a moment, stroking his moustache. 'Yes. All right, Meadows. But don't spend too much time on it.'

7

Stagg was more sober-tempered the next day, but I dared not bring up the subject again. Early that morning, I had arranged through the RAF people at Southwick and Met Office head-quarters for new instruments for WANTAC to be flown up to Stornoway and be dropped at the weather ship and for the old ones to be picked up and returned to me. The operation would use up quite a lot of resources, but one thing about being at SHAEF was that nobody outside it dared say no to you. Even so, the whole thing was going to take three or four days; it would be a close-run thing.

Once the conference was finished, I got the chance of an intimate chat with Sverre Petterssen, who of all the partici-pants was, with his strong theoretical underpinning, the near-est thing we had to a Ryman on the team. It turned out that he knew Pyke. This came up because I said Stagg wanted us to describe in some detail the chain of mental processes that led to our forecasts. Petterssen replied he knew a genius called Pyke who liked to do that, but it didn't necessarily help with the end product.

Amazed, I half turned the mouthpiece to look at it, as if the mechanism itself was responsible for this coincidence. Then, through its little grille, I told him about the sea lion at Kilmun, also mentioning 'something about ice' which I had briefly been involved in, taking care to divulge no detail.

'Oh, I know all about it,' he said airily. 'The berg ship. Project Habbakuk. But I wasn't concerned with it myself. I briefly helped him in designing a snow vehicle of high performance characteristics. It was to be powered by an Archimedean screw. I believe he is still working on it.'

'The Habbakuk project was stopped,' I said. 'Pyke just disappeared. I was left high and dry. That was just before I came here.'

'Typical Pyke. Do you know where he is himself?'

'No,' I said. 'I have heard nothing from him.'

'The last I heard he was in Belsize Park.'

There was a faint click on the line. Petterssen muttered something in Norwegian.

'What was that?' I said.

'I said, "We can hear you." Intelligence listening in. Apparently someone heard me tell Larry Hogben I am a pacifist. I had a visit from them telling me off for it.'

'*Are* you?' I asked, thinking of Ryman.

'I am a pacifist only in the sense that I believe fascism tends to war, so one must do one's best to counter it. I would fire a gun in the right circumstances. And do so in anger. My family are still in Norway, you see, under German occupation.'

'I'm sorry.'

'It is not just for them,' he said more urgently. 'D-Day has to succeed for all of us. Nazism is a kind of formless spreading horror which will eventually touch everybody unless it is stopped.'

There was a pause, during which – by the wonderful sorcery of the telephone – I imagined the huts at Dunstable from which he was speaking. 'How is Douglas?' I asked.

Petterssen's counterpart had been very quiet at the last few conferences.

'Same as ever. Well, no, he is feeling the strain just the same as the rest of us. The other day he took his baby out in its pram and walked to the top of Dunstable Downs, the highest point around here, to study the clouds. He noted the direction and strength of the wind, using the branch of a tree as a nephoscope – he told me all this later – and became so absorbed in making these observations, and thinking about what they implied for the invasion, that he went home leaving baby and pram at the top of the Downs! Do you have children, Meadows?'

'No.' Right then it seemed a preposterous idea that I might have, though I have since often regretted their absence.

'I have two daughters, Eileen and Liv,' said the Norwegian, his voice breaking with emotion. 'Trapped in my own country. I long for this war to be over, for them to be free again. When it is your own family, your own children . . . well, you would fight with your bare hands, scratch with your nails . . .'

'What we are doing is immensely important,' I said, trying to ward off the deep sadness of his voice.

'May I be candid with you, Meadows? I don't think this joint way of doing it, with the three forecasting centres, is the best way of going on. It's unscientific, over-complex – sheer madness, in fact. I should tell you I spoke to Sir Peter about it and I was stunned by what he said. He indicated to me that the reason we are doing it this way is that, if anything should go wrong with the forecast for the invasion, the responsibility could not be identified with any particular national organisation.'

His voice hardened, his accent becoming more Norwegian. 'You know that is why we have Stagg? Just to link up the views. Personally, I cannot see why Sir Peter appointed him even on that front, never mind the meteorological one, where he is hopeless. He is no diplomat. Not even at the most critical times of our talkings is he able to submerge his ego.'

I felt a need to defend Stagg. He was a bit abrasive, anyone would have to agree with that, but he was also fair-minded and very intelligent. 'Sverre, he has an unenviable task – drawing all our opinions into an agreed story, presenting it to Eisenhower, answering questions from all those formidable generals and air marshals.'

But Petterssen would not be budged. In later years he and Stagg would go hammer and tongs at each other in letters, arguing about who had said what during these conferences. I make no final judgement, except to say somebody had to bring all these warring opinions together. Yes, Stagg got people's backs up – he was at daggers drawn with the navy as well as Petterssen and Krick – but I am certain that would have been the case whoever had done the job.

8

On Wednesday evening, 31 May, the conference was still in disagreement, but again in a different mode from the previous day. Krick and Petterssen now agreed that there might be storms in the Atlantic, but Krick claimed that a finger of high pressure would by Monday extend into the Channel and protect the invasion fleet. Petterssen and Douglas still maintained that the weather would be dangerous come Monday.

Stagg and I both found this diversity of view troubling, and he consequently sought a telephonic audience with General Bull, a senior member of Eisenhower's staff.

'Pick up your handset,' he said to me before calling. 'Tell me what you think.'

I listened to him explain to Bull that the prospects for Sunday, Monday and probably Tuesday were on the poor side, but the real difficulty was that they couldn't get the forecasting centres to agree.

There was a pause, in which the whirr of the scrambler could be heard.

'For heaven's sake, Stagg, get it sorted out!' urged Bull. 'General Eisenhower is a very worried man.'

So was Stagg after that. He put down the phone and sat motionless in his chair. I suggested we eat something.

We dined on cod, chips and peas at the mess hall, washed down with strong cups of tea. That night, the hundred or so men and women in the mess were unusually silent. There was a new tension in the air as the invasion they had spent so many months planning was about to begin. I realised everyone in the room was staring at us meteorologists, as if it were our fault the weather was not falling into line.

Stagg also felt the pressure of all those solemn, unsmiling eyes. Things weren't helped by him accidentally tipping up the edge of his plate with his elbow, making his peas spray up and roll over the table. When he got down on his hands and knees to pick up his fork, his long frame bent under the table, it seemed as if he was hiding.

'Come on,' I said, embarrassed. 'Let's go.' We took our trays to the throw-out and went back outside onto a quadrangle in front of the main building. It had been covered with gravel and was parked over with vehicles. It was about 2030 hours, but there was still plenty of light to see by. The pearl-grey sky was covered with cirrocumulus. The mackerel cloud.

'Maybe tomorrow morning we'll have a breakthrough,' said Stagg, looking up at the coming moon and going sun. It was one of those evenings of pure luminosity.

'Hey, Stagg!' said an American voice behind us.

It was Eisenhower, getting out of a Packard with a US flag on the bonnet. He had a female driver, a pretty Waaf with dark hair.

Stagg straightened up and saluted. 'Sir!' Then he introduced me. 'This is my assistant, Henry Meadows.' I quickly saluted myself, realising I should I have done so when Stagg did. We stood there formally for a second, relaxing only when Eisenhower took a packet of Lucky Strikes from his pocket. Stagg declined, but I accepted.

'I've been looking everywhere for you, Stagg,' said Eisenhower. 'I'm off to London to see Churchill. We're going to have one more little talk before the get-go. I wanted to see you first. I understand from Bull you've had a lot of trouble getting people to agree.'

'I'm afraid so, sir.'

The American cigarette tasted very different from my usual Capstan.

'Well, I want you to know that you have to follow your own instincts. Trust your gut and above all don't feel you have to favour the American view just because I'm in charge. I just need the decision to be right – the nationality of whose brain it comes out of doesn't matter.'

Eisenhower's driver was studying her lipstick in the rear-view mirror. It was rumoured she shared his bed. Glancing up, she caught me looking at her. I blushed, but she just smiled and opened her compact. I thought of Joan and Gwen, wondering what had happened to them – and then of Gill Ryman. I still had not been in touch with her, and the lapse had begun to occupy my thoughts. It made me feel disgusted with myself.

'Some of my colleagues would have you replaced,' continued the commander cheerfully, 'but I know you're the man for the job, Stagg. So you just keep them forecasts coming. We need one good spell, that's all. Give me as much notice as you can. At the moment, I can confirm we are still hoping to go June 5th, assuming everything has come into alignment.'

I gulped, glancing apprehensively at the sky. It was to be Monday after all.

Eisenhower ground his Lucky Strike under his heel and got back in the Packard. With one last look in the mirror and an expression that seemed to say, 'I'm satisfied with that,' the woman put away her make-up and they pulled away, the sleek car rolling over the gravel. The Snowballs waved it straight through at the checkpoint.

'Maybe we'll have happy news for Ike tomorrow,' Stagg said without conviction.

We watched the gate of the checkpoint come down. The chance of getting the forecast right seemed as distant as a planet yet to be discovered.

June

1

At the Thursday morning conference – 1 June – Petterssen and Douglas predicted that the coming weekend's weather would form part of a long, wandering cold front that would persist for at least a week. Krick and the others at Widewing said the bad weather would clear tomorrow. By that time, I reflected, Stagg, Yates and I would be at Portsmouth, where we were to join the rest of the staff.

'Personally, I look forward to Monday with considerable optimism,' Krick said. 'You see how this protrusion from the Azores high will shield the Channel from the bad stuff. It'll be like a bubble sealing the entrance. Or a finger in the dyke.' He kept going on about this finger.

That afternoon I drove down to Portsmouth with Stagg and Yates in an RAF staff car: three extremely worried men sitting in silence. The gravity of the situation was emphasised by the lines of war traffic, which made it an extremely long ride. On the way I suddenly realised I had organised that the old WAN-TAC gauges should be delivered to Bushey, not Portsmouth. I would have to make a telephone call as soon as we got there. I wondered if they had been picked up yet. I imagined the pilot – perhaps even Reynolds himself – swooping down and hooking up the line with the bag attached, then zooming up with the package under him, to be retrieved by another member of the crew.

As we sat behind lines of military traffic – tanks, armoured personnel carriers, staff cars, and lorry after lorry overflowing with troops – the thought came into my head that I would now be very near to Gill Ryman. I was on my way to Portsmouth, she was on the Isle of Wight, just across the Solent. Again the fact that I had not yet written to her apologising for her husband's death provoked a spasm of self-disgust. It might seem irrelevant, given the moment of what I was now involved in, but in my mind I could not disconnect Ryman's death from the impending invasion. His number, meanwhile, seemed further away than ever. What stood in its place was anxiety, backed by a curious mixture of desire and admiration for Ryman's stolen bride, as Gill strangely seemed to me.

Panicking, I felt blood begin to prick in the bridge of my nose. Scrabbling around for a handkerchief in my pockets and not finding one, I had to ask Stagg, who whipped his out (he was a dab hand with a hankie, was Stagg) and passed it me. The blood flowed smoothly, turning the white material red. Keeping my head back I felt it drip down the back of my throat, until at last it dried.

Feeling nauseous, I shuddered, terrified that a dizzy spell was on its way once more: a force like a thousand magnets, pulling me to the ground as soon as I stepped out of the car. For the rest of the journey, long-suppressed memories of the mudslide mixed with a picture of Ryman hanging from the balloon, head slumped like Christ in torment on the cross, face suffused, dying crimson as if draped with a red robe, with a cruel wound developing where the wire bit below.

Was there one last chance of absolution? Answer in the negative seemed to penetrate the fleeting pane of the car window, which framed a dance of clouds over gloomy fields. Mostly nimbus, the raincloud, and nebula, the cloud of doubtfulness.

I reflected ruefully on my lapsed faith. I had become closed up in myself, refusing love, not hearing that first rule of St Benedict which the monks at Douai taught us was key to all.

Ausculta o fili, inclina aurem cordis tui . . . Listen, incline the ear of your heart. Something like that.

It was drizzling as we came into Portsmouth. I had a cricked neck from looking up at the sky. By the time we entered the grounds of Southwick Park, the rain was falling a little harder, making the leaves on the many trees that grew in the park jump and dance at irregular intervals. A big Victorian country house would have dominated the scene were there not acres of tents under the trees and up into the hills beyond.

There were some khaki-coloured caravans among the tents, one of them set back in a grove of its own.

'That's the supreme commander's quarters,' said our driver. 'Mr Churchill came the other day. And Smuts.'

A South African, Jan Smuts was Churchill's deputy in the War Cabinet. He was an interesting if now largely forgotten man, whose book *Holism and Evolution* is well worth a read; no less a figure than Einstein approved it, saying that Smuts's concept of holism, along with his own construct of relativity, would be the two main paradigms of human thinking in the new millennium.

We were a long way off that. As it was, when we pulled up outside the house that Thursday, dark clouds were swirling above us in sun-obliterating masses. Stormy weather was on its way, no question. 'It's becoming critical, folks,' Yates said as we got out of the car. 'The big ships sail tonight, come what may.'

He was right. The day of reckoning was tugging us towards it. The Allies' big battleships, set to bombard the Normandy coast on Monday, would tonight slip anchor at their havens in northern Ireland and the west of Scotland – including, no doubt, some from the Cowal – and head south to converge on the Channel. Meanwhile thousands of aircraft – Hurricanes, Spitfires, Lockheeds, Lancasters and Lysanders – strained at the leash in their aerodrome kennels, and thousands of men at their sealed-off battle stations – in tents pitched across half of Kent and most of Devon and all of Sussex and Hampshire and Dorset – were still waiting for an order to move.

We made our way to our own tents, which had already been pitched for us. Looking at the wooden pegs hammered into the ground to hold the guy ropes, I suddenly had a dreadful feeling of being pinioned by fate.

Trying to ignore it, I threw my suitcase into my tent and went up to the main house. I found the RAF section and asked them to send an order to 518 Squadron (who did the BIS-MUTH track out of Stornoway), to the effect that the package from WANTAC should now come to Portsmouth not Bushey. Later on, the message came back that the instruments had been successfully recovered and were on their way. There was still the issue of how I was going to test them. I needed wind tunnels and pressure chambers. There was nothing like that at Southwick.

Once I had organised the WANTAC redirect, I at last attended to that other communication which had been weighing on my mind. I wrote to Gill.

We had been assigned a Nissen hut on the top of the cliff to work in and it was in there, listening to the calls of the numerous gulls that soared in the grey atmosphere outside, that I mastered my own personal weather. I did so with a very short document communicating my belated condolences and straightforwardly apologising for what I had done. There seemed no point in beating about the bush with extenuating circumstances.

Explaining I was in Portsmouth, I suggested that we might be able to meet once my current commitments at work had lessened. There was still the problem of the address. Remembering her maiden name was Blackford and that Ryman had said her father worked at the Saunders-Roe factory (as, I then recalled, had the intelligence document on Ryman given to me by Sir Peter all those months ago), I addressed it Gill Ryman c/o Mr Blackford there. If he was not there, there was bound to be someone who remembered the family.

Having sealed the envelope, I felt a tremendous sense of relief. I ran down to the main house to catch the night mail, with the letter in the tunic pocket of my uniform. I can still remember the itch today – both the itch of the blue serge and the itch to be forgiven, for my sins to be assigned to a different zone. But the fact is, they tend to return, as if finding their way back home through the gates and alleys of the atmosphere.

2

As I was eating my bacon and eggs at breakfast the following Friday morning, a westerly wind was blowing through the trees outside the window. Watching the boughs move, with the thought of the Saunders-Roe factory still in my mind, I suddenly had an idea. They would have a wind tunnel at the factory: I could take the instruments there. Stagg's warning about not being able to spare me would still apply, but . . . it would only be a matter of being away for a day. Less than a day.

Even that short breadth of time we could now hardly afford. The immense machine of war, wound tight in its enforced immobility, was desperate for release. On the massive momentum of the whole operation – days and weeks of complex preparation, months of planning, years of stored-up energy, not to mention the hopes for freedom of the European nations under the Nazi yoke – on all this we, the so-called weather prophets, were now the only brake.

If we didn't go early the following week, the next available slot in which conditions could be anything close to right was a fortnight away, by which time the Germans would surely have seen through all the various movements and deceptions that were in play and reinforced the Normandy coast.

Even Yates, that phlegmatic embodiment of American courage and virtue, was rattled. He was already worried in case the enemy had spotted the big ships moving. 'The element of surprise will be lost,' he'd said yesterday. 'And where will they scatter to if we have to postpone? If there's a storm we could lose the whole fleet!'

Filled with these foretales of gloom, I climbed back up the cliff with Yates to the Nissen hut to join him and Stagg for examination of the incoming Friday charts. I and those two remarkable characters. Hidden men of war, one six-foot four, Scottish and short-tempered, the other a small, dark, patient Yank, very athletic. Heroes, really, those two. With very difficult colleagues, they had to face that array of generals knowing what a forecast meant when the forecasters themselves were in dispute. Then do it again. Day after day of charts and terrifying meetings, night after night of snatched naps and coffee cups.

The papers we spread out on the table were covered with indications of depression. 'That puts paid to Krick's forecast of calm weather,' said Stagg as we cast our eyes over the charts.

Not so. The subsequent telephonic discussion produced the by now familiar see-saw. Douglas and Petterssen at Dunstable foresaw cloud and strong winds – strong enough to make the operation of landing craft highly inadvisable, if not catastrophic; Krick and his colleagues at Widewing wouldn't budge. They were certain conditions would be 'tolerable', as Krick put it.

'All we gotta do is help the house odds be better than chance,' he added.

'But what if they are not?' I said, remembering our poker game.

'If we don't even do that we'll be busted down to privates.'

We all felt terrible, not just because of the disagreements themselves, but also because of the brutal forward pull of all those ships and armies. It was as if we were now expected not just to predict the weather but *make* it, in order that the vast ensemble of men and machines to which – let's be clear – the United States had contributed the lion's share could at last be released from its binds and unleashed upon the enemy. Little wonder there was so much irritability, which was no doubt made worse by all of us suffering from severe sleep deprivation.

Unable to extract a consensus, that lunchtime Stagg was again forced to present a hybrid forecast to Eisenhower in the library at Southwick House. As he was doing so, I went to the RAF section to see if my package from WANTAC had been delivered – it was coming by motorcycle messenger from the Portsmouth aerodrome. Through the air the radio signals washed their soundless waves; and swiftly back the answer came. Not arrived. The flight from Scotland had not even landed yet, I was told by the operator. Pressing my fists together in frustration, I walked back through Southwick's busy corridors, willing the plane to come.

On my way up to the hut I met Yates, coming down the hill. He told me that, during the morning interrogation from the generals, Stagg had clammed up, momentarily crushed by the weight of responsibility on his shoulders.

'Look after that guy,' said the kindly American. 'He's carrying a lot. He's up in the hut.'

I went in and found Stagg lying on the floor with his eyes closed, and his arms crossed on his chest. He looked like the effigy of a medieval knight lying in stone in a church. I knelt down beside him and was about to pat his shoulder when his eyes opened and his head jerked up, making me start back in shock.

'It's all right,' he said, sitting up. 'I wasn't sleeping. Just thinking.'

He drew in a series of short, sharp breaths. I helped him to his feet and made him some coffee and tried to talk inconsequentialities to him – something about my childhood in Africa, I think it was – but he would have none of it, waving me out of the room, smiling grimly.

In this atmosphere of extraordinary tension, I took the opportunity of the window between meetings to go for a walk in the hope it would shake the anxiety from my own head. As I was walking, up on the bluffs above Portsmouth, I looked up at a hill and saw that it was completely covered in odd-seeming foliage. Which, as I looked, proceeded to move. The whole hillside was alive with men. They were commandos, crawling forward in a solid mass, all wearing camouflage – 'disruptive pattern material' as the military officially call it. As they crossed the turf, turning and winding like some vast snake, the definition between each man was pruned back by the pattern. Equally, the resolution of their bodies – I mean between individual limbs and torsos – was also undercut by the tentative nature of the design.

I walked back down into the middle of the woods which surrounded Southwick. Coming into a grove, I sat down with my back against the spongy, moss-encrusted surface of a fallen tree. I noticed a snail, horns and tail out, which was making its way across a boulder nearby, leaving a trail of slime. When I picked it up there was a sucking noise, and it shrank back into its spiral shell.

I thought of something curling into being, in the very abyss of time. Before time exerted its mystery, before meaning was given to length and breadth, left and right, inside and outside, before we were able to distinguish between the edges of objects and the space around them. Before things could be bound together, or held apart, before gaps opened in cells and more cells were made and individuals were produced by that sundering. Before, before, before . . . Before all except the original vortex, whose cluster of vapour must itself have been sucked into being in order to form in formlessness . . .

I remember trying to say all this to myself, or something like it, looking inward and at the same time at the snail in the bowl of my palm. In that moment it was like I was that snail for all time and its shell, somehow, every place. But of course it all sounds quite nuts now. There are no words to convey this feeling between individuals.

Mathematics, by contrast, is universal. If you write

$$\frac{g}{T}\left\{\frac{\partial T}{\partial h} - \left(\frac{dT}{\partial h}\right)_{\text{adiabat}}\right\} \Big/ \left(\frac{d\bar{v}}{dh}\right)^2,$$

which is the formula for the Ryman number, at least you will be understood by competent mathematicians in all countries. The other truly international language is music, my other great passion. Place a piece of music in front of a piano player or a singer and you will be likewise understood, give or take a measure of interpretation. In point of which – I have just passed, listening to Haydn's *Creation* in my cabin, the moment when the fortissimo modulates to C major on the word *Licht*.

Light!

Im Anfange schuf Gott Himmel und Erde . . .

I like to practise my German exactly because it is so unfashionable. This recent takeover by English, despite the advantages it gives us and the Americans, is actually very regrettable. It makes people think in straight lines. When Heinz Wirbel, the weather scientist who jumped from the Junkers, got in touch with me after the war, wanting to correspond (he too became an academic), I said we could so long as we did so in German.

I put down the snail. Across the black bars of the trees, something moved. A person, breaking the poplars' plumb-line regularity, someone with a forward-angled stoop and rangy legs that never quite seemed in continuity with the rest.

It was Stagg, crunching impatiently across the stick-littered leaf mould. I watched him for a minute or two, pacing round and round in a circle, obscured at intervals by the trees. He took out his handkerchief and blew his nose several times. I felt impatient with myself at not being able to help, and not a little embarrassment that he was behaving like this. But who was I to talk of embarrassment?

Calling out so as not to startle him, I went and joined Stagg. He did not seem surprised to see me. We walked silently through the dripping woods until we came to a place where there was a large pond, sombre and still except where drops of water fell into it from overhanging trees.

There was a rowing boat moored there. I remember Stagg standing on the jetty and pushing that boat violently with his foot, so that it rocked wildly, oars rattling in the ribbed wood. Wild ripples pulsed over the black water. We waited till the boat came back to equipoise, then walked back to the house, still saying nothing.

My instruments from WANTAC had finally arrived, I discovered on my return. I went to collect them from the Snowballs at the secure post room (everything that went in and out of Southwick had to be checked and signed for). The instruments came in a metal box filled with straw and labelled with my name. Inside the box was a sealed rubber bag, which I presume was the very one which had been hooked up from the WANTAC ship.

Excited, I carried the bag back to my tent and, sitting cross-legged under the flysheet, took the gauges out. There were two barometers and three anemometers, all them encased in gleaming brass. It was strange to think of them hanging from storm-tossed masts.

Weighing the instruments in my hands, I sat there thinking about what form, exactly, the experiments should take, assuming Stagg would give me permission to go to the Saunders-Roe factory in Cowes, which was by no means a certainty. Then, realising I would also have to get permission from Saunders-

Roe, I rushed back to the hut and used one of the telephones to call the exchange and get myself put through to the Isle of Wight.

On being asked by the telephone operator at the factory to whom I wished to speak, I could not think of anyone but Gill's father, Chief Engineer Blackford. After a long wait, it was he who eventually announced himself at the other end of the line.

'My name's Meadows,' I said. 'I work in the meteorological department here at SHAEF in Portsmouth. We urgently need to test some instruments in your wind tunnel . . .'

There was silence on the other end of the line, so I continued. 'Your daughter, Mrs Ryman, she may by now have received a letter from me. I knew her in Scotland.'

Again there was silence. 'It really is important, sir, that I come to the factory and have use of its facilities,' I said. 'My name is Henry–'

'I know very well who you are,' said Mr Blackford then, in a stern voice. 'Your letter arrived this morning. How dare you!'

'I wrote only to apologise. If I were able to meet Gill I could do so in person.'

'She does not want to see you. You are the last person she would want . . . And I. I would not want to see you. I might not be able to control myself. Wallace and I worked together here. You are not welcome . . .'

His voice trailed off, as if extinguished by its own anger.

'I am sorry to hear that,' I said – and I *was* sorry. 'But the fact remains, for military reasons, that I must have access to the wind tunnel, and it must be tomorrow.'

'That's another matter,' he said abruptly. 'I will leave instructions that you are to be permitted entry. But do not think that excuses what you have done, Meadows. I don't just mean Wallace. I also hold you responsible for the loss of my daughter's child. She might have made it through this time, were it

292

not for the anxiety she suffered following Wallace's death.'

He put down the phone.

Shaken, I put down my own and leaned my back against the wall. I slid down, feeling my balance shifting. Was I never to be free of this event from what already now seemed like another life? Ever since it has often suddenly returned to me, covering me again; it is as if a trapdoor opens and mud comes pouring from the sky. Mud that swirls then turns solid around me, that bakes like a crater on the moon, mud which I have to break out of, move out of, snap myself out of – until the fall happens again and I am back in that deep pit, summoning up the energy to jerk myself out.

By the time of the evening conference, which began at 8 p.m. that Friday, I was feeling marginally better. But so far as the forecast went, the deadlock was the same. Widewing utterly for an invasion on Monday, Dunstable utterly against. The Admiralty, whose sea and swell forecasts were invaluable, were also pessimistic. There was uproar, a chaos of voices.

By the time it had turned half past eight, Stagg had had enough. 'This is ridiculous!' he cried. 'Listen, all of you. In half an hour I have to present an agreed forecast to General Eisenhower. Help me, please.'

Gagging, he banged down the phone and rushed outside. I heard him being sick on the ground, the retching noise making my own stomach turn.

'Boy,' said Krick. 'That is one angry man. I don't know why he's getting so pissed. Maybe we need to accept that we're never gonna agree.'

'Now that I agree with,' said Petterssen.

They both laughed, a little cruelly to my mind, and then the door of the hut opened.

'I'm sorry, Meadows,' Stagg said, coming back in, wiping his face with a handkerchief. 'It's those things.' He flapped the vomit-stained hankie at the weather charts. 'I'm not sure I can stand to look at another one. Tell them they can put their telephones down. I'm going to have to wing it again.'

He left the room. After doing as he said, I sat studying the WANTAC figures. There was a mystery there, that much was certain. Whether it had to do with the instruments themselves or was a factor of narrowly adjacent turbulent fluxes – in which case Ryman's number would come into play – I did not know. But I was determined to find out.

At about 11 p.m. Stagg came back from seeing Eisenhower. He seemed a little more relaxed. He told me that he had broadly confirmed yesterday's forecast and, therefore – at least from a weather perspective – the impossibility of invasion on Monday. 'I took more of the Dunstable view and said the situation was now potentially full of menace. Eisenhower asked me about the weather for Tuesday. I told him that would be pure guesswork at this stage, but added that the weather on Tuesday and Wednesday is unlikely to be any worse than on Sunday and Monday.'

'What did Eisenhower say?' I asked.

'Nothing. He just said nothing. And according to General Bull, D-Day is still on for Monday.' Stagg walked up to the little window of the hut and looked out into the night sky, which showed no signs of disturbance. 'You know, I have almost given up hope that we will get it right. Some of those bloody generals simply look outside, see fine weather and say, go!'

'Look,' I said, summoning up courage before that formidably tempestuous personality. 'I really think you should let me have a look at those WANTAC instruments. They have arrived now.'

'And what do you propose?' Stagg asked, gritting his teeth as if to prevent angry words from flying between them.

'There is a wind tunnel and the other necessary equipment

at the Saunders-Roe factory across in Cowes. I could be there and back in a day, taking the gauges with me. I will do some tests and the results will tell us whether WANTAC's readings have been mistakes or genuine. We will know whether it was a case of the instruments or the weather.'

It seemed like an age before he replied. I remember he appeared to shiver as he sat there in that hut on the bluff, as if trembling under the weight of the responsibility that had been placed upon him.

'Very well, Henry. One day only, mind.'

3

The wind tunnel at Saunders-Roe was octagonal in cross-section and about forty feet long. Constructed in perspex, so that experiments could be viewed from outside, it had a use-able floor area twelve feet across and there was a door at each end. Wind was blown down the tunnel by a heavy-duty electric fan. Turbulence was produced by its three vanes, shaped to act as aerofoils, the angle of which could be adjusted to produce the required frequency and amplitude of perturbation.

Earlier that morning, grateful there were not many people about because it was a Saturday, I had already tested the barometers in a pressure chamber on the site. They worked perfectly. Now it was a question of letting winds of different speeds run past the anemometers I had set up in the tunnel, to see how they performed.

I could see down the tunnel, the length of which was illuminated by incandescent lamps flaring overhead. I switched on the fan and, with a roar, the blast began. It was jolly hard work, writing down the measurements on each dial – the wind kept flipping up my notepad – but very quickly I came to the conclusion that the WANTAC anemometers, too, could be trusted.

If it wasn't a question of instrument error, then it could only be the weather itself that was responsible for the anomalous readings. I was so excited that, with the man-made wind still roaring about me, I paced up and down behind the installations like a boy on the beach pointing out ships in a storm, trying to calculate what this meant for Monday's invasion. The coming weather suggested by WANTAC was still not yet calm enough to make landings possible; but it looked as if more favourable conditions were coming, and soon.

The question was still *when?* Working out how long it would take for the calmer weather to reach the Channel would involve analysis of the range of values of the Ryman number, but there was very little time to do the calculations. How could I possibly do all that maths in one day? It seemed impossible as a solo effort.

As I was deliberating whether it might be feasible, the door at the other end of the tunnel opened and somebody walked in. At first I thought it was the tunnel supervisor at Saunders-Roe, who had greeted me when I first arrived – there had been no sign of Mr Blackford – but it was a woman carrying a small brown-leather suitcase.

She wore a woollen black coat and a long knitted red scarf tied loosely round her neck, streaming out behind her like a windsock in the onrushing gale. The coat was open, revealing a blouse with a high white collar, a V-neck jumper, and a skirt reaching almost to the floor. The suitcase was swinging like a pendulum.

I dumbly recognised Gill Ryman. She walked towards me quickly, knocking from side to side, blown off balance by the blast roaring by, her clothes flapping around her.

She looked older, and the clothing pressed hard against her body by the wind confirmed clearly that she was no longer pregnant. Her hair streamed out behind, parallel with the scarf. Behind its knitted length, tassels fluttered in turn, each one trembling its own little wake.

Immobile for a second, I felt as if my confused feelings for her, so long shut away in darkness and sighing, were about to be released; as if a squeezing hand was being released and something springing forth.

'Gill!' I cried, eventually rushing forward to embrace her. She felt extremely thin. She stood there awkwardly for a few seconds, inert in my arms with the wind tearing at us down the tunnel, plucking at our clothes and hair.

Time seemed to stand still, and then she freed herself from me – pushing me away with the little brown case. I heard myself begin to speak, 'I'm so sorry . . . I wrote, just yesterday, but I expect you haven't–'

'I can't hear you!' Shouting into the wind's roar, she staggered, almost falling down. I clasped her again.

As she spoke, we wheeled about in the rush and she had to hold on to me. I was aware of a blurring of boundaries. It was as if, in that moment, her spirit and mine were clustering together under the influence of something larger – something fundamental in which we were both intimately involved, like molecules moving in the same direction, following the flow of the medium in which they were carried.

'I'll turn it off,' I shouted back.

I walked to the control panel and reached down for the switch. With an unearthly moan, the fan slowed. The gale ceased. Suddenly, all was quiet.

As I came back towards her, Gill put down the suitcase. She came close, studying me hard, both of us still blinking from the effect of wind. 'I wrote,' I said, eventually. 'Not the right words I expect, but . . . well, I am sorry.'

She covered her ears with her hands. 'Do stop all that, please.' She was frowning as she did this, and screwing up her eyes.

'You destroyed me by destroying him,' she continued eventually, letting her hands fall and reopening her eyes, 'but I have not come here to hear you apologise. You already did that in your letter. And besides, I owe you an apology myself, for that business with the blood and . . . Embarrassing – I was not myself.'

'Of course not.'

'It only came yesterday.' She had taken my letter out of her pocket. 'My father did not want me to come here today. He refused to bring me. I had to drive myself. He was very fond of Wallace. He holds you entirely to blame for his death.'

I felt nausea in my stomach and a rising whirling in my head. 'And for your baby's, I gather. I'm so sorry, Gill – if I had thought . . .'

She shook her head. 'That was not your fault, though obviously Wallace's death did not help. But I have miscarried on many occasions previously. The rhesus factor – which is why I sat up when I heard you talk about Brecher at lunch that day. This was my eighth, so I am quite used to it by now. But each did seem to happen earlier than the last, which is why I left Kilmun when I did.' She spoke coldly, as if not about herself or her body.

'I'm so sorry, Gill, all the same. About the child as well as Wallace.'

'For God's sake!' She stepped towards me, lifting a hand as if to strike me, then reached out for my face, squeezing it hard and painfully between her fingers and thumb. Her face was inches from mine. 'Shut up. Just shut up.' Then she pushed away from me, shaking her head and falling to her knees on the floor of the wind tunnel, sobbing.

I knelt down beside her, patting her shoulder ineffectually, almost overcome by fugue-like dizziness.

She took out a handkerchief and dabbed her eyes, then got to her feet. 'It's all right, it's all right. I'm sorry. God sees all things; he shall not despise a contrite heart. That is what I keep reminding myself when I think about you, Henry.'

Despite my relief that she seemed to have recovered from the desire to mete violence on me, I recoiled from these devout sentiments. 'God!' I cried. 'I wish I knew him. If I had then I might not have had such cursed luck. I am afraid I have become like Wallace. I don't believe in God any more, after what happened.'

'Wallace actually saw God in everything,' she said, affronted. 'It's just that people didn't realise.'

The steel door at the far end of the tunnel banged open. Now it was indeed the supervisor from Saunders-Roe coming in. 'Everything all right in here?' he called out doubtfully.

'Yes, fine, thank you,' I replied. 'I think I'll pack up now. I've got what I came for.'

'What were you testing?' Gill asked, looking down the tunnel at the anemometers as the supervisor left.

'Wind speeds on ships. We've been getting errant readings. Well, they seemed errant, but actually I think they are correct. I have now got to work out your husband's number for adjacent areas of the North Atlantic and the Channel. I don't think I've got enough time. I'm afraid I must rush back for the boat to Portsmouth. Gill – I'm working on . . . well, it's the war.'

'Of course,' she said. 'I understand. I can drive you to the pier, if that is any help. You'll make the seven o'clock.'

'That would be wonderful.'

She dug in a pocket to check for car keys, then picked up the suitcase and began walking to the door of the tunnel. I gathered up my equipment, stowed it in a large kitbag, and then joined her.

'So, you live here now?' I asked awkwardly as we walked into dusky light outside the wind tunnel. One of the workers from the factory was painting the number 52 on a large flying boat mounted on trestles.

'Yes,' she replied. 'But in Seaview, not Cowes. I couldn't face going back to Scotland, not after losing another baby. I had all our belongings sent down.'

'We could meet again,' I said. 'Talk things over . . .'

She shook her head. 'Look, do you want a lift or not?'

'Yes, of course. Thank you.' We began walking towards the vehicle. 'It seems like fate,' I continued, 'you coming here like this.'

She looked at me, swinging the suitcase a little menacingly. 'Fate? Wallace hated that word.'

'But he thought everything was determined.'

'Not exactly.' We got into the car, a little blue Morris with red seats. I slung my kitbag into the back and she passed the suitcase over the steering wheel to me, so it rested squarely on my lap.

'You mean he thought everything was determined, but not exactly?'

She frowned. 'I mean he didn't think about it like that, in a religious way. He once said fate depended on the unpredictable relationship of different physical scales.'

She put the key in the ignition. 'You know what else he once said to me?'

'What?'

'That if anyone wanted to apply his number across a large space, the thing to do was to take the weather readings in the centre of each adjacent quadrant of the atmosphere, not do the whole thing.'

'I'm not sure that would work,' I said. 'There would be too many distortion errors in the rest of the quadrant.'

'But worth a try, when you are in a bind, if you could simulate quasi-random turbulence of the outside parts?'

'Yes, I suppose . . .'

I suddenly felt extremely weary. I was unable to expel from my head the vision of Allied soldiers being dragged by the rip tide, mouths agape as, raked by machine-gun fire from the shore, they were tipped out of their landing craft into the waves. A tide of men, turning the wavetops red.

Gill carried on speaking in neutral, emotionless tones. 'Well, I have brought something that might help. When we were in Scotland, and *you* came, and Wallace told me of his suspicions of you, part of me wanted him to help you. I was always a bit frustrated that he had gone to ground in Kilmun not fully recognised for his achievements. Now that he is dead, I want him to have a legacy. And that is what I have brought you. At least, I hope so. Open the suitcase, Henry.'

Perplexed, I clicked the brass clasps and lifted the lid. Inside, to my great surprise, laid out in the original green baize mould, were the eight shell cases I had last seen in Ryman's study. I looked across at Gill for an explanation. I had a peculiar sensation of impending judgement, as if I were about to go before the beak.

She smiled unnervingly, as if pleased to see me foxed. 'Wallace used these to simulate the action of turbulence round the central calculation in each quadrant. That is how he got round the problem of crossing from one weather system to the next.'

'But how?' I said, taking the largest shell case out of the mould. Even as I did so, I began to have an inkling of the answer, for inside the shell case I felt weight shift; there was also a sandy, tinkling noise, like that heard in a kaleidoscope, or a box of seeds.

'Give it to me,' commanded Gill. 'And cup your hands.' Again I had the feeling of going before the law.

I did as she said, and she began unscrewing the end of the shell. With very careful movements she tipped out some of its contents into the receptacle of my joined palms. What spilled out were tiny brass digits, pressed out of sheet metal. Inside the shell were hundreds more.

'He had them precision-made in Germany, and collected them from there after his trip to Poland in 1939. That was partly why he went to Berlin.'

Suddenly, as if in a flash of revealed knowledge, I began to see the shape of the method, but Gill was a long way ahead of me. 'It's very important you don't lose any,' she explained, touching the mound of numbers in my hands with a finger. 'Each shell case contains a different amount of digits, so within a certain range you can choose the minimum and maximum values for each set of numbers you want. Wallace used to shake the shell case like a maraca, pour out a pile of these on a table, then close his eyes to pick out an amount of digits determined by the nature of the underlying calculation.'

I was amazed she had such a grasp of it all. 'Those digits effectively become the seed for further calculations,' she continued, speaking in the same authoritative tone.

'Worked out mathematically?' I asked, looking at the pile of numbers still cupped in my palm.

She nodded. 'Right. Put those back carefully. We have to get you to the boat.'

When we got to the pier, she would not allow me to kiss her, simply turning away with a melancholy smile and heading back to the Morris. Still hopeful of possibility even then, I watched her drive away.

I spent the journey across the Solent in a whirl of emotion mixed with mathematical thought. It was as if, finally, two parts of my brain had come together . . . Full of regret and sadness, and excitement and relief, carrying Gill's suitcase in my hand and the kitbag of instruments over my shoulder, I arrived back at Southwick just in time for the Saturday night conference.

The weather outside the hut was still good, and the wartime measure of setting British Summer Time two hours ahead of GMT meant that there was still plenty of light, even at 9 p.m. To a layman it would have looked all fine and dandy to launch an invasion on Monday – but the charts confirmed yesterday's view of coming storms.

I heard from one of the navy forecasters that Stagg had become indisposed – I imagined him vomiting again – during the 6 p.m. conference while I was away. Yates had had to take over as controller.

But Stagg was back in his seat now. Things did not look good for Monday. The Admiralty's pessimism had worsened to meet Dunstable's. They also described another significant new storm which had formed in the US, to the east of the Great Lakes, which was moving towards the Atlantic and would soon come to dominate. Petterssen's upper-air work supported the rapid arrival of this 'Storm E', as we termed it.

Krick, as if beginning to accept the situation, made no mention of the 'finger of high pressure' he had maintained would insulate the Channel from the earlier oncoming Irish cold front. But he still thought it was OK to go. Out of solidarity, not conviction, he was persuaded by Stagg and Yates to allow a unanimous 'no'.

The WANTAC figures were still out of kilter, new instruments notwithstanding, which I took as further confirmation that the earlier readings were accurate.

After the conference I told Stagg what I'd discovered at Saunders-Roe. 'We can trust WANTAC, in my view. But I don't know what it means yet. I have a suspicion that a ridge of high pressure might be developing there. More like a little tube than a ridge, maybe, but something. I tried to work it out on the boat, but I need more time.'

Ignoring the technical details of what I said relating to WANTAC, he gave me a sour look. 'Time is exactly what we don't have.' There was no point in telling him about Gill and the shell cases yet.

Keeping my counsel, I then accompanied Stagg and Yates to the door of the supreme commander's meeting down in the main house. As they were about to enter, Admiral Creasy bowled up the corridor. 'Hello, chaps. Some reassuring news for us tonight? You look happier than when you went out yesterday, I must say.'

Stagg gave him a forbearing smile. 'I'm afraid I don't feel very much happier, sir.'

'Well, we'll soon know the worst,' said Creasy in reply, and they entered the meeting room. I waited outside with the other aides, but I knew what Stagg would tell the assembled bigwigs. That the weather over the British Isles in the next few days would be subject to complex patterns of turbulence, with force 5 winds in the Channel, much low cloud and risk of fog in sea areas. In fact, a series of three depressions were strung across the Atlantic and the result would be rough seas – far too rough for landing on Monday – and too much cloud for successful bombing operations or landing troops from air.

After the meeting, at about 11 p.m., Stagg told me what had happened. Eisenhower had asked if there was a chance the forecast might be more optimistic tomorrow and Stagg had explained that the whole weather situation was extremely finely balanced. Last night, he had thought that there might be the slightest tip to the favourable side, but now it had gone too far to the other side for it to swing back again. Leigh Mallory, speaking for the RAF, had enquired what the conditions would be like for heavy bombers, then Eisenhower had again asked if Stagg felt he might be a bit more positive tomorrow (Sunday).

'I'm afraid not, sir,' was all Stagg could say – adding to me, outside afterwards, 'I've a feeling they are going to postpone. I get the sense Monty wants to go whatever, but Eisenhower is listening to us.'

'But putting the ships back into harbour will cause mayhem.'

'Yes,' Stagg said dourly.

'And the Germans are bound to get wind of it.'

'Yes,' he said again, more dourly still.

As he recounted all this to me, Stagg and I were making a circuit in the moonlight round the forbidding Victorian mansion that was Southwick. Staff cars – Packards, Morrises, Lea Francises – were drawing up constantly, their tyres crunching on the gravel. Out of one of the cars, looking like Laurel and Hardy, Smuts and Churchill emerged – their faces, flashing in the porch light, were heavy with gloom. We turned away quickly, making another tour of the building, lest the PM should identify the weathermen bringing all the bad news.

'They say Eisenhower complains because Churchill eats all the doughnuts,' whispered Stagg. 'And Monty gets cross because Eisenhower smokes.'

Stagg was relieved that he had at last been able to provide them all with an unqualified forecast, even though it probably meant the invasion was off. 'I do feel a bit happier,' he said, 'but if there is good weather on Monday I'll hang for it.'

We walked round the house, then towards a lawn at the front. The moon was full, there was almost no wind, the night sky was empty of clouds. Overall, it was almost like one of Ryman's brief moments of paradise – that condition of 'just no turbulence' which is as near to equilibrium as the atmosphere ever comes. Meanwhile we were forecasting thick cloud and strong wind in the Channel by morning. It didn't seem to stack up. But these background conditions of apparent calm were, in fact, exactly those times during which powerful events fermented. Besides, it was time I crossed my Rubicon.

'I'm going to go back and have one last go at applying the Ryman number in respect of WANTAC,' I said as we looked out over the blackened grounds beyond the lawn we were approaching, where spectral lines of tents ploughed the grass and rhododendron bushes rose like sea monsters.

'Just explain again, can you, to a chump like me, why

WANTAC is so singularly important and how it ties up with Ryman?'

'I think the reason WANTAC's showing different readings is that it is in the midst of one of Ryman's thin weather boundaries, at the edge of a small area of high pressure which would give us exactly the interval we need. I am satisfied the equipment is working properly, but I still haven't managed to make the figures stack up in a synoptic model. His number again.'

'I'm sorry, but I still don't get it,' said Stagg beside me, his feet crunching on the gravel.

'The Ryman number tells you how turbulent a parcel of atmosphere is. The reason Sir Peter sent me to Scotland was to find how wide or tall is that parcel of atmosphere – the range of a given number, as it were. The importance of the WANTAC ship is that its readings may show evidence of the small high pressure interval Eisenhower needs. If it is, end of story.'

'I should get some sleep, if I were you; we're not yet at the end of any story,' Stagg said curtly.

We were at the edge of the lawn. I kicked the turf with the toe of my shoe.

'Which reminds me,' Stagg continued. 'There's something I have forgotten to tell you. Air Marshal Tedder came up to me after the meeting and said we – I mean the British – ought to put some meteorologists in with the invasion force to take measurements and check how close our forecasts are to the reality on the ground. Apparently the Yanks have two whole squadrons of battlefield weathermen. We've run plain out. Tedder spoke to Sir Peter and he rang me, wondering, since you are young and fit and know what we have been up against here, whether you'd like to go in with them? He said he thought it might be a way for you to make amends for that business with Ryman.'

'Did he now?' I instinctively wanted to say no, but instead

asked for some time to think it over. In some ways it was an honour to be asked – but I had no military training whatsoever. Feeling exhausted, and overwhelmed by the gravity of the situation, I stared up into the night sky. The stars seemed to shudder, as if feeling the same apprehension.

'I am not a soldier,' I said, as we turned to go back to the house, whose serried windows showed tiny lines of light – not visible from above – at the edges of the blackout blinds.

'That is a drawback,' said Stagg. 'But it would be tremendously helpful if someone who was actually involved could compare theoretical forecasts with actuality. Think about it, anyway, as even if we postpone today we are going to have to go in the next three weeks, come what may.'

He gave a bitter laugh. 'Come what June! Come on, we'd better get back.'

On our way back to the main house – as we approached that great Victorian lump – we heard heavy running footsteps on the gravel and soon met an out-of-breath General Bull, who said he had been looking for us.

'Don't disappear like that! I've come to tell you, Monday may well be put off. If so, we are back at D minus three again as of today.'

This meant the assault would be on Tuesday, but it wasn't quite as simple as that. 'Because of your forecasts, General Eisenhower is thinking of holding up D-Day on a provisional, hour-by-hour, day-by-day basis,' Bull continued. 'We'll meet at four fifteen tomorrow morning and, depending on what you have to say, the supreme commander will confirm the postponement or not. If appropriate, he will then, or later in the day, decide definitely whether Tuesday will be D-Day.'

It appeared provisional, from the way Bull was talking, but really that was it. Between us, Stagg and I, Krick, Petterssen, Douglas and the Admiralty, in conjunction with thousands of other Allied meteorological staff, had finally caused a decision to be made. It seemed like Ryman's forecast factory had come true – but for all that we still weren't sure whether the decision to postpone would be the right one. The sky was practically clear; there was no rain.

'Maybe it is madness to send you on a wild goose chase into France under these circumstances,' said Stagg, once Bull had gone.

'No,' I said. 'I'll go.'

A strange feeling had come over me in the general's presence. Shaking off my anxiety and tiredness, I suddenly desperately wanted a shot of the action. I wanted to be among the ranks of men whose fates our forecast would determine. I had spent too long among figures of the mathematical type.

But I still had one last set of calculations to make. It was time that everything I had worked for was met directly. This meant facing up to the forecast problems with a new purposefulness – acting on what I had learned from Ryman and from the experiment I had conducted at Saunders-Roe, and gaining new meaning and new strength from the conviction that Gill's gift of the shell cases had supplied.

So I went, that Saturday night, back up to the Nissen hut and began applying the Ryman number to adjacent parcels of atmosphere, all the way from WANTAC near Iceland down to the Channel, using the simulation method Gill had suggested. I was not entirely confident, but I had to try. It seemed to make sense: because it allowed a measure of uncertainty into the calculation, this method was the best way to future-proof the forecast.

I needed to inoculate against my dizziness, uncertainty in general as it effectively was, but were the shell cases and their contents really the medicine? They seemed in one light like another type of dizziness in themselves, but maybe that was the point. What the Africans did, in Zomba after the slide, was allow themselves to be bitten by whirligig beetles. The beetles were collected from mountain rivers and pools and held to the breast near the nipple where they bit in a defensive reaction, releasing a powerful steroid.

So the *kizunguzungu* epidemic ended.

4

In the early hours of Sunday 4 June, with the 3 a.m. conference over, I was working bleary-eyed on my equations in the hut on the bluff. Outside, the sentry stirred and the Channel fretted against the boundary shore. The far-called navy was melting towards the battle line, pushing forth tentatively, like the shy anemone, unlooked at on its ocean bed. In France, on the moon-blanched land, waves turned, foam fell, whiting more the sepulchre. Meanwhile on each page, as I was writing, the figures seemed to move. These are the images that return.

An hour or so later Stagg would attend the first of what turned out to be two crucial commanders' conferences in the library at Southwick. At the first meeting, even though the weather was still fine, Stagg told them he thought it could go bad on Monday, with wind and cloud appearing in four or five hours' time. Eisenhower confirmed the previous evening's tentative decision to postpone.

Everything was in the balance, we were indeed not yet at the end of the story. We seemed to be stuck in the middle of the end, waiting for the variables to come into alignment.

I tried not to become frozen in the terrible immobility that this provisionality can entail. Smoking heavily, I continued with my calculations, pen in one hand, cigarette in the other, shell cases and numbers on the table in front of me. I knew I needed to have patience – as every silent sheet could be the one that bore fruit. But first a tree had to grow, hurrying its rivulets of roots and fibres, each one a boundary for the next, across

311

the waiting page. An equation tree, glowing and strong.

It wasn't easy. At one point I knocked one of the shell cases off the table and had to scrabble around on the floor picking up the precious numbers. This meant I had to start all over again, just in case I had lost one of the numbers. Extremely tense, feeling as if iron hooks were being inserted into my shoulders, I decided the best thing would be to go for a walk. Stiff from sitting for so long, I hobbled down the hill into the woods, until I came to the pond.

The rowing boat which Stagg had kicked was still moored to its jetty. Dispersed through the branches and leaves of surrounding trees the moonlight was shining, honeycombing the wine-dark water and the ribbed shell of the boat's interior. It was still a gloomy place, hooded with melancholy, but now it was a beautiful gloom.

From among the trees' black bars an owl hooted, making the air tremor. On an impulse I climbed into the boat. Having released the painter, I picked up the oars and began to row round that moon-dappled pond. With each stroke, as I leaned into the resisting water, the tension went out of my shoulders, and the mental exhaustion – like muscle pain in the brain – started to lift.

With each circuit of the pond, it was as if I was making a *tour d'horizon* of the workmanship of turbulence, not just in the zones of air and water, where vapour is lifted by the sun from oceans, lakes and rivers and diversely distributed by the wind, but the uncertain edges, where curls of mixing gas give meaning to the idea of space.

The boat shivered. I became undecided again. Once you leap the limits and start on further considerations you begin wondering – since the earth is just a little prick in space compared with the galaxy, never mind the whole – where it is all going to end.

I righted the skew.

The sound of the blades dipping in and out of the water together with the rattle of the rowlocks was like music accompanying the slow song of my thoughts. Even though I was conscious that I was sitting on the cross-plank of a rowing boat, pulling myself from eddy to eddy, it was as if I were elsewhere, seeing myself from above as I made my circuits. As I might appear to the tree-perched owl. Or from below, among the myriad mansions of submerged bacterial life. Or from the side, where a moorhen anxiously called each time I passed. Or that distant rift on Venus, from within whose folds a quite alien species might watch.

I listened. Gradually, like the appearance of a new shoreline, the realisation came upon me that to see the pond I was circumnavigating as a gloomy place, or even as a beautiful gloomy place, was to impose on it as Europeans had imposed upon Africa. As my family had imposed on Africa. As I had myself. Trying to make the world speak in human terms alone was akin to making Cecilia and Gideon speak the kitchen-Kaffir English we foisted upon them.

Somehow or other I had to learn to see the limit-rich, frame-filled world as one *without* limits, *without* frames – see it, feel it, speak it in that other language of turbulence which was itself differential from the start. Promiscuous of perspective, it was less liable to the drag of bias and error. Could this programme have any place in the canon of the physical sciences? Surely that was a vain ambition.

Science is not about 'feelings'. But nor, at least at the highest level, is it the reductionist activity it is commonly supposed to be. Great scientists use their imagination, they feel their way towards a theory, then seek to prove it. With turbulence, exactly because of its intermittency and mutability, I realised that night that this 'feeling towards' was actually key. Extrapolating from *immediate* connections, we have to keep an idea of *all* connections hovering before us, as an ideal insight into the whole. Because the whole cannot be reached, we can grasp it only by intuition – by chasing not the specifics but the beautiful ghost of an idea.

Once this thought had rushed in on me, others came, relating directly to the modal variety I ought to employ in calculating the forecast. I would have to keep shifting between Ryman's, Krick's, Douglas's and Petterssen's methods to get the required promiscuity of perspective. Effectively this was what we had been doing, but no one had tried to turn the to-and-fro of the conferences into an active programme.

Exhilarated, I returned to the hut with new vigour. My hand moved quickly under the desk lamp, covering the blank sheets. I solved calculation after calculation, working methodically forward through the charts, through tomorrow to expected conditions on Tuesday.

Sitting south of Iceland, on the eastern flank of a major deepening low south of Greenland, was a small parcel of warm air thrown up by the motion of the main surface low. It was this parcel that WANTAC had been reporting. By about 8.30 a.m. tomorrow, I calculated, the Atlantic parcel would develop into a higher-pressure ridge at 300 mb. Within an hour and a half the ridge would intensify at 500 mb. It was heading east, at a rate fast enough to cause, from early on Tuesday morning, a small temporary block in the Channel from the prevailing bad weather. There would be rough seas, heavy rain and gale-force winds later on Monday, but after that (I was as sure of it as I have ever been of anything) would come an invasion-friendly haven: a brief time of immunity from storms.

Perhaps only a mathematician can understand how suddenly the treasure can come. It is as if a key has been deftly turned

314

and a casket sprung open, revealing contents within more precious than could be thought possible.

I stared at the lamp. At the paper. At the lamp. The filament of the electric light burned in its bulb, like the sun filling an arch of sky. The filigree of black figures grew, rising against the white sheet. It was as if they were the rigging of a ship setting forth on a voyage of validation, a voyage in which vessel and sail carried on into the future, somehow leaving the spars of mast and yards behind.

My tree.
That was what was left onshore.
My equation tree.

Night decayed, morning came, the sentries changed their station. A beam of dawn light descended through the hut window, beating rose-red on the page. Did the tree promise forgiveness? For killing Ryman, hanged from his balloon, arms collapsed? For damaging Gill, stranded widowed and childless in Seaview? For making myself a monomaniac, subject to an idea of change and flux that actually fixed me like a butterfly on a pin?

I could not say 'yes' to any of these. But in that moment, which seemed to win to my side both chaos *and* order, I think I came close to an ideal of life. Recognising its mutability, I experienced a moment of freedom.

As for the final calculation, it's hard to explain: you just *know* it is right. Ryman was a big reason why. What he had taught me, I realised then, was the importance of intermittency. Not just scientific intermittency, but mental and emotional intermittency, too. How, in a world of disintegration and endless renewal – a continuum, a world of flow – one must find one's own rhythm exactly by recognising the incompleteness of the melody.

It was a great gift, because incompleteness is what points to that ideal of the whole. It shows the way to whatever is emergent at the limits of any system, from an ant-lion's nest in Nyasaland to the ever-expanding edges of the universe.

I sat for some time with the full calculation of the Ryman numbers for all the adjoining areas of weather between Iceland and the Channel in front of me – along with the lamp, the piles of brass numbers relating to each quadrant, and the shell cases standing like statues on the table. Looking behind at every step was like peering into a dream of becoming – watching something inspire, move, breathe, awaken . . .

There was a danger in savouring the showing of the thing like this, I knew that. I was cautious of ecstasy, but the highest branch of the tree – God's mercy! what a stroke was there. It was not just the one forecast I saw emanating from that twig-tip but something larger, something more glorious. The jubilant intimation of a new era in meteorology, affecting not just D-Day but the whole empire of the atmosphere.

I looked at my watch. It was 9.05 a.m. and I was starving.

With a whoop of triumph I grabbed the papers on which I had done the sums and burst out of the hut, startling the new sentry, who was already dozing. I laughed into the brightening air, took a gust of it into my lungs, then ran down the hill to the main house. On the gravel outside, Don Yates was consoling Stagg about the non-arrival of the bad weather which had caused the postponement of the next day's plans. They were quite oblivious to my revelation, still worrying about the bad weather in which I believed I had spotted a future chink.

'We're in a wood, chum. We're sheltered from the wind and a cold front has definitely been measured in Ireland,' Yates was saying, rubbing the dark hair on the top of his head. The Irish cold front confirmed that the decision to postpone had indeed been correct.

'Anyway, look!' Yates's hand extended into the air. Stagg and I followed the American's pointing finger. I was breathing hard from running down the hill.

Sure enough, in the west the tree tops were swaying. Wind was bearing cloud along in threatening armadas. The clouds were of the heaped, turreted, galleonish type that often spells thunderstorms. Altocumulus castellatus. 'But it sure feels weird to be celebrating a non-invasion, however successful the forecast,' Yates continued.

'Better safe than sorry,' Stagg said.

'It's going to be all right,' I said, breathlessly. 'I've found it!'

'Found what?' said Stagg crossly.

'There *will* be an intermezzo. I finally worked out the Ryman numbers down from WANTAC to the Channel. It *is* going to be a very stormy night, and the bad weather will continue through to Monday morning. Nothing can stop that cold front coming through now, but it will be followed by a short space of more settled weather. And that means, once the cold front has passed through the Channel, that we will be clear for an invasion on Tuesday.'

I wanted to tell them how I had come to my conclusion by deliberately subduing the complete mathematics in the way Gill had suggested, and allowing in a simulation of randomness. I wanted to tell them that it was all to do with thin layers between adjacent weather systems, just as Ryman had said. But neither of them was interested in the theory.

So I explained in more detail that WANTAC, which Stagg and the others had lost faith in, was in fact the key. Its apparently discontinuous data (discontinuous with the context) was in fact a sign of a small-scale, good-weather pattern within the large-scale and extraordinary bad-weather pattern. It didn't mean Krick's generalised optimism was right – the worst summer storm series in twenty years was about to whip the

Channel and would continue to do so for a day – but it meant we had a chance.

'There will be a gap,' I said. 'I'm certain there will be an opening. WANTAC isn't wrong, it is just reporting a movement on a different scale to those we were focusing on. If the Germans see only the main depression and not the high ridge on its flank, then we will actually have a tactical advantage. Our counterparts will see only the general panorama of bad weather, not the interval in it.'

At the end of my speech I didn't get quite the heroic reception I was hoping for. Stagg looked uncertain after listening to what I had to say, but Yates's face broke into a grin. 'I hope you're right. C'mon, let's go eat.'

Over breakfast we heard that Allied troops had begun to enter Rome. It would be the first European capital to be prised back from the Nazis, but it did not stay long in our minds. We were all thinking about the D-Day assault. I confirmed to Yates and Stagg that I wanted to go in with the American weathermen as had been suggested. I told them I was sick of sitting with the telephone at my ear and that, meteorologically as well as personally speaking, it indeed would be interesting to see how local weather related to the synoptic forecasts for large areas that we had been doing.

'Maybe not interesting enough to get killed for,' drawled Yates, who was the closest thing to a man of action among us.

'You're absolutely sure?' said Stagg. 'You should feel no compulsion.'

'I am sure,' I said confidently. 'I want to see for myself whether my theory is right. The ratio I worked out, the Ryman number, it's what Sir Peter sent me to find in Scotland. And I think I have, by applying a strange avoidance of elaboration. I want to see the results for real.'

Yates said he would arrange for a car to take me up to join

the American Weather Squadron, which was waiting for the off in Berkshire.

As soon as we had eaten we went to the hut and pored over the latest charts for a few hours. During this time, to everyone's relief, the sky became overcast. In a few hours it would start to rain heavily. Then we had the Sunday morning telephone conference during which Dunstable and Widewing argued as normal.

Holzman and Krick thought a surge of high pressure, associated with but separate from my minor WANTAC high, would protect the Channel. Petterssen was concerned about the rapid evolution of the second storm – Storm E – in the Atlantic; but he now thought it might not come to us as quickly as he had previously anticipated. The Admiralty concurred.

I told people about my work with the WANTAC gauges and my positive attitude fed into the discussion, with hearty support from the American contingent. I think this, apart from getting the telephone conferences together physically, was where I made my contribution to it all. It was partly just a question of language, of *conviction*, of getting people to believe the story you were telling. Even the words you choose to represent such things can make a difference. What is the difference between 'a reasonable possibility', 'the nearest we can get to a certainty in these conditions', and 'unsafe but feasible'?

This is the marginal area we were in, reflecting the extreme complexity and rarity of the weather as set against that of a more typical June. The essential general point, which people never seem to grasp, is that volatility has a direct effect on predictability itself, as well as on whatever it is you are predicting; or (another way of putting it), don't expect the same level of predictability all the time.

This is a mistake often made by those who speculate in stocks and shares, but in fact its relevance is to the whole range of human activity: why, having been thrown into life in the first place and when everything else is so variable, should we expect predictability, of all things, to dance at an even tempo? It is just a smooth dream of comfort that life's roughnesses should yield themselves up with eyes of meek surrender like that. All the same, it is hard to live without such illusions.

I personally supported Krick and Holzman in being more forthright. There *was* a slot coming, of a day or two, which presented conditions that were tolerable for the operation. The Admiralty's sea forecasts matched this analysis. Petterssen and Douglas, on the other hand, still harboured doubts, though it would be a distortion to say they advised 'don't go on Tuesday'. It was a matter of emphasis. They fell into line with the others, predicting clear weather for bombing and 'just about' tolerable conditions on the beaches. Technically their reservations related mainly to the further outlook after 6 June, and in this they would prove to be justified.

So, anyway, Stagg and Yates went off to Eisenhower and told him they thought a fair interval would become possible from early on Tuesday morning.

The compatibility between the forecasters hardened later on Sunday, at least for a while. I myself missed the moment when peace broke out among them, leaving in the car Yates had ordered for me.

There was just enough time for me to gather some belongings and to make some further brief points to Stagg about WANTAC, which I thought he should communicate to the supreme commander. Next minute I was bumping along in a khaki Packard towards Newbury, which was one of the marshalling stations for airborne troops.

The sky was darkening, it was raining heavily, and a gale was beginning to blow – but I was smiling as I was driven along. Thousands of men whose lives depended on our forecasts had been saved from catastrophe by the postponement. Soon there would be force 5 or 6 winds on the Normandy beaches and complete low cloud cover, preventing aerial bombardment or the landing of gliders and paratroops. It would have been a complete disaster; and in making the right forecast, notwithstanding the hedged-about manner in which it came, we had turned away a calamity.

My confidence about the WANTAC signals did lessen slightly in the car, I must concede. Whether the fair interval we hoped for would actually now develop on Tuesday remained to be seen. Even if it did, the conditions would be far from the minima set out on the BIGOT sheet. Moreover, other large, unpredictable depressions were wheeling across the Atlantic. At least that meant that the Germans, observing the rough seas and strong winds now ripping across the Channel, would decrease their invasion reconnaissance ...

I sped along against a southward flow of heavy military traffic. The storm battered the windows of the Packard, which were filled with successive, half-glimpsed images of military transports, all dipped headlights, angles of metal, camouflage nets. Embouched for a moment among vehicles, I glimpsed a tank commander looking for a reason for the hold-up. Rain-lashed, he stood upright in his turret, moving from one side to the other to get a better view. Poking out of soaked camouflaged sleeves, his white hands gripped the edge of the hatch.

Yates said he had arranged for me to go in a glider. I didn't like the sound of that very much, but I supposed it was better than taking my chance on a landing craft. I hated the idea of drowning. Some of the poor buggers would have to drive jeeps off the landing craft into five feet of water. I'd seen them down in Portsmouth, dipping their hands into vast drums filled with a compound of grease, lime and asbestos fibres and coating the points and distributor with it under the bonnet, then driving down the harbour slipways into the water to practise. These jeeps had upright exhausts, like snorkels. All you could see as they moved along was the vertical protrusion of the exhaust, with its little flapper-cap going like billy-o, and the head and shoulders of the driver.

I had felt like that until very recently – as if I was just keeping my head above water. Now I was stronger, I thought, as the traffic whistled on the wet road. What I had learned, apart from the proof itself, and it was simultaneous and coterminous with it, was that all things are ephemeral, although connected by a web of marvellous affinity . . . one that stretches from the bounds of universe to those of individual being. How wonderful it would be to be some kind of scientific superhero, able to fly without let from one misty region to the next!

We passed a sign for Chobham, I think it was (the lashing rain made it hard to see), and I remember it was at more or less that moment that my conviction of total connectedness suffered a blow, as I saw the continuity between me and all the thugs and monsters of whom Hitler was simply then the most prominent. But looking back now, with sharpened eyes, I see the link to the maniacs is simply one of the facts that any system must legitimately ignore. At least, it must if it is to preserve its identity.

How rarely we see it, the full picture. Through our fogged perceptions and illusions of control, how rare is that man or woman who can stay still in the strange land of dissolving elements, constant change and unpredictable fortune that is called life; can stay still long enough to perceive an ideal of the whole. And, in becoming still, become aware of his or her own flow: the buried stream of a genuine self, murmuring quietly as it winds its course. Only another's eyes can show the way to this place, and those have now been closed to me. What's left is not the ghostly aspect of her, but that of myself – of my own former inwardness that now follows me round like a strange dog.

If, tracking me down, that figment of my past were to ask me how to tell the future, I would advise it to look for patterns within systems and perturbations at their edges. Spy out what is new and – often more important – what is disappearing. Variations of input count for a lot, as does the speed at which a system operates and at which information propagates through it. When there's a big difference between those two speeds, a shock-wave can result. Ideally, information should pass through a system at a rate which allows that system to adjust to it.

That is what we have learned. That is the news from the future, conveyed through a fountain pen to a former self, as if the pen itself were a torpedo shot into the past from the bows of the ice ship. That is what I'd tell that persistent old dog of my young self, as he moseyed his way through wartime traffic to an uncertain fate, unknowing of the love and the loss which lay before him, unaware that he was hovering between Africa then and Africa now, where he might seek the plain where his old life rose.

By 9.30 p.m. I was at Newbury among the men of the 82nd US Airborne Division, being taken through line after line of bulky young paratroopers. Some were dozing with their packs on their backs, their faces smeared with camouflage cream; others were sitting up alert, their expressions filled with anxiety by the great undertaking.

I was introduced to Colonel Tommy Moorman, head of the 21st Weather Squadron, who were going in with the 82nd. He assigned me to Corporal Eugene Jourdaine, a thickset, round-shouldered man with bushy black hairs protruding from his nostrils.

I was to act as Met liaison between the British and

Americans, but since I did not have any RAF battledress, they let me wear Weather Squadron uniform. It had a motto on the shoulder, *Coela Bellatores* – 'weather warriors' – which pleased me greatly.

I was amazed at the scale of the US Army's weather operation. There were more than a thousand men in the 21st and another squadron, the 18th, of about the same number. But it was the US Army-issue camp-bed, one of that country's greatest inventions, which impressed me most. I got some sleep that night, more than I had had for ages, conscience for once forgetting to worm its way into my head.

5

On the morning of Monday, 5 June, after a hot shower – this aspect of American technical excellence also delighted me – and a breakfast of eggs, bacon and waffles, washed down with black coffee, I telephoned Stagg at Southwick. Through that by now very familiar conveyance (so familiar I had developed a skin complaint in the cup of my ear), I learned of the extremely tense atmosphere of the previous night's forecast presentation, during which Eisenhower and his battlefield commanders in the library at Southwick House had quizzed Stagg on the interval signalled by WANTAC.

As heavy rain poured down outside and wind battered the shutters, Stagg had told them that by the early hours on Tuesday, he believed wind, sea, cloud and visibility conditions would all be tolerable enough to mount an invasion. The cold front which had brought the rain was now moving south-eastwards and would clear the invasion site within two or three hours, Stagg said, and there would now be a weather window of one to two days.

Tedder asked Stagg how much confidence he had in this forecast.

'A lot,' said Stagg simply. I knew what a relief it must have been for him to say those words, and after all that had happened in the past six months it gave me pleasure to hear them, too.

More questions were asked, until finally Eisenhower turned to Montgomery. 'Is there any reason we shouldn't go tomorrow?'

'No,' replied Monty. 'I would say – *Go!*' Leigh Mallory and Tedder were more hesitant, but Eisenhower over-ruled them.

Stagg told me that after that evening meeting Eisenhower came up to him privately in the corridor and said, 'Well, we're putting it on again; for heaven's sake hold the weather to what you told us and don't bring any more bad news.'

The further seaborne forces were already heading to France by the time Eisenhower spoke to Stagg, but it wasn't until about five that morning that the order to restart the rest of the invasion was actually transmitted. The poised power of the gigantic, wound-up military spring, already forward in its very nature, was at last unleashed.

For me it was all a bit more forward than I had imagined, for as soon as I got off the phone Jourdaine came running up to tell me that our division would actually go late that night (Monday), preceding the main invasion force, in order that the weathermen might send back their observations and their fast-moving paratrooper colleagues secure essential positions.

'D minus one is kinda D for us,' Jourdaine explained, and I could have laughed with the shock of it all. All this time I had been preparing for one day and now we were going the night before anyway. It seemed in the nature of turbulence that this should be so.

There was still a lot of preparation to be done, so far as my own survival went. His nostril hairs twitching as he spoke, Corporal Jourdaine briefed me about the forthcoming glider flight and issued me with a small radio and a personal psy-chrometer (it resembled a football supporter's rattle) together with some other instruments and an M1 carbine. Glistening with gun oil, the weapon was semi-automatic and different from anything I had shot with before, my experience of firearms being confined to small-bore rifles used to bag par-tridge and guinea-fowl for the pot.

'I've used hunting rifles in Africa,' I said, picking the carbine up from the pile of equipment in front of me, trying to seem casual. 'But never anything like this.' I could smell the cordite on the armoury, like spent firework and metal; also a faint aroma of petrol and greaseproof paper, which was the gun oil overlaying it. I felt extremely uncertain as to whether I wanted these scents of childhood back in my consciousness; but the thing about our perceptions is that they make us their prisoners as soon as we experience them.

'Don't worry,' said Jourdaine, kneeling down to sort out some straps that had become tangled in the pile. 'It's not so different. But tell me, sonny, how come they picked you for this shindig? Surely you guys must have militarily trained weathermen who operate forward in the field with infantry?'

'Well, yes, we do,' I replied, giving vent to the odd feeling of national embarrassment that, mixed with the crude stink of imperial memory, would come to be the default position in future years. 'Some. We have some. But we've run out.'

'Clean out, hey?' said Jourdaine, straightening up. 'You know, that's the thing I've noticed most about you Brits. You've run out of everything. Lucky we came along to save you, huh?'

I ignored the jibe, which already seemed fair enough in truth, and listened hard while he took me through the weapon's safety drills, and then showed me how to strip and assemble it. It was indeed not so very different from what I had learned from my father, but, as Jourdaine ominously warned, 'These Garands can go wrong sometime, if you're not careful with them.'

After explaining the weapon's operating limits, Jourdaine took me outside to a firing range and I had a go at shooting. It was fun to do it again after all these years, and I didn't do too badly in hitting the targets. In fact, my marksmanship didn't seem very much worse than that of the men around me on the range.

Jourdaine, who had packets of cigarettes strapped to each thigh, said it didn't matter too much anyway. 'There'll be plenty of troops around us to do the shooting. Our job is to get the weather news back.'

Around 11.30 p.m. that night, full of trepidation, I queued up with the others to board the giant fleet of planes and gliders. There were some nine hundred aircraft there, and three invasion-related airfields in Berkshire alone.

Coffee and buns were served to us by Waafs as we waited in the queue. They looked strange and ghosted there, ivorine amid the signal lights of the airfield and the swirling smoke from the exhausts of the lorries which had brought the troops and were now departing. The vehicles made me think of the inhuman grotesqueries taking place in Europe, of which people were now beginning to speak a little, in very muted tones.

The Yanks' comments to the girls were something to hear, each soldier outdoing the next in ribaldry as he shot his line. I remember I found myself fondly hoping that Gwen and Joan – Liss & Lamb, as they'd come to be known in their years of fame – would be among those holding out the trays carrying refreshments, but they weren't, of course. I wondered where Whybrow had sent them.

Next a general came past and looked us over, muttering words of encouragement to the lines of waiting troops – coffee-slurping, bun-eating boys from Nebraska, New York, Kentucky, all at a peak of physical fitness and mental readiness. The exception, I began to feel afraid. I started worrying whether I would get a spell of dizziness, but then to my great surprise I saw a familiar face pushing through the khaki-clad crowd.

It was Sir Peter Vaward, wrapped in a gaberdine mackintosh so white he might have just been swept, whirlwind-swivelled, out of a snowdrift.

He held out his hand to me. 'I just wanted to come up here, to see you off,' he said, looking me in the face. 'And to tell you something. Everything all right?'

'Yes, sir.' I replied. 'Well, a bit nervous, really. But you shouldn't have taken the trouble to come.'

'It was no trouble, Meadows. No trouble at all. It was something I wanted to do. Stagg has told me how hard you have worked and that your work with Ryman numbers helped pinpoint the calm interval.'

'In a manner of speaking, sir.'

Uniformed figures moved past behind him, rippling like a landscape – half green, half glinting black. The signal light flashed from the makeshift control tower, illuminating Vaward's physiognomy like a clock face in the dark. The tower itself was just scaffolding and boards, somewhere for the chief loadmaster to step above the panoply of swaying green men, beyond whom stood, in serried ranks, the black forms of the gliders that would be charged with them.

'That's what he told me. And other sources corroborate it: you should know that counter-intelligence followed you to the Isle of Wight. All you forecasters have been closely watched over the past few weeks.'

'I didn't know, sir. We knew we were being listened to on the phones but not . . .' It was unsettling to think spies had been traipsing around after us, but also faintly comic.

One of the Yanks was complaining about the hot cross buns – pointing out that for such an important operation it should have been doughnuts. The queues were very long and slow. Vaward and I were moving on as we spoke, but only by very small gradations.

'But it is other surveillance I have come to tell you about. Last night we decrypted a German signal from Paris expecting coastal winds that would make invasion too risky. Indeed,

German naval craft putting out to sea to lay mines in the Channel were forced back into harbour by the stormy conditions. The point is, they don't think there will be a gap in the weather. They don't expect any Allied action for at least a fortnight. German commanders have been stood down. Weickmann's invasion watch team have nodded.'

'That is very encouraging, sir. Those decoders deserve a medal.'

'So do the forecast teams. Even you yourself, Meadows. But you won't get one, I'm afraid.'

'Because of Ryman's death?'

Jostled by the passing soldiery, Vaward rocked slightly, as if his two heels were trying to achieve synthesis.

'No, no. Because the success of the forecast – and it really does look like it might be successful now – cannot be identified with any one nation among the Allies, still less with a single individual. Just as failure couldn't have been either. But well done, Meadows. Really well done. Even downing the plane has turned out to be useful. Heinz Wirbel is proving rather a find – it's meteorology he loves, not Nazism. Any questions?'

'No, sir. Thank you, sir. It's very kind of you to have come.'

I watched the white mackintosh disappear into the moving bodies: the swarming, variegated mass of troops which in that moment seemed emblematic of the stir of life, that circulation of bacteria into which all individuals must be subsumed.

I continued waiting with the others. With shuffling steps we approached our wooden gliders. These were fragile things, almost too beautiful to send into war. We downed our coffee and gave the mugs to more Waafs with trays.

Lots of the Met section had haversack radios, with tall wire aerials. It was behind a soldier carrying one of these that I began mounting the small steps of the glider. Ducking down to enter the cabin (the radio man had had to bend his antenna

into a curve), I took my seat in rows with the other men, surrounded by heavy packs, ammo boxes and other kit: trenching
tools, gas masks, sacks of ration tins and hand grenades – and
the rifles, of course.

Nobody spoke much, we were too apprehensive, staring at
each other's murky forms and sombre faces in the dim light of
the cabin, our chests contracting and expanding in their tunics
and webbing. Then the engines of the planes – mainly Dakotas
– started up, filling the air with fumes and roaring.

The propeller noise of big planes is like a clattering – as if a
rift is being made in the sky – and that is indeed what was happening, since the blades of the propellers were forcing apart
molecules of air very rapidly. Thunder is a larger version of the
same process, and what I heard that day was thunder. Chopped
thunder. Air that was being rent, riven, cleft. All in vain, for
new molecules quickly rush in to fill the gap.

Through the resolutely continuous medium of the atmosphere the sound waves travelled, cleaving together as they
struck the eardrum. The membrane of my glider, too, was
beating like a goat-skin drum. It pulsated with the rhythms of
all those engines, making my diaphragm beat in response in
my chest and my heart race accordingly.

With the lights shining through the membrane and all the
dark faces sitting about, the scene was reminiscent of a firelit
pow-wow in the *miombo* woods that skirt Lake Nyasa. I
remember one occasion so thick with drumbeats it made the
whole glade reverberate, as if each tree had a voice.

There was a lurch. Somebody whooped. We began rolling
behind our Dakota on the runway, faster and faster until, seconds after the motorised plane, the glider took wing and,
with an exhilarating, volatile movement, was lifted into the
air. The sound of air rushing over us was astonishing, like a
giant blowing over the plane in a constant stream.

331

My head was sweating in my helmet, going alternately hot and cold as the sweat came and then evaporated. I tried to imagine the relative turbulence around the Dakota and the glider, and how the air flow round one affected the air flow round the other, but I could not concentrate.

We seemed to circle for an age. I looked at my watch.

It was D-Day after all.

0100 hrs.

H-hour minus 5.

6

Out of the window I saw hundreds of planes and gliders, silhouetted like geese against the moon. One by one they peeled off, heading in triangular formations for the coast and Normandy. I felt my face pull as the glider accelerated. The radio aerials warped down the cabin like windblown corn.

Beneath us the surface of the Channel was covered with the shapes of ships, clearly visible in the moonlight. I had never seen so many: more than six thousand, apparently. Surely the German spotter planes would see them? It was too late now, anyway. We needed the moonlight to ensure low tides and visibility for airborne landings. It was that requirement, I recalled, which had really pushed out the odds against the right weather.

Overall, staring down at the silver stream of moving vessels and trying to judge the weather, I felt the forecast was vindicated. I was not to know that the surface wind speeds were above the Admiralty's minimum conditions and that the sea was rough and men were being sick and that much worse was to come during the run-in at the five beaches, with ships and landing craft facing steep seas and even stronger winds. Winds gusting up to 25 mph, Beaufort 5 or 6.

I could hear the boom of artillery and bombardment in the distance, and presumed the barrage had started. The man on my right took a dagger out of his boot and sliced up a lump of cheese. He offered me some, but I couldn't eat. Jourdaine, on my left, unwrapped some chocolate, its foil glinting in the dim light. I declined that, too: I already felt queasy from the coffee. I wondered if anyone else felt the same. A lot of the men around me had their helmeted heads cocked to one side, as if listening for something.

At first the flight was surprisingly calm – we were almost three thousand feet up when the Dakota released us. As dawn broke light filled the plane, and then I understood what the men were listening for. There was a stuttering of guns. Flak began to burst around us in mushrooms of dark-brown smoke.

Somebody said, 'Here it fuckin' goes.'

'I wanna go home,' said someone else.

'Easy boys, easy,' shouted Sergeant Loadmaster Iwiss from down the cabin. He was wearing a leather jerkin with a fur collar. 'Ready for the drop now.'

We swerved to avoid the anti-aircraft fire, which was bursting outside like fireworks.

'Blow noses!' came the order.

We all held our noses and blew, as we had been told, to relieve pressure on the ears. My heart was racing as we swooped downward. I had good reason to be frightened. At Southwick I'd seen aerial photos showing anti-glider stakes dug into the Normandy countryside. Somebody had nicknamed them 'Rommel asparagus'. Nine-metre long staves of sharpened wood – not the sort of thing you want to land on.

I could see the sea glittering in the half-light – changing angle and coming closer as we levelled out. We must have been going at nearly 150 mph. Then the pilot deployed his brake parachute and we were jammed forward in our seats, bodies straining against belts. I heard the sound of somebody vomiting.

There was a hard jolt as we hit the ground with terrific forward momentum. Something tore into the fuselage. Rommel asparagus: a shaved spear ripping through the bottom of the cabin, with the glider's broken nosewheel attached. It carried on ripping through the bottom of the flimsy craft, opening it up like a zip fastener. We were thrown about, some kit was lost through a void in the floor – and I was impaled at the top of my thigh.

At first it wasn't painful but I gasped all the same, looking at it in astonishment and grabbing my pierced groin either side of the wound. It was as if a tree had started growing out of my flesh. I could see open muscle fibre round wood, and then a gleaming white fragment of bone, which just seemed like another piece of wood. All slathered with blood.

Nobody heard me call. Everyone was shouting and cursing. Out of the window I saw other gliders begin to pitch up at odd angles in the dunes, as if they were models thrown by children. We are landing far too near the sea, I thought; we should be much deeper in than this. Has anyone else been stabbed by a stake like this? My trouser leg started to fill with blood. Then the pain started. Now with a spreading cold blackness, as if someone was pouring ink into the padlock of my left eye, I felt myself begin to faint.

'To me! to me!' Sergeant Iwiss bellowed. 'Jourdaine, see to that man. Call medics. Get moving! Will somebody find out where the hell we have landed?'

I could feel the heavy wet of the blood in my trousers, flowing freely now; the material was like a bag filling up. My mind became misted, the rucksack radios rose like saplings. A brightness – Jourdaine's flashlight? – enfolded me from the right, beginning to dilute the inkiness in my head. I felt I must be . . .

'Think it might be his femoral, Sarge.'

I didn't know . . .

His light. The darkness on the left side of my head seemed to be yearning to merge with his light. What the brain was summoning, I suppose, unable to cope.

I heard Jourdaine say 'two' into his radio, then some other digits and something about a dog. I glimpsed his grasp, wet from my blood, on the black handset as he said it. *Hu . . . a . . . bu,* the radio squelched back, as if searching for intelligibility. Then, and clearly, *Who?*

I thought I was going to die. Jourdaine repeated our unit number. *You're miles off the grid,* came the static-soaked reply, conveyed through the magic wand of the aerial.

Stars began to dance on the cusp of my left retina, along with little black motes. Then these whatchamacallits were swallowed up by the stars and the darkness in my head received what it required, novel immunity from itself.

Light!

It filled my field of vision. Different letters of the alphabet, fluid like molten metal, shone within this light. Fiery letters, jumping jacks, seven from this side, seven from that, eight from another place. Because of the eight, I weirdly thought, there is no longer any separation, no longer any discord. Because of the eight, the *Ilala* can sail out of the Lake Nyasa horizon and take me home.

Jolly good fellow.
Found again.
Still the furline.

Those were the strange words which repeatedly came into my half-closed mind as, partially loosed from the world, I watched myself descend the *Ilala*'s bent steel ladder. Probably it was some confused image of the fold-out steps of the glider, as I was being insinuated out by medics. They laid me on a stretcher on the ground, and gave me a shot of morphine.

They then tied tourniquets and tried to plug the wound in my groin. I resolutely remained in Africa. I will stay in Africa, I told myself, till the pain is gone. Next I was lifted, and then some Germans – I presume they were Germans – started firing at us. Little stabs of flame. Ducking their heads, my carriers were almost clipped by raking machine-gun fire as they ran erratically with me, each jolt ripping through the obscuring curtain of morphine. I passed out as I was carried hither and thither like that, as I was borne along by brave American medics jogging along in the jumble of the dunes and the general confusion, the smoke-screens and the mortar crumps and the chaos of barbed wire and concrete emplacements.

I came round, or half came round, several hours later; I don't know exactly how many, but it must have been quite a few as the amphibious landings were now well underway. The medics had moved me back to a first-aid post in some dunes above the assault beach next to which we had mistakenly landed. Other wounded men sprawled around me, some moaning gruesomely, some cracking coarse jokes, most silent, all alike in ignorance about what was going to happen. Though some faces were greyer than others, it was as if we were all waiting, with utter parity of probability, for either one of death or life.

The beach below was congested with vehicles and men who had driven or jumped off landing craft further out, the ramps of their vessels having had to open in heavy swell. In the shallows, a tank was blazing and a vicious tidal stream was carrying away dead and drowning men. Further out, there were ships as far as I could see. On the beach, under drifting clouds of smoke, crawling snake-lines of men were creeping up towards the dunes, behind a few successfully landed tanks. We were too near the German line for them to make much headway. A big gun was banging at us every few minutes, making my eardrums ache and sending vast columns of sand into the air, which then rained down, abrading our skin like glasspaper.

Jolly good fellow.

Found again.

Still the furline.

Discrete iterations, carrying the fervid mind on hollowed-out canoes up the continuum of the lake, to Monkey Bay. Where the fishermen sit cross-legged to mend their nets. Where the pestle pounds maize in the mortar. Where the iridaceous ixia grows, following its own instructions. Where, marbled and mottled, studded, speckled and spangled, the lineage of Vickers flourishes.

Jolly good fellow. Found again. Still the furline.

To block out the pain, and the appalling sights, and the noise and smell of exploding munitions, I had begun to tell myself a fantasy.

Vickers is a famous dog now, long dead but fabled for his wandering through Nyasaland in the wake of the mudslide, in vexed search for a place where the lost master, i.e. my pa, might be found again. He is renowned too for his barred and brindled progeny, which are prized by local hunters for their facing down of marauding lions and for the silence they keep when the kudu appears in the bowman's view.

Helpless, with a dressing plugged in my groin, I watched large numbers of troops being swept off their feet while wading through the breakers. Some drowned. Those who reached dry land were often near exhaustion. At that moment, I instinctively felt our forecast had failed, my optimistic feelings from the plane quite gone.

Unable to watch, or rather opening and closing my eyes, I kept returning to the protective cocoon of my African fantasy, remembering how the kudu meat was always divided, each hut getting its portion. The animal's gyre-like horn would be gouged out and polished (it has tremendous sound-carrying power and is used for sending messages from village to village, or for summoning warriors during war). The antelope's skin –

reddish brown with white, grey and bluish stripes – will be scraped with a stone and mounted to dry in the sun on two staves, which are thrust into the ground to make an X.

I opened my eyes again, to see a jeep struggling in the sand, its wheels revolving in about two feet of water. It eventually came free and began manoeuvring round a pile of logs, one of the many types of obstacles the Germans had placed on the shore. I picked up someone's binoculars to watch, only to see that the logs were in fact bodies. Somehow the driver got round them but shortly afterwards the vehicle received a direct hit from a shell. They were raining down everywhere now, together with intense mortar fire.

Crash!

A large shell, falling in the water, caused a plume of white fluid to rise up, as if a whale had spouted. Still I refused to be startled out of my dream, which I followed as if under the influence of a detective story, or some other composed mystery of that sort.

It could not be sustained. On the beach, a different sort of influence was doing its dreadful, unignorable work, as follow-up waves of the assault came in from new landing craft. Many were foundering. Landing craft were being hurled onto the beaches by the waves, smaller ones being swamped even before they could touch down. Others, flung upon underwater obstacles, were holed and beginning to sink. I realised that the onshore wind was not just above the permissible limit laid down by the Admiralty, it was near the actual physical limit which would have made landings impossible.

We really had taken a very great risk with the weather. Although the achievement of tactical surprise was undoubtedly due to just-tolerable conditions, the weather was seriously reducing our ability to exploit that surprise. Men disembarking from those landing craft that did get through were being forced to jump, rifle in hand and weighed down by kit, into a milling mass of water, only to find the dead of earlier units floating alongside them.

Although the shells fell near enough to make the marram grass tremble, I seemed to be out of danger in the dunes, in that sandy saucer full of wounded men. But I wasn't feeling so good. Knots of pain were rising from the tangled bloody mess of my groin. I disciplined myself back into the African fantasy, the comforting substitution of time and space into which I had been hurling my consciousness to stave off the spasms.

A strange business. It was as if, in trying to suppress everything that was going on around me, I had gathered two different places and times under a single weather. Scientifically impossible, to mix these two distinct realities under the one sky, but that was what was happening in my head.

At any rate, it appeared I was to be drawn into the variegated dog-pack's evening gathering in the surf, stepping out of that hideous nightmare of war into a timeless irradiance of evening sun. I could be there now as I write – not on the *Habbakuk*, nor in a scratchy, blood-soaked, screech-filled dune in Normandy, but on softer, whiter sand in Africa.

Small green waves are clinking over my feet, bribing me to get up and walk. I know you, old coin, that song you make. I take the bait and rise. Somewhere the lake stretches smooth as baize to the Mozambican side, somewhere I recognise; I begin strolling towards the dogs further down the beach. Already the gap is diminishing. As I walk, sunset is closing down, one by one, rugged ridges of cloud. Soon only a bronzish sliver of sun will be left, a tawny skein being stretched ever tighter by the pulling string of time.

And suddenly, now, I remember where all this *came* from. Something about a dog. Jourdaine calling the medics on his radio, speaking the codewords for our respective units, as I lay pinioned in my seat back on the glider, bleeding, thinking I was going to die.

'Hello, Pi Dog,' was what he said into his handset. 'This is Black Dog.'

DATE: 15 February 1980
POSITION @ 0600 LOCAL (GMT +3):
    Latitude 6° 49' South, Longitude 39° 16' East
    Dar es Salaam Harbour
DEPARTED CAPE TOWN: 13 February
NEXT DESTINATION: Jeddah, Saudi Arabia
ETA: 22 February
DISTANCE TO GO: 1668.5 nm
CURRENT WEATHER: Clear and hot
SEA STATE: Calm
WIND : 2 kt South-easterly
BAROMETRIC PRESSURE: 1009 mb
AIR TEMPERATURE: 33°C
SEA TEMPERATURE: 29°C

Hindcasting the Weather for D-Day: a three-day symposium held at Fort Ord Air Force Base, California, 5–8 June 1984, commemorating the 40th anniversary of the invasion.

Transcript of an address by Heinz Wirbel, Emeritus Professor, University of Nebraska.

Our lives take their meaning from their interlacing with other lives. I am that German or formerly German scientist whose plane Henry Meadows's ill-fated plan eventually brought down in the Scottish county of Argyll, as described in the book which I am holding in my hand. I did not like to parachute, but it is my honour and also my heartfelt desire to pay tribute to my long-time friend. We were both fascinated by the challenge of applying mathematics to nature, and, because I was quite intrigued by the connection between us, I pursued him. He was resistant at first, but we soon were writing frequently to each other. On several occasions, we met.

After D-Day, the United States recruited many German scientists to work for research programmes in this country. I was one of those figures, coming to the University of Nebraska to study turbulence: that same subject in which, working for the Zentral Wetterdienstgruppe during the war, I was tasked with discovering the involvement or not of Wallace Ryman, in connection with Allied plans for the invasion of Europe. From talking with my former colleagues I can tell you that we did not fully see the break in the weather that enabled the assault; or rather, some saw an aspect of it but were not listened to. The key to the future is rarely grasped firmly, or by all.

You can read something about similar disagreements in the pages of this book. The image of the cover here – I will put it on the display – is a contour chart for June 6th 1944 over the English Channel. It comes from the archives of the British Meteorological Office. I can tell you that June 6th was indeed the right day, even if conditions were barely tolerable. Any further postponement would have necessitated waiting until June 19th, which is when the tides were next favourable. On that day, unforeseen by forecasters, a much worse weather came – a gale of unprecedented violence whose consequences threatened the Allied foothold on the continent as it was. There is no doubt that the assault would have failed if it had taken place then.

The relation of those times . . . the story inside this book – it is, I would say, not complete. Meadows's narrative ceases abruptly, though we know he eventually joined his Highness Sheikh Said on *Habbakuk*. Or Prince as he then was. Thank you, Sheikh, for saving the manuscript and providing financial resources to enable its publication, and that is what we are here to do today . . .

Now – a single event at a symposium entitled 'Hindcasting the Weather for D-Day' cannot pay heed to all the questions that rise up out of even one book's pages. Here is not the place to cover Meadows's intervening life as a don at Cambridge University, England. I will only say that he wrote many brilliant papers and received a number of honours, which is how I first became aware that the very man who tried to bring down my plane over Kilmun became a fellow practitioner of academic meteorology.

Nor is this the place to cover all the other absent years and missing people. Even the occasion for Meadows's recollections

– I mean the journey of that astonishing ice ship – must be anticipated elsewhere.

All I wish to do now is to draw the attention of interested parties to the book – and who could be more interested than meteorologists and service personnel on both sides who were involved in the invasion? Some of you here will have known Henry Meadows. But there is one missing person I would like to mention, his beloved wife Georgia, née Clements. Henry kept up his links with the Met Office after the war and Georgia continued working there as Sir Peter Vaward's secretary; one day – he described it to me as the happiest of his life – Henry went back to that office in Kingsway and sought her out. They shared a love of music.

Although they could never have children, they had many happy years together until Georgia's death from throat cancer. This happened not long before Meadows took the commission for the *Habbakuk*, and I think it explains why the narrative written on that vessel sometimes takes on a tone of bitterness and dismay. Also, perhaps, those scenes that he witnessed on the beach; that would cause the nature of a man to become brooding, yes?

So far as satisfying such curiosity as may be aroused on the question of Meadows's own fate, I should say that, according to the Sheikh, he was last seen on the early morning of February 15th 1980, when the *Habbakuk* had nearly finished being resupplied at Dar es Salaam in Tanzania. Wearing a light tropical suit and Panama hat, he was spotted wandering round the dock area of that quiet, dusty port, but it is not known whether he rejoined the ship as it left that evening. It has been speculated that, if he did rejoin it, he may have gone overboard some time during the night. In any case, he was not reported missing until 1400 hours the next day, when he failed from the bridge to answer a telephone call. By that time the ship was well underway.

Did he seek what has been described as the faithful austerity of the sea? We must pray not. No, it is my fervent hope that Professor Meadows did stay on shore, fulfilling the long-held desire to return to Africa which is expressed in these pages. Let us all hope that his disappearance is not permanent and that we may see him again one day.

What, meantime, might be surmised of his character I leave to others, except to say that he did seem to have a rather child-like, stubborn relation to the world. That was certainly the impression I got from the artists Liss & Lamb, who saw him from time to time in the intervening years. They communicated to me – on a postcard showing a painting of theirs to be exhibited at a gallery in London's Cork Street – affection for Meadows tempered with frustration.

By the magic of PowerPoint you can see the painting on the next slide . . . it, too, is referred to in the text . . . And here is the writing of the other side. The artists say that after the war Meadows had to readjust his understanding of their relationship. They also describe him as 'a pig-headed enthusiast for meteorology', which is as good an epitaph as any weather prophet could ask for. I'd be glad of it and I'm an old man now.

As for turbulence itself, the depths are marginally less obscure than formerly. Certain patterns, we can discern. But it still casts a spell, this turbulence. When we feel ourselves approach the frontier of established knowledge on this topic, we should beware, keeping a firm evidential footing. What we think we see beyond is sometimes just a vision, like a shadow cast on an iceberg.

I have now just a quick historical comment with which to close. The outcome for mankind would have been different if scientific advice had not been heeded on this occasion. I'm very pleased, as a naturalised American myself, that the government continues to be convinced by the credibility of scientific experts. All theories await falsification, it is said, but while there is evidence for them, we ought to take proper notice, however complex that evidence might sometimes be.

In respect of which, just before we came out here to California, one of our participants – he's the senior historian for the US Air Force Weather Service and I think you can all see him sitting there, next to the Sheikh in the front row – received a telephone call from the Pentagon. It was from the team which supports Air Force One, whose duties include forecasting the weather for the destination of the President. As you know, the President is in France to commemorate, with other heads of state, the invasion we have been discussing yesterday and today and will continue to discuss tomorrow.

The Pentagon wanted to know: what was the weather on June 6th 1944, and was it as forecast? They plan to pass some supplementary notes to the President in the folder that flies with Air Force One. These notes will inform the President that the answer is, quite simply, yes. The weather on the day was essentially as forecast.

As we know, most of the troops killed on D-Day were Americans. I'm told that once a salute has been fired out to sea above the cliff-tops of Omaha beach, the President will tell veterans they shall be honoured ever and always, adding: 'America would do it again for our friends.'

One day I hope that the leader of my own birthplace, Germany, and also that of Russia, will attend the D-Day ceremony. Perhaps then the haunting memory of the danger and sacrifice of that long-ago summer may at last be put to rest. Not forgotten, or obliterated, or dishonoured; but put to rest.

There is a line from Haydn's *The Seasons*, which work is mentioned in the text in passing. It is *Sei nun gnädig, milder Himmel* . . . What? Please, sir, do not fret that I speak German on this occasion. The words mean, 'Be thou gracious, O kind Heaven'.

With that, I think we should close the launch of this book, which is available for sale in the lobby. Before we move on, as you can see up here on the screen now, to an analysis of the upper-air synoptic charts made in the days prior to D-Day by my former colleagues in the Zentral Wetterdienstgruppe, I would like to thank you all very, very much . . . Excuse me, but I suggest that those entering for the next session come round by another route, so as not to clash with those who are leaving.

Acknowledgements

The character of Wallace Ryman in this novel draws on that of Lewis Fry Richardson, one of the unsung heroes of British science. I am grateful to my father-in-law Julian Hunt, great-nephew of Richardson's wife, for his invaluable help in writing this book. The depiction of Ryman was also greatly illuminated by the biography *Prophet or Professor? The Life and Work of Lewis Fry Richardson* (1985), written by Oliver Ashford, a close friend of the Richardson family.

Of other books and papers I would like to recognise the following: *Pyke, the Unknown Genius*, by David Lampe (1959); *Forecast for Overlord*, by J. M. Stagg (1971); *Weathering the Storm*, by Sverre Petterssen, edited by James Rodger Fleming (1974/2001); *Some Meteorological Aspects of the D-Day Invasion of Europe*, edited by Roger Shaw (1984); and 'With Wind and Sword: The Story of Meteorology and D-Day', by Stan Cornford (1994). Cornford's comprehensive paper is published by the UK Met Office and I would like to thank the library of that organisation for their help and forbearance.

Many individuals helped me in the preparation of the manuscript, including: Jean Boase-Beier, Lee Brackstone, James Campbell, Angus Cargill, Mark Currie, Nicola Garnett, Andrew O'Hagan, Julius Hogben, Trevor Horwood, Kate Murray-Brown, Ian Pindar, Steven Poole, Ian Sansom, Linda Shaughnessy, Rebecca Stott, Kate Ward.

Particular thanks are due to Ben and Sue Shephard, to Derek Johns and Julian Loose, my agent and editor respectively, to John Stirling at Castle House Museum, Dunoon, and, for their kind hospitality, to the Thompson family of Kilmun.

Most of all, I must thank Matilda, for keeping everything in its proper place.

Also by Giles Foden

ff

The Last King of Scotland

Giles Foden's bestselling thriller is the story of a young Scottish doctor drawn into the heart of the Ugandan dictator's surreal and brutal regime. Privy to Amin's thoughts and ambitions, he is both fascinated and appalled. As Uganda plunges into civil chaos he realizes action is imperative – but which way should he jump?

'Audacious, shrewd and spirited.' William Boyd

'As convincing and terrifying a portrait of a capricious tyrant as I have ever read. Foden captures with absolute fidelity the fascination of a figure like Amin.' EVENING STANDARD

'A gripping tale of tropical corruption...This is a wonderful read, beautifully written.' SPECTATOR

ff

Ladysmith

The year is 1899, and Boer forces have surrounded the small South African town of Ladysmith. As shells and shrapnel rain down, British soldiers and townsfolk dig themselves in, waiting for rescue. But General Buller's relief column can't break through . . . Giles Foden's acclaimed second novel brings the drama and action of the three-month siege to life. Inspired by the letters of the author's grandfather, a British trooper, this is a powerful fictional recreation of the first modern war.

'A triumph.' SUNDAY TELEGRAPH

'A cracking old-fashioned adventure story, as well as a fascinating account of a historical period.' THE TIMES

'*The Last King of Scotland* suggested that Giles Foden has impeccable instincts for a story. *Ladysmith* confirms this absolutely.' NEW STATESMAN

ff

Zanzibar

The year is 1998. Nick, a marine biologist, is working on coral reef protection off the idyllic island of Zanzibar. While on a trip to nearby Tanzania, he meets Miranda, who works in the US embassy there. They could be forgiven for thinking they are living in paradise – until they find themselves embroiled in a desperate terrorist conspiracy. Giles Foden's gripping third novel draws on recent history to create a contemporary thriller of dazzling virtuosity.

'Wilbur Smith meets William Boyd in the warm seas and spice-scented air of Zanzibar.' NEW STATESMAN

'A riveting thriller.' Anthony Holden, OBSERVER

'Rich, complex and immensely satisfying . . . Foden's fiction is so convincing that it is hard not to feel that you are reading the real inside story.' EVENING STANDARD

ff

Faber and Faber – a home for writers

Faber and Faber is one of the great independent publishing houses in London. We were established in 1929 by Geoffrey Faber and our first editor was T. S. Eliot. We are proud to publish prize-winning fiction and non-fiction, as well as an unrivalled list of modern poets and playwrights. Among our list of writers we have five Booker Prize winners and eleven Nobel Laureates, and we continue to seek out the most exciting and innovative writers at work today.

www.faber.co.uk – a home for readers

The Faber website is a place where you will find all the latest news on our writers and events. You can listen to podcasts, preview new books, read specially commissioned articles and access reading guides, as well as entering competitions and enjoying a whole range of offers and exclusives. You can also browse the list of Faber Finds, an exciting new project where reader recommendations are helping to bring a wealth of lost classics back into print using the latest on-demand technology.